AF427386

Renaissance

E. H. Lupton

Winnowing Fan Press, Madison, WI

Text and cover copyright © 2026 by E. H. Lupton.

All rights reserved.

No portion of this book may be reproduced in any form without written permission from the publisher or author, except as permitted by U.S. copyright law.

Print ISBN: 979-8-9883944-4-0

Cover design/art by E. H. Lupton.

Winnowing Fan Press logo design by Bryan Metrish.

Author photo by Bryan Metrish.

This is a work of fiction. Names, characters, events, and incidents are the products of the author's imagination. Any resemblance to actual persons, living or dead, or actual events is purely coincidental. Where actual places, business names, and institutions have been mentioned, they should be taken as fictionalized versions of the places, businesses, and institutions in question.

No AI was used in the creation of this work. The author explicitly forbids the use of this work for training all AI technologies, including those designed for the generation of text and images, and explicitly reserves all rights to license this work for such uses in the future.

Chapter 1

I T WAS WELL AFTER midnight by the time Sam was following Ulysses up the too-many flights of stairs to their apartment in the Baskerville building. "Oh man, I can't believe your brother gets to do that every night," Ulysses said, not for the first time. "That was out of this *world*."

Sam smiled indulgently at his husband. "You're so drunk."

"I'm not! No drunker 'n you are, anyway."

"We're lucky Harry agreed to drive, then." Sam pushed his hair out of his face. "I still can't quite feel my fingertips."

Ulysses laughed, pressing him up against the door to the fourth floor. "I bet I can."

Sam snickered at that. "Get a load of Mr. Smooth here." But it was after midnight and the stairs were empty, so he tipped his head forward and kissed Ulysses.

They stumbled out onto the little common area between the two apartments on the fourth floor. Sam tried to look around as they did, because a day or two of

Vikram's exaggeratedly slow opening of his front door the last time he'd accidentally stepped out to the two of them kissing had been enough to remind Sam of the value of discretion, but there was no one around. The golden yellow walls were sickly under the anemic lights, the thin industrial carpet painted a strange gray-brown color.

Ulysses didn't notice. He was clearly still feeling playful and drunk, because he launched himself into Sam's arms, clamping his legs around Sam's waist like he was a tree Ulysses wanted to scale. Ulysses was sturdy and muscular, Sam tall and willowy, but they were about the same weight. Sam staggered badly, nearly fell, and giggled, then managed to somehow get a hand on Ulysses's ass and lurch over to the apartment without killing either of them.

"You're stronger than you look, Sterling."

Sam pushed Ulysses up against the wall and tried to fumble the key out of his own pocket one-handed. "How *do* I look?"

"Pretty good," Ulysses murmured, and kissed the corner of his jaw.

Sam lowered his eyes. Ulysses's trapezius muscle was right there in front of him, just begging to be bitten. He leaned forward, set his teeth on the other man's shoulder where thin cotton stretched over warm skin and muscle, and then remembered they were trying to enter their apartment. It took considerable effort just to get the key into the lock, which made Sam a bit dubious that either of them was currently capable of whatever Ulysses had in mind. But then again the way the other man was looking at him now, one hand on the back of Sam's neck, was definitely a vote in their favor, and—he frowned. Had the door been unlocked, or was he just not paying attention?

He managed to turn the doorknob and the door swung open, showing the darkened living room. All good then. Ulysses hitched himself up a bit, murmuring, "Are you going to carry me over the threshold?"

It was dangerous to suggest Sam engage in anything approaching a ritual when he was intoxicated, and Ulysses knew that damn well, but this was a marriage ritual and they were already about as married as they could get, and Sam had been wearing a ring on his left hand for almost eight full months, so it was probably safe. He grinned and hoisted the other man. He'd taken two shaky steps when suddenly the light went on and someone directly in front of him was saying, "Where the hell—"

That was as far as they got. Ulysses, as drunk as he was, moved *very* fast, and before Sam was even done realizing something was happening, his husband had their ambusher slammed up against a wall, one arm pinned behind his back.

A familiar back. Sam inhaled sharply. "Let him go," he managed, raising his voice to be heard over the newcomer's shouts. "It's Laz. *Ulysses.*"

Ulysses grunted and stepped back, letting his brother wrench his arm free. "What are you doing here?"

"Looking for you!" Laz rubbed his shoulder, scowling. "Where the hell have you been? Babushka's in the hospital."

"Chicago. We went to a show." Ulysses squinted at him, then looked at Sam as though seeking assurance that he'd heard what had been said. "If Babushka is in the hospital, why are you *here*?"

"Because you weren't answering your goddamn phone and I told everyone I'd come find you." Laz shoved Ulysses, who staggered backward a couple of steps. "If I'd have known it was going to take you so long to get back here, I'd have left a note."

ULYSSES DIDN'T REALLY REMEMBER, later on, the trip back down the stairs to Laz's car. He was—maybe—aware of Sam walking beside him, a hand on his elbow. Sam exchanging glances and a few words with Laz. Sam folding himself into the backseat of the Goat so Ulysses could sit up front.

They didn't speak on the drive over. There was hardly time, anyway; it was only a few blocks. And then Laz was walking into the hospital like he owned the place, and Ulysses followed along in his wake, perplexed.

"Visiting hours are over, aren't they?"

Laz shrugged and prodded him into the elevator when it opened. "Doesn't matter. They're not going to kick us out."

"How do you know?"

Laz looked a little smug. "Eli."

Ulysses shook his head, as if that would help, and glanced at Sam, who lifted one shoulder, the corner of his mouth quirking up. Eli was in private practice, wasn't he? Ulysses couldn't remember. His mind felt empty. He was sobering up, but there was nothing rushing in to fill the cleared space except fatigue and panic.

The elevator doors slid back open. When Ulysses didn't move, Laz sighed loudly and nudged him forward. "I thought you were supposed to be good in a crisis."

Ulysses had thought that too, as it happened, but it was extra galling to hear it from his kid brother. "How do you know where she is?" he asked instead.

"They'd brought her up to the floor before I left." Laz shook his head. "Get it together, man."

"Aw, fuck off," Ulysses muttered, shoving his hands into his pockets. Sam didn't say anything, just pressed one hand to the small of Ulysses's back and walked along beside him.

"Do Celeste and Obe know?" Sam asked.

"Yeah, we called them too." Laz scratched the back of his neck. "Celeste is still here, or she was when I left." They turned a corner and he knocked on a door, then pushed it open.

Babushka was in a hospital bed, wearing a light blue hospital gown, a quilt Celeste must have brought thrown across her lap. Ulysses had been bracing himself for tubes and wires, for her to look frail and weak. Instead, she was sitting up, holding a hand of cards. Celeste, in creased wide-legged trousers and a black turtleneck, and Eli, in his white coat with a bow tie pulled loose around his neck and a pair of reading glasses perched on his nose, were scowling down at whatever she'd just dropped on top of the pile.

Eli said, "You're going to clean me out."

Babushka snorted. "You are doctor. I am poor retired schoolteacher."

"*Schoolteacher*," Eli repeated.

Ulysses felt the anxiety go out of his body so fast, it was a wonder he didn't collapse.

"Shouldn't you be resting?" Sam said.

Eli tossed two cards onto the tray. Babushka didn't look up, just waved a hand. "Bah. Rest tomorrow."

Celeste studied her hand and then shook her head. "Dangerous move, Eli," she murmured, dropping a card of her own.

There was one vacant chair in the room. Ulysses dropped into it and rubbed his face. "Does anyone want to explain to me what happened?"

"Moment." Babushka set down a pair of cards on the tray and tossed one on top of the pile. "I have thwarted the parson," she said to Eli, who gave a little bark of surprised laughter. "I am afraid I win." She looked over at Ulysses. Sam was still hovering next to him, trying to press his six foot three frame against the wall unobtrusively. "Where have you been?"

"Chicago!" He held up both hands in a gesture of frustration. "We take one night off to go see a concert, and suddenly Laz is turning up like you're on death's door."

"No death, no door." She collected the cards, squaring the deck carefully. "I break leg. Tomorrow they will fix." She shuffled without looking down, glaring at him the whole time.

Ulysses examined her face, then looked helplessly at Eli. "If it's just a broken leg, why are we all gathered around like we're having a wake?"

Eli took off his reading glasses and set them on the tray table. "Shall I explain?" he asked Babushka softly. At her nod, he got to his feet.

"When elderly people break hips, what we're usually talking about is a fracture of the head of the femur rather than the pelvis."

The information wasn't all that exceptional, or perhaps Ulysses was just unable to feel anything other than the cold, sour remains of panic. He forced himself to nod. "But she broke her leg."

"It's a question of nomenclature." Eli cast about and found a small notebook and a pen in one of his pockets. "You know the shape of a femur, don't you? It's this part." He drew a rough sketch of one, plus the place where it slotted into the pelvis. Then he made a mark on the long bone. "Ekaterina's fracture is here."

Ulysses had too many questions. The first one he managed to ask was, "How do we repair that?"

"They'll install an internal fixation device." Eli added one to the drawing; it looked a little like a ladder. "She has what's called an undisplaced fracture, and from the radiographs I saw, it might not even be complete."

Sam cleared his throat. "Sorry, I don't quite understand—you can't fix it with magic? This is Ekaterina we're talking about."

There was a moment of silence. Babushka sniffed. Eli didn't look up. "It isn't unheard of to repair bones with magic. But it's a very tricky business, and—"

Babushka broke in. "—and who should I trust to do this? What would I sacrifice?"

"It would need a very large sacrifice, because of the importance of what's being done," Ulysses added. "Assuming you could find a healer with the right kind of experience."

Eli nodded. "And the prognosis from the surgery is relatively good, overall. So I don't think there's a compelling reason to seek alternative therapies."

"Wait," Ulysses said, as Eli's words registered. "What does 'good' mean?"

Eli shut his eyes for a moment. He looked very tired. "Celeste," he said when he opened them, without looking over his shoulder. "Laz. Step outside for a moment with us, if you would."

They left Sam sitting beside the bed as Babushka dealt another hand of cripple the parson. Once they were out in the hall, Ulysses glanced at Laz, who was leaning tiredly against the wall. "What time did this happen?"

Laz shrugged. "We found her at 1900."

It was past one. Ulysses frowned. "You weren't home when she fell?"

Laz shook his head. "Virgil was. He was the one who called the ambulance. We got back just as it arrived."

At seven o'clock, Ulysses had been drinking cheap beer with Sam's younger brother Troy and his bandmates. He hadn't felt a thing. How could so great an oak fall without him knowing?

Eli cleared his throat, and Ulysses looked at him. "You asked what 'good' means. There have been some important advances in treating injuries like this recently, but it's still a bad one. The mortality rate is around twenty-five percent after one year, but that isn't the only figure you need to consider here."

Ulysses glanced at Celeste's solemn face, her long hair leaking from its braid, at Laz's exhausted expression and red eyes. Eli continued: "There's a good chance she's not going to totally recover her mobility after this. The house—Gooseberry House—has a lot of stairs. If she can't walk, would she be better off in an assisted care home of some stripe?"

Celeste shook her head. "Whether she would or not, you'd never get her to move."

Eli nodded.

"Wait," Ulysses said, catching up. "The risk of mortality is twenty-five percent after a year? Not . . . acutely after the break?"

"No." Eli folded his arms across his chest. "It depends on the reason she fell. Sometimes a fall is an accident. Sometimes it was caused by something else, like cancer. Additionally, the surgery and rehab can be hard even on healthy individuals."

Laz was staring at the ceiling like he was doing complex math in his head. Celeste looked serious but calm. Neither spoke.

"Does she know?" Ulysses asked.

"She grilled the orthopedic surgeon when he came to see her," Celeste said, smiling wryly. "I don't think Dr. Alderkin expected her to be quite so aggressive."

Laz chuckled, suddenly back with them. "He kept looking at Eli like he was hoping for evac, or—" He coughed. "Anyway."

Ulysses snorted. "You trust this guy?"

"I don't know him. But he and my sister Ayala did a fellowship together and she recommended him." Laz was watching Eli intently as he spoke. "She offered to come up and look at the X-ray films if we wanted."

"Your sister is a surgeon?" At the question, Laz shot Ulysses a disappointed look, as though he was supposed to have remembered that. "Could she do the surgery?" Ulysses wasn't entirely sure why he was asking, but Eli seemed to understand.

"Not unless we have Ekaterina transferred to Chicago." He smiled sympathetically. "I think the trip would probably be unnecessarily hard on her."

There was still something no one was saying. Ulysses could feel it, like a splinter just under the skin. "Is there a problem?" He glanced between the others. "Did she ask for something unusual when she was grilling him, or—"

"She's happy to be operated on here," Laz said. "*If* Eli will stay in the operating room."

"She doesn't trust the doctors?" he asked, but even as he said it, he realized: "She'd have to be unconscious, wouldn't she?"

"It's a very long surgery," Eli said. "Of course patients are sedated for it. Is there a contraindication she hasn't mentioned? She was very emphatic, but she wouldn't explain—"

Ulysses glanced at his siblings. "She worked for Russian intelligence during and after the revolution through to the thirties. Under sedation, she wouldn't be able to defend herself."

"I see." Eli rubbed his forehead. He opened his mouth like he wanted to say something and then shut it again two or three times. Finally, he said, "Is it just Soviet intelligence we should be worried about? She hasn't worked for anyone else since she defected?"

Ulysses started to say no but stopped, frowning. He glanced at Celeste, who shrugged and said, "Not that she told *us* about."

After some consideration, Laz said, "I don't think I have the clearance to find out anymore."

After another long pause, Eli said, "I'll speak to the surgeon. Is it all right if I explain this?"

Ulysses had told Sam early in their relationship, casually, like it was a joke. It had always occupied that space in family lore, nothing serious, just something *known*: Babushka had enemies. That was one reason Gooseberry House was warded so well. Now, the secret felt unwieldy and dangerous. Celeste said, "Keep it on a need-to-know basis," and Ulysses nodded. He was relieved when Laz agreed too.

Ulysses went back into Ekaterina's room. Apparently she'd been caught cheating outrageously at cripple the parson, and she and Sam were discussing it.

No, he realized belatedly. She was teaching Sam how to deal seconds.

"Lyosha," she said when she noticed him, a childhood nickname she hadn't used in two decades. Why dredge it up now? Before he could ask, she corrected herself. "Ulysses. I wish to speak with you."

Ulysses sat down in one of the other chairs. "You should get some rest." When she scoffed at him, he added, "Send Eli and Laz home. They're exhausted. I'll stay here overnight if you'd like."

After a long moment, she nodded. "Send them all home."

Ulysses looked over at his husband. Sam looked about as tired as Ulysses felt. "You should go too. No sense in both of us being wrecks tomorrow."

"I'd rather stay," Sam said. He glanced at Babushka. "If you don't mind."

Babushka gave him a long look. "It is a family matter." Ulysses turned from Sam to her, frowning, but she only gazed back impassively.

What the hell kind of thing was that to say? And how was he meant to respond?

Whatever she wanted to talk about was probably important; that was the main thing. He composed his face. "Come on," he told Sam.

When they were alone in the hall and the others had gone in to say their goodbyes, Sam rounded on him. "I don't want to leave you."

"It'll be fine."

"I know it'll be fine," Sam said, leaning closer to speak in a quiet voice. "I just don't want to leave you alone in a hospital. You hate hospitals."

Sam also hated hospitals, but Ulysses didn't say that. "It's just a couple of hours." He squeezed Sam's arm gently. "Eli will be back here for the surgery and I'll come home and get some sleep. It's just . . . my family, you know?"

"But I'm your—"

Laz appeared at Sam's elbow. "We're gonna split. You coming?"

Sam looked at Ulysses in mute appeal. Ulysses tried to keep his face implacable and straighten his shoulders. After a long moment, Sam went.

Ulysses went back into the hospital room and settled into the chair Eli had vacated. Babushka nodded and began shuffling the deck again.

They played three rounds in silence—Ulysses won one and drew one—before a nurse came in to check the monitors and offer Babushka more painkillers. When it was just the two of them again, Babushka shuffled for the fourth with a new vigor.

"Are you still in touch with anyone from the bad old days?" he asked idly, watching her gnarled hands snap the cards together.

She pursed her lips. "I haven't seen anyone since we left." Meaning defected, meaning not since 1935. He thought that was all she was going to say. But she must have been in a talkative mood, or maybe it was whatever drugs they'd given her, because she added, "Of course, I see their photos in"—she made an elegant gesture that Ulysses took to encompass various forms of media—"from time to time. Some of them have left now as well. Or they were sent to the West. I do not know, so it is safer not to meet. These things . . . can be tricky."

Ulysses chewed on that idea for a while, staring absently at his cards. In the West, being a magician was generally accepted. Behind the iron curtain—who knew. "Is that what you're worried about?"

Babushka gave him a focused look. "Them? Nyet."

"Then what?"

She dropped a two of diamonds in the center of her tray as an opening bid. "What did he tell you?"

"Who?"

She sniffed. "Doctor Sobel."

Ulysses looked at his cards and dropped a three of hearts. "You don't like him?"

"No, no. He is a good man. He is a good doctor. Young. Bright." She drew a card and set down a pair of kings, leaving Ulysses to draw and top his own bid. He managed a five of clubs.

"But?" he asked warily.

"He looks at me and he sees a fragile old lady."

Ulysses paused. "This is a trap, isn't it."

"Yes, trap. Well spotted." She gave him a disappointed look.

"It's past two in the morning," he said, but sat with her words for a moment anyway. He considered the clever, quiet man who'd neatly absorbed so much of Laz's attention over the past seven months or so, whom Ulysses had gradually been getting to know. "When you say Eli sees you as frail . . ." It took him a moment to complete the thought. "He's a good doctor, but he's only looking for the proximate cause of what happened."

Babushka nodded sharply.

"He's . . ." She watched him. He was abruptly aware of how exhausted he was, and how much he didn't want to be playing games. "What happened, then? You didn't fall?"

"Of course I fell," she snapped. "The question is what caused the fall. He cannot answer that question."

"Well?"

She gave him a steady look, and his heart sank.

"No. That's not—"

Babushka snorted. "So much education, so little sense."

Ulysses sighed. "Be fair, I would be like this even if I hadn't gotten a PhD." He rolled his neck, wishing away the hours spent in the back of Harry and Ellen's Datsun. "The . . . what are you suggesting? Something *made* you fall."

"The magic shivered. Like a jelly." She frowned at the two cards she held. "Someone tried something big, and failed. I want you to figure out what happened."

He stared hard at his hand of cards, trying not to think about the sheer scope of the investigation. "That could be difficult."

"But not impossible." Her voice was stern. "I cannot look into it. You must be my eyes."

He licked his lips. "A spell big enough to affect the magical background of the city."

The statement sounded absurd, but Babushka nodded. "A tricky proposition, but given enough motivated magicians . . ."

"Motivated," Ulysses echoed. He drew a card without really registering what it was, saw that it was the right suit and dropped it on the pile. "What motivation? Do you think they were trying to hurt you?"

Babushka thought about this. "There are more straightforward ways to hurt me," she said eventually. "But they are more defended against." After a silence that very nearly drove him out of his mind, she added, "Perhaps it is nothing. Natural phenomenon." She shrugged, an exaggerated gesture, palms facing the ceiling.

"I'll look into it." He tapped his remaining cards on the tray restlessly. "But the amount of time that's passed . . . I don't know if I'll be able to find anything."

"You are *my* grandchild, Lyosha. You will succeed." She smiled and dropped her cards: three queens. "Another hand?"

Chapter 2

I N EARLY JUNE IN Wisconsin, the temperatures were still turning cool at night. It would have been wonderful weather for sleeping, except that Sam was angry. He straightened the kitchen, grumbling under his breath. When that didn't work, he stretched out on the sofa and stared at a book until his eyes stopped focusing on the words. Then he went to bed and slept a few restless hours, wondering how it could feel so odd to be alone in the apartment when he'd spent most of his life alone in various apartments and never much cared.

Vikram knocked on the apartment door at five thirty. Although Sam had not planned to run, he was, arguably, awake, and after a brief argument with himself wound up going out anyway.

It didn't help clear his head, but it knocked some of the sharp corners off his frustration.

Sam was about ready to go back to bed when Eli and Laz arrived to pick him up around seven. Neither of them seemed especially tired, though they couldn't have gotten much more sleep than he had. The benefit of being an ex-fighter pilot and a doctor, instead of a librarian. They were sharing a large thermos of coffee between them. None was offered to Sam, which was a relief. The idea of drinking anything made his stomach turn over.

Laz was skinny, pale, dark haired like Ulysses, walking the line between unshaven and bearded. He had pulled on an old T-shirt, jeans, and a cardigan. Eli, who was short, tan, and clean-shaven, was wearing blue scrubs.

"You convinced the surgeon to let you observe? Or did he convince you?" Sam asked, following the pair of them back down the stairs.

"Some of both, I suppose," Eli began.

"It's actually not that hard to talk him into stuff like this," Laz said, voice affectionate. "He *likes* operations and autopsies and suturing people."

Eli sniffed. "You make it sound *weird*."

"Maybe there's a reason for that." Laz had parked his car in what was probably a no-parking zone directly in front of the building. Sam folded himself into the backseat and leaned against the window, watching Laz slide behind the wheel and fasten his seatbelt.

"Is Ayala coming up?" Sam asked Eli as they pulled away from the curb.

"She called me an hour and a half ago when she got in."

Sam whistled. "That's pretty early."

Eli shook his head. "Most orthopedists start rounds early. I know I can always call her when I'm awake at four in the morning."

Sam didn't ask why Eli was up and making long-distance phone calls at four in the morning. Laz didn't seem surprised by the revelation, but then again, he probably already knew.

They rode in relative quiet to the hospital, where Sam again followed the two of them up to Babushka's room. Ulysses was there, half sprawled on an uncomfortable-looking vinyl chair, looking unshaven and hungover and delectable.

Ayala was there too, a woman in her early thirties—Eli's age; they were twins—dressed in a sharp pantsuit. She was nearly a foot shorter than Sam, with the same wiry dark curls and gray eyes as Eli. She was explaining something about an X-ray when she saw the three of them and broke off to hug her brother and Laz.

Sam, feeling awkward, hung back, hands in his pockets, though Ayala flashed him a bright smile when Eli introduced them. Sam smiled, then turned to work his way over to Ulysses in the suddenly crowded room.

"What's your opinion?" he heard Eli ask.

Ayala's face lit up, and she gestured at the X-rays and resumed her lecture.

It was good news, on the whole—Ekaterina did have a broken hip, but there was every chance the operation would be successful and she would recover entirely. Sam could tell that this point was beginning to sink in when he saw Ulysses's shoulders relax a bit. He put a hand on the back of Ulysses's neck and leaned down.

"We should get out of here," he murmured.

Ulysses nodded.

Leave-taking was always a prolonged procedure among the Lenkovs, and it took even longer today than it usually did to disentangle themselves, but eventually Sam was standing on the sidewalk next to Ulysses and Laz in the early summer sun.

Ulysses grumbled and winced, and finally accepted a pair of sunglasses from Sam.

"Breakfast?" Laz said, peering at his brother. "You can't have eaten yet."

They washed up at a greasy spoon on Park Street called the Circle. The sign had the word EAT in large bold letters directly beneath the name. When they walked in, the green and white linoleum floor and green vinyl booths triggered some sort of sense-memory of the last time Sam had been in a diner like that. He remembered it like he was watching himself from the audience: Howard making nervous chitchat with some old man at the bar, Sam sitting quietly in a booth, waiting for—

Ulysses touched his shoulder and Sam jerked out of his reverie. "All right?" he mouthed.

Sam nodded unsteadily.

Laz had already slid into a booth and was inspecting one of the menus that had been left there like it held the key to deciphering the Rosetta Stone. Ulysses took the seat next to him, and Sam sat opposite. Ulysses immediately reached out and tangled a foot between Sam's long legs, as though he had sensed somehow that

Sam needed grounding. Or maybe it was the other way around, and Sam was keeping Ulysses tethered.

They weren't the only people who had decided to go out on this Sunday morning. There were a handful of hungover grad students hunched around one table in the back, a single man at a table near the window who seemed to be deeply in his own world, and a woman reading while her child devoured a stack of pancakes.

"How was it?" Laz asked, not lifting his eyes from the menu. "Long night?"

Ulysses grunted. "We played cards. We reminisced. She told me all her crazy conspiracy theories." He tipped his head back, stretching his neck. "I'm never playing cripple the parson again."

Sam said, "Conspiracy theories?" and then the waitress arrived.

She was wearing an aqua polyester dress that didn't look good with her complexion and an expression of moderate pissed-off-ness. "Coffee?" she asked, brandishing a pot and a fistful of mugs. They all nodded, and she somehow deposited the mugs on the table without breaking any of them, then poured.

"What can I get you boys?"

Laz got an omelet of some description, bacon, and a side of hash browns. Ulysses had the same. Sam ordered pancakes.

The waitress made no move to write anything down. "You want blueberries?"

"That sounds lovely."

She snapped her gum and sauntered off, taking the time to pour more coffee for the man by the window. He seemed to neither notice nor care.

Laz was the one who broke the silence after her departure. "Well?" He gave Ulysses a speaking look.

Ulysses was focused on putting sugar and cream in his coffee. "She wants me to figure out why she fell," he said.

"She doesn't . . . accept . . . that old people fall down sometimes?" Sam asked.

"No. Or—the elderly might, but that's not what happened here. Or—" Ulysses looked down at the sugar shaker, turning it on the table. "She thinks something happened."

"Something magic," Sam clarified, and Ulysses nodded. Sam licked his lips. "And you believe her?"

Sam felt something sharp spark between them, gone before he could put a name to it. But Ulysses just said, "Anything is possible," in a somewhat distracted tone, as though he were still mostly thinking about his coffee.

Laz fished a large coin out of his pocket and spun it like a top on the table. The light glinting off it was hypnotic. "I thought if someone did a spell, it's done, and there's not a way to track it unless there's an ongoing aspect. Is there a way to find out now?"

"I have a student who set up a zaubergraph." Ulysses sipped his coffee. "I don't know where they found it. It's based on old research about magic detection. Very touchy, but it does keep some kind of record."

Sam's brow furrowed, but before he could say anything, Laz slapped his right hand down on the table, covering the coin. It was a big, loud, theatrical gesture, and Sam jumped. Ulysses took another sip of his coffee, one eyebrow raised. Laz was looking intently at his hand, but after a moment he snuck a quick look at Sam.

No, not at Sam. At a point about six inches above Sam's left shoulder. Someone in that vicinity giggled, very quietly. Laz raised his hand and the someone gasped. The coin was gone. Laz boggled at this turn of events.

Sam bit the inside of his lip and glanced at Ulysses, then quickly away. Laz was carefully searching everywhere, moving the ketchup bottles and salt shaker and taking the sugar from in front of Ulysses, always with his right hand. Slowly, he turned his attention to his left hand, which had been sitting in a relaxed fist since almost the first moment.

When he opened it, there was the coin.

Laz grinned and picked it up. It had a star on one side and an eagle on the other—some kind of military thing, maybe. He rolled it along his knuckles, then flipped it into the air and caught it right-handed.

Sam looked behind him. The small child he'd noted earlier, about five or six years old, light haired and of no particular gender, coated liberally in syrup, was peering over the back of the seat. When they saw that Sam had noticed them, they gasped and ducked down behind the booth.

Sam looked back in time to see Laz grin and vanish the coin again, up his sleeve or something. It was sleight of hand, not magic; Sam could imagine Laz lying in a tent somewhere in Thailand, practicing the movements over and over until they were flawless.

Ulysses just shook his head and tried to hide his smile in his coffee cup. Meanwhile, the waitress arrived with their breakfasts.

The pancakes were thick, cakey, and sweet. Ulysses and Laz appeared to approve of the bacon and eggs as well; by the time they'd finished, Ulysses looked less hungover, though still in dire need of a nap and a shave.

"You know," Laz said, wiping his fingers on his napkin, "you could talk to the house."

"I could," Ulysses said, in a tone that clearly meant he didn't want to.

Sam blinked. "You love talking to buildings."

Ulysses shrugged unhappily, which Sam understood to mean 'later.' "We'll see what the zaubergraph says."

Laz waved at the waitress for the check, smirking to himself.

Sam said, "What are you going to do today?"

"Walk the dog," Laz said promptly. "I have to re-wire a lamp, too. And then I guess I'm going to hang out at the hospital for a while, wait for Eli."

Sam suddenly, guiltily, remembered the operation. "I suppose someone has to stay with her tonight."

"Probably." Laz picked up the crust of a piece of toast and looked at it. "Let's see how she's doing when she's out of surgery."

Ulysses grunted. "Did Eli say when that will be?"

"Not really his area," Laz said shortly. "But not too long, if the prognosis is as good as they were saying. A few hours."

Ulysses lifted his coffee cup again. "Is it going to be me or Celeste on duty tonight?"

There was a long silence. "It depends on where she winds up," Laz hedged. "Sometimes when patients are sicker, they get assigned more one-on-one nursing care. In that case, no one's going to turn a blind eye to our being there like they did yesterday."

"But if she's not?"

Laz shrugged. "Celeste could take it."

But she had an eight-month-old. Neither of them said it, but Sam could tell they were both thinking it. Baby Lila was adorable, but she didn't have a reputation as a good sleeper. *And* she and Obe had a business to run, unlike Ulysses, who would be on summer break in another few days.

Sam looked at the circles under Ulysses's eyes. "What about Virgil or Cass?" he asked. Both brothers looked at him in surprise. "Her actual children."

Laz nodded. "I'll talk to them when I stop home. I don't know how long she'll be hospitalized for, but maybe we can set up a rotation."

Ulysses looked down at the table. "Yeah, maybe."

U LYSSES HAD HIS HAND on the handle of the car door when Laz grabbed his elbow, startling him out of the postprandial haze he'd begun to sink into.

"Look," Laz said, drawing him aside. "Be careful."

"What?" Ulysses caught the urgency in his tone well before he registered the words. "What's going on?"

Laz's face was angular under the beard, and his eyes were tired. "I had a vision."

"Of what?"

There was a long pause. "I don't know. There was—it was pretty chaotic. A lot of screaming. Blood. It—" He broke off, looking away from Ulysses's eyes, like he didn't want to think about what he was saying anymore.

With exaggerated patience, Ulysses said, "What's your point?"

"I have a bad feeling, and it's related to you somehow." Laz punched him in the shoulder. "There was a full moon, if that helps. I don't have any other details."

They stared at each other for a moment before Ulysses managed a wan smile. "Full moon's not until next week," he said, ignoring the unpleasant twisting in his stomach. The whole thing was so distant and absurd, and he was already so tired. "C'mon, man. Nothing's going to happen to me."

Laz rolled his eyes and went back around to the driver's seat. "Just be careful."

He left them outside their building, which was right in between helpful and not helpful. Ulysses wanted so badly to take a nap. He also wanted to go check the fucking zaubergraph in the magic building. Maybe then he'd know how worried he should be.

Sam was standing in the middle of the sidewalk, hands in his pockets, expression of concern on his face he was trying to hide. Ulysses glanced around, trying to remember where he'd parked the bike.

"Do you want to lie down?" Sam sounded hopeful.

"I need to go over to the magic building," Ulysses said. "It won't take long."

"Should you be driving?"

Ulysses rubbed his face, yesterday's stubble rasping against his palm. He'd shaved before they'd left for the concert. Hadn't he? It seemed like such a long time ago now. "What time is it?"

Sam stared at him for a long moment before shifting his gaze to his watch. "Nine-thirty."

"I've only been up since seven yesterday morning, so that's twenty-six hours. No problem." He forced a smile and shoved his hands in his pockets to stop himself fidgeting. "I've been up longer and ridden. When I was an undergrad—"

"You're not an undergrad anymore." But then Sam sighed, evidently concluding that arguing with Ulysses would just waste valuable sleeping time. "I'll get the helmets."

The zaubergraph was about the size of a large breadbox, albeit one made of glass and half filled with electronics. Above all the circuits and vacuum tubes and transistors that Ulysses was ill-prepared to deal with, there was a flat table with several thin pens scratching out spidery lines on a long roll of paper. Some of the pens moved a lot, and some wiggled only a bit—when Sam came near, for example. The box was topped with glass to keep out people who didn't know what they were doing. The paper exited through the far end in a long strip and wound up coiled on the counter. The current strip was quite long; it appeared that in the general hustle and distraction of finals, Peregrine hadn't been in to check on it over the weekend.

"Is that it?" Sam asked, intrigued.

"Yes. Basically, the pens detect magic occurring at different distances from the detector." Ulysses pointed at the bottom two. "Long distance." The next two were medium distance, with close range on the top.

They were in the magic department's main lab space, a large windowless room on the twelfth floor across the hall from Ulysses's office. Sam hopped up on the bench and the uppermost needle twitched and jumped.

"Sorry," Sam said, peering at it. "Did I jostle something?"

"No." In some distant office, a phone was ringing. Ulysses frowned at the lines and wondered if he was supposed to note somewhere that they'd walked in.

"You're just . . . casting a shadow on it. So am I, for that matter. It's supposed to do that." He skimmed back along the strip. "Laz said they found her at 7 p.m. yesterday, right?"

Sam nodded. "But Virgil had already called an ambulance. That means she fell sometime earlier."

"How much earlier, I wonder." Ulysses looked again at the pens and tried to gauge how fast it was scrolling.

"Hopefully it's obvious," Sam offered.

"Hopefully." Ulysses glanced up at Sam, who offered him a wry smile. "Let's see . . . it's quarter to ten now . . . so seven was almost fifteen hours ago . . ." He counted backward. "Here we go."

"How are you counting?"

"These tic marks represent the top of the hour"—he pointed—"I think. I should ask Peregrine. It's their project."

Sam nodded. "Someone should combine it with that electroencephalogram Eli had."

Ulysses looked at the zaubergraph, then at Sam. "Clever." He poked Sam's thigh. "You should talk to Laz and Eli about that."

Sam made a face. "If it's that clever, someone has probably already thought of it."

"Could be." Ulysses shrugged, moving to the next section of strip. "But you've heard Eli rant over the last six months, right? No one is studying this stuff."

Sam exhaled. "I guess."

Ulysses went back a little farther. Then a little farther than that, and on until he realized he must be looking at two in the afternoon. "Damn it."

"What?"

"There's no smoking gun." He tapped the page at about half past five, where the lines went a little shakier. "If something happened, this is probably it. But it's hard to tell what's noise." There were plenty of lines, a small thicket of things going on in the environment, some near the detector and some far away. Nothing jumped out at him. Nothing looked like a bomb going off.

Sam nodded. "There's magic happening all the time, and the detector couldn't hear the putative attack over the—the background noise?"

"I wonder." Ulysses scanned further back through the record. "If you were building a machine like this, wouldn't you want to filter out the magical background?"

"That just means that if whatever got Babushka wasn't large, it might also get filtered out." Sam hesitated, then added, "What was Laz being so weird about?"

Ulysses opened his mouth and realized he didn't know how to answer. Or, rather, he didn't know how to explain in a way that would prevent Sam from worrying more than the prediction merited. "He had a vision," he said finally. "You know what he's like."

"A vision of what?" Sam asked, eyebrows drawing together. "Babushka, or—"

"It was nonspecific. Death and destruction and really wild things. During the full moon. *A* full moon." Ulysses shrugged helplessly.

Sam's face went still, his eyes wide. "About you?"

"I—yes. But when in the last few years couldn't one have had some kind of vision like that about me?" Ulysses looked down at the zaubergraph and cleared his throat. "Do you think—even if this was targeted, there have to have been *some* witnesses—"

Sam reached out to put a gentle hand on the back of his neck. "Let's get some sleep first." Ulysses leaned into the touch despite his annoyance, eyes fluttering shut for just a moment. Sam smelled nice, like fresh air and rain; the bond lay between them, quiet but warm and comforting. "I need a nap. And that means you probably need one twice as badly."

Ulysses sighed, and said, "I'm not getting out of this without a fight, am I?"

He tilted his head back, and when he opened his eyes, Sam was smiling down at him, but trying to keep his amusement at least a little bit hidden. "No," he told Ulysses. "Probably not."

Chapter 3

Sam dozed for a while before his always-treacherous body decided he was done sleeping. It was noon or thereabouts, and even with the curtains drawn the bedroom was too bright. Ulysses was deeply asleep, curled loosely on his side of the bed. His face was relaxed, although worry still clung to him. It took Sam a while to realize he was sensing it through the bond.

He got up and wandered around the apartment. Unfortunately, nothing needed doing; he'd already washed all the dishes, the plants were watered, and even if he'd felt like vacuuming, that would wake Ulysses. This was why Laz had a dog, probably.

Eventually, he found the copy of *The Lathe of Heaven* Celeste had given Ulysses for his birthday. Ulysses didn't twitch when he padded back into the bedroom, feet tan against the rather lurid cactus-green shag rug. It felt self-indulgent to read here instead of the office, but he climbed back into bed anyway, arranging the pillow so he could lean against the headboard. A few minutes later, Ulysses rolled over and threw an arm across Sam's thighs.

Well, it wasn't like Sam had anywhere to be.

He had a brief image of reading quietly for hours while Ulysses dozed, providing silent support. In reality it was about forty-five minutes before Ulysses stirred and opened his eyes.

"Hmm?" he managed, eyes not quite focusing on Sam's face.

"Hey." Sam ran a hand through Ulysses's hair. "How do you feel?"

"Mmm." Sam thought Ulysses might shut his eyes and go back to sleep. Instead, he rolled partly onto his back and stretched. "What time is it?"

"Not quite one. You could sleep longer if you want."

Ulysses sat up slowly and leaned back against the headboard with a groan, shoulder to shoulder with Sam. "I'll never manage to sleep tonight if I do that."

Sam studied him. He looked less tired, but still somewhat brittle. His face was strained. "Want to go for a walk?"

"Sure." Ulysses looked up at the ceiling for a moment. "State Street? We could sit in a coffee shop for a few hours."

"Sounds nice," Sam said. He cast about and found a scrap of paper on the nightstand to act as a bookmark. "Do you want to shower first?"

"Let's just go. Run away." Ulysses didn't move.

Sam touched his arm, then shifted, running a hand down his side. "Ulysses?" he murmured when Ulysses looked over at him.

"I don't—" He shook his head. "I don't know, Sam." Ulysses looked lost.

Sam put an arm around him. "Ssh."

Ulysses curled forward, elbows on his thighs, face in his hands. "I knew this was going to happen sometime. She's not immortal. But I didn't think . . ."

"This isn't the end," Sam said, even though he didn't know if that was true. "All will be well."

Ulysses nodded. Sam felt him inhale. "I don't—"

The phone rang.

Ulysses pressed his face against Sam's shoulder and cursed when the phone very inconveniently continued to ring. He carefully slid off the bed and padded out to the living room.

"Hello?" he said, voice testy.

Sam got up and leaned against the doorway, watching Ulysses with the receiver pressed to his ear.

"No, sorry," he was saying. "You just woke me up. Yeah. How is—okay. I see." He exhaled. "That makes sense. All right. We'll be down in a bit." There was a longer pause, and Ulysses's mouth quirked up. "I thought maybe I'd shower, that's all. Okay. Yeah, see you." He hung up and turned to Sam. "That was Laz. Babushka's out of surgery."

"Good?"

"Yeah." He scratched the stubble on his jaw absently. Sam waited to see if some of the tension would leave him, but it didn't, not really. "She's back in her room. Laz is on his way over. I guess Virgil is already there, and Aunt Cass has been and gone."

"Do they need you?" Sam asked, even though he already knew the answer. "You were there all night. You could—"

Ulysses shook his head. "I said I'd go."

For a moment, he and Sam stared at each other, and Sam felt suddenly that he'd erred somewhere, although he wasn't sure quite where. Ulysses smiled tightly. "I'm going to go shower."

The hospital was exactly as they'd left it, although there was more activity in the halls. People clutching balloons and teddy bears shuffled uncertainly from elevator to rooms and back. Husbands and wives and children, lovers and best friends. How many ghosts were wandering this building that Sam couldn't see, passing through visitors and staff? Ulysses claimed that ghosts usually abandoned places like hospitals and nursing homes in favor of more familiar places, but . . . there had to be some. Right? It was a big hospital. There had to be some.

Babushka's room was already pretty full when they walked in. Virgil was in a chair next to the bed she was sleeping in, and Eli was asleep sitting up in another, arms crossed, head thrown back in what couldn't be a comfortable position. Laz had perched on the foot of the bed.

"There you are," he murmured when they came in. "Thought I was going to have to go find you again."

It hadn't been long since he'd called, forty-five minutes at the outside, and Sam could feel Ulysses bristling. "We got here as fast as we could," he said, hoping he sounded conciliatory.

Laz glared at both of them, then seemed to back down, shaking his head minutely. "I'm going to take Eli home. Celeste cleared her schedule to be here during the day tomorrow, but Virgil and Aunt Cass have to go to Milwaukee on Babushka's behalf for a meeting, so that leaves you on tonight."

Ulysses nodded resignedly. Then the implications of what Laz was saying caught up with Sam, and he made a noise of protest. "You can't—"

"Sam," Ulysses said in a low voice. Virgil was looking at them now, much to Sam's chagrin, eyes sharp and inquisitive. Ulysses grabbed his elbow and dragged him out into the hall.

"You've had *three hours* of sleep." Sam thought he sounded reasonable, but the pinched look on Ulysses's face wasn't reassuring. "You can't stay here another night."

Ulysses looked back at the door to Ekaterina's room and then squeezed his eyes shut. "There's no one else, Sam."

"There are plenty of other people! There's Obe, there's me, there's—"

"There aren't." Ulysses exhaled. "I'm sorry, I have to stay. Laz can drive you home." He turned away, then added over one shoulder, "Rain check on that café, okay?"

Was that an attempt at consolation so this whole embarrassing argument wouldn't feel like quite such a blow? Hopefully. Before anything else could happen to drive it all deeper under his fingernails, Sam turned on one heel and walked out of the hospital.

T HE NEXT MORNING AT half past six, Celeste arrived, which was a relief. She even brought Ulysses a small bag of donuts so fresh they were still warm through the waxy paper bag.

"Bless you," he muttered, standing up to take it from her. The movement made his muscles protest.

She smiled. "Thought you and Sam would be hungry." She glanced around the room as though he'd found a place to hide a man Sam's height somewhere she hadn't immediately noticed.

"I sent him home," he said, opening the bag. "No reason he should have to endure this too."

Celeste gave him a curious look but didn't say anything, which was probably for the best. "Do *you* get to go home and sleep?" she asked instead, settling into the chair he'd occupied most of the night.

"I get to proctor an exam," he said, mouth half-full of pastry. "And then four hours of meetings and some grading."

Celeste made a face. "Better you than me. But doesn't that make for a long day?"

Ulysses shrugged. "*I have been one acquainted with the night.*"

"That doesn't mean you have to be acquainted with it here, alone." She dug through the canvas bag she'd brought in and pulled out two knitting needles and a skein of blue yarn. "It can't be very exciting, sitting here by yourself while Babushka sleeps."

He shoved the other half of the donut into his mouth. "I got a lot of reading done." Celeste made a face, and he added, "What's wrong with reading?"

"Nothing!" She raised her hands. "I just know what you were probably reading, and it wasn't anything fun. More like some dry academic brick with a title like *Ghastly Grievances*: *Ghosts and the American Revenge Fantasy.*"

"No comment."

Celeste grinned. "I've called a bunch of local folks, so we should have some more people to sit with her soon. And I sent Mariah a telegram."

Ulysses blinked. But of course letting their mother know made sense. "Do you think she'll come?" he asked, his voice unexpectedly wary. "It's a long way." And Mariah and Babushka had a long history he didn't completely understand.

"She might come. She's good in this type of crisis." Celeste considered, and added, "And she could meet Eli!"

"Do you think Laz will thank you for that?"

They both thought about it. Finally, Celeste said, "She'll love him," which wasn't really an answer.

"Yeah," Ulysses said, and yawned.

Celeste smiled and put a hand on his arm, gently pushing him toward the door. "Go home, Ulysses. And tell Sam I said hi."

Ulysses did not go home. Instead, he went to the magic building.

He couldn't recall ever having been in the building at seven in the morning, but it was very quiet, even accounting for it being the last day of finals. Magicians were largely not morning people, he supposed. Well, you didn't earn a reputation for midnight sabbats and then get up at the crack of dawn.

He was going to explain that to Sam, someday.

Ulysses set the bag with the remaining donuts on one corner of his desk, dropped his helmet on the shelf behind it, and slumped down in his chair, closing his eyes. The exam was in the same building, in a lecture hall on the third floor. He had close to forty-five minutes to shut his eyes and pretend the rest of the world didn't exist.

He got ten minutes before someone knocked on the door. As though she could hear him considering not answering, Dr. Lesko didn't wait for an acknowledgment before she came in.

She was about fifty, with long curly hair and orange eyes she kept hidden behind blue-tinted glasses. She was wearing a light blue suit today. She'd once been his PhD advisor, and before that Babushka's student and possibly some kind of coven member. Now she seemed to fancy herself Ulysses's mentor, whether he would or not.

"Bad time slot draw," she said, leaning back against the closed door. "How are you doing?"

"I'm fine." He rubbed his face, aware that he hadn't shaved in two days and probably didn't look fine anymore. "Don't take this the wrong way, but why are you here?"

"Celeste called. I just wanted to see if there was anything you needed."

Ulysses shrugged helplessly. "You should go see Ekaterina. She'll be in the hospital for a while."

Dr. Lesko gave him a tight, concerned smile. "Do you want me to proctor your exam for you? I have some time."

"I've got it." He sat up straight and cast about for his pile of empty blue books. "Really. Thanks, but—"

She stared at him like he was a question she was trying to answer. "No one is going to think less of you if you go home and rest."

"I'm not worried that they will." He glanced at his watch, but of course it was too early to go find the lecture hall he'd been assigned. "If I go leave now, I'll get at best ninety minutes of sleep before I have to come back here for the staff meeting. If I can make it until two, I can go home and sleep for as long as I want." Or until Laz called him at seven to ask him to do another night shift. But that was a problem for later.

Dr. Lesko looked skeptical, but she didn't say anything. Usually that meant he was doing something deeply thoughtless or, occasionally, actively reckless. "How's Ekaterina doing?"

He swallowed against the sudden choking feeling in his throat. "She's . . . I mean, the surgery went well. She slept most of the night, so I didn't get much chance to talk to her."

"Mm." Dr. Lesko glanced over her shoulder, as though checking that the door was closed. "Do you know what happened?"

"She fell." He hesitated. "She said something made her fall, something in the magic. Did you feel anything?"

Dr. Lesko was quiet for a long moment. Then she shook her head.

"Nothing?"

"No. But she always was more sensitive." She rubbed her chin. "*You* didn't . . .?"

"I was in Chicago when it happened." Ulysses felt a pang of something between guilt that he hadn't been around and jealousy that he'd missed it.

Lesko didn't waste time on that. "Did you check that magic detector in the lab?"

"Yes. But it's difficult to tell if it picked up anything important." He found a pen and made a note on the blotter. "I should talk to Peregrine. It's their project." He looked up at the drop ceiling, then pulled himself together and got to his feet. There was probably coffee in the department kitchen by this hour. "If you see them, would you tell them I'd like a moment?"

"Sure."

He thought she was going to say something else, but she just rose and followed him out into the hall.

S AM HAD BEEN AT work for an hour, just long enough to get caught up on the whirl of tasks that always needed attention first thing. Unfortunately, once he'd sorted through all the mail and memos and interlibrary loan requests, there was a lull.

After Ulysses had all but kicked him out of the hospital, he'd walked for hours, too annoyed and proud to wait for Laz and Eli to be ready to leave. He'd had a lot of time to think, mostly about how it was possible to be right and yet get a situation so badly wrong.

It hadn't been an especially pleasant walk. But it had been time to think.

Ulysses hadn't come home that morning, which was unsurprising but at the same time felt like a slight. Realistically, there were a lot of reasons Ulysses might have been delayed at the hospital and had to go straight to work. Nothing worthy of concern. *Sam* wasn't going to spend his time worrying about it. Even if Ulysses desperately needed some sleep and a decent meal. He was a fully grown adult and perfectly capable of getting them for himself. He didn't need Sam fussing over him.

Sam had been paging through a recently acquired volume of poetry from the late eighteenth century for some time, trying to figure out when it had been purchased and who he was supposed to inform of its arrival. Dr. Edith Pearlman, head of the special collections department, had acquired it, probably for someone in the English department, but she was on vacation, and her notes were unfortunately sparse. Just when he decided to put it aside for the time being, he heard a sniffle and looked up to see Buttercup standing in the doorway to his office.

Buttercup Diaz was a young Black woman, a year or two younger than Sam, today wearing a knee-length dress the color of a sunflower. She also looked like she was on the verge of tears. "Can I talk to you?"

Sam stood, fishing his handkerchief out of his pocket. "Are you okay?"

She nodded, but the corners of her mouth turned down. "I'm fine."

"You don't look fine. Please, sit." He waited until she'd taken the visitor chair to settle into his own again. "What's going on?"

"I wanted to ask . . ." She twisted the handkerchief between her hands. "I have to go out of town unexpectedly. Is it all right if I start next week instead?"

In all the excitement, Sam had rather forgotten she was scheduled to begin a summer job working for him. "That's fine. What's going on?"

Buttercup rubbed her forehead. "Galadriel had a bad trip. We were down by the lake on Saturday, and she fell in, and—" She took a deep breath to steady herself. "Anyway, she got scared. We decided it's best if she goes home for a spell. So I'm driving her. I don't know if getting out of Madison will help, or . . . maybe her family will be able to do something." She blew her nose noisily. "I'm really sorry I won't be here."

He waved the thought away. "The job will still be here when you get back. Please don't worry about it."

"Thanks." She dabbed at her eyes with the handkerchief.

"Have you told Uly—Dr. Lenkov?" Ulysses was, somewhat unofficially, her advisor; he was on her committee; and she'd been sitting in on some sort of reading club his other grad students ran since her return from the UK in April.

"I don't know what he'd do about it," she mumbled, looking down.

Sam nodded slowly. "Are you going to be okay? Where's Galadriel from?"

"Detroit." Buttercup gave him a thin smile. "I'm from the same area. That's where we met."

"Well, drive safe. If there's anything you need that we can help with, call us." He fished one of his business cards out of the top drawer of his desk and jotted Ulysses's office number on the back.

"Thank you." She tucked it away into her little yellow purse. Sam watched her hesitate, as though wanting to add something, and then get to her feet. "We're heading out right away. Can you tell Dr. Lenkov I won't be at the end of the year thing this Friday? I don't have time to go out to the magic building."

Sam stood as well. "If it's any consolation, I don't think the get-together is going to happen. Ulysses's grandmother is in the hospital."

Buttercup's eyes grew wide. Sam wondered if she knew who Ekaterina was, or if that was just an instinctual response to the idea of sick or injured grandmothers. "I hope she'll be okay."

Sam nodded. "I'll tell him you said so."

He felt absurdly better after she'd left, the relief of having dealt with one problem—any problem—to the best of his ability. He turned his attention to a stack of letters, starting with one from an antiquarian book dealer Edith liked.

Four hours later, someone in the doorway cleared his throat and knocked gently, and Sam looked up.

It was Ulysses.

Chapter 4

U LYSSES LOOKED MESSY, ALTHOUGH Sam didn't want to say that. Hair going in every direction as though he'd been running his hands through it for hours, yesterday's clothes, thick five o'clock shadow, rings under his eyes. It was all Sam could do not to jump up and hug him.

"I brought you a donut," Ulysses said, holding up a little paper bag, and Sam suddenly realized what time it was.

"I worked through lunch." He felt unaccountably embarrassed by that fact. Ulysses laughed, voice a little rusty but beautiful all the same.

"There are still some food carts out on the mall," he said, setting the bag down on the corner of the desk. "Can you take a break?"

Sam squeezed his left hand slightly until the wedding ring pressed against the insides of his third and fifth fingers. "Yeah," he told Ulysses. "I can."

Ten minutes later they were relaxing on the grass on Library Mall with sandwiches. The afternoon sun was still high in the sky and the day was almost perfect, temperature in the sixties with a cool breeze off the lake.

"It feels strange," Ulysses said, looking around with a huff.

"What does?"

"The weather being so beautiful when everything else is . . ." He made a general motion with one hand.

Sam nodded. "How was last night?"

"Probably exactly how you think it was." Ulysses sighed. "Babushka slept, mostly. They have her on some pretty heavy medication right now, so she was confused when the nurses woke her up to check on her, and that was . . . I mean, I've never seen her not lucid in my life. Rationally, I know she'll be fine. Eli can tell them to reduce the painkillers today, and she'll go back to normal, but . . ."

"She's not the type of person who shows her mortality," Sam said quietly.

Ulysses nodded. "She's seventy-four this year, but she's never acted frail." He stared down into his sandwich like there was some way to use chopped vegetables and slices of turkey to divine the future. "I mean, it's obvious that she's never been hospitalized before, because we don't have a goddamn clue what we're doing. If we'd ever done this, we'd have a plan of some kind."

Helplessly, Sam reached out and put a hand on the back of Ulysses's neck. Ulysses didn't look at him. "I suppose that means you're on for the night shift tonight, too."

"Depends. Dr. Lesko might go over there, but—" There was a silence between them. Not strained, exactly, but loaded. Sam didn't like it. "Who else is going to do it?" Ulysses said softly. "Celeste can't be there all night, she's got Lila, and Obe has to be able to run the shop, or vice versa. Virgil and Cass are out of town. Eli's already there during the day as much as he can to liaise with the other doctors. And Laz is getting the house ready."

"He's what?"

Ulysses set the sandwich back on its wrapper. "The house is going to need a ramp before she comes back. Better handrails. I talked to him about it earlier—it's a big project just to fix the place up enough that she'll be able to use the ground floor." He leaned into Sam's shoulder, a warm weight against Sam's side. "Obe is helping him with the boundaries. I should try to go over there, see if there's anything I can do."

Sam shut his eyes and forced himself to take a few measured breaths. "I'd better send you home to sleep for a few hours, then."

Ulysses said, "Sam—"

Sam couldn't meet his eyes. Instead he looked down at his sandwich. It smelled appealingly of hummus and cucumbers, green and earthy. He pulled the waxed paper wrapping back over it. "I'm not trying to cause you more problems."

"I know." Ulysses sat up and the cool air flooded in between them.

Sam was drying dishes at seven o'clock in the evening when the phone rang. He knew it wasn't for him—he had no idea what Ulysses had done to the phone, and he was absolutely sure that the phone company would not approve, but almost immediately after it had been installed, he'd started sensing who the caller wanted to speak to. He'd also noticed the moment of confusion he provoked when he persisted in picking up the receiver despite the caller plainly seeking Ulysses.

It happened now, again—the brief pause after he said "Hello" before Laz replied, "Hi, Sam. Is Ulysses there?"

"He's asleep," Sam said, because it was true, and because he had half a mind to tell Laz exactly what he thought of what they were doing to him. "What's up?"

"Is he doing all right?"

Well, that was a surprise. Sam hesitated. In one sense, there was nothing wrong with Ulysses that about twelve hours of sleep and an actual meal or two wouldn't cure. On the other hand, that afternoon Ulysses had looked like he was about one more night shift away from openly hallucinating, which seemed unlikely to help anyone. On the third hand, the family was having a crisis, and Ulysses was probably not wrong that he needed to pitch in. And on the fourth hand, Sam was a little resentful that despite having been married to Ulysses for nearly a year, *he* apparently wasn't qualified for Ekaterina-sitting duty.

He said, finally, "Comme ci, comme ça."

"Can you—"

Ulysses slid an arm around Sam's waist and pressed his face into the spot between Sam's shoulder blades. He also took the receiver from Sam's unresisting fingers. "Yes?"

His voice was sleep-rough, and Sam shivered at the vibrations against his back as Ulysses exchanged a few short volleys with Laz, then hung up with a loud, frustrated groan.

"You're going back," Sam said. It wasn't really a question.

"I'm sorry," Ulysses said, releasing him. "I had hoped—but they need me. I'm sorry."

Sam sighed. "I'm not angry at you." He turned around to look at Ulysses, whose eyes were wide and searching. "Look, what if I go with you?"

"What?"

"I'll go," Sam said. "We can split the night, like we're taking watch or something. Four hours each. That way you can get some sleep." He tried to count how many hours Ulysses had slept in the last forty-eight and came up with a number close to seven.

"Taking watch," Ulysses repeated. "Is this the army or something?"

Sam shook his head. "Do you not want me to go?"

"Sam, no. It's not that." He looked stricken. Sam reached out and took his hand, fingers ghosting over Ulysses's ring.

"So what is it?"

"You just don't have to. It's boring, it's . . . I mean, it's my family bullshit. Why should you have to deal with it?"

Sam frowned, both at the content of Ulysses's assertion and because it seemed like Ulysses was, if not lying, at least not telling him the entire truth. But if there was one thing he remembered from his college years, it was that people running on very little sleep were not in a good position to make decisions or have emotionally complex discussions. So he tucked his doubts away for the time being. "Good. Then I'll come. Do you want to change before we leave? Are you hungry? I made muffins. I could brew some coffee, too."

Ulysses frowned into this torrent of questions. "What kind of muffins?"

"Blueberry."

Ulysses looked down at their linked hands, smiling faintly. "That sounds nice."

Ekaterina's hospital bed was halfway reclined, putting her at what seemed like an uncomfortable angle, but she was dozing when they arrived. She had an IV in one arm, and a couple of wires snaking out from the top of her hospital gown led to softly beeping monitors. Sam was surprised by how small she looked. When she was awake and standing, he was aware that he towered over her, but it never felt—

He'd never thought about how much space she really took up.

Someone, possibly Laz, had dragged a sofa, upholstered in mustard yellow vinyl, from one of the waiting rooms into Ekaterina's room in place of two of the chairs. It was a crowded setup, but at least there was someplace to rest. Sam shoved Ulysses onto the sofa, then sat down to read *The Lathe of Heaven* in the remaining chair, next to the bed. It didn't take long before Ulysses was asleep.

For a while, there were only the muted sounds of the machines and footsteps as nurses went up and down the hallway outside. Ulysses breathed deeply. Sam turned a page.

Two and a half chapters later, Ekaterina made a small noise, and he looked up to see she was awake and taking him in.

"How are you doing?" Sam asked.

She scoffed. "All day they fuss over me."

"They're worried about you," he replied, not sure if they were discussing the nurses or the rest of the Lenkovs.

She peered at him, lips pressed together in a thin line. "I will not break."

That gave Sam a momentary pause. "I'm glad you're feeling better," he said eventually. "Have they told you any of your test results?"

"No. Eli said he will make inquiries." She motioned to the little tray table she'd been using for playing cards that first night and he moved it into range for her. She picked up the cards and shuffled. "You play durak?"

It was a trick-taking game, not that different from cripple the parson or sheepshead or any other game of that type. Lower cards were defeated with higher ones, which were topped by still higher cards. Attack and defense passed back and forth between Sam and Ekaterina. Nurses drifted in and out, and Ekaterina trounced him several times before he managed to put together a coherent hand.

She seemed normal. Sam kept watching her, waiting for some sign that she was becoming senile or fragile or—old. But there was nothing. Just those ice chip eyes in a wizened face, watching Sam right back in a way that made him uneasy.

Ulysses rolled over on the sofa, and Ekaterina paused in her shuffling to look at him. They'd been there for two hours or so and Ulysses had been unconscious basically the entire time.

Ekaterina looked like she wanted to ask Sam a question, but she wasn't quite sure how. That was a first. After a moment, she shook her head. "He is a good boy."

Sam was completely sure she would never have said such a thing if Ulysses was awake. "He is," he said, and passed her the deck.

She separated the deck into two stacks and bridged them together, hands moving carefully. She was on a fair bit of medication—Sam had seen the nurses administer it. But he would never have guessed from the precision of her movements. She watched him while she shuffled, eyes intense. The air between them felt heavy, somehow. Like the moment before a summer thunderstorm broke. Then she dealt each of them six cards—he knew now to keep an eye on her hands when she did—and set the rest aside.

Sam picked up his hand and blinked. The game was played with a reduced deck in which 2 through 5 were left out. She'd dealt him 6, 7, 8, 9, 10, jack. All clubs, all in order.

"Did you do that on purpose?"

"No." She lowered her hand to reveal the same sequence in hearts. After a moment's consideration, she picked up the rest of the deck and fanned them out face-up on the table. All the cards were arranged in numeric order by suit, laced together so that dealing six cards alternately would net them each what they'd received. Sam looked up at her, sure that his face mirrored Laz's astonishment at the vanished coin back at the diner, except Sam's feelings were all genuine. Ekaterina shook her head, frowning.

The temperature in the room dropped by thirty degrees, very suddenly.

Ekaterina pointed at Ulysses and snapped, "Wake him. Now!"

Sam scrambled to obey. Dimly, he heard the chair he'd been sitting in hit the floor as he leaped out of it. "Ulysses!" he hissed; speaking aloud would have felt like shouting in a cathedral. Ulysses stirred, slow to wake, and Sam shook him gently, crouching in front of him. "We need your help."

Ulysses opened his eyes. For a moment, he was confused and drowsy, staring at Sam as though he couldn't figure out where they were. And then his gaze shifted. Sam was close enough that he caught the moment when Ulysses inhaled quietly and tensed. At first, he had no idea why.

Then Ulysses grabbed Sam's hand with his own and he saw them.

How many ghosts surrounded them he didn't know, but it was a lot, all crowded into the little hospital room like a group of protesters encircling him and Ulysses.

I T WAS AN EERIE moment to wake to, and that was saying something; Ulysses had been seeing ghosts since his youth. His threshold for weird was pretty high. But opening his eyes to see dozens of ghosts staring at him—it was unsettling.

He sat up slowly, taking care not to startle Sam, who had flattened himself against the edge of the couch and was scarcely breathing. The ghosts were silent and staring, but what surprised him the most was that they were all from such different eras. There were women in flapper dresses and women in miniskirts. Women in pigeon-fronted gowns accompanied by men with their hair slicked back and cravats neatly tied. Women with long hair loose around their shoulders and women with victory rolls. Men in bowler hats or long, homespun robes or bell-bottoms. People of indeterminate gender dressed like cowboys and doctors and every other way.

The temperature was continuing to drop. Ulysses looped an arm around Sam's chest, leaning forward against him for warmth as much as to offer reassurance.

"Why are you here?" Ulysses asked finally, looking from face to face. "What's going on?" Somewhere beyond them, he could hear Babushka muttering, feel the breathless tightening of a spell being wound up.

From out of the crowd stepped a woman with a familiar face. Long hair, glowing slightly and woven with feathers. Yellow eyes. Vertical pupils. "Hey, U," she said, and winked. "How ya been?"

"Abbie," he said.

"I gotta tell ya, stuff's been real weird by us—"

She drifted closer, and he got a whiff of—what? Malevolence? Discontent? He stood up, trying to put himself between her and Sam. "What do you mean by weird?" Was she the source of the malice he felt, or simply awash in it? Sam was standing now too, silent, one hand on the back of Ulysses's neck.

"We were just minding our business," Abbie said. "And—hey, wait a minute, I know you."

Ulysses wondered what Babushka was doing. If he could get a step closer, he could help—but the ghosts between them didn't seem inclined to shift aside.

"You're the one I told him to stop fooling around with." Abbie didn't have a voice, exactly, but her tone grew a little colder with this revelation. "What are you doing here? Still fooling around?"

Sam cleared his throat. "Afraid so."

Abbie took a step closer, and Ulysses moved to intercept. He remembered Laz's prediction—his death beneath a full moon—and wondered if that meant he was safe to take risks until then. He nearly laughed.

Abbie raised a hand and reached toward Sam. Her arm passed through Ulysses on the way, and it felt shockingly cold, impossibly bleak. Ulysses opened his mouth, not sure if he was going to scream or attempt a spell—

Behind Abbie, Babushka chanted four or five words in a hissing crescendo and she flung something into the air. Water, Ulysses realized, from the cup next to her bed. It froze into snow as it arched upward and spent an odd, weightless moment hanging in the air. Ulysses lunged, shoving Sam to the floor and throwing himself on top of him. Then, in a silent implosion, the ghosts vanished.

He heard a sizzle as the water hit the linoleum and evaporated.

When Ulysses opened his eyes, Sam was staring at him. He smelled good, clean and a little bit spicy. That was a hell of a thing to notice at a time like this. "What the heck," Sam said, having apparently decided that regardless of the ghosts and the fact that Ulysses was lying on top of him, the most important thing was not to curse in Babushka's presence.

Ulysses, already lightheaded from the ebbing magic in the room, pressed his face into Sam's chest and started to giggle.

Eventually, they managed to untangle themselves. Ulysses found a bag of lemon drops in his satchel underneath the exams, and they sat with Babushka in silence. A nurse came in to check on them and Babushka requested another glass of water. She didn't try to explain where the previous one had gone—the entire glass had vanished during the spell—and after a tense moment or two, the nurse clearly decided not to ask.

"So what happened? What was that?" Sam asked. His voice had steadied, but his eyes were still a little wild, occasionally darting around the room as though he expected more ghosts to appear. That felt fair. Ulysses had never seen that many in one place either.

He took Sam's hand in his, trying to be reassuring. "It was . . ." Abruptly, he realized he didn't really know. "I think I told you at one point that some magic practitioners are sensitive to the psychic tides of the world?"

Sam blinked. "*That* was a while ago. I suppose I do remember that, yeah."

"Consider what just happened to be high tide."

"That's . . ." Sam shook his head. "No, I have no idea what you're talking about."

Babushka looked at Sam. "Where do souls go after they die?"

"To Ulysses's bedroom," Sam grumbled, and then remembered to whom he was speaking and turned bright red. "I don't know. Ulysses said sometimes they go to the nexus."

She shot Ulysses a look. "It is a theory." Babushka leaned back against the pillows she'd propped herself up with. "The real answer is no one knows for sure, which is not satisfying."

Ulysses managed to admit, "I was a bit glib, I suppose." Babushka snorted at that. He cleared his throat. "There's not a good way to measure where souls go, because we can't really sense them using traditional instruments. The idea that they wind up inside a nexus is like— Think about groundwater sinking into a reservoir. We can see the rain, and we can see the underground lake. But we can't correlate a single raindrop hitting the earth with a rise in water levels."

Sam tapped the fingers of his free hand on his knee in a staccato pattern. "Does the nexus move around at all, or is it stationary? Are there multiple or just the one?"

"They're stationary; there are many of them but only one in Madison that I'm aware of. Remember that place Livia took us to, out behind the old sanitarium?"

"The—is that what it was?"

"She said the nexus was nearby." Ulysses frowned at him, feeling his confusion bright and sharp. "You don't remember this at all."

They were both silent for a moment. Sam said, "I think you're talking about conversations I wasn't there for."

Ulysses tried to replay the night in question in his mind. His memories were a bit hazy, to say the least; there had been a lot of drugs involved. "Possibly," he admitted after a moment. And then, pressing on. "The nexus is like a basin." He cracked a few knuckles one-handed while he thought. "When Dionysus was here, he raised the water level, like throwing a big rock into a lake. Now something is disturbing it again."

"Not Dionysus?" Sam asked warily, and Ulysses shook his head. "But it's scaring the ghosts out of the nexus. Or that's what you think."

"I don't know if *scaring* is the right word, but . . . essentially. They're flotsam."

Sam took his hand back so he could rub his face. "Why? What's raising the water level, so to speak?" He fell silent for a long moment. "Could it be a natural phenomenon?"

Ulysses glanced at Babushka, who shook her head. He thought of Laz's vision, then pushed the idea away as hard as he could. "I don't know. I've never seen anything like this before."

Chapter 5

THE NIGHT GREW OLD and restless long before they were permitted to leave. They played cards for a while, until Babushka grew too tired and Ulysses finally prevailed on her to rest. Then he sat on the couch next to Sam and graded exams while Sam dozed, his feet in Ulysses's lap.

Ulysses was glad to have time to think, although he wished it wasn't coming at the expense of another few hours of sleep. The evening's events had rattled Sam, and Ulysses didn't blame him. He still felt the chill of Abbie reaching through his shoulder. The appearance of so many ghosts was . . . well, it hadn't happened to him before, and that made him suspicious. He needed to go look at the zaubergraph output again, maybe finally talk to Peregrine about it. He needed to figure out how this fit in with what had happened to Babushka. He needed to . . .

Sam shifted in his sleep, muttering, and Ulysses absently patted his ankle. It was coming up on five. A few moments later, the nurse came in. She was young, with dark hair pulled up beneath her cap and light brown skin. She gave him a professional nod and crossed to the bed to check on Babushka. Ulysses watched the interaction in silence, the vital signs the nurse scribbled down on a small card she was carrying, the pills she offered Babushka when the older woman woke. Then the nurse turned and went out.

In all of their discussions about Ulysses staying at the hospital, Sam had been too polite to mention the futility of Ulysses's presence. If one of the nurses had been compromised and decided to take advantage of Babushka's helplessness to poison her, there was no way he would know. Eli *might* have a chance if he stood over every medication administration and checked every pill, but Ulysses wasn't sure even that would be enough. There were so many types of medications, so many ways they could be tampered with or switched. Yes, if someone attempted direct violence, Ulysses could stop them, or at least try. But Babushka's enemies were subtler than that.

If they tried magic, though. Which, given who she was, what she'd done . . .

Ulysses thought about the ghosts again, and then about the zaubergraph. He didn't like it.

Sam stirred and opened his eyes. "Hey," he murmured, squinting up at Ulysses.

Ulysses smiled a little, feeling Sam's post-sleep fuzziness through the bond. "Sorry, was I thinking too loudly?"

"You really weren't." Sam sat up and stretched, and Ulysses heard several of his vertebrae pop before he settled, head on Ulysses's shoulder. "What's up?"

"Nothing," he said, not that he thought Sam would believe him. Ulysses checked his watch; the minute hand had inched along a few notches since he'd last looked. "I'm hungry."

Sam snorted and took the bait. "I'm not surprised. We should grab breakfast when we get out of here."

"What's open this early?"

"That diner, I think. It always smells like bacon when Vik and I run past in the morning."

Ulysses considered that. "It probably always smells like bacon," he said finally. "Like an aura."

Sam chuckled, and Ulysses elbowed him, because Babushka was still trying to sleep, but gently, because he was laughing now too, punch drunk from stress and exhaustion.

"I don't think that's how it works," Sam said finally. "I think someone has to be actively cooking for the place to smell that way."

"You haven't eaten bacon in, what, a year and a half? How would you know?" It struck him suddenly that a year and a half was practically the entire length of their relationship. Sam gave him a quizzical look. Possibly his face was doing something regrettable.

"I ate bacon for most of my life before I turned twenty-five," Sam said.

"Yeah." Ulysses looked down at his hands, still holding the exam he'd been grading.

"What?"

He didn't know, that was the problem. He was just full of feelings that seemed unmoored from reality, and there was so much going on that he could barely figure out what had rattled him. "We'll have known each other for two years this September."

Sam pulled back so he could turn his entire body to face Ulysses. "Is that a problem?"

"No! Not at all," Ulysses said. "I just—"

The door opened, and Laz came in, carrying the same plaid thermos he'd had the other day. He paused for a moment just inside the doorway, looking at Sam and Ulysses, and then jolted back into action, shutting the door quietly behind him. "Thought you might like to hit the road early," he said. "I couldn't sleep, so—"

Ulysses stared at him for a long moment, but Laz seemed fine. If he'd had another vision, he was keeping it to himself. "Thanks," Ulysses said, shoving the exams back into his satchel and shouldering it. "It's been a long night."

Sam grabbed their helmets. Laz smirked, but didn't say anything. He didn't need to. One evening they'd gone out for drinks; Eli had slid into the booth next to Sam and innocently told one story about his time working in the emergency room. Sam had bought them both helmets the next day.

"Anything to report?" Laz asked when they were almost to the door.

"There was a haunting earlier," Ulysses said.

Laz's brow furrowed. "Here?"

"Where else?" Ulysses shrugged. "Babushka dispelled them."

"I wasn't aware they travel in packs now." Ulysses had also been unaware. The idea made him shudder anew.

"They were . . ." Sam stumbled, apparently unsure how to finish the sentence. Finally he said, "They were mostly interested in Ulysses. And everything was quiet after Babushka got rid of them."

Laz nodded slowly, digesting this. "Do we know why they came in the first place?"

"No," Ulysses said. "Not yet."

Laz, miracle of miracles, relented and let them go.

The sun was coming up as they made their way out to the parking lot. There was still fog hanging around at streetlight level, giving the world a gauzy, blurred feeling, like an impressionist painting.

"Breakfast?" Sam asked.

Ulysses weighed bacon against sleep. Sleep lost. "Can you drive us there?"

Ulysses could feel Sam worrying without touching him. "All right," he said at last. Ulysses had suspicions about what might be lurking underneath that easy agreement and decided to ignore them for now.

Instead, he kicked the starter to life for Sam, then slid back to make room. Sam climbed onto the front of the bike; Ulysses wrapped his arms around Sam's waist and shut his eyes in prayer. He didn't know what god he was hoping would hear him.

They got to the Circle in one piece, and it was open, the same waitress on duty. Somehow Ulysses managed to eat a couple of banana pancakes and a strip of bacon and to drink a cup of coffee, and Sam kept up half a conversation about nothing in particular while he did it.

Eventually, Ulysses sat back, cradling his mug, and Sam sat forward, leaning his elbows on the table between them. "About what happened . . ."

Ulysses scratched his jaw. He needed to shave, and probably shower and go lift weights for a while, not in that order. When Sam didn't continue, he suggested, "With the ghosts?"

"I've seen ghosts before." Sam's voice went soft. "But Abbie hasn't come around for a long time."

"Not for years." They'd been in bed together the last time they'd seen her, near the beginning of their relationship. That was when they'd discovered Sam could also see ghosts if he was touching Ulysses, a strangely nostalgic memory. "She thought something was going on."

"I suppose she would know," Sam said slowly. "But . . . ghosts do what they want, right?"

Abbie had once upon a time been an often stoned remote viewer; someone who'd helped Ulysses with cases occasionally. Then she'd died, and as a ghost she was somewhat more sober, if not especially helpful. "In practice, that just means trying to get them to do anything is like trying to get consensus from an academic steering committee." Sam gave a surprised bark of laughter, and Ulysses grinned. "I don't think she'd have any reason to lie about this."

Sam sipped the dregs of his coffee. "Do you think whatever happened last night was big enough that the zaubergraph recorded something?"

"Maybe." Ulysses stared down into his cup. "Or . . . the house or the nexus might know something."

"You should probably get some sleep if you're going to talk to either of those places." Sam gave him a small smile. "Can I take you home?"

Ulysses looked at Sam through his eyelashes, hoping he looked heated rather than about to fall asleep where he was sitting. "You want to take me to bed?"

Sam laughed and said, "Yes," like there was nothing he'd wanted more all week.

THERE WAS A CERTAIN thrill to driving the motorcycle, Sam had to admit. Even taking it slowly down the mostly deserted early-morning streets, he felt a surprising rush of freedom. It beat the hell out of cars, that was for sure.

They made it up the stairs to the apartment without seeing anyone. Inside, Sam steered Ulysses toward the bedroom before he could get distracted, much to his husband's obvious amusement.

"Is that how it is?" he murmured, as Sam pushed him down to sit on the edge of the bed.

"Evidently," Sam told him. Ulysses laughed, but he raised his arms as Sam stripped his shirt over his head.

Sam examined Ulysses's chest for a moment, searching for marks from the earlier incident and finding none. Then he touched the scars on Ulysses's shoulder from their run-in with Livia's plant zombies, an almost superstitious gesture. The marks were quiescent now, no longer harboring any magic, malign or otherwise, other than the energy Ulysses had always carried. The full moon—harbinger of Laz's annoyingly vague vision—was still twenty-four hours away. This had been nothing. Sam ran his finger along the ridge of Ulysses's collarbone to the notch at the top of his breastbone, and then Ulysses reached up and caught his fingers.

"Are you trying to seduce me?" His voice was soft, tired, rough at the edges. Sam could feel the bond between them shiver as Ulysses fought to keep it contained.

"Lie down," Sam told him.

Ulysses hooked a finger through Sam's belt and tugged him closer. "Sam—"

"I know." Sam leaned forward and pressed his forehead against Ulysses's, breathing in the smell of him, sweet and a little medicinal, like the hospital. For a moment it was all there fizzing reassuringly between them, warm desire and old, sour fear. Ulysses's breath hitched, and Sam kissed him. "Come on, lie down," he murmured, pressing Ulysses back onto the bed, feeling his tense muscles slowly give way.

"You too," Ulysses said when Sam tried to pull away. "I just—I want—"

"I know." Sam crawled in next to him and settled the quilt across their shoulders. "I can stay for a while."

"Stay forever."

"I have to work."

Ulysses made a muffled, drowsy noise, not quite objection and not quite agreement, and pulled Sam closer, curling around him like he was going to protect him from the world. And for a moment, it was enough.

Eventually, Sam got up and went to the library. Partly because he was supposed to be working, and partly for the comfort of the building, the books, the routine.

At noon or a little after, there was a knock on the door to his office and he looked up to see Harry. He had a sudden sinking feeling.

"Lunch?" Harry had recently cut his hair and beard to celebrate having finished his dissertation, and it was still a bit surprising. Not that he was clean cut now by any stretch, but his hair was earlobe-length instead of down to his collar, his beard no longer that of a nineteenth-century Russian mystic. "Unless you're waiting for Ulysses."

Sam put down the book he'd been leafing through. "He's supposed to be sleeping." He got up and stretched, felt something in the middle of his back crack. "It's a long story. Where's Ellen?"

"That's a long story too."

They sat on the steps outside the Historical Society, watching a few harried grad students trekking from the humanities building to the Union.

"Ulysses's grandmother broke her hip on Saturday while we were in Chicago," Sam said eventually. "He's been running himself ragged ever since. We were at the hospital all night last night."

"How'd you work that out?" Harry took a sip of his Coke. "Aren't there visiting hours or something?"

"No idea. I think Eli talked to them." Sam cleared his throat. "Anyway, sorry I missed tennis this morning. With everything else, it slipped my mind."

Harry laughed. "We tried to call you about it, actually. Both of us got asked to pitch in last minute. One student in my department got in a car wreck on Saturday night and couldn't be around on Monday for the final he was supposed to proctor, so I got stuck with that plus the grading. Then this morning, really early, someone called Ellen to see if she could help with *their* grading, because they'd developed a migraine overnight and couldn't do anything but lie in a dark room." He paused and made a face. "I'm not sure that excuses calling El in a panic at five thirty in the morning, but . . ." He made a 'what can you do?' gesture.

"Of course," Sam murmured. After a moment, he said, "Car accident?"

Harry nodded. "He's going to be fine, but I think he was pretty banged up. They might still have him over at Wisconsin General. I went to see him yesterday." He grinned. "If I'd known you and Ulysses were hanging around, I'd have come by and said hi to his grandmother as well."

"Yeah." Sam looked down at his soup. "I'm sure he would have been happy to see you."

Harry looked a little taken aback at Sam's tone. "Trouble?"

"Not exactly." He exhaled. "I'm just . . . this isn't the type of crisis I'm good at."

Harry did not say, 'What kind of crisis *are* you good at, again?,' but Sam felt he would probably have been well within his rights to. What he did say was, "He has other family around here, doesn't he? Are they not helping?"

Sam shrugged. "They *are* helping. But . . . Ekaterina is really the one who raised him and his siblings, and she holds everyone together. Ulysses is barely sleeping. It's a mess."

Harry nodded, face serious. "His grandmother is the matriarch?"

"Yeah, no question." Sam turned his little plastic spoon in his hand. "It's a big family, and everyone has been pitching in, but—during the day."

"Leaving Ulysses on nights."

Sam scrubbed a hand through his hair. "He's a night owl. But I can't help worrying—"

Harry held up a hand to stop him. "Are you about to say, 'I'm worried they're taking advantage of his good nature'?"

"Yes."

"You want my advice?" Sam raised an eyebrow, because yes, of course, that was why he'd brought the whole sorry topic up. "Don't say that to him."

"I'm not a complete fool."

Harry gave him a level look, and Sam turned away. "Just make sure he's eaten. That's your job until someone tells you differently."

Sam said, "Why—"

"Most people who can't be convinced to take three to eight hours away from a sickbed to sleep *can* be convinced to take fifteen minutes to eat some ziti or something." Harry shrugged. "He'll sleep eventually. His body will force him to."

"You sound like you speak from experience."

Harry fiddled with the bezel of his watch. "Ellen's mom got really sick when we'd been together for about a year." After a moment, he cleared his throat and added, "You didn't hear it from me, but Ellen likes to be in control of situations. Telling her to take a break was asking her to give that up at a time when her mother's illness was making her life even more chaotic than usual. But food just feels like food."

Sam nodded slowly. "How long have you guys been together?"

"Six years." He shot Sam a mischievous look. "Most people date for a while before they get married so they can learn things like how to deal with each other during times of crisis."

"We've been through crises," Sam said primly. "You were there for some of them."

"And yet." Harry had a rakish grin, and when he pulled it out it was delightful. Sam could see why serious, sardonic Ellen had fallen for him. "You know we're happy for you guys, right?"

"Sure. Just bitter you never got to embarrass me with a big speech." Sam's stomach had unknotted a bit, enough that he took another bite of soup.

Harry laughed. "As an actor, if I needed an opportunity to do that, I'd create one."

Chapter 6

ULYSSES WAS LYING ON the chaise longue in his office, listening to the title track of *The Man Who Sold the World*, when Sam got home. He'd been trying to empty his mind in preparation for everything he had to do, let Mick Ronson's guitar run through him and replace all the apprehension he couldn't bring to a ritual. And it was working, at least up until he felt Sam return. Ulysses's control over the bond was thinner than usual, and Sam was like a spark at the edge of a newspaper, glimmering and growing stronger until he could practically see him through closed eyelids.

He waited, and after a while, Sam came in.

Ulysses opened his eyes and pulled off his headphones. Sam was leaning against the doorway, still in the gray suit he'd worn to work. "Feeling better?" he asked, voice casual, as though he weren't oozing worry. Ulysses frowned; Sam probably didn't know he was doing it.

Maybe Ulysses could give him a lesson or two.

He stretched. "I slept, I went to the gym, I showered, and I handed in my grades. I feel as good as possible, under the circumstances."

Sam's gaze had strayed to the strip of skin visible where Ulysses's shirt had ridden up. "Sounds like a productive day," he murmured. "Do you want something to eat?"

Ulysses eyed him. "What did you have in mind?"

Sam snapped his eyes to Ulysses's, looking vaguely embarrassed. "Dinner. I could make a casserole."

Ulysses stood, closed the gap between them in two quick steps, and backed Sam into the doorjamb. Sam gave him a little half smile, tilting his head down, and Ulysses kissed him. "I don't have time to eat right now," he said when he'd let Sam go. "I have to head over to Gooseberry House and do the rite of communion."

Sam didn't respond, just followed Ulysses with his eyes while he turned off the stereo and put his headphones away. It wasn't an accusation, but there wasn't much he did that merited this degree of scrutiny. Well, not safe things. But this was safe-ish. Safe as houses, as Eli was wont to say.

He waited, holding his tongue. Finally, Sam said, carefully, "We could grab something at Nick's afterward."

Ulysses exhaled. "That sounds good."

They were sliding off the bike in front of the house before Ulysses managed to ask, "Is something wrong?"

Sam looked down at his helmet, tracing the gold racing stripe with one finger. "Why don't you want to do this? It's Gooseberry House. You love this place."

In Laz's mouth, those words would have sounded like a challenge. But Sam's tone was gentle and curious. Ulysses reached out and squeezed his hand. "I'm pretty sure the house is—" He hesitated. "With the caveat that places don't have emotions the way that humans do, that is—"

Sam made an encouraging noise.

"I'm pretty sure the house is mad at me. All autumn, when I was coming here to see Laz, I had this feeling . . ." He looked down at their linked hands, then tugged Sam away from the bike and up the front steps. "To say nothing of how it probably interprets Babushka's absence. If I have to do the rite of communion, all that emotion gets mixed up with me, and it's not very pleasant."

Whatever feelings Sam had about this confession, what he actually said was, "Why not call the watchtower instead?"

Ulysses paused in the middle of opening the front door. "You *have* been paying attention."

Sam rolled his eyes. "I'm not one of your undergraduates," he groused, following Ulysses in and up the stairs. "The watchtower is like a guardian of the house, right? An intermediary. I just thought it would be a more detached way to get information."

"Detached," Ulysses repeated.

"Emotionally uninvolved?"

"You're not wrong." He rubbed his jaw thoughtfully. "All right, let's try it." He led Sam to the second floor, along the hallway with the rather loud black and pink wallpaper and up the back stairs. Sam already had one hand on the doorknob to Ulysses's former bedroom when Ulysses shook his head and gestured at the access hatch set in the ceiling. Sam must have noticed it before, but he looked a little surprised. Ulysses tugged on the rope to release the ladder.

"I always thought this was some sort of crawl space access," Sam said, watching Ulysses ascend.

"My room was the attic." He paused, halfway out of the hatch. "Strictly speaking, I think it was an old servants' dormitory that got converted into an attic." He stepped through into the early evening air. Sam emerged a moment later. "We turned it into my bedroom when I went to college but decided not to live in the dorms."

Gooseberry House had a large, flat roof, punctuated by a tower on the street side. "I always wondered how to get up here," Sam said, wandering over to the edge.

Ulysses sat down in the lee of the tower. "I used to come up here to look at the stars."

"Not to get high with your friends?"

Ulysses could hear the smile in Sam's voice. He pulled the blanket he'd brought from his satchel and spread it on the roof. "At the time, I was trying to save my law-breaking for when it was really important."

"Not everything was illegal back then." Sam flopped down on his back on the blanket, not quite touching Ulysses, gazing up at the sky with his hands behind his head. Ulysses smiled at him.

"I don't know how anyone was ever surprised that you were Dionysus." He shook his head.

Sam grinned broadly. "I don't know either. The name was right there the whole time."

The ritual didn't take much setup. A sigil sketched on a sheet of paper, the stub of a candle stuck on a board, a quarter for a sacrifice, and he was ready. Kind of.

The lighter smelled of sulfur and carbon, and it was heavy and cool to the touch. Sam watched him turn it in his hand for a moment. He was quiet, but Ulysses thought he was wishing they could just get started. Or maybe Ulysses was projecting.

He opened it, flicked the wheel to watch the sparks dance, then closed it again. When he raised his eyes, Sam was kneeling at the edge of the blanket. The sky above them was still bright, the temperature comfortable. Perfect weather for a ritual. Ulysses exhaled.

"What do you want me to do?" Sam asked, and Ulysses blinked.

There was danger in having Sam too close. There was danger in having him too far away, too. He wasn't powerful, exactly, but the way power surrounded him, bending the world as he walked through it. . . .

Ulysses said, "Why don't you sit across from me?" Sam moved closer, crossing his legs. For a long moment, Ulysses sat, contemplating the ritual objects. He wondered if Sam was getting restless. But Sam didn't say anything, even if he shifted around a little.

Ulysses forced himself to clear his mind.

He lit the candle. And then he took Sam's hands, so their arms encircled the candle. "Watchtower of this house, I summon thee."

The spirit came to them quickly, almost before Ulysses was ready. Watchtowers weren't visible spirits—at least, Ulysses had never seen one—but they could be sensed. The one they'd called at Sam's family's house had been young and tenuous. Gooseberry House was older, and it had been inhabited by magic people for the better part of thirty years now, if not longer; Ulysses had no idea who the previous occupants had been. The spirit was clearly out of sorts when it arrived, bringing with it a sharp scent of vinegar and smoke.

Sam made a soft noise, as though at some sort of revelation. How must this appear to him? At least Ulysses had been around the block enough to know such epistemological inquiries rarely ended well, so he didn't ask. Instead, he focused on what he had to accomplish.

"I—" Ulysses began, not entirely sure what he was going to say, and it nipped him. "Ow!"

"Wait," Sam said, "what did it—"

It went for him again, and he cringed backward, jerking away from Sam's grip. Even without being able to see it, he knew teeth when they closed around his flesh. It bit down again and he yelped. "I'm sorry!"

There was a pause, as though it were listening.

"I wanted to apologize for Babushka's absence," he said in a rush. "I realize this must be difficult for you. She's fine. She'll be home soon."

He had a sense that the watchtower wavered. Or at least its franticness seemed to ease somewhat, so he added, "And I'm sorry I left so abruptly when I moved out last year. I was—my family—" He looked up at the sky, wishing it would give him some inspiration. "I was in a hurry."

Sam was definitely giving him a look, but Ulysses got the feeling the watchtower was paying attention now. He wasn't, by any stretch of the imagination, forgiven, but it was willing to talk.

"On Saturday, when the magic moved . . ." Ulysses felt the watchtower radiating confusion and hesitated. How to discuss the magic background with something that was, in some way, a part of it? He was trying to describe a wave to a fish. "Were you attacked?"

Outrage, hot and sharp, and pain. It surprised Ulysses. He couldn't tell exactly who or what had injured it or why it was angry, but the emotions were there. Sam looked taken aback, perhaps by the vehemence, or the idea that a protective spirit could be injured at all.

Ulysses said carefully, "From which direction did the attack come?"

He could feel it pulling toward Lake Mendota, almost directly north. Shit. He murmured, "Thank you. That was what I needed. You may depart." The sacrifice vanished with a little pop, and he let the spell fall closed.

It was Sam who, after a time, pinched out the candle. "Are you all right?" he asked, leaning close to Ulysses.

Ulysses rubbed his arm where the watchtower had bitten him. "I'm fine," he remembered to say.

"Are you?"

Ulysses shrugged uneasily. He got to his feet and paced to the edge of the roof to look out over the lake, one hand on the tower. The late afternoon sun played on the water; he could see the faraway mound of Maple Bluff, trees running along the shoreline away from it in both directions. "It's nothing I didn't expect. Or—I should have. If I'd been paying attention." He sighed and slouched against the tower, letting his head fall back against the brick, his eyes shut.

After a moment, he felt Sam's presence in front of him. "What do you mean?"

"The sanitarium, the nexus, they're both over there." He opened his eyes. "I don't want to go back there. Not—"

Sam frowned, stepped a little closer. "You don't have to do this."

Ulysses stared at him. "Of course I do. Somebody has to. We've established at every turn—"

"Ulysses—"

"—that something weird is going on—"

"Ulysses."

"And it would be dangerously naïve to assume that things will simply fix themselves without attention."

Sam shook his head. "*You* don't have to do it. We could hand the investigation off to someone. You're going through a lot right now."

They looked at each other. The moment stretched. Then Ulysses sighed and closed his eyes. "There's no one else." He sounded to his own ears like he was pleading with Sam. Maybe he was.

Sam leaned forward, pressing his forehead against Ulysses's. "Of course there is," he said, voice pitched low. "There's Laz. There's Cass. There's Celeste and Obe. There's m—"

"What the hell is all the stomping—oh." Laz pulled himself through the hatch onto the roof. "What the hell are you two doing up here?"

Ulysses looked over at his brother. "What are *you* doing here? Aren't you on Babushka duty?"

Laz snorted. "Since five o'clock this morning? Are you high?"

Ulysses heard Sam laugh at that, but it was a quiet, sad noise. "Who's with her now?" Sam asked.

Laz said, "Eli," but as he said it, Eli came trekking across the expanse of roof between them and the hatch. Laz frowned at him.

"A woman named Nadiya Lesko showed up," Eli said, shrugging. "Ms. Len—Ekaterina sent me away." He looked between the three of them. "Sorry, did I muck something up?"

Ulysses shook his head. "It's fine. Dr. Lesko was my thesis advisor, and Babushka's student back in the day. Did she say how late she was planning to stay?"

"Midnight."

Ulysses groaned inwardly. That was late enough that he didn't have any excuse *not* to go around the north side of the lake to investigate the nexus. But calling the watchtower had been more taxing than he'd expected, and it *was* the full moon—whatever else, Laz would kill him if he wasn't careful, but—

Sam put a hand on his forearm and said, "Before whatever you're planning, let's get dinner."

Ulysses . . . was actually pretty hungry. He looked up at Sam's face, which was tired and slightly pinched, then over at Laz and Eli. "Nick's?"

➤➤➤ ◄◄◄

S AM SLID INTO THE booth next to Ulysses in time to hear Eli finish a sentence like, "—almost every migraine patient in the last two days."

Laz frowned. "Is that unusual?"

"Statistically unlikely." They smiled at each other, at something in the shared language between them that Sam couldn't hope to penetrate.

Then Laz said, "A lot of Eli's patients are bloodline magic users," and Sam felt Ulysses stiffen beside him.

"Ah," Sam said neutrally.

"I think we need to consider that this may be related to Stricker's group," Laz said. "There aren't very many people out there with the capacity to do large-scale, high-power magic, which is really what the attack was—"

"There's a whole *department*," Ulysses said, but half-heartedly.

"Remind me who Stricker is?" Eli asked. "Laz told me once she'd been making life difficult for you, but he was not very specific."

"She tried to kill us," Sam said absently, watching Ulysses fight some sort of internal battle. "She was the daughter of my grandfather's research partner. She wanted to recreate some of their work."

Eli looked a bit lost. "Work on what?"

Sam frowned. "Immortality, mostly."

"We have no proof," Ulysses said at last.

"Someone is messing with the magical seabed, or whatever you're calling it these days," Laz said. "What more proof do you need?"

"Every time something weird has happened in the last eight months, we've thought it was related to Julie Stricker," Ulysses snapped, dropping his menu onto the table. "No one has seen her since the night we burned down the Quonset hut. Her followers were arrested. There's nothing to suggest that she's even in the city anymore."

The waitress appeared to take their orders before Laz could pick a fight with his brother.

"You're very dismissive," Laz snapped when she was gone. "It's your *husband* she was gunning for last August. I'd think you'd be more concerned."

"That's . . . not a terrible point, actually," Sam said, half turning toward Ulysses. He meant it at least partially in jest, but when he caught sight of Ulysses's face, something stopped him. "Are we sure it's not her?"

Ulysses made an aggravated noise under his breath. "That's not what I mean. Of course it *could* be her. Of course she *could* be after you. I just don't want to fly off the handle without some kind of proof."

Eli frowned. "What kind of proof would you need?"

"Knowing she was still in the area would be a good start," Ulysses drawled.

"It's not like she's listed in the phonebook," Laz said.

"Didn't you used to do all kinds of military intelligence shit?" There was a definite edge to Ulysses's voice now. Sam looked down at the table, pressing his fingers to the wood. It wasn't very old, as tables went. The trees had been older.

Why had he thought that?

The waitress came back and set a round of beer on the table. Sam took his glass and then looked at his companions, all of whom were at different stages of exhaustion, and shook his head. "If we go over to the . . ." He hesitated and took a swallow of beer. "To the sanitarium, could there be any clues there?"

"Possibly," Ulysses said. On the other side of the table, Laz and Eli exchanged a puzzled glance. The disaster with Livia had taken place before Laz had returned from overseas. Ulysses continued, "But unless someone left an envelope with her name on it lying around, I don't think we'd know if Stricker was involved just from wandering around there."

Laz snorted. "You don't know her magical signature by heart at this point?"

"I've seen her do magic exactly once, and I was a *bit* preoccupied." Ulysses picked up his beer and took a long, thoughtful swallow. "You know, why don't you take over that side of the investigation?"

He was definitely issuing a challenge to Laz, but the way he said it suggested he was also voluntarily letting go of something. Sam put a hand on Ulysses's knee under the table and squeezed gently, trying to hide his relief.

Laz wasn't as excited. "And do what? You said you can't trace her signature. She left her house. For all we know she left town, changed her name. What makes you think I could find her?"

Sam considered this. "If she's here, she hasn't vanished," he said slowly. "She still has to go to the grocery store. If she needs followers, she has to meet people somewhere to recruit them. Aren't there . . . I don't know, bars or something?"

"Magician bars," Ulysses muttered under his breath. And then, more loudly, he said, "Yes, go round the Gramarye Tavern and ask if anyone has seen her."

From the look Laz was shooting at their side of the table, that wasn't the benignly helpful comment it could have been.

"She had at least a bachelor's if not a PhD or something. She changed her name from Barth to Stricker, suggesting she got married. At some point, her photo was probably in the paper," Sam continued, trying to ignore whatever was going on between his husband and his brother-in-law. "If we could find it, you could take it around and show . . . whoever. Like a private eye."

"By 'we,' I assume you mean me," Laz said levelly. "Ulysses needs to keep his head down for the next day or two. My vision—"

"I promise I will stay at the hospital all night, safe and sound," Ulysses said dryly, "if that will make you feel better."

Sam smiled, but his throat felt abruptly tight, and he had to take a breath to steady himself before he spoke. "I'm happy to help," he told Laz. "The library is pretty slow between the end of classes and the beginning of summer term."

Laz looked like he wanted to say something snappish in response, but the waitress returned and set a burger in front of him, so he shoved a french fry into his mouth and bit down angrily instead.

Sam was waiting for Ulysses next to the motorcycle when a man with long hair and a clipboard walked up to them.

"Hey, man," he said, not quite looking at him. "We're collecting signatures for a proposal to turn State Street into a pedestrian mall."

A man standing outside Nick's smoking a cigarette shouted, "Don't sign that. It's going to turn the place into a haven for hippies."

"We're just trying to get some change around here," the man shouted back. "The place will be better without cars, man."

Sam raised an eyebrow. "Sure," he said, and took the clipboard. It was a simple form, asking for his name, address, and signature.

They'd been married for nearly nine months, and it wasn't as though he'd been stymied by the idea of writing his name every time the subject had come up. He was Sam Sterling, the same as he had been since he'd been old enough to decide. But on the other hand, they'd never really talked about their names, a fact of which Sam had grown all too aware since Babushka's fall. It was hard to ignore all the little hints that he stood somehow outside the family.

Quickly, feeling oddly rebellious, he signed *D. Samuel Sterling-Lenkov* and then stood there for a moment, staring at it. Almost before he realized what he'd done, Ulysses arrived and took the clipboard.

He looked at the list of names and then up at Sam, and Sam held his breath. But eventually, Ulysses just signed his own name and handed the clipboard back to the stranger. "Maybe a little change would be a fine thing," he said, and slid onto the motorcycle.

Chapter 7

THEY WOUND UP ON a tiny beach near the Warner Park boat launch on the northeast shore of Lake Mendota, the closest Ulysses could bear to get to the sanitarium. It felt remote, a thick stand of trees separating them from the nearest houses on either side, but they could hear the distant shouts and whistles of a game being played elsewhere in the park.

"Baseball," Sam murmured after a particularly loud cheer. He settled on the edge of the grassy sward where the land dropped away toward a narrow strip of sand running down to the lake.

"You think so?" Ulysses couldn't hear any particular noise that would suggest one sport over another.

Sam shrugged. His gaze was fixed on the western horizon, where the sun was beginning to set, the light dancing orange and yellow, too bright to look at for long. "I only know it's baseball season because Vikram keeps trying to convince me to go to a Brewers game with him." He made a face.

"Not a fan?" Ulysses forced himself to sit down, next to Sam but not touching. He stretched his legs out into the sand.

"Not really." Sam smiled wryly. "I don't know if Vik is either. He just really likes statistics mixed with storytelling."

"Did you tell him you'd go?" Ulysses watched Sam slip the coat off his shoulders, fold it neatly on the grass next to him, and loosen his tie. He looked good. It felt like early days for summer, but Sam's olive skin was already tan when he rolled up his shirt sleeves. He looked like he should be sunning himself on a beach in Naxos, not fucking Warner Park in Madison, Wisconsin. And god, Ulysses wanted to give him that. Wanted to whisk him away to somewhere they could relax, alone, and not be dragged through this terrible drama, whatever it was.

"I told him if he went to the opera with me, I'd go to a game with him." Sam tugged at his cuff. "The opera season doesn't really start until fall, though, so I guess I'm going to a baseball game in July, and then we'll see if Vik follows through on his end."

Ulysses felt—hurt was probably not the right word. Stung, perhaps. "I'd go to the opera with you," he said, trying to keep his voice neutral, aware of his own absurdity.

Sam blinked at him. "I know. I thought you probably would. I just . . ." He trailed off, giving Ulysses an odd look. Ulysses lowered his eyes, focusing on the strip of dark, wet sand a few feet away, the seaweed that had washed up. After a moment, he heard Sam sigh before asking, "What are we doing here?"

Ulysses was no longer sure. It felt like the moment before a migraine, when the world was too much of everything. The sounds from the game were shrill, the clothes on his body were uncomfortable and itchy, the light hurt his eyes, and the gentle tug of the bond, normally a soothing reminder of Sam's presence, was like a cheese grater on his nerves. He was halfway to hoping something *would* come kill him at moonrise. "The sunset is nice," he said, somewhat nonsensically, hoping to distract Sam.

Sam looked at the lake again. "It *is* nice," he said. "Clearly, its pulchritude is why you're still wearing your shades." He reached for the sunglasses, and Ulysses moved his head away without thinking. Sam froze and then lowered his hands, hurt radiating off him.

Ulysses pressed his fingertips against the ridge of his eyebrows, where the pain of his migraines usually gathered first. He tried as hard as he could to dial the bond down to zero. Not that it made much difference; Sam was still broadcasting his emotions as loudly as ever, and Ulysses made a mental note to teach him some shielding, not *maybe someday* but as soon as he felt better.

"We are here," he said after a while, "so that I can try to commune with the nexus."

Sam looked hard at him, then around, as though expecting to spot it. "Is this where it is?" he asked. "I thought from the way you described it . . ."

"It's . . ." He tried to think of how to describe the nexus in space and ran out of words. "I thought I could reach it from here." If he knew how. But he didn't. The nexus had always just been there, like the grass they were sitting on. He couldn't *talk* to it any more than he could have a conversation with a tree. And yet, here he was.

If Sam caught the undercurrent of despair in part or in full, he didn't say anything. Instead, he sat with his eyes fixed on the sunset and stretched out his hand on the grass between them, palm up. An invitation. A peace offering.

Ulysses took it, and for a while they sat side by side, to all appearances just watching the sun sink slowly toward the horizon. After a while, Ulysses let himself lean sideways, resting his head on Sam's shoulder. The pain began to sneak up the back of his neck. He tried to quiet his mind, to reach out to the nexus—but all he could feel was the park around and behind him. It was an old one, and—well, it wasn't what he was there for. Eventually he dropped the line of inquiry all together, trying to push the worry away.

"Sterling-Lenkov, eh?" he said instead, and felt Sam go tense again.

He wasn't sure why. A moment later, Sam said, "I believe it's fairly normal for spouses to take their partners' names when they marry."

Of the married couples they knew, only Obe and Celeste had the hyphenated Lenkov-Démosthène; Ellen and Sita were professional women and had kept their maiden names. Ulysses didn't bother to point this out, because Sam was no doubt already aware. Instead, he said, "Be careful calling yourself a Lenkov."

Sam pulled away. "It's nothing *you* don't do every day," he said, sounding defensive.

"I don't have a choice," Ulysses said. "It's my name."

"But it's my . . . I mean, I wanted . . ." Sam trailed off and fell silent, as though the fight had gone out of him all at once. For once, Ulysses didn't feel a thing, like Sam had shoved all his emotions into some dark cave.

Ulysses waited, but Sam didn't say anything else, so eventually Ulysses got up. "Come on," he said. "Let's get you home."

❧ ❦

S AM LOOKED UP IN dull surprise when Laz appeared at the library late the next morning. Despite their conversation, he hadn't really expected the man to show up. Laz was dressed reasonably nicely, too, in clean, non-oil-stained jeans and a short-sleeve button-down shirt, neatly tucked in. His hair and nascent beard were still wild, though. That was reassuring.

"How did you get in?" he asked, although he knew from experience that it was hard to keep the Lenkovs out of anywhere they really wanted to be, for good or ill.

Laz just snorted. "I have an ID." At Sam's obvious confusion, he said, "I'm registered as a non-degree-seeking graduate student for the summer term."

"You are?" Sam blinked. "Does Ulysses—I mean—"

Laz bristled. "My academic credentials are impeccable, I'll have you know." He crossed his arms in front of his chest. "The Air Force Academy is highly rigorous, and I graduated at the top of my class."

"That's not what I meant." Sam took a deep breath. "All right. Newspaper research. Let's go."

They went across to the Historical Society, and Sam showed him where all the microfilms were.

"How old was Julie Stricker?" He tried to bring her face to mind and felt himself flinch away. Most of what he recalled from their meeting was the fear and her curdling dislike of him, of gods more generally. He cleared his throat. "About ten years older than Ulysses?"

Laz shrugged. "At least. Maybe twenty, twenty-five. Hard to tell with some people even under the best conditions, and when we met her—"

"Not really the best conditions." Sam looked at the cabinets of microfilm. "If we take twenty-five years older than Ulysses as the outside, that makes her fifty-five-ish. That means she was born around 1916. So we should presumably look for a wedding announcement sometime after 1934."

"You want to look at *forty years'* worth of papers?" Laz squinted at him. "I guess if we each take twenty—"

"It's eighty, actually," Sam said. "We have to look at the *Cap Times* and the *State Journal*."

"The *State Journal* endorsed McCarthy!" Laz hissed, horrified. "Multiple times!"

They stared at one another for a long moment, Sam fighting the impulse to rub his forehead. Finally, he said, "I'll take the *State Journal*, all right?"

"Fine."

Both papers had been dailies for most of their existence, which meant that a single roll of microfilm contained hundreds of issues that had to be scrolled through. Sam decided to start with the most recent issues and work backward, in the hope that Stricker had been mentioned in some UW-related article. But no dice; two hours later, he'd reached 1954, and Laz had worked his way forward to March of 1941.

Laz sat back and groaned, rolling his neck. "There has to be an easier way to do this. Isn't this indexed somewhere?"

Sam shook his head. "Not marriage announcements, I don't think. Not here."

"Shit," Laz said, drawing the vowel out along a lengthy exhale. He rubbed his face. "I have to go walk the dog. And you probably have other work. Why don't I meet you back here in a couple of hours?" He bounded out the door almost before Sam could acknowledge the plan.

Sam had been enjoying the mindlessness of the task; it kept him from thinking about how the rest of his life was suddenly falling apart.

No, that was an exaggeration. It wasn't falling apart. Ulysses had still kissed him goodnight, lingering for a moment at the door of the apartment, murmuring "I love you" despite that bizarre interdiction against calling himself a member of the family. Then he'd run off to spend another night alone at the hospital. It didn't make any sense to Sam. He kept looking at all his different premises and thinking . . . what? It was like being in free fall. He couldn't locate himself in space. They were married, everything was fine, Ulysses wanted him around to go to concerts and dinner with, wanted him around to fuck, but Sam couldn't . . .

He could only really be a Lenkov if he was willing to follow a set of rules he didn't understand. Possibly no one could explain them, either; certainly not Ulysses, not right now, half-crazed from sleep deprivation. It was not, in some respects, any better than being part of his original family had been.

Of course, none of the Lenkovs had tried to sacrifice him to Dionysus.

Sam came to the end of the 1954 reel and started to rewind it, only to pause as a familiar face he'd missed the first time flashed past. He scrolled the machine along manually and found himself staring at a grainy photo of Julius Sterling. It was unmistakable, those dark eyes and heavy eyebrows, unsmiling lips beneath a walrus mustache . . . Sam remembered standing in the man's study, on the weathered Persian rug, feeling almost unable to breathe because his grandfather was staring at him.

Died suddenly, the obituary ran. *Julius Sterling was born on July 8, 1890 in Madison, Wisconsin, to Howard and Agatha Sterling. Julius followed family tradition and attended Harvard University, graduating in 1912. He then worked as a pharmacist's assistant. When the United States entered World War I, he enlisted in the Navy and served in the Mediterranean. It was there that he met and married Alexandria Sophia Konstantinou. On his return, he studied at the University of Chicago, eventually earning a PhD in biology and biochemistry. In 1920, Alexandria and their young son Howard joined him in the United States, and in 1924 the family settled in Madison, Wisconsin, where Julius took a position as a professor with the University of Wisconsin–Madison. He became well-known as a researcher into issues affecting women's health after Alexandria suffered a difficult birth when their daughter was born in 1925, with complications that would lead to her own death several years later.*

He is preceded in death by his parents and wife. He is survived by his children, Howard (Francine) and Joanna (Richard), and by his grandchildren, Maxwell, Alyson, Dionysus, Troy, and Stephanie.

That was it. The old man with piercing eyes reduced to less than two hundred words. And yet . . . Unbidden, a different image rose in Sam's memory, a photograph hidden in Howard's office. It showed a dark-haired woman in old-fashioned dress whose face held a ghost of Sam's own. She was perhaps twenty-five, smiling, her dark eyes dancing. She'd raised Howard until he was seven or eight. And here she was again, a ghost in the background of her husband's obituary. Had he started experimenting before she died? Would she have known?

Howard had *hated* Julius. But what the hell did the rest of it mean?

Sam went back to his office and buried himself in cataloging a newly donated copy of *Micrografia*.

Laz showed up there at three, clutching a photostat copy of an old clipping.

"Hey!" Sam blinked, suddenly realizing what time it was. "Did I forget to come down and meet you? I thought—"

"Nah. I called the *Cap Times*." Laz dropped the sheet of paper on Sam's desk and sat down in the visitor's chair, grinning. "Told them I needed a copy for my sister's anniversary present and asked if they kept an archive or something. Turns out there's a lady who works in the layout department. Her name is Mildred, and she's been there since 1942. Anyway, she found it." He tapped the date on the top. "Nineteen fifty-one. You think Mr. Stricker here got drafted or something?"

"Or he was about to be." There was a certain adorable quality to Laz when he was excited. Sam decided never to tell him that. "I wonder if he came back." The page had been copied on an elderly photostat machine, and the text was blotchy, although the photo of the happy couple was clear enough. "What's next?"

Laz drummed his fingers on his knee. "I'm gonna go check out some places, see if I can figure out if she's been recruiting. Maybe tomorrow night. You busy?"

"Probably not." Sam smiled wryly. Laz didn't ask for details.

"I'll pick you up at eight." He bounded to his feet and grabbed the paper. "Don't wear a suit."

"What do I wear, then?"

"Not a suit," Laz said over his shoulder, and he was gone.

* * *

ULYSSES LOOKED UP MID-AFTERNOON to see Peregrine hovering in the door to his office, clutching a folder to their chest. "You wanted to see me?"

"I did." Peregrine seemed to be constantly in motion through the department, always just ducking out of one meeting to rush to class or run an errand, and Ulysses had learned that spreading the word that he wanted to see them worked better than trying to track them down. Ulysses gestured Peregrine to a seat. "How was your semester?"

Peregrine shrugged. "I think it went well."

Ulysses said, "I've heard good things from Dr. Lesko." It was a bit of an understatement. Peregrine had been in the department for only one term, but they were by all accounts quite as brilliant as their application had made them seem. They were interested in studying geography and the topography of magic, and Ulysses had been excited to take them on as a student. Now he was sure it was just a matter of time before someone in the engineering department caught on to the clever machines they were constantly working on and poached them.

They looked pleased at the praise. Peregrine was small, graceful, full of an irrepressible energy, like a bottle full of fireflies. They seemed to be constantly in motion; they didn't sit so much as perch at the edge of furniture, giving the impression that in a moment they'd be up and about again.

Ulysses wondered if he'd ever had that much energy in his entire life.

"Was there something you wanted to discuss?" Peregrine was looking at him curiously. "You don't usually summon me."

"I—" Well, he had summoned them, in a roundabout way. "Yes. I had some questions about the zaubergraph."

"Is it a problem?" Peregrine asked immediately, poised to hop to their feet. "I can move it. It's—I wanted it to be somewhere high up, but I'm not sure that makes too much of a difference—"

"No, no," Ulysses said. "I mean I was looking at the output from last Saturday, and I had some questions."

"Oh!" Peregrine opened their folder and flipped through the papers inside. "I haven't had a chance to check it yet. Did something happen? Was there a problem?"

"Possibly." Ulysses looked at them carefully. "Were you in town?"

"No, I was in St. Paul for a friend's graduation." They found the page they were looking for and pulled it out. From a distance, it looked like every other page of tracery Ulysses had ever seen come out of the zaubergraph, but it apparently meant something more to Peregrine. "Well, this is . . . I see what you mean."

"You see something? I wasn't sure."

Peregrine looked up at him. "It's subtle, but—" They gestured at a line. "This is a little unusual. Were you here?"

Ulysses shook his head. "I was in Chicago." Peregrine dropped the page on the desk and Ulysses looked at it, upside down this time. "I don't have a lot of experience with zaubergraphs, and I'm not too familiar with what you've done to this one." He paused, considering the mystifying tangle on the page. "Do you have the one from Monday night, or early Tuesday morning?"

"This past Monday?" Peregrine found the page with the abnormality quickly this time. The lines were not as dense in the top of the chart, but in the middle section they were much spikier. "It's odd, isn't it? I haven't seen anything like that before."

Ulysses nodded, thinking of Abbie and the other ghosts. "No chance of a natural phenomenon?"

"I don't know. Seems unlikely." Peregrine tugged at their hair, which was shaggy in a neglected sort of way. "I suppose there's a chance something malfunctioned. . . ."

They trailed off, and Ulysses guessed that the aforementioned chance was probably pretty low. "I see." He looked at the two pages next to each other, but other than a few wiggles that looked subtly different from the rest, he couldn't see any patterns. He handed the graphs back to Peregrine. "Do you know if it's possible to refine the spells to give information about where the magic is coming from?"

Peregrine looked thoughtful, then shook their head. "The zaubergraph isn't really designed for that." They sat for another few long moments, frowning. "I've been working on ways to make it useful for detecting magic residue. But I would have to make it portable for that to really be worthwhile."

"You mean you'd need a battery?"

"Essentially." They sat forward in their seat, sounding more confident. "Something with more juice in it than your standard nine volt, but car batteries are too heavy to lug around."

Ulysses nodded slowly. "You know, my brother is designing a new battery. Let me give you his number."

Chapter 8

I T WAS PAST ELEVEN by the time Sam followed Laz into the Gramarye Tavern. They'd already been to four other bars, and he was no longer feeling much in the way of pain.

He'd been wearing jeans and the Stumbling Blindly T-shirt Troy had given him on Saturday—had it only been Saturday?—when Laz arrived to collect him. The outfit had received a skeptical look, which Sam felt was probably deserved—he looked awkward in short sleeves, his arms were too long, his elbows were knobby—

"What's Ulysses think of that getup?" Laz had a way of asking certain questions out of the side of his mouth, like he was some sort of Sam Spade private eye.

"I don't know," Sam said. "He hasn't been home." He'd returned from work to a note informing him Ulysses had gone to a meeting and was off to the hospital from there. 'Don't wait up.'

Fine.

"Do you have a leather jacket or something?"

He did. Ulysses had gotten it for him after Madeline Island, a *glad you lived, now that you're not a god you have to be a little more careful on the motorcycle* present. It was boxy on Sam's lean frame, made him look bigger than he was. Tougher.

"Is this why you're bringing me along?" he asked a little later, catching sight of himself in the shiny side of Laz's car. "Muscle?"

Laz sucked his teeth and said, diplomatically, "In a sense," which made Sam laugh.

"But in another sense?"

"Eli's busy and I thought it would be boring to come alone." He clapped Sam on the shoulder and went into the bar.

The Gramarye Tavern was a seedy dive bar, far enough down East Wash as to be firmly out of the student area of town. It was housed within a square brick building with a cement stoop and a few neon beer signs in the high windows. Inside felt charged as soon as they stepped through the door. There weren't too many people there on a Wednesday night, but they were all magicians, and as far as Sam could tell they were all giving him and Laz the hairy eyeball.

Sam slid onto a barstool. "This place is like if the Hells Angels did magic."

"Who says they don't?" Laz leaned against the bar with scruffy insouciance. "I take it my brother hasn't brought you here before."

Sam shook his head, aware that he was radiating the sort of wide-eyed naïveté that was likely to get them stomped. He tried to summon the version of himself that had gone drinking in Brooklyn Heights once or twice. "Do you bring Eli here?"

Laz rolled his eyes. "I like Eli. I don't want to frighten him off."

Sam wasn't sure how to take that. Eli had never struck Sam as the type who scared easily. He had once decided to negotiate with dybbuks that had been commanded to murder him. But before Sam could respond, the bartender slid over and said, "Don't I know you from somewhere?" Her manner was not that of someone launching a pickup line or greeting an old friend.

"I don't believe I've had the pleasure," Laz said smoothly. "But—"

"You're a Lenkov, aren't you?" When Laz blinked, she whooped. "I knew it. What are you doing here, buddy?" She was tiny, barely clearing five feet tall, and thin, with dark brown skin and short black hair. She wore glasses with thin tortoiseshell frames, a black vest, and black pants.

"I just wanted some information and then we'll be on our way," Laz said, recovering quickly.

"Buy a drink," the bartender said, and smiled. She had a lot of sharp white teeth. It wasn't exactly a happy smile.

"Whisky, neat," Laz said.

"And your friend?"

Sam shrugged. "Sounds good to me."

The whisky appeared quickly. The bartender took a five-dollar bill from Laz and went down to the end of the bar to ring them up. Laz lifted his glass in a mock salute, and Sam clinked his against it.

"Does Ulysses come here a lot?" he found himself asking. "Or—did he?"

Laz took a sip of his whisky and grimaced. "What do you think?" He looked around at the bar's interior, one eyebrow raised, taking in the dart board, the pool table, the pinball machine blinking in the corner, neon lights, a card game going on in the corner. The walls were covered with wood paneling, decorated here and there with a few taxidermy ducks and one deer head. It was like any townie bar in the city, except for the clientele.

"It's probably more happening on a Saturday night." Sam tasted the whisky. It wasn't good, that was for sure, but it had a strong bouquet of smoke and forgetfulness.

When the bartender came back with Laz's change, he set it deliberately on the bar in front of him and pulled out the photo of Julie Stricker. "I'm looking for this woman. Has she been in?"

The bartender studied the image silently. Helpfully, Sam added, "She'd look a bit older now." And much meaner. He didn't say that part out loud, probably. Instead he took another drink of the whisky.

He was struck by an intense desire to find Ulysses. He usually had some of that, but this was ten times stronger than usual, a fishhook sunk beneath his sternum, pulling him vaguely west. It wasn't that late. He would go and find Ulysses and apologize for—he wasn't entirely sure what he'd said back at the park, but apologizing would probably help. And they could go get ice cream or something. And talk. How late was Rennebohm's open? He looked down at his left hand, wrapped loosely around the short glass, and at the silver wedding band he'd worn daily since last September.

He slid off the barstool as gracefully as he could, and turned to look toward the exit. The bartender was saying something to Laz; across the room, a rather large man in an old blue work shirt scowled at them from behind the pool table while his friend lined up a shot. Another man, alone at a table, was also clearly keeping an eye on them. One of them was about to come over, put a hand on Laz's shoulder, and say to the bartender, "Are these guys bothering you?" and that wasn't going to end well. Sam met their gazes in turn. Nothing to worry about here, fellas. Let's all just—

The world shivered sideways for a moment, and Sam staggered into Laz, who was suddenly clutching his temples.

"What the hell," Laz said, loudly. "Sam, how much have you had?" Laz was strong enough, but he still nearly fell under the sudden application of Sam's unwieldy body.

"Sorry," Sam said. Something squirmed in his inner ear and the world lurched in the other direction. "I'm—I'll be outside."

He barely made it to the alley behind the bar before he threw up.

There was less in his stomach than he'd imagined. A beer, a brandy, two whiskies, and one onion ring he'd regretted almost as soon as he bit into it. Maybe that was why the world seemed to be trembling slightly, tipping over his ears as he straightened up.

The alley was really the space between the back door of the Gramarye Tavern and an outbuilding on the same property, an old brick icehouse or something. Maybe the door into the bar led to the kitchen, because the whole alley was overhung with the nauseating scent of bacon and old fry oil. There was a dumpster at one end. At the other, his hand on the wall of the icehouse, was Sam, miserable now, flushed and shivering. He looked up, but the sky was cloudy. Ulysses was—who knew. Somewhere down the isthmus where the normal people stayed, not angry men with dagger eyes.

His stomach reiterated its anger, and he bent forward. A moment later, the world shivered and heaved again, and he staggered sideways into the icehouse, face first.

Sam opened his eyes and found that he was lying face down on the ground. The asphalt was cool and gritty, and there were tiny flowers growing up in the cracks. He felt like he was dreaming, or like he'd just awoken from a brief nap, and the disorientation made him want to close his eyes again.

"Oh no you don't," Laz said. Sam hadn't even realized that Laz was there. He rolled over and regretted it. Laz's pale face swam into view. Beyond him was a distant and pale moon, thirty-odd hours past full, bright but mostly shrouded in clouds. Laz tugged hard on Sam's arms, trying to get him upright. "The car's right over there. If you can get up, you can lean on me. It's ten, twelve steps."

Sam considered his options: continue lying on the pavement until he died, or get up. Neither of them was great, so finally he forced himself up and let Laz lever him to his feet. This time the shorter man didn't stagger.

"The bartender," Sam said. "I didn't mean—"

"Later," Laz said.

Sam experienced the ensuing ride only vaguely. He remembered watching the streetlights outside, yellow-orange in the sky, the too-loud click of the turn signal. His face hurt.

Then they were out in the air again. Eli was there, wearing soft pajama pants and a white shirt, frowning at them from the top step of his back stoop. Laz looked apologetic and charming. Sam sat at Eli's yellow kitchen table and shut his eyes while Eli gently cleaned the blood he hadn't noticed off his face and gave him a couple of stitches to close a cut.

"Where's Ulysses?" Eli asked.

"Downtown somewhere," Sam said. Then it occurred to him that Eli might be asking Laz.

Laz said, "I'll find him," and slunk off.

"I'm not drunk," Sam told Eli. The lights in the kitchen were too bright, and his voice was too loud, making him flinch. Laz had carried the phone's receiver into the hallway, but even the distant murmur of his voice in the background was grating.

Eli shrugged, still looking for additional damage. "You're drunk."

"Okay, but I'm not *that* drunk." He wondered where Ulysses was. Safe, hopefully.

Oliver the dog came and put his head in Sam's lap, so Sam scratched him behind the ears.

"Ulysses wanted to rush over here." Apparently Laz was back; Eli nodded. Sam nodded too and regretted it. Laz went on, "I tried to tell him not to head out until after the moon sets. I had another vision in the bar, and if something is going on—"

"What?" Sam said, louder than he'd meant.

Laz glanced at him. "I had another vision. Same as the first, but more so."

Sam's nerves were too shot to react to that revelation with anything more than a single horrified twitch. He tried to decide whether saying what again would be helpful. Probably not. "Can you drive me home?" he asked instead. Was that where Ulysses was? Or maybe he could walk to the hospital after they left, or—

"It's late," Eli said, exchanging a look with Laz over Sam's shoulder. "Why don't you lie down in the guest room and wait for Ulysses? I'm sure he'll be here soon."

Sam didn't want to, but it was the kind of suggestion he didn't get much say in. The two men helped Sam upstairs. He brushed his teeth and washed his hands, discovered another scrape he hadn't noticed before by virtue of getting soap in it, and then tumbled into bed, feeling sad and lonely and hurt.

Chapter 9

S AM DOZED FITFULLY. ELI came in once to poke him and shine a light in his eyes, making him hiss. When he woke up again, it was early morning, and there were voices downstairs, none of them entirely happy. One of them belonged to Ulysses. But as much as he wanted to leap up and fling himself down the stairs and into his husband's arms, his body was not up for fast movement. The room was too bright and the light hurt his eyes, lanced straight through his brain and set things roiling everywhere in his body. He buried his face in his pillow.

He'd become too accustomed to being a god, or at least god-adjacent, looking on Ulysses's aches and pains and hangovers and illnesses with sympathy but a certain inward smugness that *he* didn't feel like that. It was hubris. It was chutzpah. It was arrogance.

This was terrible.

There was a soft grumble, and Eli's little cat got up, stretched, and left. Sam hadn't realized she was there; his thrashing must have dislodged her. He felt absurdly like he should apologize, but the words caught in his throat.

At some point, the door opened quietly, and Ulysses came in, his feet quiet on the carpeted floor. Sam felt him pause. Then Ulysses went around to the other side of the bed and lay down beside him.

Sam cracked one eye to look at him. Ulysses was unshaven, with dark rings under his eyes. He was staring at the ceiling.

"I'm sorry," Ulysses said eventually. "I should have been there."

Sam unwrapped an arm from around his pillow and draped it across Ulysses instead, pulling himself closer so he could press his face into his husband's shoulder. Ulysses smelled like old sweat, the hospital, anxiety, soap, coffee. "I don't know what happened," Sam said. His throat was scratchy and his voice sounded like someone had taken a file to it. "I wasn't—I fucked up somehow." He wasn't even sure what he was asking, and he felt like a huge baby for needing some kind of reassurance, but that was the world he was living in.

Ulysses nodded. "The magic moved again."

A few things clicked into place for Sam. "If that's what it was like when Babushka fell, I am not at all surprised she broke her hip." He reached up and felt his own face; the cut Eli had sutured was puffy and sore, safe beneath a square of gauze. A few other little scrapes were still healing. "I ran face first into a brick wall," he admitted. "Not my greatest moment." He rolled onto his back and looked up at the ceiling Ulysses seemed to be finding so absorbing. The plaster was bright with the morning light coming in through the windows, and Sam winced and shut his eyes.

Ulysses rolled onto one side and pulled Sam close, curling around Sam as though trying to shield him from the world, gathering his too-long limbs and aching body to his chest. Sam sighed and shut his eyes.

He was on the verge of falling asleep again when Ulysses said, mostly into the back of his neck, "I was at the hospital when it happened. And I was worried about the possibility of a secondary attack on Babushka, and Laz wanted me to wait, and it took me a while to get ahold of Obe to come down, and . . ." Silence. Sam could feel Ulysses gathering himself. "At least Laz was with you."

Sam just breathed for a few moments, thinking about that. "When we were in Carnac last winter, Titania read my tea leaves. She said something bad is going to happen."

"You didn't say anything." Ulysses didn't sound accusatory, at least. "You could have told me."

"I didn't believe her." Except that wasn't it. He tried again. "I didn't *want* to believe her." There was a long pause.

Finally, Ulysses made an affirming noise. "I like to believe that I'm capable of thinking about the world without self-delusion, but I suppose I'm as human as the next person."

Sam wanted to look at him, but he was afraid if he rolled over again, he would spill himself, somehow. "How did it happen, last night?"

He expected Ulysses to say he didn't know. Instead, he said, "I wonder if they managed to weaponize snap back somehow. Cast a big enough spell, let it fail, and then let the ripples take your foes out at the knees."

"How does that work? I was just in a bar. I was drunk, but I think I would have noticed a ritual of that magnitude."

Ulysses chuckled. The sound vibrated through Sam, making him feel absurdly better. "No one too near you, I don't think. You're just fairly sensitive."

"Wouldn't the spell caster get hit by that too?" Sam flinched just imagining it. "Do you think they lived?"

"How much do you care?" Ulysses pulled away, carefully tugging Sam onto his back.

"Not a lot," Sam admitted. "But it sounds painful."

"It does, doesn't it." Ulysses propped himself up on one elbow. Sam felt Ulysses's eyes searching his face, taking an inventory of his injuries with that piercing blue gaze. Ulysses shook his head. "I didn't hear any nurses gossiping about an ambulance bringing in little tiny pieces of some magician, so I imagine that they survived. There are ways of mitigating the damage if you're prepared for it." He relaxed again, settling his body against Sam's side, and rested a gentle hand on his chest. "When you're feeling better, I'll try to teach you some techniques."

"Will you?" Sam felt his left eyebrow twitch upward. Ulysses started to laugh, at first with genuine mirth, then shading over to something a little tighter, a little more hysterical, as though something was catching up with him. Sam found that he was laughing too, and couldn't stop, even though there was nothing especially funny about this, until Ulysses slumped wearily against him, still snorting.

"Thanks," Ulysses said quietly. Sam ran his fingers through Ulysses's hair, knocking it even more askew, and the other man groaned.

Sam relaxed and shut his eyes again. Ulysses touching him was a balm; everything hurt a bit less, and the clenching stress of what had happened seemed further away, more manageable.

After a while, Ulysses sighed and sat up. "We should go downstairs. Eli was making coffee when I came up, so it'll be ready by now."

"Do we have to make small talk?"

"No, but he'll probably want to examine you again." Ulysses slid off the bed and picked up the T-shirt Sam had unceremoniously dropped on the floor before he passed out. It was covered with blood and vomit. He made a face and turned it inside out, carefully folding it. "He was worried. When I got here, he was about to wake you himself." Ulysses picked up Sam's jeans; he looked like he wanted to burn them, but instead he folded them up as well.

Sam forced himself to sit up. It wasn't quite as bad as he'd expected, although his stomach gave an experimental lurch sideways. "I don't suppose you brought anything for me to wear?"

"Of course." Ulysses picked up a paper bag from beside the door. He fished out a clean shirt and a pair of sweatpants and tossed them to Sam, then dropped the filthy things in as a replacement.

Sam looked down at the shirt, a soft, old, long-sleeved thing, and then up at Ulysses. He felt like he was fighting to keep all his emotions off his face, and then wondered why and let go. "Thanks."

Ulysses gave him a bewildered little half smile. "Get dressed."

ULYSSES KNEW HE WAS hovering as Sam made his way downstairs. He was vaguely aware that he was always like this when Sam was injured. It happened rarely enough that he hadn't had much chance to get used to the idea; Sam was obnoxiously healthy. He hadn't picked up a single cold over the winter, or in the entire time Ulysses had known him. He'd been high a few times, and stabbed twice, but that was really about it. He'd come back from the dead once. Now he looked like he would have preferred to stay there.

Eli's kitchen was not large. There was an avocado-colored refrigerator shoved into one corner, an electric stove across from it, a small yellow table with yellow and chrome chairs, and a large metal bowl of water on the floor. Laz's dog, Oliver, a rangy, dingo-colored mutt, was sitting at attention in the doorway that led to the back of the house. He looked vaguely concerned that there were extra people around, like he wasn't quite sure whether he should protect Laz from the newcomers or ask them for attention.

Sam slid into a chair with a pained noise. "Is this what being hungover is like?" he asked, resting his forehead on the table.

Eli, who was in front of the sink, turned and fixed him with wry look. "It's probably good for you to understand what it's like for us mere mortals." Laz, at the stove, choked on his coffee, and Ulysses had to stifle a smile. There was something reassuring about Eli's insouciance; it felt like proof that nothing terrible was going on.

Eli set a couple of mugs on the table and stood in front of Sam with a small penlight, moving it horizontally in front of his eyes.

"Ow." Sam tried to turn away, but Eli held him in place with a hand on the jaw. "What are you doing? I didn't hurt my eyes."

"Checking that your pupils contract equally on both sides." Eli held up the penlight. "Follow it with your eyes."

"Do you have an aspirin or something?" Sam asked.

"You can't have aspirin." Eli was carefully untaping the gauze from Sam's eyebrow. "Do you still have a headache?"

Sam nodded. He looked a little better now that he was up and moving around, but still pretty miserable.

"You must have hit your head pretty hard." Eli frowned and glanced over his shoulder at Laz and Ulysses.

Ulysses raised his hands. "Neither of us actually saw him go down." The admission brought with it a fresh wave of guilt that he quickly stepped on.

"I realize that," Eli said patiently. "I was going to ask if there was any reason to believe his ongoing symptoms were related to the—the magical background, is that what you call it?"

"The magical proscenium," Sam muttered, and Eli chuckled.

"I don't know," Ulysses said. "But I still have a pretty bad headache, so it's possible."

He realized belatedly that he shouldn't have said it. Eli's attention was on him like he was a shark and Ulysses was blood spilled in the water. "Is it a localized headache, or general?" He grabbed Ulysses by the arm, guiding him to the chair next to Sam. "I mean, is it everywhere, or is it on a particular side?"

"Localized."

"Where?"

Ulysses tapped the right side of his head. Eli flashed the light in his eyes quickly, a stab of pain that was gone almost as soon as it registered. "Do you often get headaches like that?"

"Once in a while," Ulysses said, fighting the urge to squirm uncomfortably. The headache wasn't actually too bad, as these things went. The aspirin he'd taken was kicking in, and the coffee would help. He would be okay in an hour. His headaches certainly weren't bad enough to need Eli's attention.

Eli glanced over at Laz, who shook his head. "I don't know what you're looking at me for. I don't get migraines."

"Mm." Eli turned back to Sam. "You should rest until your symptoms resolve. I'll pull those stitches in a few days." To Ulysses, he said, "Do you get prodromal symptoms, or just a headache?"

Ulysses shrugged. "What counts as a prodromal symptom?"

Laz said, "Could you hand me some plates?" and Eli turned away to grab a couple out of the cabinet.

Ulysses felt relieved to be out of the line of scrutiny, but Eli was still speaking over his shoulder: ". . . aura, like blurry vision, or sensitivity to light or touch, nausea, sleep problems . . ."

Laz set a plate of scrambled eggs with a slice of toast on the side in front of him. Ulysses looked down at it, trying to ignore the thought that dwelling on the headaches gave them more power. "I get most of those occasionally."

Now Sam was looking at him. "You never mentioned any of this!"

"It barely happens!" Ulysses rubbed his face. "I don't think I've had a bad headache since November—"

He forced himself to stop speaking. Eli was looking at him speculatively, but all he said was, "If they get worse, or you just get tired of dealing with them on your own, come see me."

Laz set a plate of eggs and toast in front of Eli and one in front of his own empty chair. Sam received only toast, and looked grateful.

Ulysses didn't blame him. The food was acceptable, even appetizing; he was just so exhausted that the idea of spending energy eating seemed absurd.

"The bartender said she'd seen Stricker around." Laz set Eli's French press on the table in between Ulysses and Sam, along with a sugar dish and a quart of milk. Ulysses watched him walk around to sit beside Eli.

He asked, "Which bartender?"

"Maeve."

He could see Sam mouthing the name out of the corner of his eye. "What did she say?"

Laz shrugged. "Much less than I would have liked. But she thought Stricker had been recruiting."

Ulysses forced himself to take a bite of the eggs. Laz had scrambled them in butter and added some sharp cheddar, and they were as good as they smelled. When had Laz learned to cook? "Anything else?"

Laz sipped his coffee. "That's all I got. Honestly, we weren't there for very long before everything went all to hell and I had to drag your—I had to pick Sam up off the pavement and get him help."

Eli hummed to himself. "The rest of the bar's patrons . . . how were they?" He picked up his own teacup and looked at the pattern of tiny birds that covered the outside. "I mean, was Sam the only one to suffer such ill effects?"

Laz said, "There wasn't exactly a statistically significant sample there, Doc."

Sam snorted, and Ulysses looked over at him. He appeared to be staring blankly into his coffee; Ulysses suspected that he was on the verge of falling asleep again. But he was listening.

"After the first wave went off, I thought a couple of them looked rattled. There were only six or seven people there, mind you."

"*You* didn't feel it?"

"I felt . . . something. And I had another vision, like the last. That might have influenced my impression of what was happening." Laz looked like he wanted to say something else, but eventually he just took a jaunty bite of his toast. "It takes something pretty big to move me." He winked at Eli.

After breakfast, Ulysses helped Sam down the concrete steps of the back stoop, not because Sam needed his assistance, but because it gave him an excuse to ignore Laz's murmured conversation with Eli.

"I'll meet you at 1400," he heard Laz say, and then his brother came bounding out to catch them. "Get in the car."

"The bike's right there," Ulysses said. He'd parked behind Laz in the driveway.

Laz rolled his eyes. "Do you trust him on the back of that thing right now?" he said in an undertone.

Sam straightened up. "I'm—actually, I'm still pretty dizzy."

"I'll drive you back to pick it up later," Laz said.

"Is this a roundabout way of saying you don't think I should be driving either?"

Laz shrugged very casually, but what he said was, "You look like you're about to fall over, man."

Ulysses scowled. But he moved the bike.

It was a short drive back across the isthmus, but halfway there Ulysses could see the drugs Eli had given Sam start to take hold. He relaxed with a sigh against the passenger side door, his eyes flickering shut.

"Fine," Ulysses grumbled. In the rearview mirror, he saw Laz grin. So he asked, "What happens at two?"

"Eli wanted to look at a property. I said I'd go with."

Ulysses thought about the little brick house with its cozy kitchen. "Doesn't he own that house?"

"Yeah." It took Laz a moment to get his drift. "It's a commercial space. He's thinking about moving his practice."

"Off the Square?"

Laz shrugged. "He's got plans. Ask him sometime; I'm just around to check out the mechanicals."

Ulysses said, "Why do I doubt that?" and Laz laughed.

Ulysses got Sam out of the car and up the stairs, an arm around his waist for support. Sam muttered something as they paused outside the door. He wasn't exactly dead weight, but he was unsteady on his feet, and increasingly cuddly.

Once they were inside, Ulysses had to let go in order to lock the door and take off his boots. When he turned around, Sam had wandered off. Halfway to the bedroom he found a discarded shirt. A shoe lay on the rug a few steps later, and then a sock, and inside the bedroom door was the other shoe, and there was Sam, sprawled across the whole mattress, face down. He still had one sock on, and the gray sweatpants Ulysses had brought him.

Ulysses nudged him in the ribs. "Roll over so I can pull the blanket over you."

Sam made a noise but rolled over, looking up blearily at Ulysses. "Will you stay with me?"

Ulysses glanced over his shoulder. The curtains were drawn, but the brightness outside made them glow slightly in the dim room, reminding him that other things needed his attention. "I can't," he said gently. There was plenty of administrative garbage that needed to get finished up before the semester formally ended, to say nothing of checking in with Peregrine about the zaubergraph.

Sam was having none of it. "Sure you can. You still have a headache, right? Come lie down."

Ulysses looked down at him, the warm tan skin on display, the half-lidded green eyes, the mouth turned down at the edges, and sighed. "Sure. All right. But you have to move, you're taking up the whole bed."

Sam arranged himself under the blanket. Then he lay there quietly while Ulysses walked around the bed, pausing to strip off his jeans before he crawled in beside Sam. He was so quiet that Ulysses thought he had fallen asleep, and was nearly there himself when Sam rolled over onto his side.

"Thanks for coming to get me."

"Sam . . ." He shut his eyes against the guilt that whispered all of his sins. "Go to sleep."

"I just know this hasn't been easy for you," Sam continued. He put one hand gently on Ulysses's bicep. "I don't mean to be a burden."

"You're not," Ulysses said, more strongly than he'd meant to. "You really aren't. You didn't know this was going to happen. Neither of us did. If we had, I would've been with you, or—" He forced himself to take a breath. "Go to sleep, okay? We can talk later."

Sam looked at him for a long moment, and Ulysses was sure he wasn't going to let this go. But then he nodded and draped an arm across Ulysses's chest. "Yeah, okay."

"Okay," Ulysses echoed, and watched Sam's eyes flutter shut.

❧ ⟫⟫⟩ ⟨⟨⟨❧

S AM STEPPED OFF THE elevator into a forest.

It was an old forest, and there was something delicious about it, a certain satisfied air from the trees, or the scent of pine and yew, the distant murmurings of birds. Sam hadn't been in a really old forest in years. A deep sense of happiness and relaxation he hadn't known he was capable of settled over him.

And it had been in Memorial Library's basement all this time! He shook his head.

There was a trail through the undergrowth, possibly a deer track, and he followed it as it meandered along past where he thought the preservation department had been before. Looking up, he saw no pipes or electrical conduits, no stained drop ceiling, just the dark green of the crowns of trees seen from below, and patches of vivid blue where the leaves parted. A bird—something very large, like an eagle—swooped past to the right, making him jump. A moment later, the bird returned, sailing on near-silent wings, and dove quickly into the undergrowth. Sam listened to it thrash for a moment, and then stepped backward as it took off again, some small mammal dangling from its talons.

There was supposed to be a conservation lab here, where books were mended and rebound, part of the preservation department. And the depository for theses and dissertations. He remembered that much; he'd gone with Ulysses to deposit his dissertation last year.

Instead, he came to a bridge.

It was made of wood, and arched so high in the middle that he couldn't see where the other end came down from where he was standing. Full, leafy bushes obscured the creek the bridge spanned, but Sam could hear the cheerful rushing of its water. And from somewhere, a fell little tune filled the air. Perhaps he'd been hearing it all along, growing louder as he walked.

"Played by the picture of nobody," he muttered to himself.

He wondered, suddenly, about Ulysses. Was he all right? If he was, where was he? If he wasn't, why didn't Sam know?

Why didn't he know where Ulysses was? He always knew.

There was a tug beneath his breastbone that he associated with his husband. It seemed to draw him toward the other side of the bridge. He stepped forward, but hesitated just before setting foot on the first board.

There was nothing obviously weird about it as a structure, but suddenly Sam didn't think he wanted to cross it. Evil couldn't cross running water, right? Someone had said that.

Who had said anything about evil?

As he stood trying to think through this, he felt again that something was on the other side, waiting for him. Ulysses? Or—something else?

The posts of the bridge were carved ornately, although the longer Sam stared at them, the harder time he had making out what they actually looked like. Maybe they were oracle script? Ogham? Some kind of tally system? A complex type of hieroglyphics?

He was stalling. Meanwhile the music grew slowly louder.

Sam squared his shoulders and raised his chin. Above the chasm there were fewer trees, and he had a better view of a sky that was shading darker and darker, until on the far side of the bridge, it was a velvety blue-black so deep it felt as though no light could escape from it. There were no stars.

But Ulysses was over there somewhere.

Sam took a deep breath and stepped onto the bridge.

Chapter 10

S AM WOKE UP TO Ulysses leaning over him. He must have made a startled sound when he opened his eyes, because Ulysses sat back abruptly.

"Sorry, I thought—" Ulysses shook his head. "You seemed distressed."

"I was having the weirdest dream. There was a forest in the basement of the library . . ." He yawned.

Ulysses stared at him hard. "Is that all it was, do you think?"

Sam closed his eyes for a moment, tried to focus. The details were fleeing, but the sense of urgency remained. "I guess," he said uncertainly. "How would I know?"

"I don't know." Ulysses relaxed back onto one elbow. "I suppose there's nothing especially provocative about one dream."

"I mean, you've had visions before. What distinguished them?" Sam traced the line of Ulysses's shoulder with his eyes.

Ulysses weighed this. "Someone trying to stab me, usually."

"Then we're safe." Sam yawned again. "What time is it?" It felt like they'd slept a long time, but the room was still bright.

"Elevenish." Ulysses stretched and sat up. "You should go back to sleep if you can."

That sounded like a decent idea, but—"What about you?"

"I have to go. No rest for academics." He slid off the bed. "I've been working on ways to figure out where Stricker might be operating from."

Sam wanted to ask a lot of different questions, but instead, he said "How's that going?"

"Not much to report yet." Ulysses grabbed his jeans off the foot of the bed. "Peregrine is kicking around a few ideas. Filtering out local interference on the zaubergraph might help with longer-range detection. I thought if we could use a few of them, maybe we could triangulate sources, or if we could boost the signal more . . ."

Sam nodded, but slowly so he wouldn't make things worse for himself. "That sounds complicated."

"Probably." Ulysses stepped into the pants, not looking at Sam. "There's a lot we don't know about how magic propagates through space, so detecting it is complicated. This is a long shot. It's just the best idea I have right now."

"We'll figure something out." Sam bit his lip. "Or *she'll* find *us* and it won't matter."

Ulysses hesitated. "I suppose so." He came around the bed and kissed Sam gently on the lips, then on the forehead. "Now go to sleep, before your brain starts to overheat."

The ringing phone woke him.

It was—what time—Sam didn't remember what time Ulysses had left, but it hadn't been more than an hour or so ago.

He got up too fast and staggered as he tried to take a step, dizzy and weak-limbed. But his legs held, and he made it to the bedroom door, into the hall, and all the way to the phone.

"Hello?"

"Why aren't you at work?" The voice was authoritative and annoyed.

Sam panicked. "What day is it?" He twisted around to see the calendar. "Shit." Then he recognized the voice. "Howard?"

"I called the library but I didn't get any answer."

"I'm out today," Sam said. "And Dr. Pearlman—"

Howard made a dismissive noise, which was probably for the best, because Sam genuinely didn't know what he was about to say. "I need to see you."

"Today?" He tried again to figure out what time it was, then discovered he was still wearing his watch. It was just past noon. He shut his eyes.

"As soon as possible."

Sam took a deep breath. When he opened his eyes, the world was just about as he'd left it. "I'll see what I can do."

He showered and put on a suit—his favorite, in fact, the seal gray one—and a lively green tie he'd found in a market in France. It made him feel, if not precisely whole, then at least prepared to face Howard. His scrapes were much improved from the previous night, and when he took the gauze off his stitches, they looked . . . unremarkable, not too bruised or puffy.

Reaching the man was a different problem. Sam was by no means foolhardy enough to ride his bicycle the six miles to Howard's office in his present condition. Ulysses was busy. They didn't have a car, and anyway Sam thought Eli would have disapproved of him driving so soon after a head injury. So he called Ellen.

She was skeptical and intrigued in equal measure—as far as he could remember, she'd never met any of his family—but she was also bored, or at least sufficiently at loose ends that she agreed to pick him up. He refused to watch her face as he made his way from the doorway of the Baskerville to the passenger side of her old green Datsun. By the time he'd gotten in, she'd schooled her features again.

"You weren't kidding," was all she said.

"Afraid not." He glanced sidelong at her, but she was focused on checking her blind spot as she pulled away from the curb. "You're taking this well."

Ellen shrugged. "I considered what Ulysses probably did to whoever did this to you, and I felt as though justice had probably been served."

Sam smiled faintly. "We don't know who caused it."

"But Ulysses is going to figure it out, right?" She looked away from the road for an instant to assess him. Her hands stayed tight on the steering wheel.

"He's trying." Sam thought of the pavement behind that terrible bar, rough against his cheek, and the little plants. "He's trying," he said again.

"Well then." Ellen had long hair the color of tomato soup, and today she was wearing it loose around her shoulders. She pushed it impatiently out of her face when they stopped at the next light and said, "We're doing a little last-minute thing. A staged reading of that shortened *Hamlet* I showed you. At the party."

Sam frowned. "That's a month from now."

"I know." She shot him the placating expression of a director with a vision that was in no way in touch with reality. "But it's a reading, and we've got time for four or five rehearsals. We've got a cast ready to go."

"And you want me to do . . . what?" He considered her description of the project. "Music stands, I suppose. There was a lot of double casting in that short version; do you want nametags or something?"

"And weapons for the final fight. Not swords, but maybe water pistols?"

They were on East Washington Avenue now, rolling past old brick storefronts, a few warehouses, a tenement, the smokestacks of the electric plant visible out his window. They were going to go right past the Gramarye Tavern. He shifted, crossing his ankles. "Something a little flashy?"

Ellen nodded. "Funny, but also kind of serious. We don't have a stage, so it has to be visible."

Sam nodded. "I'll pick up some silver spray paint." He wished he had a piece of paper to make a list on. He wished he had anything to be doing other than driving back toward the Gramarye. "Anything else? Full costumes, or are you doing stage blacks?"

"What do you think about crowns?" He was holding his breath. Ellen didn't notice. "Or some kind of hat for Claudius, Gertrude, and Hamlet." She drove with both hands on the wheel, eyes fixed on where the car was headed, which was very responsible of her.

"Baseball caps," he suggested. "They could be one team, and Fortinbras could be a different one?"

Ellen laughed. The car sailed past the bar. Sam breathed out.

The Sterling Enterprises office was the same as it had ever been—an industrial exterior hiding a vaguely modern design sense inside. But this visit, instead of Howard's secretary attempting to prevent his entry, she smiled at him. The smile was rather forced, but it was an effort. "Good afternoon, Mr. Sterling," she said, getting to her feet. "Miss . . .?" She looked at Ellen uncertainly.

"Dr. Balfrey," Sam said. He'd asked her to come in, partly because it seemed rude to force her to hang around the parking lot, and partly because he suspected it would piss Howard off.

The secretary handled everything professionally. "Of course. Just one moment." She sat down and picked up the phone to announce to Howard that his next appointment had arrived.

Sam whispered, "The last time Ulysses and I were here, the security guards nearly threw us out."

Ellen smirked. "Good luck."

The walls of the outer office were lined with photographs: Howard accepting an award for leadership, Howard and Sam's siblings Max and Alyson on the rostrum at a biotechnology conference, Max and Alyson at a groundbreaking ceremony somewhere, a few other corporate VPs presenting awards to underlings and community members. Further back along the line, there was a black and white photo of Julius in full academic regalia, wearing the tam favored at the University of Chicago rather than a mortarboard. He was about the same age as in Sam's memory, in his late fifties or early sixties, but somehow no longer ancient—he was about the age of a lot of Sam's colleagues, and that was strange and unfair.

Ellen said, "This the old man?"

"My grandfather." He wanted to say something else, but he wasn't sure what.

"He doesn't look evil."

They considered the portrait together. Julius looked robust, with gray hair and a broad forehead above a straight nose and wide gray moustache. Sam saw echoes of himself in the man's thick eyebrows and cheekbones. "What," Sam asked quietly after a few moments, "would you expect evil to look like?"

Ellen shrugged, discomforted. "Not like someone's grandfather."

Which was fair.

Something crackled with static behind them and the secretary said, "You can go in now."

Howard looked up from his desk, where he was writing something with a gold-nibbed fountain pen. He'd taken off his suit coat at some point and rolled up his sleeves, leaving him a bit less imposing than usual. If there were echoes of Julius in Sam, here was a man with whom he had little in common. Howard was closer to Ulysses's height and naturally broad-shouldered, with dark hair and eyes. He looked irritable as usual, but also worried about something. Both emotions were smoothed away by the time Sam and Ellen had reached the desk, but Sam remained concerned. Howard didn't worry about things. When he had problems, he took care of them.

"Samuel," Howard said, getting to his feet. "It's good to see you." He might have almost meant it, too. Their relationship was slightly less icy than it had been a year or so before. Howard had provided a warning about Julie Stricker and a referral to a very good lawyer when Ulysses had requested one, and he'd taken the news of Sam and Ulysses's sudden marriage with equanimity. It was probably the least one could expect from a parent, and yet it was more than Sam would have thought possible on the day Howard sacrificed him in a frozen northern graveyard.

Howard turned to Ellen, a little surprised by her presence but willing to be charming nevertheless. "I don't believe we've met."

"Dr. Ellen Balfrey," she said, holding out her hand.

They shook. "Lovely to meet you." He motioned them to the chairs in front of his desk. "May I offer either of you a drink? I have coffee, tea, soda, brandy . . ." He waved a hand at the crystal decanter that sat on a shelf.

Sam shook his head tightly. Even if it hadn't been explicitly against Eli's orders, he had no stomach for brandy or anything else here. Ellen said, "Water," and they sat silently as he resumed his seat, pressed a button on the intercom, and spoke into it.

Howard's office had changed little since Sam's last visit. It was bigger than any space of that name had a right to be—bigger than some apartments Sam had lived in—and fashionably appointed. Howard had a vast mahogany desk with two study chairs on the opposite side. There were more chairs in the corner of the room where the two walls of windows met, so that Howard could have a drink with whomever was visiting him at sunset. At one point in Sam's childhood, there had been a long table in that part of the office, but now it had its own room somewhere else. There were file cabinets along the far wall, so many that it almost felt like a library.

"How have you been?" Howard asked, jerking Sam's attention back to him. After a moment, he added, "Do you have *stitches*, Samuel?"

Sam put a hand to his face, as though he'd forgotten. "I . . . I fell, yesterday, and cut myself." He smiled, off-kilter. Ulysses would have caught the lie, even without the bond. Perhaps Howard wouldn't spot it. "Clumsy of me."

Howard tilted his head. "You first got glasses when you were six, and we must have replaced them twenty times over the next ten years." He glanced at Ellen. "Probably lucky he doesn't need them anymore, eh?"

Ellen smiled awkwardly, darting a look at Sam, and shrugged. "I suppose it does make life easier," she suggested.

Howard smiled back, and started to ask her about herself. How had she met Sam, what her research was on, was she still looking for a job. She was reticent at first, but Howard persisted; he was very good at being interested in people's interests, and she did love a chance to talk about differential geometry. When the secretary walked in with three glasses of water on a tray, Ellen looked almost disappointed.

"Thank you, Mrs. Palmer," Howard said as the secretary handed him a glass. "I wonder if you could take Dr. Balfrey here and show her the gallery. I need to chat with my son privately for a moment."

Ellen glanced at Sam, and he raised one shoulder slightly. "I'll come find you."

When she was gone, Howard sat back in his chair, studying his water glass like he was searching for imperfections in it. "Where's Ulysses?" he asked eventually.

Like he was just asking after an absent friend. Sam fixed his gaze on the pen stand on Howard's desk. "He had to go in to the office today. Graduation is Monday, so . . ." Sam made a gesture that he hoped conveyed—he wasn't entirely sure what. For whatever reason, he felt like a recalcitrant teenager today. Maybe it was the head injury.

"How is he? How's Ekaterina's hip doing?"

"Ulysses is fine," Sam said slowly. "How do you know her name? How did you even know she'd been hurt?"

There were, realistically, a million ways he could have found out. He could have seen it in the newspaper. He could have looked her up in the phone book. He could have called the Lenkov home looking for Sam.

Howard offered none of those explanations. Instead, he said, "You must have told me. It sticks in the mind, a name like that."

It had stuck in Sam's mind, but that was different. He was reasonably certain, despite his head injury, that he had never breathed a word about Ekaterina Lenkov to his father. But that was not a discussion he was prepared to have. "She's doing well," he said, in lieu of everything else that wanted to tumble out.

Finally, Howard set his glass down and said, "Were you in Forest Hill Cemetery last night?"

Sam stared at him. "What?"

"Someone entered the tomb," Howard said slowly. "I need to know if you and Ulysses are up to something."

"How was it opened?" Sam hesitated, not wanting to tip his hand about his previous misadventures. "There's a spell on it, isn't there? No one can get in unless they're a blood relation of the family. So how—"

"That is what I would like to know." Howard pressed both palms against the desk blotter, his dark eyes hard on Sam. "Where were you last night? Where was Ulysses?"

"He was at the hospital," Sam said. "I was—I went to a bar."

Howard's expression didn't change, not really. He was good at keeping a poker face; he had to negotiate international contracts. But Sam thought he looked—disappointed, maybe. Or dismayed. "Alyson and Max also deny having any business in the graveyard."

"And Troy?"

"Was on stage in front of a crowd of almost three thousand people in Detroit."

Sam half smiled, then recalled what they were talking about and stilled. "And you're certain someone was in there?"

"The sarcophagus was open."

"The—Julius's sarcophagus?" Sam was out of his chair before he realized what he was doing. "But—it—did they—the body?" and if Howard hadn't believed him before, that string of gibberish probably proved it.

"The body is missing," Howard said.

Sam forced himself to take a deep breath. "What does this mean? What do they want?"

Howard shook his head. "I was hoping you would know."

Chapter 11

"WHAT ABOUT YOUR COUSINS?" Ellen asked after Sam had explained the whole thing. "Don't you have an aunt?" They were caught in a construction slowdown on Gorham, and she was slumped back, looking unhappy and too warm. The leather seat was hot under Sam's legs.

"She lives in Connecticut," Sam said. He tried to remember where her child was these days. "I have one cousin on that side and I think she lives in Maine. Haven't heard from her since her wedding. I don't know why she would be interested in my grandfather's corpse."

"Fair enough," Ellen said. "What about Julie Stricker? Didn't she take a sample of your blood or something?"

"Last September." Sam's stomach churned at the memory. "The sacrifice has to be fresh. As in minutes old, not months."

She did not ask how he knew that. Instead, she hummed to herself for a moment, then asked, "Is that it?"

"For cousins who are directly related to Julius, yes. My step-mother Francie has brothers in the area. They have kids, but they wouldn't be able to do this. And my mother had an older sister who lives in Massachusetts." He sighed. "I have nieces and nephews too, but I think they're all under ten years old and not involved in magic."

Ellen sat, tapping out a rhythm on the steering wheel that made an interesting counterpoint to the old Sam Cooke song playing quietly on the radio. "Could Julius have any other kids we don't know about?"

"If he did—"

"We wouldn't know about them," Ellen finished. She rolled her neck. Traffic inched forward.

"He was only married once." Sam's stomach turned over for no justifiable reason. "He met my grandmother on shore leave in Rhodes. They got married in 1917, and they only had two children. I just read his obituary."

Ellen snorted. "Do you think out-of-wedlock sex was invented in 1962?"

"I—" Sam squeezed his eyes shut. "I'd hoped so."

Sam tried to call Ulysses as soon as they got back to the Baskerville, but he wasn't answering at the office. He was probably in a meeting—it was too early for him to have gone back to the hospital. Sam hung up and stood with his forehead pressed against the smooth, cool living room wall, thinking.

"Maybe you should rest," Ellen said uncertainly. She had thrown herself onto the living room sofa when they came in. Now she was frowning at him, concerned. "You look like you're about to fall over."

Sam ignored her. "I have a better idea. We should go down to the cemetery."

"Why?" She sat up, crossing her ankles. "What do you hope to learn from that?"

He shook his head, opened his mouth, shut it again. "Something Howard was unaware of," he said finally.

"Come here." She patted the sofa next to her. After a moment, he came and perched at the edge of the cushion. "God, you're like a nervous cat. All right, you're not Ulysses. What do you expect to find there that wouldn't have been reported to Howard?"

Sam didn't say anything for long enough that she added, "Something that would be obvious in broad daylight from a distance, since I'm guessing they have the place roped off at the moment."

"I don't know." He was abruptly aware of the exhaustion he'd been pushing against since she'd picked him up, the emotions bubbling too close to the surface. After an anguished moment, he let himself slump, resting his head on her shoulder. "I just—Ulysses is already so busy. If I tell him about this, he's never going to have time to sleep again."

"I see." Her voice was softer than he'd expected. "Where is he, on campus?" Sam nodded. "I'm heading down there anyway. I'll see if I can find him and get him to give you a call, on the condition that you lie down until that happens." Sam tried to protest and she cut him off. "I guarantee Julius Sterling is not going to get any more dead if this has to wait a couple of days to be looked into.

And you're not going to be good for anything if you don't give yourself time to heal."

He sat on the sofa for a long time after she left, then dragged himself back to bed.

Ulysses did eventually come home, and sat on the edge of the bed listening to Sam recount what had happened.

"The—the body, you say? The whole . . ." Ulysses looked surprised in the dim light. "It was—the man died quite a while ago. I wouldn't have thought . . ."

Sam tried to wake up more so he could understand, Ulysses's distress setting off things in the back of his mind Ellen had soothed earlier. "I assume whatever was in the sarcophagus was taken. Probably just bones at this point." He pushed himself slowly up to a seated position. "Is there a way to circumvent the ward on the mausoleum?"

Ulysses hesitated, considering. "No," he said finally. "That's blood magic. No way around it."

"So Julius Sterling had another child that we don't know about."

Sam had been hoping that Ulysses would contradict him. Instead, Ulysses said, "That seems likely."

Secrets upon secrets. None of them were any good. Howard hadn't known, but what if Barth had known, and had told his daughter? Sam bit the inside of his cheek. "If Stricker knew, and they've fallen in together . . . could they be trying to bring him back from the dead?"

"No! That's very complicated magic." Ulysses sounded certain, but something niggled at Sam. Maybe it was niggling at Ulysses, too, because he added, "You can't bring someone back just by taking their body."

Sam leaned back against the headboard. "What would you need?"

"A ritual, for one. I know I did something very ad hoc, back when Hugh . . . but you can't count on getting fucked up and deriving something from thin air and desperation."

Sam stared at him. "They have that book they stole—"

"We don't know what's in it." Ulysses looked away. "You'd need his soul, too, which is going to be difficult given how long he's been dead. And you'd need a tremendous amount of power."

"How much power?"

"On the order of sacrificing a god, I think. That's what I did."

The emotions he was getting were Ulysses's—dread and concern, mostly. Things felt so strongly he couldn't stop them from leaking across the bond. Sam shuddered. "So they have a book and the body—"

"We don't know *who* has the body," Ulysses said.

"Uh huh." Sam waited.

"Even if she *did* have both of those, she doesn't have the soul or the power."

"Nothing to worry about, then," Sam said dryly.

Ulysses must have left at some point, because when Sam woke up on Friday morning, he was alone.

He was feeling better, though. Still headachy, but not like the top of his skull was about to fall off. Ibuprofen and a bowl of oatmeal helped, and by nine o'clock he was dressed and strolling across the isthmus on a beautiful summer morning.

Special collections was quiet, and Sam spent most of his day going through the mail and taking care of some cataloging that had been pushed aside during the semester. It seemed that with Dr. Pearlman still out, no one had noticed his absence except Howard.

Late in the afternoon, he locked up and went over to the Union to wait for Ulysses and the grad students.

The Terrace was fairly busy, which was unremarkable considering it was the start of graduation weekend. It was probably prime time for a drink with soon-to-be-graduating friends, especially those in danger of getting called up.

Sam got himself a beer and claimed a couple of bright orange tables near the lake. For a while he sat there and wound his way through *La Disparition*, a book about an odd lacuna in a man's history. He'd picked it up in France and read the first half, then set it down on their return and forgotten about it.

An hour later, he realized he was reading the same page over and over again and closed the book.

The lake was wide and sparkling in the golden afternoon sunlight.

If there was another child—if Howard had a half-sibling somewhere—Sam assumed Howard wasn't aware. There had been nothing in his face when Sam had denied being in the graveyard except concern.

And skepticism. But Sam was used to that.

Presumably, if Julius had gotten someone pregnant before he'd gone to war, his parents and hers would have made sure they got married. Wasn't that how these things went? Or if she'd refused, she would have been sent away and the baby adopted, and they wouldn't know they were related to Julius. And if Julius had dated someone after Howard's mother had died, wouldn't Howard have known about it, or at least suspected? The man was many things, but no one would have called him unobservant. Furthermore, by that point in his life, if Julius had knocked up another woman, wouldn't he just have married her? The hit to his reputation if he were caught doing anything else would have been too great to risk, probably.

Sam tried to ignore the feeling that people knowing Julius had intentionally sacrificed his daughter-in-law as part of an unhinged plot to make a deal with a god and become functionally immortal would also have been quite a hit to his reputation.

That gave Sam a relatively small range of years during which it could have happened, from about 1916 to Julius's wife Alexandria's death in 1928.

He could ask Howard for whatever documents might still be held by the family, but that would probably require Sam to spend a lot of energy explaining. Some of Julius's papers were held by the Historical Society, but it was almost all related to his work. Perhaps he could—

He forgot whatever it was, because Ulysses arrived.

He came up quietly behind Sam, although Sam was aware of his presence long before a hand touched his shoulder. Ulysses said, "You didn't have to come."

"Faculty Spouse of the Year, remember?" Sam said, smiling up at him.

Ulysses claimed the seat next to him and slung one arm across the back of Sam's chair. "You getting bored over in special collections all by yourself?" He leaned closer and stole Sam's beer.

"Less than you'd think," Sam said easily, and watched Ulysses make a face as he took a drink from the half-empty pint glass. "It's probably warm; I've been sitting out here for a while."

Ulysses grumbled to himself and got up, letting his fingers brush against the back of Sam's neck. "I'll get you a refill, how about that?"

Since assuming his post as an assistant professor, Ulysses had become the de facto history of magic scholar for the department; he was also the resident expert on gods and had done some work on subjects that included ghosts and magical geography. As such, he had attracted a small gaggle of grad students. Sam had met most of them when he and Ulysses hosted a get-together at the apartment one night in January, shortly after they'd returned from France. At that point, there had been three of them: Manaow, Leo, and Buttercup, plus Buttercup's girlfriend Galadriel. He found himself thinking of them as good kids, even though at twenty-six he was almost certainly only a year or two older than them at best.

But as they straggled over, that was the closest he could get to explaining how he felt: protective and concerned. Leo Ma looked distinctly green around the edges; he hadn't gotten a beer but was carrying a glass bottle of ginger ale. Manaow arrived not long after, wearing a large pair of sunglasses.

Ulysses didn't seem too surprised by this, although he was clearly concerned. He withdrew his arm and leaned forward to look closely at each of the students in turn. "Wednesday?" he asked quietly, and they both nodded. "East side?"

"Woke me up," Manaow said. "Felt like another bomb going off."

Ulysses drummed his fingers on the tabletop. "Where's Buttercup? Has anyone seen her?"

Sam realized belatedly that he had. "She left on Monday to drive Galadriel back home. She was having some kind of problem that started Saturday night." He looked sidelong at Ulysses. "She stopped by the library before she left, because she was supposed to start interning for me this week."

"Canaries," Ulysses muttered, just loud enough for him to hear. Then he looked up and waved. "Hi, Peregrine!"

Peregrine was short and slight, with pale skin and red hair, wearing a short-sleeve button-down shirt and a pair of jeans. They looked tense to begin with, and it got even worse when Sam looked at them. Ulysses said, "I don't know if you guys have met Peregrine. They're here studying geography."

Sam blinked. "Oh, the zaubergraph. That's yours?"

Peregrine nodded. "You saw it?" Their gaze slipped nervously from Sam's face to Ulysses's.

"We stopped in on Sunday to see what it recorded on Saturday night." This explanation didn't drive the concern from their face. "I'm a librarian," Sam said desperately.

Ulysses pressed a hand to his own face, possibly to hide the fact that he was laughing. At Sam. "Peregrine, this is my husband, Sam. He works at Memorial, if you ever need help finding something."

Sam watched Peregrine's eyes widen. They had a certain je ne sais quoi. Something sparkling, taut, unyielding . . . something he'd seen before.

He desperately wanted to hug the kid, and also to run away without explanation. He wanted to be wrong about them.

Peregrine seemed to accept, finally, that Sam wasn't some sort of heretofore-unknown rival. Then, evidently realizing what had just transpired, they raised their hands. "Sorry, I didn't mean to—it isn't top secret or anything, what I'm doing. I just—you know, things happen, and if you were a student—" They grinned desperately at him, eyebrows drawing together. Then they held out their hand.

Magic people did not, as a rule, shake hands. It was one of the first customs Sam had learned. Today he decided to make an exception. Peregrine's hand was smooth and cool, their expression a tentative smile.

Sam smiled back. Under the table, he gripped his own thigh, hard, digging his fingers into his quad. "When's your birthday?"

Peregrine blinked. "July."

"What year?"

"Nineteen forty-six." Their cheeks were slightly pink. "I'm turning twenty-five."

Sam nodded, feeling a little bit like he was about to explode. "I'm not that much older than you. You have every right to think I'm some sort of academic spy—" Sam noticed Ulysses's deeply unimpressed look and tried to pull himself together. "Where are you from?"

"All over." Peregrine looked more relaxed now, perhaps realizing that things could be smoothed over with chitchat. "My dad was in the army, so we went everywhere. West Germany, Japan, American Samoa, Hawaii . . . I think that's why I got interested in geography, actually."

Sam tried to look interested. "Why did you choose UW–Madison? Not that Ulysses isn't worth coming here to work with"—Ulysses made a rude noise beside him, and Sam rushed on—"but he could only barely have started his position when you were applying."

"My mom's from here. This is where she and my dad met. They got married in a little church out on the north side." Peregrine looked a little sheepish. "My gran said if I came here for school, I could live with her. I spent a little too much on a trip to Tunisia over the summer, so . . ."

Sam tried not to react at all. It was a perfectly normal thing. Many people were from Madison. He had no idea whether Peregrine's folks had seen Dr. Barth before or during his mother's pregnancy, and he couldn't think of any ways of asking that didn't sound entirely deranged.

Instead, he asked Leo what he was planning to do after graduation (a postdoc at UCSB with someone Ulysses agreed was very good), and then asked Manaow about her work on curse tablets for a while. Eventually, some guy farther down the lakeshore sat down with a guitar and started to sing a John Prine song, and the students were distracted.

Sam got up to get a round of beers and Ulysses followed him.

"What was all that?" he hissed when they were waiting at the bar.

"What?" Sam hoped he didn't look quite as caught out as he felt. "Just talking."

"Bullshit." He looked more closely at Sam's face, eyes narrowed. Then he reached out to touch Sam's hand.

Sam sidestepped him. "Later," he murmured. "This is—public."

He hated the flash of hurt in Ulysses's eyes, quickly covered over. But he couldn't get into this now. "When's moonrise?" he asked instead, glancing toward the window, as though it weren't still an hour or two until sunset.

"After ten. Sam—"

"Later," Sam repeated.

Ulysses exhaled loudly. "Fine."

THE SKY WAS CLEAR on their walk back, and the moon was bright, still nearly full. Ulysses had drunk two beers, enough to feel warmly relaxed, and he wondered why Sam was clearly not feeling that way. After that weird bit of back and forth with Peregrine, he'd been perfectly pleasant, although with a brittle undercurrent; occasionally Ulysses caught strange looks flitting across Sam's face when he thought no one was looking. Ulysses would have teased him about it, except that he didn't seem like he would find it amusing at the moment.

The mood lingered while they walked up the steps to the apartment, while Ulysses unlocked the door, while Sam shrugged out of his suit coat and went into the bedroom to hang it up.

Ulysses followed him, leaning back against the bedroom door, hands in his pockets. "Is something wrong? Is this about Peregrine?"

Sam huffed, not quite laughing. He was facing away, hands on his narrow hips. "Were you going to tell me about them?"

"I did. Back in France!" Sam turned around, shaking his head. Ulysses pointed one finger at him. "I said, 'I finally got a student who's interested in places,' and you said—"

"I remember," Sam snapped. "You didn't mention they were a god!"

Ulysses froze. "They're not a god," he said, although his voice sounded weak. "They're . . ." He trailed off, remembering the questions Sam had asked. "No. *No.* That is circumstantial evidence, Sam."

Sam took a step toward him. "You know that if anyone knows—"

"Sam!"

Sam stepped closer. "You know that I know," he said, and lowered his voice as though someone might be listening. "I've been right about this before."

Ulysses swallowed. "Once."

"Twice. Hugh—"

Ulysses snorted. "Hugh doesn't count. A blind person would be able to tell he'd had a god shoved into him."

"Identifying Sita wasn't any different." Sam glowered, but standing this close the emotion it provoked in Ulysses wasn't matching irritation or concern. "There was something about Sita. Something about how she sparkled. Peregrine has the same thing, and they're from Madison, during the right time period, they're about to turn twenty-five—"

"Their parents met here. That's not the same as saying their mother saw your grandfather and his co-conspirator during her pregnancy."

"It would explain the ghosts," Sam said. "If the psychic seabed or what have you is responding the way it did when I was . . . whatever you'd call that. A demigod? An embryonic god?"

Ulysses nodded and rubbed his face. "You've clearly been paying attention," he said reluctantly. "And you have a point."

"I'm very clever," Sam grumbled, hooking a finger into one of Ulysses's belt loops.

It was, terribly, true. Sam was clever and he learned quickly and retained everything. Ulysses was always a little relieved when he saw him with a novel, because when he read nonfiction he tended to get ideas.

"But you're here with me," Ulysses said. "Suggests your judgement is questionable at best."

Sam laughed. "Shut up," he murmured. "My judgement is unassailable." He was standing very close, a gap of a few bare centimeters between his rangy body and Ulysses's more muscular one. Ulysses didn't have to look down to know that if he swayed forward, they would be pressed together. He felt like he was holding his breath, caught in between two moments, watching Sam waver between frustration and something else, his eyes lighting on Ulysses's mouth.

Then Ulysses tipped his head up, just enough to kiss him.

Sam leaned into him, kissing back, hard and open-mouthed until Ulysses could hardly breathe. When he pulled away, hands on Ulysses's chest, Ulysses caught a hint of his unsettled apprehension, and said, "Wait, wait, you—"

Sam made a disgruntled noise, pressing him more firmly against the wall. Ulysses managed to say, "You're not worried about this, are you?"

"Of course I am," Sam said.

"Why?"

They were close enough that he felt Sam's slow inhalation. "If this goes the way it went when I was turning into Dionysus, it could be very dangerous."

Ulysses kissed him before he could continue. "I know." He kissed him again, one hand gentle on the back of Sam's neck. "I'm sorry."

Sam made a low noise in the back of his throat and knelt. He rucked up the old Dylan shirt Ulysses was wearing and swayed forward, pressing his lips to the exposed skin. Ulysses's mouth went dry.

"In a way, this is the best case scenario," he said, probably unwisely. "Because we know what we're doing now, and we can help—"

Sam's fingers were on his belt, on the top button of his jeans, on the sensitive skin beneath the waistband. "Ulysses."

Ulysses shut his mouth. Sam was so close that the space between them vibrated with arousal and possibility. A second ticked by, and then Sam leaned forward and nipped the flesh beneath Ulysses's navel. Ulysses jerked back against the door, surprised, pressing his palms to the old wood. Sam spoke almost against his skin, and it took Ulysses a moment to parse what he'd said. "Open the bond."

"I—" Was it a bad idea, or a good one? The world had narrowed to the room they were in, the distance from Sam's sock-clad heels to Ulysses's. So he did it.

Ulysses had never wondered how a piano felt mid-concerto, but it couldn't be far off from the sensation of Sam's mouth, tongue, hands on him right now. He saw Sam's feelings, smelled magic, heard pain as everything lurched sideways. It was like getting the sensation of pins and needles in his liver. It was like being a cloud. It was like being so happy he couldn't inhale. Ulysses's head clunked back against the door, but he hardly felt it over the sensation of Sam easing his pants down, running gentle fingers over his exposed cock, taking him into his mouth.

Ulysses swore.

Sam kept going.

Ulysses shut his eyes, trying to block out some of the stimulation. It didn't help. He could barely breathe with Sam touching him. He wanted to curl into the sensation and never let it go, and he wanted to crack open his own ribs and let Sam crawl inside. He wanted—

Sam stopped and pulled back, looking up at Ulysses questioningly. His eyes were gorgeous, thin rings of green around huge dark pupils, and it took Ulysses a moment to register that anything was even being asked. Had he been speaking aloud? "What—"

"You said stop." Sam's voice was a little rough.

His fingers were knotted in Sam's hair. "I did." It felt like he was losing track of his body. He opened his mouth to say so, and what came out was, "I want you to fuck me."

Sam blinked, and then said, "Yes." He surged to his feet, putting just enough distance between them that Ulysses could think again. Ulysses shucked his clothing, tripping over his own feet on his way to the bed, and then Sam caught up and tumbled him down onto the mattress. He wrapped his arms around Sam's shoulders and told him quietly, into his ear, that he was never letting go.

He felt Sam shiver when he said it. Sam kissed the side of his neck. He kissed the soft spot right beneath Ulysses's sternum, then dragged his scratchy five o'clock shadow across Ulysses's chest. When he raised his head to meet Ulysses's eyes, Ulysses felt something tighten between them, hot and spice-scented. For an absurd moment, he wished he was a wave, returning to the ocean.

But Sam wasn't a god, he was a human. Ulysses reminded himself of it when Sam ran his fingers over one or another of Ulysses's scars and kissed him far too earnestly, when he tumbled Ulysses onto his hands and knees and draped himself over Ulysses's back. And when Ulysses said, "Don't hold back," and Sam growled and bit his shoulder, he wasn't sure whether he was saying, "Remind me who I am" or "Remind me that I'm yours."

He wasn't even sure those were different anymore.

Sam after sex was relaxed and calm, as though all the starch and tension had gone out of him. Ulysses supposed he was like that too, once he'd screwed the bond back down, because he was staring vacantly at the ceiling while Sam scratched his fingers through Ulysses's chest hair. Sam's head was pillowed on Ulysses's shoulder in a way that might eventually be painful, except that he was going to have to get up in a minute, and that was going to be worse.

"You're going," Sam said after a while, like he was picking up a conversation from earlier. "Back to the hospital."

Ulysses sighed. "I have to. I need to talk to Babushka."

"This is what you do for the people you love."

Ulysses could recall all his feelings about their earlier discussion of Peregrine, the frustration and concern, without really being able to feel them. He'd left those emotions on the floor, along with his clothing, his superego, and possibly most of his sanity. "I'm sorry," he said. "If it were you, I'd do the same. Hell, I wouldn't leave the hospital."

"If it were me, I think I'd make you." Sam kissed his shoulder, bittersweet and tender, and let him go. "Just remember, you're no good to anyone if you coin yourself and give it all away."

Chapter 12

THE NEXT MORNING, SAM felt normal—as normal as he usually felt, anyway. He lay on Ulysses's empty side of the bed for a few minutes, trying not to feel sorry for himself. The pillowcase smelled faintly of Ulysses. The sheets were cool on his skin.

At six in the morning, the sun was already above the horizon when Sam stepped out of the apartment in his running clothes. Vikram was stretching in the hall.

"How far do you want to go?" he asked Sam without looking over.

"What are you up for?" Sam locked the door, then knelt to thread the key onto his shoelace.

"I was thinking twenty."

No wonder he wouldn't look at Sam. "We just did that." He fixed his other shoe while he was kneeling.

"Three weeks ago," Vikram said. "Besides, I heard they're doing a marathon in New York now. It's in the fall. We could make a weekend of it, bring Sita and Ulysses."

Sam frowned. "In Manhattan, you mean?"

"Yeah, around Central Park." Vikram spared him a glance, then started toward the staircase. "Come on, we can go around Lake Monona and then maybe down to Picnic Point and back."

After not seeing Sam all week, Vikram had apparently stored up a full three hours' worth of chatter. This was good, because Sam's brain was full of static, weird dreams, and the memory of a naked Ulysses bending down to pick up his jeans off the floor.

It was a nice day, sunny but not too warm, clouds on the horizon suggesting there might be rain later. The miles went by faster than he'd expected. After a while, his brain shut off and he found himself enjoying the simple pleasure of movement and the rhythmic slap of their sneakers against the pavement. Occasionally he laughed or offered a remark as Vikram told an involved story about a prank a few undergrads in his department had pulled off that involved extremely realistic cow hearts molded from different colors of gelatin.

They were crossing Park Street just past the humanities building, heading toward the path that skirted Lake Mendota all the way to Picnic Point, when Sam said, "You know what, I'll try the marathon with you."

He wanted, suddenly, to have plans. He wanted Ulysses to have plans. He wanted them to have so much on the calendar after July that they had no choice but to go on living.

Vikram made appropriate noises of enthusiasm. A few minutes later, he said, "Is the grandmother not doing well?"

"What?" Sam blinked, replaying the last few hours of conversation in his head. "No. I think she's recovering as expected. They'll probably let her come home next week."

"That's good." A few steps went past. "So what's bothering you?"

"What?"

He wasn't looking at Vikram, so he couldn't see the shrug, but there was something in his voice. "You're very quiet this morning."

Sam had known Vikram for nearly a year. They'd had dinner together with their spouses now and then, and been through one séance together, but for the most part, they'd run. They knew each other well enough, but he'd never thought Vikram had his number quite so clearly. "I'm that obvious," he said after a moment.

Vikram laughed. "We are cut from the same cloth, you and I." He paused for a moment while they navigated the hill next to the Union leading down to the Lakeshore Path. "As someone who has been married for far longer than you—"

"Nine months longer!"

"—let me give you some advice." He paused, long enough that Sam started to wonder if there was anything else coming. Then he said, "You cannot save Ulysses from himself."

Sam tripped, scraping his palms on the gravel path. "I'm sorry," he said, getting up slowly. "What?" Because Vikram didn't know about Laz's vision—Sam hadn't told him, and Ulysses certainly wouldn't have mentioned it, but—

"Ulysses is his own person, and even if you're right about what he should do, you can only tell him that. You can't make his choices for him." He patted Sam's shoulder.

"What do I do, then?" Sam asked finally.

"Be patient." He broke into a jog again, and Sam followed. "He'll figure it out."

"Sure." Sam must have said it too dryly, because Vikram laughed.

"I know, easy for me to say. But whatever is going on with the grandmother—he isn't doing it to you on purpose. That isn't about you." Vikram waved vaguely in the direction of the hospital. "And she'll be home soon, right? So keep your chin up."

Sam nodded slowly. For a moment, his palms still stung, but when he looked down at them, they were already starting to heal.

Sam came home to an empty apartment, showered, ate a bowl of oatmeal, and left again. He wound up at the library. He wasn't totally sure why; he'd come down to campus to use the microfilm reader-printer to make himself a copy of Julius's obituary. Then he'd crawled through the papers from last September until he'd found the obituary of Julius's co-conspirator, Alfred Barth. It was about what he had remembered—born 1881 in an affluent area of Massachusetts, studied biology and then medicine, wound up in Wisconsin in the early 1920s where he married a woman named Lilian. Survived by daughter Julie. Died at age eighty-nine after a brief illness.

The photos didn't print especially well from microfilm. It was hard, placing the obituaries side by side, to reconstruct the conversations these two must have had in their lab. Had Barth realized that they were doing evil? When he and Ulysses had met him, he'd seemed angry at Julius, still, years after the man's death. Well, he'd been angry at everyone, but the animus toward Julius Sterling had seemed to burn the brightest. Was that because he regretted what they'd done, or because Julius had made promises he hadn't kept?

Sam's office was quiet. He had nothing that needed to be done urgently, and he could easily go back home and spend the afternoon reading on the balcony in the sun. On the other hand, there was nothing at the apartment to keep his mind off the fact that Ulysses was still at the hospital.

He went through the mail quickly with nothing to distract him, left a stack of it on Edith's desk for her return on Monday, and then slid down into his desk chair. The building was quiet in an unfamiliar way on the weekend before graduation; no students were in, and any staff were down in circulation. It was a bit eerie.

Sam liked it. There was a reassuring pressure from the presence of so many books. He'd always felt that way about libraries when he was a kid. He lacked Ulysses's affinity for places, but Sam felt *something* when he was at Memorial.

Today it was like a tickle, or an itch happening in a different room. That was odd.

He was tired from the run, and the sunlight streaming through the window had warmed his office. It didn't take much time sitting with nothing to do before his eyes started to drift shut. The library seemed to press a little closer, wrapping him in a warm, comforting blanket. It wanted something. He'd known that for a long time. He thought briefly of trances, and watching Ulysses talk to buildings, the way he seemed to effortlessly take his mind off the hook. Sam leaned back in his chair and shut his eyes, waiting.

For a moment, he felt like he was floating. Then, with a little stomach-twisting lurch, he was being pulled down through the treetops and toward the forest floor. He felt the air growing cooler and more humid as he went, heard the murmuring of small insects. When his feet touched the ground, he could smell the soft earth beneath them, hear water in the distance.

He had a very strong sense of where he needed to go. It was like when he was trying to find Ulysses, that persistent aching thrum in his center. He let it pull him along, toward the bridge. Toward—

Something brushed his leg and he lurched awake with a barely restrained shout.

"Hey, I've got you," Ulysses said.

Sam opened his eyes and discovered that he was still in his office, leaning back in his desk chair. Ulysses was kneeling on the floor in front of him, one hand on Sam's knee.

For a moment, they just stared at each other. It seemed absurd that Ulysses would suddenly be here in front of him, and yet, here he was. Sam reached out a hand and touched the side of Ulysses's face, gently, letting his thumb trail along his jaw. He wanted to say, "Hi." He wanted to say something clever. He wanted to say something disarming, or seductive. Instead he said, "There's something in the basement."

Ulysses got to his feet and bent forward, blue eyes intense. "I know," he murmured.

Sam leaned back, trying to keep his husband's whole face in view. "You do? What's down there?"

"Something bad."

Sam blinked. "What?"

Ulysses stepped closer. "Someone bad," he said, and then with a loud bang he dissolved into dust.

Sam jerked backward and found himself falling.

"Sam?" Ulysses was in the doorway now, somehow. "Are you—what the hell?" He bounded across the room to Sam's side.

Sam had landed on the floor, sprawled in an ungainly heap atop his old wooden desk chair. His head ached like he'd been hit; he supposed he had, in a sense, been hit by the floor. "Don't tell Eli I did that," he groaned.

Ulysses dropped his satchel and reached out to help Sam up. "Why not?"

"I wasn't listening too closely, but I'm pretty sure one of his instructions was not to hit my head again for a while." What Eli would say about Sam running twenty miles and *then* slamming his head into the floor didn't merit thinking about.

Sam made it to his feet but staggered dizzily sideways when he tried to step away from the chair. Ulysses caught him and wrapped an arm around his waist. Ulysses certainly felt solid. And he smelled right, warm, like cedar and leather and antiseptic.

Ulysses dragged him to a clear spot in the corner and helped him sit down on the thin rug with his back against the wall. "What happened? Why were you sleeping here?" His voice was gruff, and he turned away to pick up the chair.

"The library," Sam said. "I wanted to talk to it. I thought if I tried the rite of communion . . ."

For a moment, Ulysses just stood there, staring, mouth slightly open. "Sweetheart," he said. Then he fell silent, like he couldn't think of anything else to say. He sat down shoulder to shoulder with Sam, leaning back against the wall. "Did anything happen?"

"There's something in the basement." Sam leaned sideways, resting his head on Ulysses's shoulder, but the angle bothered his neck and he shifted so he could lie down with his head in Ulysses's lap.

"Did the library tell you that?" Ulysses's voice sounded a little faint.

Sam huffed. "It might have. I guess I was hoping it could be more specific."

"It might have," Ulysses repeated. "How did you know how to do it?"

"I've watched you."

Ulysses was quiet for what felt like a long time, staring straight ahead, combing his fingers through Sam's hair. He was clearly being as guarded as he could be, but this close there was no way for Sam to mistake the turmoil inside him.

"Did I do something wrong?" he asked quietly.

He tried to sit up, but Ulysses put a hand on his chest. "You're fine. This is—it's the opposite of a problem. I'm just thinking."

Sam made a noise of assent and stayed where he was. After a while, Ulysses said, "I'd like to teach you something."

"The basement," Sam said, and tried to get up again. "We should—that's more important."

"It isn't." Ulysses kept his hand on Sam's chest, a heavy weight. "If you're going to be messing around like this, you need some protection."

"I don't—" There was a tension to Ulysses's voice that made Sam subside. "All right."

Ulysses cleared his throat. When he spoke again, it was in a lighter version of what Sam thought of as his professor voice, engaged but a little detached. "Picture something with a knob."

Sam snickered, and Ulysses poked him in the ribs. "I'm not letting you hang out with Eli anymore."

"Sorry." Sam shut his eyes. "A knob like a record player, or—"

"Sure. I usually think of an amplifier, but anything familiar that you can picture vividly is fine."

It took a while to form an image in his mind. Sam thought of the radio they'd owned when he was young, back in the hazy days before his father had married Francie. It had been a very tall piece of furniture, at least compared to three-year-old Sam. The cabinet was made from different colors of wood, with a beautiful art deco speaker grill down the front, a round dial in the center, and a volume knob below that. Little stylized wooden wings peeked out from the sides of the dial. He walked through it all slowly, remembering the textures he'd run his fingers over, the way it hummed when it was warming up.

"Okay," he said, when he realized Ulysses was waiting for him to say something, and told him about the radio.

"All right." He could hear Ulysses's breathing, easy and measured. "Think about the knob as controlling the intensity with which you feel the bond."

"I don't—"

"Ssh," Ulysses said, hand on his chest. "You're going to learn. What you do with your knowledge is up to you."

Sam said, "Fine," and Ulysses laughed at his tone.

"The dial turns, right? Quiet to loud. So think of the all the way in the left position as you being totally unable to feel the bond. Picture the rightmost position as you being able to feel everything. Me sitting here, my emotions, the feeling of my leg with your head on it . . . all of that. Like last night. It may help to assign some arbitrary units, one through ten."

Sam nodded slowly. "What are we at right now?"

Ulysses shrugged. "On my side, about a three."

Sam said, "Okay."

"This is the hard part." Ulysses took a deep breath. "I want you to picture turning it up and down. Just practice that."

It took Sam a long time to figure out how to turn the knob, even a little bit. At first, he tried to imagine the knob turning, but there was resistance. He could tell that that turning it could change something without being able to imagine the movement. Eventually, he pictured himself standing in front of the radio—which was still as tall in comparison to him as it had been when he was a child. Then his fingers kept sliding off the dial.

His brow furrowed, and Ulysses reached over and took his hand. "Relax, Sam. I've got you."

He wasn't sure what Ulysses meant by 'relax' until he noticed he'd been clenching his jaw. "I can't. I mean, I see how it works, but—"

"Then you're almost there."

He didn't offer any more advice. Sam frowned. "How do I—"

"Make sure your visualization is very clear," Ulysses said after some thought. "And whichever way you're trying to turn it, try the opposite."

Sam sighed. But he shut his eyes and pictured the damn radio as clearly as he could. The wood grain going in different directions, the chrome around the dial, even the little buttons on the left and right that looked like laurel leaves and whose purpose he couldn't remember. It had had a specific smell, too, a little like ozone. He mentally set the radio at the edge of a cavern, with a wire running from it out into the darkness beyond.

And then he looked at the dial again. It should have had numbers on it, but instead, it just had one station. WULY, he decided to call it, and smiled to himself.

He looked at the volume knob. It was also the on/off switch. Turn it to the right, and the radio would click on, and then there would be a pause while the tubes warmed up. Not a great metaphor for the bond, because it was always on.

He frowned. Maybe his fear of it getting switched off was why he couldn't move the damn knob. Maybe he should separate the functions. It was a little absurd, but the whole thing was, really. And there was something pleasing about the idea that if he manipulated the metaphor, reality would follow.

He assigned on/off to one of the little leaf-shaped buttons and then returned to the volume knob. It was also made of wood, with an inlaid compass rose pattern. He'd been trying to turn it to the right, because he'd been thinking about radios.

But it wasn't really a radio, it was just radio-shaped. And if he hadn't really been filtering *anything* before . . .

He turned the knob to the left, and suddenly the feeling of the bond . . . quieted.

He opened his eyes. Ulysses was looking down at him, a surprised expression on his face. "Like that?"

Ulysses nodded. "Like that." He grinned crookedly. "It took me hours to figure that out."

"I had a good teacher." Sam mentally twiddled the knob back and forth, just to make sure he could. When he focused on Ulysses's face again, the other man was blushing, just a little, along the tops of his cheekbones.

"You can use this for other things," Ulysses added after a moment. "If the library is . . ." He hesitated. "If it's bothering you, you can block it out. Or—lots of types of magic work like that."

"Are you always focusing on it?" Sam felt like he was constantly looking back at it, checking that everything was still set up correctly. "Seems like a lot of work."

"It gets easier. I usually don't think about it now."

"Except when you're tired."

Ulysses shrugged. "Except when I'm exhausted."

"Speaking of which, did you sleep last night?" Sam sat up slowly. "You can't have been home yet."

"I slept at the hospital," Ulysses said. He looked sheepish, a little guilty. "Dr. Lesko and Dr. Pearlman were both there with Babushka when I arrived, and I wound up talking to them. I passed out after they left, I guess. Cass didn't wake me up when she arrived, so . . ." He rubbed the back of his neck. "I woke up at eleven. Probably slept about seven hours."

"That's . . . not bad." Sam smiled. "What did they have to say?"

"Nothing good." Ulysses looked down at the short gray industrial carpet. "We know something weird is going on but not what. Given what happened last fall, a connection with Julie Stricker can't be ruled out, to say nothing of this unknown person of Sterling bloodline. Why anyone would want Julius Sterling's body, no one is sure, although almost every possible reason we came up with was bad. Similarly, it's well within the realm of possibility that Peregrine is one of Julius Sterling and Alfred Barth's experiments." He rubbed his face, an anxious, tight gesture that looked somehow very young. "I feel like they're keeping something from me. I just don't know what."

"Secrets all over the place," Sam murmured. Impulsively, Sam rested a hand on the back of Ulysses's neck. When his husband looked at him, Sam leaned forward and kissed him. Ulysses made a muffled noise and leaned into him, gripping the lapels of Sam's coat, and Sam felt warm, tingling, tender. For a moment, he wanted to drag Ulysses back to the apartment and not let him leave. Or just shift a little closer and take him right here; it was private enough, and Ulysses had enough of an exhibitionistic streak that he wouldn't object.

And then Ulysses pulled back, eyes still shut, hands still clutching at Sam's clothing. Sam studied his face, the faint lines around his eyes, the darker bruises beneath them.

"I guess we should go look for the thing in the basement," Sam forced himself to say.

Ulysses exhaled and let go. "I guess we should."

Chapter 13

ULYSSES LOOKED AT THE elevators with a little thrill of memory and then at Sam, his mouth twisting into a grin. "Stairs?"

Sam led the way, trailing his hand along the wall as they descended. The stairway was concrete and cinder block, walls painted white, handrail painted black, the kind of industrial place designed largely for emergency exits. Rounding the switchback on the first floor, Ulysses heard a quiet yet purposeful hum of activity from the circulation desk. "What are they up to? It's Saturday."

"They're trying to finish checking in all the books that got returned last minute, so anyone with a library hold can graduate on time." Sam glanced over his shoulder. "It's like a minor Olympic event."

Ulysses snorted.

The basement was quiet. On the right as they stepped out of the stairwell were more stacks. The hallway ran to the left and then turned, leading past the elevators and the Preservation Department. Sam turned right again at the hall's far end and led him down a corridor that was clearly not intended for the public, with a concrete floor and bare pipes overhead. They passed a door that said Conservation Lab, currently shut, and another door that said Depository that stood open. A radio was playing somewhere distant; he caught a brief burst of Bobby Darin before they passed out of range. Sam led him around another corner, down the hall, and then made an abrupt turn and went through a double metal door. There was a large storeroom on the other side full of odds and ends—card catalog drawers, boxes of blank cards, a handful of broken chairs and desks, a shelf of books with papers sticking out of them, various dusty sheet-shrouded shapes. Finally Sam stopped in front of the far wall. "Here."

Ulysses looked around. "Sorry, the—?"

"Right behind here." Sam pressed his palm to the drywall. "Can you feel it?"

Ulysses shut his eyes and pressed a palm to the wall, just beside Sam's.

He could feel . . . something. Not directly, but perhaps because of where they were, the building was pressing on him, drawing him toward *something*. After a moment, Sam took his hand, and he felt it much more clearly, like a lump under his skin.

It was concerning. As was Sam's weird affinity with the library, and the fact that he'd apparently tried the rite of communion without any formal instruction and had some kind of result. Sam decidedly shouldn't have been able to do that. "What does it feel like to you?" Ulysses asked. He let go of Sam's hand.

Sam gave him an odd look, then turned back toward the wall. "Like a splinter."

"Huh." He looked at the wall, the drop ceiling above them. "Is this the edge of the foundation?"

Sam looked around, scratching his jaw idly. "I think so."

Ulysses nodded and cupped his hands together. "Here, I'll give you a boost."

With Sam standing on Ulysses's shoulders, the two of them together had a combined height of tall enough for Sam to move a ceiling tile and look around. There was a long silence, and then a sneeze. "There's not enough of a gap between the wall and the foundation to get in this way," Sam said, slightly muffled. Ulysses braced himself so Sam could jump down. "If there's something there, we'll have to cut through the drywall to get at it." He sneezed again.

"Okay," Ulysses said, fishing a handkerchief out of his pocket. "We're going to need some tools."

They found Laz and Eli out front at Gooseberry House. Laz, sweaty and shirtless, was driving wooden stakes into the ground to the left of the front porch while Eli worried over a sheet of notebook paper and the dog chased bumblebees through the flowers. They both glanced up as Ulysses parked the bike at the curb. Ulysses thought Laz might have rolled his eyes.

"I think that one needs to be moved," Eli said as they approached, pointing at one of the stakes with a screwdriver. "I think the maths are wrong."

"The math is fine." Laz dropped his mallet, wiping his face with his arm as he made his way back to Eli. "Where is it wrong?"

Ulysses peered over Eli's shoulder at the paper. "What are you working on?"

"Ramp," Laz said. He took the page and frowned at it. "It's going to be tight—there's not very much space."

Eli stuck the screwdriver into the back pocket of his jeans. "Look, the distance is measured away from the wall of the house, but I think the stake—"

Laz glanced at the lawn and sighed. "Bring it forward?"

"Just by six inches or so."

Laz grumbled something about precision and squatted down to dig a tape measure out of a pile of discarded clothing and tools.

Sam looked between the porch and the sidewalk. "What's so difficult about putting in a ramp?"

"Degree of the incline." Laz measured the distance from the house to a mark he'd made on the railing and nodded to himself. "If it's too steep, it becomes dangerous for its users. So it's going to have to go back that way, make a U-turn, and then head back this way." He turned, letting the measuring tape retract into the metal housing. "Also, there's a question of the boundary stones. We're changing the way the porch is accessed, so that needs to be accounted for. But there's city requirements about setbacks for boundary magic."

Ulysses tried to envision this. "You sure you don't want to just run it to the driveway? That way you could just extend that line laterally—" He waved a hand describing it.

"Well . . ." Laz sucked his teeth. "Fewer turns, but I'd have to go back to the hardware store for more wood. And more stones."

"Did you check in the shed?"

"Yes, I checked the shed," Laz snapped, sounding harassed enough that Ulysses took a half step backward. "You're only the third person to have suggested it. There isn't anything useful in there, for the record. There are a few pieces of rotting plywood, one and a half croquet sets, parts of three bicycles and two motorcycles, and a cauldron I have absolutely no desire to touch."

"There used to be a bunch of two-by-fours in there," Ulysses insisted.

"Feel free to go look yourself. Or pick up a hammer and make yourself useful." Laz motioned sharply toward the pile he'd, then took another step away and measured a line from the edge of the house to the stake he'd just put in. "I think it's fine," he told Eli.

"Are you about to adjust everything else in the plan by six inches to avoid moving a single stake?" Eli asked.

"It wouldn't just be one."

Laz's mood was understandable; he had taken on the large, very physical task of getting the house ready.

Ulysses felt a little twist of guilt at not being there to help. This was clearly a lot more taxing than sitting watch over Babushka. He reached for a hammer as Laz had asked—until he caught the look on Sam's face.

Ulysses straightened. "Could I borrow some hand tools?"

"And stuff for patching drywall," Sam added.

Laz frowned. "What are you two planning?"

"Nothing," Ulysses said, raising his hands in possibly the least convincing defense ever. "We just—"

Eli sidled closer and peered at Sam. "Sit down, would you?"

"If you were doing work in that apartment, you'd probably want power tools. Or you'd ask me to come over. Ergo, you're doing something in a place with no electricity or you want to be quiet. What fits into either of those categories, includes drywall repair, and is aboveboard?" Laz crossed his arms and stared at them.

Ulysses didn't believe for a moment that Laz had started using the word *ergo* on his own. It was also probably Eli's fault that Laz was asking questions at all, rather than just volunteering to help with whatever Ulysses had in mind. "Don't worry about it," he said. "We'll bring everything back in one piece. Shocking as it may seem, we're responsible people."

Eli scowled at Sam until he sat on the stoop, then stood over him, penlight in hand. Ulysses glanced at the two of them, shifting from one foot to the other, trying to let go of his immediate impulse to follow. When he looked back at Laz, his brother was smirking.

"Did you hit your head again?" he heard Eli say, pushing Sam's hair off his forehead.

Sam muttered something Ulysses didn't catch.

Eli sighed. "Because your eyes are moving like you're dizzy."

Sam hadn't mentioned being dizzy. Laz took pity on Ulysses and took a few steps closer to Sam and Eli so he could hover more effectively. "When are we going?" he murmured.

"We?" Ulysses said, eyes on Eli, who was waving the screwdriver back and forth in front of Sam's face. "Don't you want to know what we're doing?"

Laz shrugged. "Is it legal?"

"I don't think it's technically illegal."

Laz gave him a look, but it was Sam who said, "Mmm," in a skeptical way.

"It's not illegal to repair a wall," Ulysses said. He folded his arms in front of his chest. "It's also not illegal to open a wall up."

"Who exactly are you trying to convince?" Eli asked, not looking at him.

Ulysses huffed to himself. "We could go Monday night. Babushka will be home by then, and Virgil can take care of anything that comes up."

Sam nodded, which drew a low chastising sound from Eli. "It should be deserted by then."

"Where?" Laz asked pointedly.

"The library," Ulysses told him, still watching Sam and Eli.

"Fine," Eli said. "As long as you go home and rest for the remainder of the weekend."

SAM DID WHAT HE was told, although by Sunday morning he felt fine again—at least, he didn't feel dizzy anymore. Ulysses got back from the hospital at seven in the morning and let Sam cook him breakfast before he stumbled off to bed. It was all very calm. Downright quotidian.

He wondered if he'd simply run out of energy to fight against the upheaval Ekaterina's crisis had caused, or if things were slowly falling into a pattern he found predictable and therefore less disturbing, or if—well, he'd known for a long time how much he was willing to give up for Ulysses. He supposed that was the start and end of it.

It was drizzling outside and sixty degrees, a nice temperature for a run and a crummy one for doing anything else. After he'd straightened up the kitchen and watered the few plants he kept in the dining room window, he paced around the apartment, trying to decide how serious Eli had been about the rest he'd prescribed.

Pretty serious, probably. Also, Ulysses was asleep in the bedroom, which was where Sam's running clothes were, and Sam definitely did not want to risk waking him.

He'd left *The Lathe of Heaven* in there too. It all left him rather out of luck.

He found himself standing in front of the bookshelves in Ulysses's office.

There was a small collection of rather beat-up hardboiled detective novels that Ulysses seemed to accumulate when he traveled. A few reproductions of books Sam recognized: an illuminated Greek manuscript called *Hemera ton Theon*, and a Latin one called *Irae Animōrum Caelestium*. A bound copy of Ulysses's dissertation. And a lot of other books that Sam had occasionally seen him reading, or seen in footnotes in his papers: *Hauntings of Newfoundland*, *The Ghost and the Jetty*, Newberg's *Experiences in the Mountains*. And then, he happened upon a textbook.

It was called *Cultural Magic: An Introductory Framework*, and it was what the department had chosen for the introductory seminar. Sam knew this because Ulysses had been handed one of the lectures and the honors section during his first semester as a professor, and he'd spent a lot of time flipping through the book and sighing, scribbling notes in the margins, and making trenchant comments to everyone who would listen.

Sam pulled it off the shelf and sat down on the chaise longue.

It became apparent that the course was really Magic the Long Way Around. The book began with a lengthy discussion of magic and the ways in which it was culturally embedded. Having watched Obe call down a spirit to ride him, Sam had firsthand knowledge that magic was culturally embedded. He skipped ahead. Chapter two dealt with the universal properties of magic. Chapter three was entirely about sigils, and chapter four was about spellcraft. A sidebar caught his eye as he paged through:

Bloodline magic users are often thought to avoid the spellcraft portion of the sigil-spellcraft-sacrifice triskelion, but this is inaccurate. It would be more correct to say that their spellcraft is often deeply internal, personal, and non-language-based. So personal, in fact, that it can be difficult to get them to explain how they performed a certain spell except by metaphor, which can be acutely frustrating for non-bloodline magicians. "I let the magic waft through, like the scent of jasmine tea" is one example. Research has suggested that—

Sam shut the book and stared at the wall for a while.

He had been Dionysus. Not just during the—the original event. Last summer, when they'd been captured by Julie Stricker and her goon squad. He'd somehow—Ulysses had even said—

It was a hard moment to recall, not least because of how intoxicated he'd been. At the beginning, Ulysses had suggested Sam could borrow Ulysses's power, the way he had that time they'd broken into Julius's tomb. But at the end, he'd grown vines. He remembered it very clearly—the frustrated seeds beneath the tarmac, the way they'd sung to him. And although he'd been touching

Ulysses when he did it, it had felt different from just using himself as a bridge between his husband and the door to unlock it.

Sam got up and went back to the bookshelf, exchanging the textbook for Ulysses's dissertation, *Empty Mirrors and Open Doors*: *The Historical Problem of the Demigod*.

At the time Ulysses had been working on the thing, Sam had read several drafts. Mainly, his job was to ensure that any details relevant to his experience were accurate and fairly presented. But now, he turned to a section of analysis he remembered vaguely, part of the concluding chapter.

In amongst a lengthy discussion of how Sam was basically a normal human after falling through the demon's archway, Ulysses had written, *Initial testing suggested the subject was rendered human after the events of December 21st, with no more magical affinity than the average non-bloodline magician. When testing concluded, their status appeared stable; however, given the complex and shifting nature of such connections, a continuing bridge between the subject and the god cannot be excluded.*

Sam had ignored that part the previous time he'd read it. It was at the beginning of a long section about avenues for future research, and he'd wanted to believe this was just ... a way of keeping all paths open. Graduate committees liked to see that in a dissertation.

Now it hit him very differently.

"At least I know where that bridge idea came from," he grumbled, shutting the book.

He leaned back and put his feet up on the chaise. His gangly legs extended over the edge when he slumped down, but it was surprisingly comfortable. Or, perhaps, comforting. He could hear the rain, harder now, drumming on the fire escape.

Sam thought about the radio as a metaphor. It was imperfect, because if he changed the station, his connection to Ulysses persisted. At least, that was his understanding; if the bond could have been switched off, he was pretty sure Ulysses would've just done that back when it had gone so haywire they wound up getting married to fix it.

Sam didn't really know how radios worked, either. There was no particular change in the antenna when he turned the dial, was there? So perhaps the antenna passively picked up whatever signals were around, but the radio only played what he was interested in.

It was the type of question Laz doubtless knew the answer to. Sam wasn't going to ask him. Instead, he looked carefully at his imagined radio. The letter WDIO now appeared on the main dial, off to the right of WULY, as though Dionysus was just a slightly different wavelength.

Most radios didn't put call signs on the dial. He sighed.

Still, the station was there now. Or it had always been there, and now he was paying attention.

He wondered what switching over to it would mean. Would it be obvious, when he turned the volume up, that there was a connection? Might that invite Dionysus to take him over again?

The thing was, Sam remembered what had happened in the Quonset hut. It hadn't felt like someone else puppeting his body around. It had felt like him. Like everything he did had always been available to him and he just hadn't wanted to do it before.

He hesitated, hand over the dial, and then a noise made him open his eyes.

Ulysses was standing in the doorway, shirtless, with a blanket wrapped around his shoulders. His eyes were heavy-lidded, like he'd just awakened. Sam sat up to make room on the chaise for him. "You should go back to sleep."

Ulysses sat down heavily beside him. "Weird dreams."

"Weird?"

"Bad," Ulysses translated. After a moment, he said, "Is that my diss?"

Sam looked down; he'd forgotten he was holding it. "Yeah."

"What've you got that out for?" He leaned sideways, resting his head on Sam's shoulder, and slid an arm around his waist.

"Just checking if I remembered something correctly." Sam ran a finger over the gold embossed letters on the cover. "Are you going to revise any of it before you publish?"

Ulysses groaned and closed his eyes. "I told that editor I was going to add a chapter each for Hugh and Sita."

"Are you going to revise the stuff about me?"

Sam hadn't quite registered his own inquisitive tone until Ulysses started to laugh. "I probably should. Parts of it, anyway."

"And the rest of your research into gods has to wait for when you get tenure?" Sam suggested, and glanced over to watch Ulysses grin.

"Or until someone pisses me off in a committee meeting and I decide I need a little table flipping moment," he mused. "I could publish all of it, the sex magic, the bond. . . . Sure, it's a one-way ticket to being shut out of academia forever, but it'd be worth it to see Dr. Pretherie's face."

Sam considered this. "It might not shut you out of academia entirely," he said after a while. "Berkeley would probably take you."

"You think?"

"They're hiring Harry and Ellen. I'm sure they'd put in a word for you." He paused, tapping his fingers against the cover of the dissertation. "Not that your ability to kill demons is especially relevant to your research program."

Ulysses tilted his head until he was smiling against Sam's neck. "There's always a catch."

Monday was commencement. Vikram knocked on the door at eight o'clock in the morning, already wearing his academic regalia, and with some grumbling Ulysses downed the last of his coffee and went off with him.

Sam took his time getting dressed. He stopped at Memorial to check in at the office, but no one was around. Graduation was held at the football stadium; by the time he'd walked all the way there, the graduates were lined up outside, a long stretch of people of all races and genders and sizes standardized into anonymity by black robes and black mortarboards. He found a spot in the stands and watched the faculty members already inside fussing around. There was something delightfully medieval about the whole process—the gowns, the colored hoods and stoles, all these remnants of the early thirteenth-century universities that had somehow managed to persist for eight hundred years, because deep down, people liked pomp.

Ulysses would have said people liked ritual. Sam frowned to himself, because there was something to that. This wasn't a magic ritual, not anything close, and yet it was certainly transformative.

Someone sat down beside him before he could start trying to remember Ulysses's rules about rituals.

"Samuel." It was Sita, wearing a smart tea-length dress with a belt and a shirt collar. She leaned closer. "You have wisely opted out of the traditional attire, I see."

Sam snorted. "Likewise."

"I wouldn't want them to think I was some kind of academic," Sita said, and they both laughed. "I see Vik over there. But where is Ulysses?"

Vikram, a tall and gangly figure in a black gown embellished with gold trim, was at the edge of the platform that had been set up on the football field, gesturing to one of the chairs as he spoke to a man in dark coveralls. Sam looked around for Ulysses. The magic department's hoods were a deep blue-purple color, hard to find in the swirl of incoming academics. "He's here," Sam said, "but I don't—oh, never mind. He's over there." He gestured to where Ulysses was talking to a guy with a face like Edward R. Murrow.

Sita leaned forward. "He looks tired."

"He probably is." As though he sensed they were discussing him, Ulysses glanced out at the crowd, his eyes sweeping over their seats. Sam half raised a hand. "Did Vikram tell you about Ulysses's grandmother?"

"He did. I hope she is recovering." Sita paused for a long moment. "Could I ask . . . is something else going on?"

Sam spotted Ellen weaving through the crowd and caught her eye. She changed directions, started up the stairs to where he was sitting. "What do you mean?" he asked Sita.

She pursed her lips. "I'm not sure. I just noticed things have felt unsettled lately. The magicians I know are all jumpy. You have stitches on your face, and Ulysses looks like hasn't slept in a month . . ."

"Unsettled," Sam repeated, and looked away.

"You know what I mean. Like the air before a thunderstorm."

"I do." He took a deep breath and exhaled. "I don't know what to tell you. You're not imagining it. I just don't have a good explanation for what's happening."

"Are you in trouble?"

He licked his lips. "Maybe."

Sita looked at him severely. "Keep it to yourself." After a second, she grinned, and then stood up to greet Ellen. "Dr. Balfrey!"

"Dr. Lakhani!" Ellen grinned and they shook hands. They'd met at a dinner party Sam and Ulysses had thrown in the spring and hit it off. "You didn't get roped into the festivities?"

"The medical school does its own thing," Sita said, waving a hand. "I mostly came to say hello to Samuel. And to watch Vik strut around in that getup." She gestured, and they all looked.

"That getup doesn't look half bad on him. It must be nice to be tall," Ellen quipped, sitting down to Sam's right.

"It is," he said, and she elbowed him.

"Sita, we're having a party the evening of July eighth, in honor of Harry's graduation and our anniversary, and as a going-away party," Ellen said, leaning past Sam.

Sam added, "The theater troupe is doing a staged reading as our last hurrah."

"You should come," Ellen continued. "Bring Vikram." Sam snorted, and Ellen added, "You can come too. Bring that weirdo you're always hanging around with."

"I think Harry's already going," Sam told her, and she laughed until she had to lean on his shoulder for support.

Chapter 14

ULYSSES WASN'T EXACTLY SURPRISED when Laz met them outside the library around midnight. But he was pleased.

"Been a while since we did this," he said, and caught Laz's crooked smile in the beam of his flashlight. Library Mall was painted with dark shadows and darker ones; a few street lights on Langdon Street shone a valiant orange against the gloom and accomplished almost nothing.

"Ill met by moonlight," Sam drawled from where he'd been sitting on the steps up to the main entrance. And yes, there was a moon, a waning gibbous visible here and there among drifting clouds. "Where's Eli?"

"Sleeping," Laz said, with a certain finality. "Long day at the migraine clinic. We are asked not to do anything that would require medical care this evening."

Sam made an amused noise.

"We'll do our best," Ulysses said dryly. "Shall we?" He held out a hand and pulled Sam to his feet.

Sam kept hold of him as they approached the door. Ulysses watched Sam raise his free hand and press it to the frame. There was a long pause. The sensation of Sam borrowing his power always felt odd, like the pinching feeling just before a sneeze. This time, there was almost nothing—a dull tickle behind his eyes, very distant. What was Sam trying to do?

"Does he have to be stoned to do it?" Laz whispered. Ulysses glared at him. Laz's eyes widened. "Is he stoned now?"

Sam laughed, a surprised sound that felt out of place bouncing off the granite of the entryway, and let go of Ulysses's hand. "Why, you want some?" Sam fished the key out of his pocket and opened the door. Ulysses checked that it was locked behind them before he followed Sam across the darkened lobby.

Laz took two quick steps to catch up as they reached the staircase. "You feel it too, don't you?"

"Laz," Ulysses said quietly. Laz shot him a look in the dim light, and he sighed. "Yes." By night, the library had a different, much more sinister feel, as though something was watching them. Ulysses was being paranoid. It was a library, for crying out loud. There weren't even any ghosts in it, because they'd all decided to go somewhere more exciting.

"It's unhappy," Sam said without turning. "I thought it was because I lost that book."

"What—oh." Ulysses bit the inside of his cheek, remembering the prophecy they'd received about that volume. "The ivory and ink." Laz inhaled sharply in recognition. Ulysses said, "You thought?"

"It's unhappy for a lot of reasons."

Once they were safely underground, Sam flipped a switch and the hallway fixtures flickered reluctantly on. The wan, unsteady light did little to dispel Ulysses's unease.

Walking in front of them, Sam looked tense. Something about the set of his head, the stiffness of his arms. Ulysses thought he must be picking up Ulysses's own forebodings, but when he tried the bond, it was as cranked down as it could be. He frowned. Sam wasn't much given to hiding his feelings. Or he hadn't been before now, at least.

The drywall that Sam pressed his palm to looked the same as every other part of the wall, but when Laz knocked on it, the sound was different. Hollow.

"All right," Laz said, setting down his bucket. "Give me a few."

Sam watched Laz, face drawn. After a moment, Ulysses reached out and took him by the arm. "Are you okay?"

"What if this is a terrible idea?" he whispered. He reached down and took Ulysses's hand; the moment their fingers brushed, Ulysses got a pulse of Sam's anxiety. Not that he needed it, but feeling it was almost a relief. It gave him something else to think about.

"Why would it be a terrible idea?" Ulysses asked, pulling Sam farther away so Laz could work.

"First, someone could figure out what we're doing and I could lose my job. Second, a forgotten object someone sealed up in a wall? I don't know if you ever read any Edgar Allan Poe, but that's not good news."

Ulysses grinned at the reference. "I don't think anyone will fire you. Certainly not Dr. Pearlman. And I don't think it's one of Julius's enemies bricked up in there."

Sam pressed his lips together. "Yeah, but it's something the library doesn't want."

"So it's like we're lancing a boil." He guessed from Sam's face that he should have come up with a less alarming simile. "Whatever it is, it's better that we know about it, rather than leave it here for someone else to find."

Sam looked, if anything, more unhappy. "Do you think anyone else knows?"

"It's a distinct possibility." It wasn't like the library had been especially restrained in trying to communicate at any point. If it had told Sam, it had doubtless tried with others over the years. To say nothing of whoever had put it there to begin with. "When was the library built again? Nineteen fifty-four?"

Sam cleared his throat. "The cornerstone was laid in 1950, and the building was finished in '53."

"And Julius died in—"

"Nineteen fifty-four."

They stared at each other for a moment. Because they were still touching, Ulysses felt it when Sam started to spiral, the sense that all the air in the room was fleeing from him, that he was somehow very tall and cold and alone, that—

Ulysses grabbed him and walked him backward until his back hit the end of one of the tall metal shelves. He leaned forward until their bodies were pressed together, trying to let Sam feel his weight. Sam's eyes widened, but at least he was looking at Ulysses. "Look," Ulysses growled, "we are going to figure this out."

Sam inhaled sharply and nodded.

"If you two are quite finished," Laz drawled, giving the two of them a raised-eyebrow glance over one shoulder.

They separated. Ulysses dropped Sam's hand reluctantly, and then found that without it *he* felt suddenly, strangely adrift.

Laz had used a long, thin saw to cut a square hole in the drywall. Now he removed it, revealing a small alcove.

"How did no one notice?" Sam muttered, peering into the hole. "I mean, you couldn't just stick it in at night and hope someone would hang the drywall over it without asking questions."

Laz ran a finger around the inside of the opening he'd made. "Someone waited until the drywall was hung and then did exactly what we did." He glanced over his shoulder at them. "This has been patched before."

Someone had cut into the foundation. Or it had been poured to have a little niche in it—an abandoned electrical junction box? Ulysses didn't know which version was more likely. There were old rituals that included small objects and pseudosacrifices in the foundations of buildings to avert evil or bring good luck. But they were rare nowadays, and used mostly for holy sites, churches and the like, places that needed to be sanctified to some sort of deity.

Some sort of deity.

He wondered who had been responsible for building the library. How had this space appeared?

In the niche was a small wooden box with rounded corners about the size of a pack of tarot cards. It had no feet and no obvious lid or hinges, although there were inlaid geometric shapes all over it, done in a fine white material, perhaps mother of pearl or ivory. Some looked almost floral, while others twisted around, intersecting like stylized sigils. Ulysses leaned closer, frowning, then reached to grab it and pull it out into the light.

As his hand passed the edge of the niche, something sharp prickled over his skin. Sam and Laz both shouted; Laz grabbed his arm and yanked it back.

"Let's not touch that," Laz said, and twisted his head around to shoot a look at Sam. "You don't know what it does."

Deep down, Ulysses was proud of them. Probably.

Sam reached past with a handkerchief in hand, like he was picking up something objectionable. Perhaps he was. As he touched it, Ulysses felt the pressure in the room shift, like his ears had popped. There was clearly some kind of spell protecting it—not just a good luck charm, then.

"It's lighter than it looks." Sam sounded surprised.

"Is it cursed?" Ulysses asked.

The silence went on longer than he would have liked. Finally, Sam said, "Maybe."

The word hung between the three of them. Laz looked at Ulysses, then at Sam. "What does that mean?"

"It feels—" Sam licked his lips. "You know those apotropaic marks on the walls back at Gooseberry House? This feels like the opposite of those." He wrapped it in his handkerchief, tying the cloth tightly around it. "Here, give me yours too," he added, snagging it out of Ulysses's pocket.

"What are you doing?" Ulysses asked.

Sam didn't look up. "We don't have time to study it here, right? But we should keep it hidden."

"Yeah," Ulysses said, frowning as the box vanished into the center of a knot of linen. Next to him, Laz was digging in his bucket for supplies to repair the hole—screws, a few little bits of wood, joint compound. A surprisingly large tub of joint compound, actually; was he planning to plaster the whole wall? Ulysses looked back at Sam. "Actually, that's a good idea."

S AM LISTENED WITH HALF an ear to the argument the brothers were having on the way out, something about whether they should get the box to Gooseberry House immediately, or if Sam and Ulysses's apartment—"Which has equivalent warding,

Laz!"—would suffice for the time being. It all seemed painfully academic to Sam. After all, the thing had been sitting essentially unprotected in the wall of the library for years, possibly decades, and no one had bothered it.

They crossed the lobby. Sam heard the slap of Ulysses's boots on the marble behind him, the low creak of the handle of Laz's bucket swinging as he walked. He pushed open the door and they followed him out onto the broad steps that led to the mall. The air was warm and pleasantly humid after the basement. He took a deep breath, feeling for a moment like he imagined a tree might, expansive and calm.

Then he lowered his gaze from the star-speckled sky above them to the steps he was approaching and stopped so suddenly that Ulysses walked into his back. The library door clunked shut with an ominous finality, locking automatically behind them.

"What?" Ulysses said irritably, stepping back half a pace and peering around Sam. "Oh." Five men were arrayed at the foot of the four short steps leading down to the mall. They were all pretty large in both height and breadth, and Sam really didn't like the way they were eyeing the three of them.

"Hands where I can see them," said one of the men. He was a ruddy white guy, hair cut short and shellacked into place, wearing camouflage pants and heavy black boots. The others looked like hairier carbon copies of him, similarly attired in army surplus. One of them was wearing a Brewers cap and holding a bat. Another had a bandage across the bridge of his nose. None of them looked familiar. The man added, "Now."

Sam had been walking with his hands in the pockets of his windbreaker. Now he drew them out, slowly. No one was holding a gun, so he didn't raise them up, but held them open at his sides.

He remembered the seeds under the earth last fall, the vines he'd been able to produce, and tried to reach out to them. Ulysses glanced over, but he was too far away to touch. Sam could almost smell the life of the plants. It was so close. He *knew* it was there. All he had to do was reach out and tell it what to do.

Just a little bit more—

To his right, Laz growled something in Russian that Sam registered, belatedly, as *Run!* He replied, "Chto"—what—and then, "Nyet!"

Ulysses stepped forward, putting himself between Sam and the men. "Take some with you," he said in Russian.

There were no vines. There were no other choices.

Sam touched a hand to the outside of his left jacket pocket and zipped it shut. The lead camo man said something inaudible to one of the men to his left, then fixed his eyes on Sam. "Whatcha got in there?"

Sam smiled thinly and forced himself to move his hand away. "Nothing that would interest you."

"I'm sure." The man looked around at a couple of his fellows, catching their eyes. Not everyone. Some of them were looking pretty intently at Ulysses and Laz. Sam didn't like that.

There was a little tick noise as Laz set down his bucket, rolling his neck like a boxer warming up. It would have been more threatening if Laz didn't look like he lived on a diet of black coffee, whisky, and cigarettes. In front of him, Ulysses cracked his knuckles, suddenly not a nervous gesture.

"Sam," he said, a warning in his voice. "Get out of here."

For a moment, everyone held their breath.

Sam darted forward, grabbed the hat off the baseball bat guy, and sprinted away toward State Street.

Behind him, he heard the guy in camo pants shout something indistinct. Probably "After him!" A few of his colleagues took the bait and came thudding along the pavement behind Sam.

Running recreationally with Vikram and running for his life really had very little in common, except that through the former he'd gradually become a bit faster at a dead sprint. Now he tried to measure his pace, moving fast enough to draw them on without letting himself be caught. He hadn't had a chance to do up the front zipper of his jacket and it flapped around him, the bottom edge brushing his hands with every swing of his arms.

He crossed Lake Street, stumbled on a pothole but didn't break an ankle, and then suddenly they were hard on his heels and he had to speed up. His heart pounded hard, and he felt the air burning into his lungs, or maybe his lungs were on fire around the air, refusing to process it at the speed that he needed. There were at least two of them back there, maybe three. He was hoping for three.

It must have been bar time or just about, because the sidewalks were overrun with people. They flashed past as he wove between them, mostly colors and sounds: a laughing figure in pink microskirt; someone in a silver jumpsuit balanced precariously on top of a garbage can; very long black hair; the flare of a cigarette lighter in the darkness. He pulled one arm back and threw the cap, let it sail out into the street among the wide sedans driven by the tipsy and tired. There was a muffled curse from behind him. A loud murmur rolled through the crowd as people were jostled or pushed aside.

Sam wanted to shout 'help,' or 'leave me alone,' something to draw attention to his pursuers, enough to get the bystanders involved. But he didn't have breath to waste. If they caught him, he was going to be in trouble. Eli had said no more head injuries.

'Stand up straighter.' Vikram's voice echoed in his head, from the last time they'd hopped the fence down at Memorial High School to use the track. 'It'll feel like you're leaning backward, but you're not. Shoulders back, open your chest.'

Sam tried to open his chest, regretting every joint he'd ever taken a drag off of, even though his body couldn't possibly remember them all. He started bargaining: Could he make it all the way to the capitol building, huge and shining at the end of the street? Could he make it to the Orpheum? Could he make it even another block to the intersection of Gorham and State? Maybe.

He heard one guy behind him say, "Shit," and the pursuing feet sounded a little quieter. He dodged across the street against the light at Gorham and a car honked its horn first at him and then presumably at whoever was still following him. Some other vehicle's brakes squealed.

A hand grabbed his jacket right between the shoulder blades, shocking him. He hadn't realized they were so close. He let his arms go limp and put on another burst of speed, leaving the guy standing there with the empty windbreaker.

Damn it, that had been a nice jacket.

He went another block before he realized he was alone. He slowed as he trotted past the Orpheum. Either they knew now he didn't have it, or they were too tired to restart the chase, or. . . . He shook his head. How long had he run for? Hopefully he'd drawn them off for long enough.

He wasn't sure what to do when he reached the Square and realized he had well and truly made it away. His immediate impulse was to circle back to help Ulysses and Laz, but the chances of meeting one of his pursuers again seemed high.

Sam sat down on the capitol steps at the corner of Carroll and Mifflin and looked down along State Street the way he'd come. The street had emptied pretty quickly, the drunks toddling off to their homes or others', to parties they'd heard were still going on down on

Bassett Street, to frat houses on Langdon. Above, the sky was clearing, and he could make out a vast sweep of stars that made him feel dizzy when he tipped his head back.

He'd been waiting for a while when it dawned on him that something had gone wrong. The thought was stomach-churning. They'd led Stricker's goons—or some other, unknown foe—right to that box, whatever it was.

Worse, Laz and Ulysses must have been hurt in the fight, or killed. Sam had assumed, because the full moon had passed, that they were safe from Laz's prophecy for the month. But could Laz have been off, and the moon he'd seen was actually waning rather than full—

Before he could sink any deeper into this reverie, a red 1969 GTO convertible pulled up at the curb in front of him and honked to get his attention.

Laz and Ulysses were both grinning, although Laz's lower lip was split and Ulysses's right eye was swollen shut. "Success?" he asked, leaning in through the window.

Ulysses kissed the side of his face. "You were perfect."

The high spirits lasted until they tumbled from the back steps into Eli's kitchen and found they'd awakened him. Preferable to waking up Babushka, probably. But he was standing next to the icebox, supremely dignified despite his bathrobe, arms crossed in front of his chest, his expression so perfectly disappointed that Sam felt guilty. Laz didn't even officially live with Eli, and yet the doctor had to deal with a lot of Lenkov nonsense.

Ulysses glanced back at Sam, one eyebrow raised: leave or stay? Sam shrugged. Without Laz, they would have to walk almost two miles home. Sam was probably up for it, but Ulysses looked like he needed an ice pack and maybe to sit down for a while.

"It's not what it looks like," Laz said, somewhat nonsensically; Eli pinched the bridge of his nose. Laz dropped the bucket and stepped forward, reaching out toward his boyfriend, then stopping himself. "Eli, I didn't—" He stopped. "Are you laughing?"

Eli grabbed the kettle off the stove. "Tell me it was worth it, at least."

"Ah hah," Laz said. "It was worth it." He dug the container of joint compound out of the bucket and set it on the table. "Behold." With a flourish worthy of one of his coin tricks, he removed the lid and pulled out the handkerchief-wrapped box.

"What is that?" Eli watched as Laz unwrapped it and set it carefully on the table without ever touching the wood with his fingers. "That was hidden in the wall?" Apparently forgetting any annoyance with Laz, he reached for it, then stopped himself. "Is it safe?"

"I wouldn't touch it," Ulysses said from where he was leaning against the sink.

Sam saw the moment when Eli registered that Ulysses had been hurt too. He waved toward a chair and turned away, rummaging through the freezer. "What does it do?" Eli asked, ceremoniously offering a bag of frozen peas to Ulysses.

Ulysses took the bag but frowned down at it like he didn't understand why he'd been handed it. "We don't know. But given how much they wanted it, I'd bet it's important."

"I see." Eli pressed on Ulysses's shoulders until he sat in the proffered chair, then gently helped him position the makeshift ice pack. "Interesting night you lads have had."

To Sam, it looked like a wooden box. Just a box. It sat on the table like a wooden box. It had pretty inlays, and probably if he looked closely enough he'd find a hidden catch somewhere, but it was in essence no different from a jewelry box. Yet somewhere underneath those thoughts, a part of his brain was quietly screaming that it was very bad.

He felt skittish about it, like a deer that had caught the wrong scent. Maybe it was simply that knowing someone had chosen to hide it in the library, and it had bothered the building, was making him uneasy. It certainly didn't smell as obviously strange as Laz's cursed painting had, and the nazar remained stubbornly at its regular temperature. But there was something off about the box nevertheless.

Sam shook his head. When he looked back up, Ulysses was staring at him.

"Sorry," he muttered. "Did you say something?"

"We were debating trying the Griswold test." Ulysses looked over at Laz, sitting in the chair opposite him, and then back at Sam, quirking an eyebrow. "It's frequently inconclusive and might damage the box, though, so I think we should save it as a last resort." Sam followed his gaze.

Eli leaned forward and caught Laz by the chin, peering at his split lip. Laz stared back, lips half-parted, eyes wide, as Eli traced the spot where the skin was broken with one gentle finger. Finally Eli shut his eyes and exhaled.

Sam let one of his own eyebrows raise in response, and Ulysses smiled.

Chapter 15

S AM WOKE UP IN Eli's guest room at a time that was nowhere near as early as his body was trying to convince him it was. He reached out and blindly put a hand on the nightstand where he would have put his watch, but it wasn't there. He moved his hand an inch or two both directions, then opened his eyes. He was still wearing the watch. He was still wearing his wedding ring. By the time Eli had chased them off to the guest room, Sam had been so tired he'd barely gotten his jeans off.

"It's almost seven," Ulysses murmured. Sam turned his head to see his husband lying on his side, watching Sam.

They'd slept four hours, maybe five, depending on what almost meant. "Did you get any sleep?"

"Some." Ulysses smiled wanly. "You?"

Sam didn't feel especially rested. "Probably, yeah." He moved closer, draped a leg over Ulysses's hips. "Is anyone else up yet?" On a normal day, Sam would be back from his run and showering by now.

Ulysses shrugged. "Haven't heard any movement." His face didn't look as bad as Sam had expected it to, but it was still a little shocking. The delicate skin beneath the eye was puffy, the skin painted a dark red-purple color almost up to his eyebrow and down the side of his nose.

Sam said, "We should get up." He shut his eyes again.

"I know," Ulysses said mildly. Sam heard the sheets rustle, but when Ulysses moved it was to wrap an arm around Sam's shoulders. "Soon."

"It's Tuesday. I have to work," Sam murmured. He trailed his fingers up Ulysses's arm to his shoulder. Ulysses's body was heavy, warm where it rested against Sam's.

Ulysses buried his face in Sam's neck and mumbled something. Sam took a deep breath and exhaled, his whole body relaxing. After a few moments, he reached out carefully and fumbled at his mental radio's volume knob, cursing internally; then something clicked and he was able to turn the volume up until he felt aware of Ulysses's emotions at the edge of his consciousness. Ulysses made a sleepy, inquisitive noise, but didn't move. Sam's skin sparkled where Ulysses's bare arm brushed against it. He was warm and comfortable; they both were. Sam let the feeling grow up around him like a grove of trees, blocking out all the anxiety and fears from the previous night.

For a while, they floated on an island somewhere far from reality. Sam had a passing thought that maybe if they never left Eli's guest room, they'd never have to deal with the thing downstairs.

That brought him back down to earth pretty quickly.

"What are we going to do with it?" he asked softly.

Ulysses hummed. "It's safe. I mean," he added when Sam shifted, "safe enough. They don't know where it is."

"They know we have it." Sam opened his eyes. "They've clearly been keeping an eye on us, or why were they outside the library to greet us?" He shook his head. "And they know what it is, while we don't."

Ulysses grumbled something and sat up, the comforter still pulled up around his shoulders. It was an absurd image; his face had a red crease from Sam's undershirt down the side, and the bedspread was the ugliest floral pattern Sam had ever seen. "It's not as simple as all that to break into our apartment."

Sam raised an eyebrow. "We have windows and doors like anyone else."

Ulysses snorted. "What do you think all those wards do?" He considered things for a moment, and then added, "There *are* ways in. But the wards will buy us time."

"That's good. Time to do what, exactly?"

Ulysses didn't answer. "I'll take it by Celeste and Obe's and see if they have any advice." He grinned crookedly, slid off the edge of the mattress, and stretched, rubbing his left shoulder.

Sam sat up and watched Ulysses pull on last night's jeans. "Is that wise?"

"They know a lot about magic objects." He picked up Sam's pants and laid them across the foot of the bed. "It isn't as though they could hide their association with me, anyway. Celeste is my sister. At least Stricker's group seemed to have compunctions about injuring humans, as opposed to—" He stopped abruptly, as though realizing what he was saying. "I'm sorry."

"Yeah." Sam bit the inside of his lip. "I know."

Down in the kitchen, someone had put an empty vase upside down over the box, like it was a bug to be taken outside. Eli was sitting quietly at the table, drinking a cup of tea, a medical journal open in front of him.

"Coffee's in there," he said, gesturing vaguely toward one of the cabinets. "I'm heading to the office soon. I can give you a lift if you're ready."

The Americanism in his accent made Sam smile to himself and look away. He grabbed the kettle off the stove and refilled it.

"Laz not up yet?" Ulysses asked from the doorway.

"Oh, he left about half an hour ago." Eli dog-eared the page he'd been reading and shut the journal. "Things to do, I'm afraid. It's his day off from the gallery."

Sam wanted to ask what Laz did when not working at the gallery, but Eli pressed on before he could: "He thought those were lotus blossoms," he said, gesturing toward the vase.

Sam lifted it to examine the object beneath. The flowers were skillfully made, and looked familiar, but he couldn't easily identify them. Water lilies, perhaps. "No idea," he said cheerfully, and covered it again. "Is it important?"

"Lotuses are associated with rebirth in Buddhism," Eli said. He tapped one finger on the table, eyes still locked on the box. "Or so Laz says." He sipped his tea.

"I would have thought of the Lotus Eaters," Sam said. He glanced at Ulysses, who nodded at him in a professorial, 'go on' manner. "The—it's a place Odysseus mentions visiting, isn't it? Where people eat the lotus fruit, which is a narcotic."

"So either something mind-altering or with religious implications. I shudder to think what Marx would say." Ulysses slid into the chair across from Eli. Sam couldn't face sitting still, so he bustled around the kitchen, finding Eli's French press, scooping coffee into it. Ulysses lifted the vase again and peered at the box. "Cass would know what they are." He sighed and leaned a little closer. "Or do I just want to believe that plant identification is not one of my brother's many talents?"

"If he's right, what would it mean?" Eli asked.

"My—" Sam broke off abruptly, feeling sick. "Julius Sterling had a plan to extend his life indefinitely by taking on my body. And we know that there are ways, given sufficient power, to bring the dead back to life." He stared down at the coffee grounds.

"Under very particular circumstances!" Ulysses was looking at him now; they both were. "This is not like what happened to Hugh."

"For a rapidly dwindling list of reasons." Sam looked back at Eli and saw that he was frowning. Of course, Laz hadn't been there when Ulysses had brought Hugh back.

Neither he nor Eli had even been in the city at the time. "Don't worry, Ulysses isn't planning to infringe on your territory."

Eli chuckled dryly. "I should hope not. Although I do hope you'll tell me what happened someday."

"Someday," Ulysses echoed, sitting back on his chair. "The important part is that the dead stay dead. I told you before, that's rule one."

"Ninety-nine percent of the time," Sam said.

Ulysses nodded. The kettle began to whistle, and Sam made coffee, watching the grounds twist and foam into new, unfamiliar patterns under the hot water.

ULYSSES'S FIRST IMPULSE ON their return home was to go back to bed. He'd barely slept at Eli's and was still exhausted, even with the coffee jangling around his system. But after Sam had rushed out of the apartment, pulling his tie on as he went, and Ulysses could finally lie down again, he found himself unable to relax. Sam, for all his claims to need only four hours of sleep per night, made very strong coffee.

When he realized sleep wasn't on the menu, Ulysses showered and went over to Celeste and Obe's store.

It was on East Dayton, a little hippie shop tucked away among a little collection of hippie shops that had sprung up unexpectedly in the middle of one of the older east side neighborhoods. There was a corner grocery that specialized in health food across the street, next to that a bicycle mechanic, a place that fixed string instruments, a laundromat, and Crystal Revolution. The inside was bright and cheerful: sitar ragas on the stereo, racks of gauzy, colorful clothes, hand-woven blankets, and tapestries. There were paintings by local artists on the walls and display cases full of crystals and polished semi-precious stones, big lumps of salt, geodes, leather and metal necklaces, silver jewelry findings, lumps of incense.

Ulysses heard a giggle as he stepped through the door and looked to his left. It took him a full thirty seconds and more laughter before he bent down to find Lila hiding underneath a rack of skirts.

"Does your mom know you're under there?" he asked, crouching down. Lila crawled out, showing off a gummy grin and several small, sharp teeth. Ulysses carried her to the counter at the back, where Celeste was organizing necklaces.

"Was she getting into trouble?" Celeste asked, glancing up and smiling at the two of them.

"She's fine." Ulysses set the baby on the counter. She immediately turned around and grabbed his leather jacket in her chubby fist, trying to pull herself to a standing position. "On the move, huh."

"She's got big plans." Celeste handed the child a string of fat love beads and she made a happy noise. "What brings you round?" She looked at Ulysses's face for the first time and then looked again, eyes widening. "Oh god,

U, what have you—" She reached out to angle his face toward hers; he pulled his head out of reach.

"It's just a black eye. Eli already looked at it." He reached into his pocket and pulled out the box, which they'd wrapped in a paper bag like a liquor bottle. Ulysses felt a little clandestine putting it on the counter. Then, on second thought, he moved it as far away from Lila as he could. "I was hoping to talk to you and Obe. We found something yesterday."

Celeste looked at the bag, then at him, and shook her head doubtfully. "Obe just went across the street. He'll be back in a few."

"What are these?" he asked, leaning over the counter, in part to prevent Lila making a beeline for the new object.

"Charms." They were sigils, cast in silver on little leather necklaces. Ulysses saw one that meant peace and another that meant love. What kind of spellcraft they required was anyone's guess—as was the end effect.

"Isn't this dangerous to sell?" He fingered the common rune for fire.

"No one is going to be able to do more than spark a candle with that," Celeste said. "And we warn all our customers."

"Hmm." He picked up one he didn't recognize. "What's this?"

Celeste snorted. "It's the Chinese word for radio, apparently. It must've gotten into the shipment by mistake."

"*Radio*?"

"That's what Laz said." She shrugged. "You want it? I don't want to sell it to anyone under false pretenses."

It was small and intricate, two characters stamped on a lozenge of silver, polished to a high sheen. "Did he say how it's pronounced?" He looked up. "Wait, when was Laz here?"

"He came by this morning. He was on his way to the hardware store for something and wanted to check on the dishwasher, because it needs a new hose." Lila babbled something and Celeste laughed. "Yes, did Uncle Laz come to visit you?" To Ulysses, she said, "He just said the top part means *radiates* and the bottom means *electricity*."

Ulysses frowned. "How does that add up to radio?" It took him a moment. "Oh, you mean *to radio*, like 'to transmit.' A verb."

"Probably. Ask Laz." She raised an eyebrow and waited.

"I'd like it," he said finally. Sam would probably find it entertaining. Ulysses reached for his wallet. "How much?"

Celeste made a face at Lila. "Do we need Uncle Ulysses's money? No we do not. Can you tell him?"

Lila blew a raspberry and giggled again. He took the necklace and slipped it over his head. The charm dangled at the collar of his T-shirt, unfamiliar against his chest. "Thanks."

The door jingled behind them and Ulysses turned to see Obe, carrying a small paper bag. "Dous, they had those cookies you like, so I got—" His eyes lit on Ulysses, and he sighed. "Bonjou, Ulysses. Why have you come to darken my doorstep?"

"I can't come by just to say hello to you and Celeste and admire how adorable my niece is?"

Obe raised an eyebrow. "Not to say that you cannot, but typically you don't." He frowned. "Is Babushka well?"

"Yes," Ulysses said quickly. "As far as I know, anyway. I haven't been over there yet this morning."

"All right." Obe shifted, glancing at Celeste, at his daughter, and then at the bag on the counter. "Is it about that?"

Ulysses nodded. Obe grimaced. "I can already tell I'm not going to like this."

Ten minutes later, when Lila had been spirited off to nap in the back room, Ulysses watched Obe and Celeste's faces as he opened the paper bag and let the box slide out onto the counter.

"Oh *Ulysses*," Celeste said, looking at it, "where did you get that?"

"The library."

Obe grinned darkly. "Did you check it out? When will you return it?" He fished around under the counter and came up with a pair of thin cotton gloves. "Do you know what it is?"

Ulysses crossed his arms. "I was hoping you two might help with that."

Celeste and Obe exchanged a look. Celeste said, "I'll get the book," and went into the office.

Obe, meanwhile, put on the gloves and picked up the box. "It's pretty. Where was it?"

"Inside a wall." Ulysses cracked the joint at the base of his thumb, then rubbed the knuckle. "Whatever you're thinking—"

"You deserve whatever I'm thinking."

Celeste came back with an old, heavy book and set it down. "Anything notable?"

Obe turned the box over. "This is not my area of specialization, but I suspect you should consider how it got to where you found it." He gave Ulysses a hard look that he must have picked up from Babushka. To Celeste, he said, "Would you look up this sigil, dous?"

Celeste peered at it, then started thumbing through the book.

Ulysses tried not to sigh. "It was bothering Sam." He looked down at the elegant little flowers. "Or it was bothering the library, and once the library worked out how to talk to Sam, it started telling him about it."

"The—" Celeste squinted at him. "Has Sam always been able to talk to places like that? That sounds like your weird thing. Or are you—"

"I don't think he talks to it," Ulysses corrected her. "The library talks to *him* in a way that seems to be qualitatively different from my interactions with buildings."

Celeste nodded slowly. "What are your concerns about this piece?"

He wasn't sure how to answer that, and his ambivalence was probably plainly visible on his face. Celeste tried again: "Why was it being hidden?"

"We don't know. We don't know how long it had been there, either; possibly since the building was finished." Ulysses licked his lips. "A couple of people tried to take it away from us last night, and that is a coincidence that makes me distinctly nervous."

"Hence the eye," Celeste murmured.

Ulysses reached up and touched the puffy skin. "Indeed."

They were all silent for a few moments, as though collectively contemplating what a fool he was. Finally, Obe sighed loudly. "Ulysses, you have the—" He shook his head. "Why are you here? This is so far outside of our expertise, I'm not sure what we can do for you. Whatever this is, it's something out of myth."

"Here," Celeste said, pointing at the page in front of her. "The sigil. It's protective."

"How so?" Ulysses asked. He craned his neck, trying to read upside down.

Celeste turned the book around for him, then started to gather up the now-sorted necklaces and put them on a little display rack. "It keeps whatever is inside the box in there." She glanced at her husband.

Obe flicked the box and nodded at the dull sound this produced. "It's a blood lock."

"It's a curse," Ulysses said flatly.

Obe shook his head. "Not quite. Just . . . protection." He shrugged. "Get it out of my shop now though. Go put it somewhere safe. And then go ask your grandmother like you should have in the first place." He smiled to take the sting out of his words and set the box back down on the counter, peeling off the gloves.

"Thanks." Ulysses scooped the box back into its bag. Even wrapped in paper, there was something delicate about it, and he had a sudden anxiety that he would fumble and see it smash to pieces on the floor. He quickly returned it to his pocket for safekeeping. "Sorry to have bothered you. Give Lila my best when she gets up."

"It's not a bother," Celeste said. "Take care of yourself, okay?"

Ulysses felt the cool metal of the little radio necklace brush his skin as he shifted. "I'll try."

Chapter 16

S AM TOOK HIS BICYCLE to campus, but he was still late. At a quarter after nine, he walked into his office to see Buttercup sitting uncomfortably in the guest chair.

"Oh," he said, coming up short. "I'm so—I didn't realize you were coming in today."

She gave him an uncertain half smile. "I just got back from Michigan, and I thought . . . Dr. Pearlman said I should wait here."

"Yeah, no, I'm happy to see you." He was babbling. He sat down behind the desk, where Edith had already left a stack of mail. "How was your trip?"

Buttercup's orange dress made her skin so glow prettily that, when her mask shifted, the exhaustion in her face hit him hard. "Galadriel is doing better."

"That's good to hear." Sam looked down, tried to shuffle the papers on his desk into some kind of order. "Ulysses thinks there's a—I don't know how to explain it. A higher level of background magic right now. And people who are sensitive to that might have trouble."

Buttercup opened her handbag and fished out a handkerchief. "I see," she said, and touched it daintily to her eyes. "What raised the level?"

Sam hesitated. It didn't seem right to name names; Peregrine probably didn't even know what they were yet. And anyway, who was to say they were even the cause of it all? There was a lot going on. "I'm not sure," he said eventually. "You'd have to ask Ulysses. It's not my field."

She gave him an odd look but dropped the subject. "Since I'm here, what do you want me to work on?"

"Oh!" Sam had, back when they'd gotten the funding to hire a summer intern, made a list of all the tasks he and Edith thought could be offloaded to such a person. Most of them required some training, though. "How long are you here today?"

"Until noon." She gave him an uncertain look. "I have to go deal with our landlord. I forgot to pay rent before we left town."

Sam winced. "Is that going to be a problem?"

"Probably not. They've always been decent. I just don't want to do it." She sounded resolute, but her expression was sad. He thought about how he'd feel if he and Ulysses were forced apart, and wondered if it was wrong to offer her a hug.

"If they give you any trouble, let me know," he said instead. He wasn't sure what he could do on her behalf, but he'd try.

Buttercup gave him a long look and then nodded. "You're okay, Dio."

"Thanks." Sam got up. "Let's start with something easy for today."

Sam left Buttercup filing catalog cards and went back to his desk to try to beat back the rising tide of entropy.

He was partially successful. By ten, he'd been through all his mail and sorted out the reference books on his desk from the stuff he was actively trying to catalog. The surface of the desk was visible, which felt like a victory.

This procedure had also revealed Sam's decorative touches, including a couple of photos in a double frame. He picked it up; one of the pictures was him with Harry and Ellen after a show, still in their stage blacks, in front of the boathouse in James Madison Park. The other was a black and white one of him and Ulysses standing on the balcony at the apartment in Carnac they'd visited for their honeymoon, the vast gray Atlantic Ocean behind them. They'd taken it using a timer, and Sam thought his expression betrayed an uncertainty about whether it would work. He was wearing that ridiculous poncho he'd picked up at the market, and Ulysses was smiling at him, a sort of indulgent, fond look that crinkled the corners of his eyes. Both of the photos made his heart clench, for different reasons.

There was a polite knock and he looked up to see Edith standing in the doorway.

He set the frame down and cleared his throat. "Come in. How was your vacation?"

"Lovely." She lingered where she was, eyeing him. "How was graduation?"

"The weather was nice. And we were all very proud to see Harry finally get to walk."

"Harry," she said musingly. "The medievalist, right?" Sam nodded. "I'll be sad to see him go. Where's he off to?"

"Berkeley."

Edith nodded approvingly. "They have a reasonably good history collection. I think he'll like it. I met their head of rare materials at a conference a few years ago. She runs a tight ship." Before he could respond, she waved a hand as though dispelling a cloud of smoke between them. "How is Ekaterina doing?"

The change in topic took Sam a moment. "She went home yesterday." And immediately growled at all three of her grandchildren to leave her be for a while. Ulysses's reaction had been one of such intense relief, Sam had barely been able to feel his own over it. He tried to remember if he'd told Edith about the fall before she'd left on vacation. But no, hadn't Ulysses said she'd been visiting? "As far as I know, they didn't find any underlying pathology. It was just bad luck."

"Do you believe that?" Her gaze was clear and steady.

Sam fought the impulse to react guiltily. "I think there's a lot going on."

Edith's mouth twitched, like she was going to smile and stopped herself. "Sorry. That's the sort of answer I'd expect from Dr. Ulysses Lenkov."

He pressed the fingers of his left hand together, feeling the ring hard against the soft skin of his middle finger.

But before he could think of a response, she swept on, changing the topic. "There's a rumor that someone was snooping around last night, maybe looking to break in."

Sam said, "What?" He hoped he somehow hadn't gone as pale as he felt. "Why?"

She shook her head. "It's not clear." She fixed him with a sharp look he wasn't entirely sure he deserved.

Sam shrugged. "Kids, do you think? Just playing around?" The words felt awkward in his mouth.

"Maybe." There was a silence between them. Sam wondered if this was some sort of warning. Tread carefully. "Are you on the expansion committee?" Edith finally stepped properly into the office, looking around at the shelves he'd been rearranging with vague interest.

"Do you mean building remodeling or collection development?"

"The former."

He actually sat on both committees, because Edith found them extremely tedious but felt that someone from the department had to be there, and as his boss she could tell him what to do. She wasn't wrong in any of her opinions. "I am."

"It's been moved to one o'clock." She picked up the photo frame and looked at the pictures for a long moment, face unreadable. "Would you tell Dr. Lenkov?"

"Tell him what?"

"About the kids." She gave him an anemic smile and set the frame down again.

INSTEAD OF GOING STRAIGHT home from Crystal Revolution, Ulysses pulled up in front of the magic building mid-morning with some vain hope that he might find Dr. Lesko there. Or maybe hope was the wrong word. But he had a feeling she knew more than she let on about the whole situation with Julie Stricker and all the Julius Sterling-related activity, and he wanted to speak to her before attempting a conversation with Babushka.

What he wound up finding was Peregrine.

They were bent over the zaubergraph when he opened the door to the lab, and he would have turned around and left them to it except that they made a low, surprised sound and turned to stare at him. "Everything okay?" he asked.

"I've been trying to recalibrate the zaubergraph," Peregrine said, and motioned to him. "Especially refining the short-range detectors."

Ulysses crossed the lab and peered at the squiggles. It looked as though Peregrine had turned up the gain—all the peaks were significantly higher and the valleys lower than they had been when he and Sam had visited a week ago. "All right," he said. "Is that—"

"That's you."

He raised an eyebrow. "What's the radius on it now?"

"Roughly? This floor." Peregrine went over to a filing cabinet they'd commandeered and started digging through it. "You just stepped off the elevator, right? You can see where the line starts to move." They pulled out a folder and flipped through the output strips within. "It's not normalized yet, but this is your last visit."

Ulysses looked down at the lines, which seemed to be a magnitude smaller. "So you made it more sensitive."

Peregrine looked uncertain. "Not that much more sensitive."

On Sunday he'd been here with Sam. Ulysses tried to remember the last time he'd been in the building on his own. "Do you have the records from last Monday?"

"Let me check." They dug through the cabinet. "What time?"

"I got here around seven."

Peregrine shoved a sheet of paper at him. "Here."

He looked at the line, tried to compare it to the previous day's. "Did you come up to the lab?"

"Around the same time." Peregrine raised their eyebrows. "I said hello to you."

Ulysses blinked. "Oh, you're right. I'm sorry. Slipped my mind. I hadn't had much sleep."

The two pages were difficult to compare. Ulysses hadn't come inside the lab on Monday, but the line appeared to change around the time he'd stepped off the staircase. Meanwhile, the reaction to Peregrine, who must have been closer to the detector, seemed quite strong. Not the same as the day Sam visited, but similar.

Peregrine was right, too, that Ulysses had a strong effect on it. He reached into his pocket and touched the paper bag, frowning.

"How do you plan to normalize it?"

"You mean, standardize the new data against the previous?" Peregrine shrugged. "I don't know yet. When I'm done with the adjustments and have a few weeks of data, hopefully it'll be clearer." They leaned over, peering at the page he'd been examining. "That might help me develop an algorithm for comparison. But it may be that I just wind up with new data going forward." They looked back at the filing cabinet, a vaguely pained expression on their face. "I'd like to take the zaubergraph to purportedly highly magical spots and measure them directly. See how it does."

"That's an impressive project." He leaned on the counter. "Is that going to form the basis of your dissertation?"

"If I can get it working. I'd like to choose a few places and examine the myths about them compared to the actual measurements I get." They were speaking faster now. Nervous. "I thought it might be interesting. It could say something about hereditary memory and the way knowledge gets passed down in the magic community."

Ulysses nodded slowly. "Do you have a plan if you can't make the necessary modifications yourself?"

"I have a degree in engineering, and I've been studying the zaubergraph pretty closely." They bent a wire out of the way and frowned at the machine.

"Did you wind up talking to Laz?" Ulysses asked.

They hesitated. "I called him the other day. He's going to—he has a battery I can use, I guess."

"He might know more about this kind of problem." Ulysses looked at how Peregrine had drawn themself up and realized his inquiries were probably coming off as an academic challenge. He changed course: "Remind me, where did you do your undergrad work?"

"King's College London." Peregrine did not look substantially more relaxed.

"Because you grew up in West Germany?"

Peregrine shook their head. "We were living in England when I was looking at colleges, and I had some friends who were applying." They shrugged. "My parents didn't go to college. Dad joined the army right out of high school and Mom worked up until I was born. They didn't know what to tell me."

"Good for you." Ulysses looked down at the zaubergraph. "This is going to sound odd, but . . . Did your parents know anyone named Julius Sterling here before they left? Or Alfred Barth? They were both associated with the university, but Barth was a doctor."

"I might have heard Barth mentioned once or twice." They gave Ulysses a curious look. "Why? Friend of yours?"

Dr. Lesko would have shrugged it off, but Ulysses felt compelled to say, "He was a high-level member of the magic community I've been looking into."

To his relief, Peregrine seemed to accept that. "My parents weren't magic people," they said. "I'm kind of a mutant or something in that regard."

Ulysses smiled weakly. "You know, I've heard that story before."

S AM WAS SITTING BEHIND his desk, staring at a book written in Esperanto. It was relatively new by special collections standards—published in the 1920s—but because it was out of print and rare, it had come to him. Now, as he flipped through to catalog it, he began to wonder if it was a translation of something older.

Unfortunately, reading Esperanto consistently felt a little like having a stroke. The vocabulary was just similar enough to Latin and French that he should be able to read it, but then it pulled in false cognates from other places, and he would belatedly realize he'd gotten the wrong end of things and needed to start again. Was there such a thing as an Esperanto dictionary, or was he doomed to tracking down etymologies for hours?

He leaned back in the chair, rubbing his neck. His shoulders were stiff, and so was every muscle all the way down his spine; Vikram claimed that was the wages of being tall, which seemed entirely unfair. He'd been an altogether normal height before Dionysus had intervened.

There was a knock and Buttercup came in. "Sorry, have you seen my pocketbook—there it is." She looked relieved to see her purse sitting on the chair where she'd sat earlier. "I'm going to head out now," she told him, picking it up.

"Sounds good. How did the filing go?"

She shrugged. "It was uneventful."

"I'll have something more exciting for you tomorrow," he promised, getting to his feet.

"Pace yourself, Dio." Buttercup fanned her face with one hand. "Putting cards in alphabetical order was almost too much of a thrill for me."

"I believe I'm being mocked," Sam said, grinning, and Buttercup laughed.

"Maybe a bit." She opened her bag and pulled out an envelope. "I almost forgot. Galadriel wanted me to give you this."

He took it. It was small and cream colored, sealed shut, with his name—his proper name, Dionysus—scrawled on the front. "What is it?"

She shrugged. "She said it was for you and Dr. Lenkov. Beyond that I don't know. Could just be ramblings, but . . . sometimes when she rambles, smart stuff comes out."

When she was gone, Sam stood staring at the envelope for a long few moments. He needed to go find a dictionary; whatever intrigue Galadriel was up to, he didn't have time right now.

He walked behind his desk to stash the envelope in the top drawer. And then, just before he could, he opened it and read the letter within.

Ulysses wasn't waiting for him at the end of the day when he left the library, which although expected was disappointing. Instead, Sam found his husband back at the apartment, stretched out asleep on top of the bed, fully clothed.

There was a certain rawness to the sight, like Ulysses had been too exhausted to even crawl under the covers. Sam shut the bedroom door and went to the kitchen.

He examined the contents of the refrigerator and compared them to the recipes in their battered copy of *Mastering the Art of French Cooking* until he found the recipe for quiche, which seemed to fall in the center of a Venn diagram between the domains of ingredients in the house and relatively easy to cook.

Ulysses wandered in forty-five minutes later as the quiche came out of the oven. "That smells good."

Sam glanced over his shoulder. The other man was leaning casually against the doorway, smiling fondly at Sam. "The edges got a little too brown, but it's probably fine," Sam told him, setting the pie plate on the top of the stove. After a moment, he added, "I always find making pie crust therapeutic, somehow."

Ulysses raised an eyebrow. "Did something specific happen, or . . ."

Sam had the letter, replaced neatly in its envelope, in his shirt pocket. He handed it to Ulysses and watched his face as he read it.

The note inside was written in an uneven scrawl in cheap pen on cheap paper, like something from a motel. But it was legible; Sam had spent most of the afternoon committing the lines to memory.

> He knows the breath, he knows the
> Beat, he knows the underground.
> Beyond the death, beneath your feet,
> The nexus has been found.
> Between the lies and lives of those who
> Fought the war before,
> The age-old weapons rest forgot,
> But yearn for use once more.

Ulysses exhaled. "Where did that come from?"

"Galadriel."

"All right." Ulysses rubbed his jaw. "Well, that's something to think about."

Sam remembered again the last prophecy they'd gotten from her, and their failure to protect the book it had mentioned. He shivered. "She's been right before."

"The ivory and ink," Ulysses murmured. "The advantage this time, I suppose, is that we know what she's referencing."

"Do we?" Sam studied his husband's face. "What happened to that box?"

Ulysses pointed at the cabinet under the kitchen sink. "The age-old weapons rest forgot."

"If this is some complex joke about soap," Sam muttered, but opened the cabinet door to reveal the box. "Interesting choice of storage location." He crouched down and reached a hand toward it. Something prickled over his skin, sharp enough that he jerked his hand back. "What the hell! Did you put some extra spell on it?"

"Extra warding, just in case." Ulysses looked pleased with himself.

"In case of what?" Sam waited, but no explanation was forthcoming. "Did you find out what it is?"

"Not exactly." There was a brief pause, and then he went on in a rush, "It has a lock on it."

Sam paused in the act of straightening up. "A lock?"

Ulysses looked troubled. "It requires blood to open. I'm not sure what the other requirements might be—is it a specific person's blood, or a family's, or—" He shook his head.

The room reeled around Sam, and he clutched at the edge of the sink. "That." He shut his eyes. "Like the—like the spell on Julius's tomb."

"Same principle," Ulysses agreed, stepping closer. "Are you all right?"

"I don't know." Sam shut his eyes for a moment. Ulysses's fingers were cool on the back of his neck. "What's inside the box?"

"No idea. But presumably—"

"Something powerful."

Chapter 17

ULYSSES HAD KNOWN THEY'D be back to the Gramarye Tavern at some point. That didn't mean he was fond of the idea. The Gramarye made him uneasy; it wasn't really the kind of place to bring a date, unless you were seeing a very different sort of person than Ulysses typically went for. Or perhaps you could take whomever you pleased, provided you hadn't angered many of the regular patrons by poking your nose into various wrongdoings based on the testimony of ghosts. To choose an example at random.

Sam also seemed apprehensive walking in, but with something much closer to restrained glee underneath. He clearly thought this was just like old times. As though this wasn't an investigation into some sort of terrible, world-shattering conspiracy, but just date night.

The place wasn't overrun, but there was a decent enough Saturday crowd that Maeve just glared in their direction instead of fully coming over to give him some sort of tongue-lashing. Sam caught the look and raised an eyebrow. "What did you do to her?"

"Nothing!" He realized he had raised his hands defensively. He lowered them, then started in cracking the knuckles on his right hand because he couldn't hold still. "I've sometimes attracted attention from unsavory parties."

"Seems unfair to blame you," Sam murmured loyally, although his sharp gaze suggested that he had a few questions.

"When you're the bartender, it doesn't matter so much who started the fight," Ulysses said by way of explanation. "Feel like a game of pool while we wait?"

Sam agreed. Ulysses managed to flag down a waitress and ordered a couple of bottles of beer, on the assumption that Maeve would feel more generous toward him if he spent some money. When the waitress came back, it was with raised eyebrows.

"I've never seen her make that face," she said, setting down the bottles. "Not toward anyone who was allowed to stay, anyway."

Ulysses sighed and handed her a couple of bucks. "Tell her I'm sorry."

They hadn't played pool since the end of April, when they'd gone out with Ellen and Harry after Harry's defense. Ulysses had won two games to Sam's one—or at least, that was how he remembered it. So Sam got to break, and Ulysses got to lean against the rough cedar paneling of the wall and watch Sam circle the table, bending over it, his hands moving efficiently as he brought the cue around to line up a shot. He was wearing dark pants with thin white pinstripes that made his legs look impossibly long, and that leather jacket Ulysses had bought him. After the first shot, he shrugged out of it, revealing a long-sleeved button-up shirt and a dark vest that matched the pants.

He was gorgeous, although the word felt too small to contain someone like Sam within its confines. He was glorious. He shone. If they hadn't already been together, Ulysses didn't know whether he would have found the courage to approach him.

And yet. He rubbed his thumb against his wedding ring, which was heavy and warm and felt like it had been on his hand forever.

Sam finally missed a shot and straightened, smiling ruefully. "You're up," he informed Ulysses, coming back to lean against the wall. "You got solids."

Ulysses picked up his cue and stepped up to the table, surveying the wreckage Sam had left for him. Unfortunately for his ability to focus, Sam followed, hitching his hip up on the edge of the table to watch. Ulysses glanced up as far as the beer bottle dangling from his fingers, then shook himself minutely and returned his attention to the shot he was lining up.

"Something's bothering you," Sam said.

Ulysses forced himself to take the shot before he answered. There was really a lot on his mind that he could have deflected with: He was concerned that Peregrine was more interested in engineering than in scholarly magic. The department was going to make him teach the honors section of the intro to magic course again in the fall, if he lived that long. The box under the sink and the book they'd lost. Peregrine possibly turning into a god. Sam's continuing unhappiness, which clung to him like cigarette smoke. The grinding background guilt of whatever was wrong with Laz that Ulysses hadn't managed to fix. But what Ulysses eventually said was, "I don't have a death wish."

"No?" Sam said, and then blinked. "We had that conversation over a year ago."

Ulysses shrugged. "I've been thinking about it." He lined up another shot, standing next to Sam, almost bumping against him.

"So what is it?" He heard Sam take a swig of beer. He was close enough that Sam was practically in his nostrils and prickling across his skin. It was beautiful. It was distracting.

He took the shot and stood up to watch the cue ball knock against the dark green one, careen into the yellow one, and then come to rest somewhere useless in the middle of the table. The green ball shuffled itself over to a pocket but refused to drop in. The yellow ball just wandered away.

"I always thought I would die young," he said. At Sam's sharp look, he shrugged. "I spent my childhood with dead people! It gets to you, you know?" He glanced over, but Sam didn't move. "Eventually I realized I was probably too old to die young, but I think the habits remained."

"Habits?" Sam slid off the edge of the pool table. Ulysses felt pinned by his eyes. "The curious disregard for your own safety in the name of protecting the people you love?"

He managed to shrug. "I just want to keep everyone safe."

Sam swayed forward. For a dizzying moment, Ulysses thought Sam was going to kiss him. In public, in the *Gramarye Tavern*. But in the end, he just leaned down and murmured, "We want you to be safe, too."

"In the words of the Rolling Stones . . ." he began brightly, and Sam groaned and turned away.

Ulysses watched him line up his next shot.

When he looked up again, Maeve was glaring at him.

Well, that was invitation enough. He set his cue down and went over to the bar, sliding onto one of the empty stools.

"I *specifically* told you," she began. A couple nearby patrons looked over, interested, and Ulysses made a quelling motion.

"I'm not here to cause any trouble. I wanted—"

Maeve's face was closed, angry. "I told your brother I didn't know anything about anything." She set a coaster on the bar and put a pint glass on top of it. "You're messing with something dangerous."

He watched her fill the glass with a dark liquid without really registering what he was being given. "I know. Sometimes you just have to poke the bear."

She shoved everything across the bar to him. "Make sure you know what kind of bear you're poking." He held out a dollar and she took it, disdainfully, like he'd offered her a crumpled napkin with his phone number on it.

He lifted the pint glass and said, "Cheers," feeling somewhat ironic. The beer within was dark and bitter, but he was distracted by the coaster, which had something scribbled on it. He pulled it closer and tried not to peer at it—he really wanted his reading glasses, and he really wasn't going to get them out in the fucking Gramarye. It was an address, although he couldn't immediately place it on his mental map of the city. Somewhere on the north side. He tucked the flimsy cardboard thing into his inside pocket and nodded a thank you to Maeve.

"How wary should I be if I pay these folks a visit?" he asked in a low voice.

Maeve grinned in a downright predatory way. "You should definitely not go over there."

Sam raised an eyebrow when he came back and reclaimed his cue. "Get what you were hoping for?"

Ulysses looked at the balls left on the table. Sam had cleaned up a lot of the stripes already, and the remaining solids made a strange constellation under the low-hanging lamp. "I got something. That's more than I expected."

"Should we head out?"

"In a bit." He shrugged out of his jacket and draped it across a chair, then bent forward to line up a shot. "If anyone is watching, I don't want it to look like I was using her as a source."

Sam made an agreeable noise. "Is anyone watching?"

"Most of the bar." He tried to focus his gaze on the purple number four that was just beyond the cue ball. "You—people want to look at you. You're a fox."

Sam leaned forward to place a hand on the center of Ulysses's back, right between his shoulder blades. "I think you're overestimating," he murmured, directly into Ulysses's ear.

"Dirty pool," Ulysses mumbled, shutting his eyes to stop his brain spiraling off in multiple directions.

Sam laughed and stepped away, dragging his finger across Ulysses's shoulder and down his deltoid before he was gone. Ulysses gave in and just took the shot, listened to the balls clack against each other without looking.

He heard one go in. "Not bad," Sam said, and he opened his eyes to see the purple ball was gone—just in time to watch the cue ball drop into one of the other pockets.

❧ ➤➤➤➤ ❮❮❮❮❧

THEY STAYED FOR ONE more game of pool and one of darts. Sam drank bad beer and flirted shamelessly with Ulysses. Maeve didn't look at them again. Eventually, the sense that they were being watched by everyone in the bar started to diminish. Probably they had failed to do anything spectacularly interesting, like pick a fight or turn the light fixtures into snakes.

Out in the parking lot, the breeze was cool and pleasant against Sam's face. He slid onto the Triumph behind Ulysses and leaned forward, wrapping his arms around his husband's waist. He could feel Ulysses laughing, and okay, maybe he was a little drunk. He rested his chin on Ulysses's shoulder, and heard him say, "All right, cowboy, let's get you home," voice full of restrained laughter.

The motorcycle had a lever that Ulysses had to kick in order to start the engine. He unfolded it, put one booted foot on top, and froze. Sam looked to find Ulysses staring out into the parking lot in front of them.

"What?" Sam grabbed Ulysses's hand that loosely gripped the handlebars.

A ghost was crossing the parking lot toward them. She wore a long peasant skirt and a loose blouse, and her long hair was woven with colored feathers and beads. But it was the eyes that he recognized first, gold with vertical pupils. Snake eyes.

Ulysses slid off the motorcycle and Sam followed, pulling off his helmet as though that might help him think on his feet better. Ulysses let Sam keep hold of his hand, but he put his body between Sam and the ghost as she drew close.

"Hello, U." Her voice was pleasant, on the low side but friendly. She glanced at Sam. "Still keeping bad company, I see." Sam wasn't sure which of them she was addressing.

"Abbie," Ulysses said, his fingers tightening around Sam's. "I was wondering if I'd see you again."

"After that little performance in the hospital," she said, and shook her head. "Makes a girl feel unpopular." She looked fainter than she had. Sam glanced up at the streetlight, then back at her. She wasn't just washed out by the light. She was flickering. He'd never seen that before.

Ulysses shrugged unapologetically. "Nothing to be done about that. What's going on?"

"We're upset."

Sam said, "We?" and then looked up and stifled a gasp. The rest of the ghosts they'd seen at the hospital—or more?—were encircling the two of them. Some walked through cars, some around them; beneath their feet, a thin rime of frost spread across the pavement, coating the pebbles and cigarette butts and all the little plants that stuck up through the cracks. They had the same staticky quality, like a TV channel after hours.

"What's happening?" Ulysses said, jerking Sam's attention back to him. "I can't fix a problem I don't understand, Abbie."

She didn't breathe, which meant she didn't snort, but she did scoff at them. "The nexus has been disrupted," she said, edging closer. She had an unsettling way of moving now, not quite walking but not quite gliding. That was new; Sam was pretty sure she'd walked before, albeit with silent steps. But then again, he'd learned some new tricks in the last year. Perhaps it wasn't a surprise that she had as well. "Do you understand what that means?"

"What is the nexus, anyway?" Ulysses asked. "The souls that make it up? An ecosystem for magic? A gestalt of the two?"

Abbie shook her head. "Not sure I'm going to be able to help you on that, my man."

"Then explain what you mean by disrupted."

Abbie gestured at the other ghosts as if to say, 'You know what I mean.' Gnomically, she added, "The way is closed to us."

"How? By what?" Ulysses asked, leaning forward.

"Not what," Abbie said. Then she froze, head half-cocked to the left, eyes wide. She looked like an animal that had heard an unexpected noise.

Sam glanced around. All the ghosts were looking in the same direction, motionless, some clinging to each other.

"Abbie?" he asked, and flinched when she looked at him. There was something in her eyes, the way the vertical pupils were just slits now, despite the darkness. He couldn't put a name to it, but he didn't like it either. "What's going on?"

"We are hunted." Abbie's voice was rougher than before, and the ghosts pressed in around them. "Our power is consumed. Our safety is gone."

Ulysses was silently, quickly, chalking a sigil onto the leather seat of the motorcycle. Sam didn't recognize all of it. There seemed to be a near-infinite number of sigils; any conversation among magic people inevitably led to them directing each other to various codices and grimoires to look up the damn things. What Sam did recognize was a complicated, lacey ring around the main sigil Ulysses was tracing. And he recognized it because it was blood magic.

He felt very solid on that point, in the depths of his beer-addled brain. He had seen it in one of Julius's notebooks and thought it looked pretty until Ulysses had explained it. It took blood sacrifices and . . . intensified them, somehow. Because the biggest problem in magic was power—how to get it, how to channel it.

Sam leaned forward until his chest was pressed up against Ulysses's back and he could hiss in his ear, "What are you doing?"

"Protection."

"Don't you hear it?" Abbie's voice was staticky now. Sam tried to listen, but there was nothing to be heard above the cars out on East Washington.

"I don't hear anything," Ulysses said. He was still drawing, focused on the sigil that was taking shape.

Abbie grabbed his wrist. "It's coming."

Sam hadn't realized that ghosts could do that. Then he felt her fear coming through the bond. He had never felt anyone's emotions but Ulysses. This was different, and it hit him like a wave, filling his nose with despair and clogging his lungs with persecution and exposure and powerless rage until he couldn't breathe.

Ulysses jerked backward, knocking his head into Sam's. Sam recoiled, letting go of Ulysses's hand to grab his nose. The ghosts vanished from his view as he stumbled backward, tripped over his own feet, and fell. Simultaneously, there was a loud noise, and a wave of power washed over them both, sending Ulysses staggering back. He tripped over Sam's feet and fell heavily on top of him.

Sam groaned. "Are they gone?"

"Yeah." Ulysses leaned back, resting his head on Sam's shoulder for a moment. "No thanks to anything I did. I think they fled."

Sam glared at the motorcycle as though *it* had somehow failed them. It stood its ground, the chrome exhaust pipes staring back at him, blameless and unflinching. "Whatever they were running from . . . is it related to the attacks?"

Ulysses got to his feet. "It would be a hell of a coincidence if it wasn't." And with an impatient, unceremonious gesture, he wiped his hand across the sigil, erasing it.

Chapter 18

Ulysses called Gooseberry House the next morning while Sam was out running. Laz answered, sounding wide awake despite the early hour. He arrived at the Baskerville thirty minutes later, unshaven and smelling of old whisky and sawdust and tobacco. Oliver the dog padded in at his heels. Ulysses wasn't sure how a dog could look tired, but Oliver was also walking like he'd slept badly or not at all.

"You all right?" Ulysses asked, handing Laz a cup of coffee.

"Gunshots all night," Laz said. He accepted the mug gratefully and took a long swallow. "I don't know what's going on. But every time I dozed off, another one went off. I tried to call the cops and they just laughed at me." He sighed deeply. "It's all those fucking students. I should've stayed out at Eli's. It's quieter."

Ulysses stared at him for a moment, picturing his brother in another fifty years. "Fireworks?" he suggested.

Laz blinked. "Is that—fuck's sake."

"The Fourth is coming up."

"It's still June!" Laz's hands were shaking a little, the surface of the coffee shivering.

"I'll let the student body know to hold their fire until July first," Ulysses said, and grinned when Laz practically growled.

"Why'd you call me, anyway?" Laz took another gulp of coffee, so Ulysses topped off the cup and poured a bit more for himself.

"Come on, we can talk in my office."

They walked down the hallway, and Laz threw himself down carelessly on the chaise longue in the corner. Ulysses paused for a moment, one hand on the back of his desk chair, watching Oliver sniff around the edges of the room before lying in a puddle of sunlight, sighing as he put his chin on his paws.

"Well?" Laz asked when the silence had gone on too long. "I have stuff to do, you know."

"Such as?" Laz sipped his coffee and didn't reply. Ulysses got the coaster with Maeve's scrawled note from his desk and passed it over. "Word is that Stricker's group has been meeting in this area."

The actual address—on Northport Drive, north of Lake Mendota—didn't seem to mean anything to Laz, but he drew in a breath at the mention of Stricker. "Where'd this come from?"

"Maeve."

Laz nodded slowly. "You trust her? She didn't seem like your number one fan when I saw her last."

"I apologized. Water under the bridge. And I think she understands how serious the situation is." He sipped his coffee. "I'd like to go over there with you to investigate."

"With *me*?" Laz paused, mug halfway to his mouth, eyes narrowing. "This is the sort of thing you and Sam do, isn't it? You get a lead and go investigate." He looked around theatrically. "Where is Sam, anyway?"

Ulysses resisted the urge to roll his eyes. "Sam cannot come." He said it more forcefully than he meant to, earning an intrigued look. "Whatever Stricker is trying to do, I want Sam as far from her as I can get him." He got up and carried his mug over to the window so he didn't have to look at his brother.

"Sam's not going to like it." Laz sipped his coffee loudly. "He doesn't want to be"—he took a long moment to consider what he was about to say, and finally decided on—"left out."

"You protect Eli; why shouldn't I protect Sam?"

There was silence in the wake of what he'd said. "I don't protect Eli," Laz said at last. "This just isn't his entire life." There was something in the way he said it that gave Ulysses a momentary pause, but Laz didn't elaborate. Instead, he asked, "What about that zaubergraph?"

"Peregrine's been in the lab for a week. Won't tell me anything. Don't know if they've got it portable, or if they'd let me take it out of their sight if so." Ulysses crouched down and scratched Oliver behind his ears. He made a little questioning noise and stretched a leg. "I think they're nervous I'll revoke their admission if they say something wrong."

"Can't get out of the draft with grad school anymore," Laz said, seemingly automatically.

"They'd be 4-F anyway." Probably. He hoped.

Laz grunted. For a long moment, he didn't speak, the only movement that of his eyes flickering back and forth as he thought. "All right. I'll see what I can do."

"You—what?"

He sat up and drained his coffee. "I'll stop by and see them. That thing I gave them was basically a prototype; wouldn't be surprised if it wasn't working quite right. Maybe there's something I can help with." He stood, and so did the dog, watching Laz's face attentively.

"I can come along if you'd like.

Laz shook his head. "I'm a grad student helping a peer with a problem. It's a different dynamic."

"Is it?" The corner of Laz's mouth twitched. "Wait, you are?"

"I'm just taking accounting." He sighed and scrubbed one palm over his face. "Give me a couple of days."

"Thanks." Ulysses followed Laz back to the apartment's small entryway. "I appreciate your help."

Laz looked up from tying his boot, eyes narrowing as he inspected Ulysses. "Shit, are you going to try to hug me or something?" He stood, frowning.

Ulysses forced himself to take a deep breath. "Look, if something happens to me—"

"I'll make sure you get buried at sea," Laz said, smacking him on the shoulder.

Ulysses almost laughed. "That's not what I mean."

Laz stared at him for a long moment, expression grave, and then in one fast move had him slammed up against the closet door. He pressed one forearm across Ulysses's throat, not quite hard enough to stop him breathing, but it got his attention. Laz leaned forward and growled, "You bastard, you don't get to die on my watch." He stepped back, pulling his jacket straight with a little snap. "I'm not going to have any of these little just-in-case conversations. If you're on your fucking deathbed, I'll listen. Anything else, you have to take up with Sam. Understood?"

Ulysses stared at his brother. "Understood."

Laz nodded and swung the door open, and there Sam stood, sweaty and dusty, fumbling with his key.

❧❧❧ ❧❧❧

S AM WAS AT A Wednesday-night rehearsal at Harry and Ellen's place, and secretly dying inside.

They were doing a staged reading, so the setting was very casual: a few of their actor friends in chairs around the fire pit in the backyard. Sam had a folding chair next to Ellen and his clipboard, and at least a quarter of his attention was focused on making notes for the performance.

Harry and Ellen hadn't moved house in the year and a half since the night he'd brought Ulysses along to a cast party and been attacked by demons. They were still in the same yellow bungalow near the river—not far from Eli's place, as it happened. In theory, that should have felt weird. It had been the worst first date of his life. He'd had nightmares for weeks afterward, jumped at sudden noises. And yet, with his feet stretched out toward the cold fire pit, listening to a bunch of the actors who had become core members of Harry and Ellen's company read from an extremely condensed version of *Hamlet*, all he could think was how much he was going to miss it.

What was he going to do with Harry and Ellen gone? He'd thought about the question in small pieces. There were other community theater groups around, even others associated with the university. Some of them were doing actual *guerrilla theater*, which was intriguing. Probably any one of them could use a stage manager. But it wouldn't be the same.

He wondered if they'd keep producing plays in Berkeley without him.

"What are we going to do here?" the actor playing Hamlet asked suddenly, glancing up from her script. "Are we going to do a sword fight?"

"No." Harry glanced over at Sam. "Do you have them?"

Sam pulled the two water pistols he'd painted out of his bag and tossed them to Hamlet and Laertes, who were at opposite ends of the row of actors.

"Very Flash Gordon," Laertes said, looking down at the silver gun. "I like it. Can you add some more pointy bits?"

Harry glanced down at his script, and said, "You'll fire at each other just after Claudius says, 'And you, the judges, bear a wary eye.' "

Laertes started to say, "All right," but trailed off into a squawk in the middle when Hamlet hit him with a jet of water to the side of the head.

"Sorry," Hamlet said, giving Harry a wide-eyed, unrepentant look. "I thought that was the cue—aaah!" She turned and glared at Laertes, who hid his squirt gun behind his back.

Things devolved from there.

Sam was packing up the props afterward when Ellen came over to him. "How's it going?"

He shrugged and didn't look up. "It's, you know. Things are more or less what they always are."

"That's—" Her eyebrows drew together. "That bad?"

"I don't know." He drew Ellen aside from the departing crowd of actors. "Something is afoot, and it seems to be related to my grandfather, and that makes me very nervous."

Ellen groaned. "Is it bad that I was hoping this was just . . . I don't know, Ulysses's grandmother had a setback or something? The sort of problem I could solve by making you a loaf of banana bread."

"If I had a dog, I'd ask you to walk it," Sam said, and she chuckled.

"Can you tell me what's going on?" Ellen drifted over to the back stoop and sat down. Sam joined her a moment later.

"You mean, can I tell you in a coherent way, instead of through . . . primal screams or something?" He took a deep breath. "The biggest problem in magic—as a disciple, not as an area of academic study—is power. As I understand it, my grandfather . . . he had this plan to create gods, and then use their power to move his consciousness into one of their bodies, and—"

"This isn't hypothetical," Ellen interrupted. "He would have done that to you, right?"

"If he'd lived." Sam looked down at the toes of his shoes. They were brogues, in dark brown leather, worn in enough to be comfortable. At some point, he'd scuffed the left one across the instep; he needed to fix that. He said, "I benefited from the fact that no one else knew what the hell he had planned. Nobody else would have been able to pull off a stunt like that."

Harry came back from seeing the actors out and leaned against the porch railing. "Speaking of, where is Ulysses this fine evening?"

Sam didn't even try to keep the bitterness out of his voice. "He and Laz took a field trip." Sam glanced at his watch and got to his feet again, but didn't follow the action with anything like walking toward the edge of the yard. "There's been—I don't know. There's a . . . a power reservoir somewhere on the north side, and we think someone's been trying to use it for malevolent purposes, so they went to check it out."

Ellen rested her chin on her palm. "That seems safe."

"Why aren't you with him?" Harry asked. "That's usually your bag, isn't it?"

Sam gave him a halfhearted smile. "I had rehearsal."

It was only about two miles from Harry and Ellen's to the apartment. About ten minutes by bike—nearly no time at all. Sam still managed to go six blocks before he realized the unease he was feeling was his own, not something reflected from Ulysses's misadventures.

That was reassuring. Or . . . well.

He took Willy Street, cruising past jazz cafés and tiny galleries, performance spaces and studios, warehouses and supply hubs. It was a neighborhood that was starting to change; when Sam was a kid, it had been full of industrial stuff. Factories. Breweries. Not the kind of place you went on a Saturday night. Unless you were looking to get jumped, maybe.

King Street was all uphill, and he had to stand up on the pedals as he went past the seedy clubs there. He'd been spending too much time running, not enough time on the bike, and his muscles were unaccustomed to the different motion. It was a relief to turn onto the flatter loop around the capital. There was something deeply, hilariously pathetic about running twenty miles for fun but struggling to bike up a steep hill. He was never going to mention this to Vikram; the man would have him running uphill sprints in penance.

It was while he was cruising past the intersection with West Washington Avenue that he passed a payphone with a man standing at it. He looked up as Sam went by, a movement that started as the aimless glancing around of someone who was mentally more engaged with the conversation he was having than with his environment, and ended in a moment of shock as he spotted Sam.

Sam cranked his neck around to stare at the guy as he sailed past, his mind racing through the *who was that* possibilities. By the time he realized the payphone man has also chased him outside the library a week ago, he was halfway down the block, man and phone rapidly retreating into the distance. A car honked its horn and he startled, twisting back to keep his eyes on the road as he turned the corner.

There was a parking garage across the street from the Baskerville. Sam slid off his bike in front of it and stood catching his breath for a moment. Of course it had been a coincidence. The man had only looked like one of those guys. Or he'd been in the neighborhood for other reasons. Lots of people came up to the capitol.

Sam's hands were trembling.

He forced himself to walk down the alley next to the parking garage, pull out his lock like this was a normal evening. He pushed his bike into the rack and closed his eyes. Inhaled. Exhaled. He opened his eyes again. Something moved in the shadows and his attention locked on it, his pulse kicking up again. There was someone there, watching him.

"Hello?" he said, trying to decide if he was being foolhardy or brave. Or both, possibly. The watcher stepped out of the shadows before he'd reached a conclusion, and Sam—Sam knew him. A tall, dark-skinned Black man with clever eyes, wearing a well-tailored blue windowpane suit. "Hugh?"

Hugh raised his hand in a little wave, but by way of greeting he said, "What kind of wards do you have on your apartment?"

Sam blinked. "How did you get our address?"

Hugh's mouth twitched at the corner. "I asked Celeste."

"Oh." Sam had assumed that after Livia's attempted sacrifice of Ulysses, Celeste would no longer be on speaking terms with her. But perhaps that didn't mean she wouldn't talk to Hugh. Or—who knew, really. "Celeste and Obe did our wards, as it happens."

"Hmm." Hugh looked over Sam's shoulder at the front door to the building. "Ulysses is out, I take it?"

"Yes." Sam twisted around, but there wasn't much to see, just the outside of the Baskerville building, its tan bricks and stonework. "Why?"

"I've been watching the most suspicious motherfuckers I've ever seen in my life walk back and forth in front of your building like they lost something."

Sam looked back at him, then at the Baskerville again. "Stricker's guys, do you think?"

Hugh shrugged. "They have a cultish air to them."

"How did *they* get my address?" Had the university given it out? Had they learned earlier, when they'd tried to attack Sita in the fall? Or was it more recent? He remembered the petition he'd signed and groaned. Sterling-Lenkov indeed. "What the fuck do they want?"

Hugh shook his head. "I'm not sure. You got something important to them in there?"

Sam opened his mouth to say no and remembered the box. His stomach turned over. "Shit." He started for the front door, moving without thought, pulse racing. The world was flung wide in his panic, the colors of the cars along the street and the bricks and the sky obscenely bright. Sam could hear the distant cries of birds and sirens, smell the rush of the wind. Distantly, he heard Hugh mutter something.

Sam nearly fell, wrenching something in his back, and discovered his shoes were stuck to the pavement. Abruptly he was back in his body, and mad. "What the hell!"

Hugh put a hand on his arm. "Don't go in there."

"I'll be discreet! I just need to know—"

Hugh stepped closer. "Look, if it was Ulysses in there, I'd let you go. Hell, I'd lead the charge. But these guys won't hesitate to kill you—I speak from personal experience—and nothing you have in there is worth dying for." His tone was so deadly serious that it cut through Sam's panic.

Sam forced himself to take a deep breath. Hugh was right; Sam had been in a few fights but he'd never been the one who won them. He said, "We can go up the fire escape. I just want to get a look inside." Hugh didn't answer and Sam added, "I'll go myself. Let me go."

Something in Sam's voice must have convinced Hugh that he was prepared to do it, because after a long, tense moment, Sam felt the pavement let go of his shoes.

It wasn't dark yet, not even twilight, but the sun had fallen low enough in the sky that there were a few shadows for them to skulk through on their way over to the building. Not that two men, both over six feet in height, were really capable of moving unobserved. In their favor, the goons all seemed to have gone into the building and left no lookout.

The Baskerville had been built in 1913, and the builder had cared enough about both aesthetics and human life to put stairs between the wrought iron balconies that ran along either side of the building. There was a ladder that could be extended from the second-floor balcony to the street. It wasn't very far off the ground—just high enough to discourage casual miscreants. Sam watched Hugh reach the lowest rung without even jumping; apparently most Madison ne'er-do-wells weren't very tall.

Sam went up first, crouching low. Which was absurd, because he was in plain view of anyone who came outside or even looked through their windows, but he couldn't stop himself. As he went up, he started to get the feeling that he shouldn't be there. It was like hearing a fire alarm. His body *knew* he should be doing something else, and each step got harder to take as he edged closer.

"What do you think the wards are for?" Hugh hissed when Sam told him. "They're an alert system."

"I thought they kept evil out!" Sam protested.

Hugh nodded. "They do, to some extent. But can you imagine the power it would take to defeat sufficiently motivated evil? These are passive wards we're talking about."

The balcony ran the length of the apartment. They didn't use it much, because it was pretty narrow and only accessible by climbing out a window. But it wasn't difficult to crawl along it until he was beneath the living room window. There were no suspicious noises coming from inside, but then again what did tossing a home sound like?

Hugh flattened himself to the bricks between the living room window and the office. "You going to look or should I?" he whispered.

"I will." It was his house, his neck on the line. "On three."

The countdown was simultaneously too slow and the most rapid descent Sam had ever experienced. Sweat prickled along his back in the space between three and two. His own ragged breathing filled his ears, drowning out the rush of his blood. And then he was up and looking through the window at the scene within.

Five men were standing on the living room carpet. They were all still wearing their boots, which—absurdly—infuriated him, and they had their hands joined, eyes closed. Some kind of magic. None of them seemed to notice him, even though he looked for far longer than he should have.

"What are they doing?" he asked Hugh, dropping out of sight again.

"Location spell, I think."

The box. Sam nodded, trying to keep himself under control as he edged back toward Hugh. "What are the chances they find what they're looking for?"

"Pretty good." Hugh crouched down and spoke almost into his ear. "Let's go grab a beer while they do whatever it is. We can't stop them just the two of us. Let them have your stamp collection."

"It's not—"

"I'm sure it's important. But be realistic. You won't be able to get it back if you're dead."

Sam hesitated—but what was he going to do alone and unarmed against people who wouldn't hesitate to kill him? In desperation, he reached out to Ulysses along the bond. But Ulysses had his end clamped further down than Sam had ever felt it before. No luck.

He sighed, the fight abruptly going out of him.

They descended and walked quietly together to the Fret Not Bar, which was funny, because Sam was definitely fretting. He claimed a table on the patio, looking around warily while Hugh went inside and ordered. There was no sign of the man who'd been at the payphone. That wasn't very reassuring—or surprising.

The ashy taste of defeat was still in his mouth, even though he couldn't really be sure what it meant to have lost the box. Maybe it had just been some odd keepsake, or the remnant of a ritual. But Sam didn't think so. The thought of Stricker's people having it was nauseating.

He breathed, and sat for long enough to start feeling chilled, the sweat from his earlier alarm drying in the breeze. Eventually, Hugh brought back two pints of beer and settled into the chair opposite. He looked much better than he had when they'd last met; then he'd been skinny, his dark skin bloodless. A year later, he'd put on enough weight to look healthy. His hair had grown out into an Afro, and his eyes glittered behind his sunglasses. "Being alive seems to agree with you," Sam said, and raised his glass.

Hugh clinked his against it. "Getting the support group back together, eh?" he quipped.

Sam managed a weak smile, but he meant it. "It's good to see you."

"How's Ulysses?" Hugh took a drink of his beer. "Heard you two got hitched."

"We did." Celeste again? Or was the magical world really that small? "It's—he's good. Yeah. A year ago in September, actually."

Hugh smiled, the corners of his eyes wrinkling. "Congratulations, man."

"Thank you." He took a long drink and forced himself to say, "How's Livia?"

There was a moment of hesitation. Livia was not Sam's favorite person, to say the least. But he wasn't going to let her become a conversational third rail, either. "She's doing well. We took a long vacation, you know? When I came back. Went down to Guadalupe and lay on the beach for a while. We had to figure out who we were after what all happened."

"You mean, after what Ulysses did to you," Sam said before he could help himself. After Ulysses brought you back from the dead, he couldn't say. Impulsively, he reached out to the bond again. Still nothing.

"Yeah." Hugh didn't bother to look embarrassed, which Sam was grateful for.

"Did you?"

Hugh's face softened. "We did."

Sam wondered a bit about their relationship. He himself had somehow stumbled from meeting Ulysses outside the Historical Society building to marrying him without much in the way of forethought or planning, so he'd never really sat down and tried to list out what qualities were important to him in a partner. Now if he tried, he had a bad feeling it would just be a list of the things he liked about Ulysses: smart, hot, kind, strong, good at sex, talks to ghosts. Thinking about Hugh and Livia made him wonder if *willing to actually attempt murder for you* was considered a turn-on. Maybe, from the look on Hugh's face, it was.

Sam said, "I'll drink to that," and Hugh laughed again and drank.

When he was down to the dregs of his beer, Sam sat back. "What brings you back to Madison?" he asked.

"Training, officially. I was asked to come up here and meet with some of the local magicians." Hugh looked down into his glass. "I'm involved in organizing within the magic community." There was a long pause before he added, "Similar to what Ulysses's grandmother does."

Sam frowned. "Did you come up to meet with her?"

"Among others." Hugh traced a line in the condensation on the side of the glass and then set it down. "It's odd, though. When I was driving up here, I thought . . . I should go talk to Sam." He fixed Sam with a knowing stare. "You must be able to feel it. There's something going on around here."

"I—yeah." Sam cleared his throat, thinking of the box again. "Some of it I'm aware of."

"I just wanted to let you know I'm around for the next two weeks." Hugh shrugged and downed the last of his beer. Sam watched his hand as he lifted the glass, the silver wedding ring on his fourth finger bright against the dark skin.

"Thanks." He looked down at his own hands, thought about the radio in his brain. "Say, do you ever feel . . . are you still connected to Arawn, in any way?"

Hugh considered this, then shook his head. "I don't think of it that way. I don't think of us as two different people. I am who I always was."

"I see." Sam picked at a stray thread on the leg of his pants. "So you don't ever worry about what would happen if he came back."

"I worry about a lot of things, man. But that's not one of them." But his voice was warm, and Sam understood the unspoken apology there.

Sam shrugged. "Maybe things would be different for me if I remembered being Dionysus, or if I hadn't met Ulysses back when I was just me."

Hugh tilted his head to one side, but in the end he just nodded. "Don't worry. You'll figure it out."

When Sam looked up again, he spotted Vikram and Sita coming along the sidewalk from the direction of the capitol. They were holding hands, Vikram bending slightly toward her as she spoke. Sam raised a hand and waved to them; after all, they lived on the fourth floor too. Probably best to keep them away from the building for a while.

Hugh twisted around in his seat to look, then glanced back at Sam, a question on his face.

"Someone I want you to meet. She's another member of the support group."

Chapter 19

"THE PROBLEM HASN'T BEEN scale," Laz was saying. "It's more that the magico-chemical linkages are difficult to manage." They'd decided to take Eli's car out to visit the nexus, since it was the least likely of any of their vehicles to be recognized. Laz was driving.

Peregrine, sitting shotgun, was checking and rechecking the wires that ran between the zaubergraph and a black box about half the size of a car battery. They seemed to understand what Laz was saying and even, god help them, to be interested in the subject. "How do you manage the power fluctuations?"

Laz looked extremely pleased with the question. His answer started out, "After I realized—" and then continued through twenty words that Ulysses thought he'd need another PhD to figure out.

"Sorry," he muttered to Eli, who was sitting next to him in the back, absently staring out the window, even though the scenery on Northport Drive wasn't very exciting.

Eli shrugged. "It's good for him to have someone new to discuss it with." He shifted so he was facing Ulysses, then darted a look at the seat in front of him. "Does Sam know about them?"

"They've met," Ulysses said, voice a little rougher than he'd like.

Eli nodded. "And Sam knows that—" he gestured at Peregrine, who was bent over the machine's new readout.

Ulysses had to remind himself that Eli couldn't know about Sam's suspicions and was probably mostly concerned Ulysses was dragging a student into danger. "They wouldn't let me bring the machine without them, and I need their help." It definitely wasn't the sort of thing Dr. Lesko would have done with her advisees, and the specter of danger made it worse, but there didn't seem to be any way around it. "Sam knows what we're doing," he said, and then added, "and he *trusts* me." He'd meant to put the emphasis on *he*, but at the last moment his treacherous brain switched it, so that it came out not as a quiet rebuke but as a statement of wonder and confusion. Sam trusted him to keep everyone safe.

They pulled into a parking lot, and Ulysses was saved from further conversation.

Not for long. "Where are we?" he asked. Laz had parked midway up a hill next to a small brick church with a few arched windows and a white steeple; at one end of the parking lot, slightly downhill from them, was another church, much larger and newer, made of stone and wooden siding. Ulysses would have assumed it was some sort of professional building except there was a chimney-like brick steeple with a cross at the top. He frowned.

Laz, getting out of the car, gave him a look. "Don't you have any sense of direction at all?"

"I know where we are geographically," Ulysses snapped, "but . . ." He trailed off. He'd spotted a tall, imposing building at the crest of the hill to the northeast. It was barely visible through the trees, but he remembered it. Five stories, a prominent central section with a wing on either side, austere windows and terrible, neat brickwork. The sun was low enough in the sky to make all those windows flash orange. The sanitarium. He shivered. "Never mind."

Laz turned, then looked back at him quizzically. "This is the address you gave me." He gestured up the hill at a small graveyard. It was neatly mowed, but many of the gravestones looked to be in poor repair. As Ulysses drew closer, he realized that they were the narrow obelisks of early settlers, with dates from the 1840s. Each listed an entire family, the members spread across the four sides of the monument. Some of the inscriptions were in German; others were worn nearly to the point of near-illegibility, although it could have been only a century or so since they were placed there.

Everything was green. The lawn was a wide stretch of grass punctuated by occasional flowers set alongside the headstones. It reminded him of visiting Forest Hill Cemetery with Sam one cold, wet spring night more than a year ago, but this place was—he wanted to say peaceful. He wanted it to *be* peaceful. Someday, they were going to have to dig a grave and stick Babushka in, and he desperately wanted to feel like it was a peaceful place, because any god knew she hadn't had enough of that during her life. But this particular graveyard was unsettled, full of a low-pitched hum of anger, fear, and regret, and he tensed.

Toward the back, there were signs of more recent burials, flat military headstones noting the individuals therein had served in World War II, Korea, or Vietnam. Laz stopped in front of one of them and his mouth did something horrible at the corners. Eli stood beside him for a moment, hands in his trouser pockets. Ulysses wasn't sure where to look, or if he should say something. And then Peregrine came laboring up the hill, carrying the portable zaubergraph, and the bubble burst silently.

Laz and Peregrine set up the zaubergraph on a stone bench and started fussing with it, talking in low, excited voices about what adjustments could be made on the fly, what the readings meant, how it could be normalized and tested. Ulysses drifted off and found a spot under a pine tree. The ground was covered with needles, and the sweet scent rose up around him as he settled and crossed his legs, willing himself to relax.

The last time he'd tried this trick, back on the lakeshore, he'd wound up with a migraine, tasting Sam's displeasure sharp on his tongue. This time it was easier to sink down, unnoticed and silent. He felt guilty for thinking that, unhappy with the knowledge that sometimes magic was easier without Sam around. Well, you couldn't bring a cannon to a duel. Sure. That sounded plausible.

The nexus was not a welcoming place. That was interesting in itself. It felt like a snake, coiled in a defensive knot. Ulysses didn't know what to make of that. Places could pick up some of the attributes of the people who lived there. That was most true of buildings, because people actually spent their lives inside them. The cemetery, on the other hand, was outdoors, and even a century or more of occasional visitation wasn't going to charge it up much, psychically speaking. So it had to be the nexus itself that was somehow causing the unease he felt. The nexus was feeling the unease, and he was brushing against it.

It was lukewarm, with an unpleasantly acidic taste, and Ulysses could have sworn it flinched away from him as he reached up a hand.

He tried to think how to explain that he came in peace. That he meant it no harm? None of that seemed quite right when what he really wanted to ask was, 'What the hell is going on?'

There was a scuffling noise, far too close to his ear, and Eli said, "Someone's been using the area for bonfires."

Ulysses fell out of the trance and landed in an ungainly sprawl. It was an ugly exit, and it stung like having a bandage ripped off. "What?" he managed, opening one eye. The light stabbed in.

Across the cemetery from them, Laz and Peregrine were still bent over the zaubergraph, crowing to themselves about the readouts. Eli was crouched about ten feet away and looking sheepish, like he hadn't quite realized that Ulysses would be able to hear him. "There was a bonfire here. Not too long ago, I don't think." He poked at something Ulysses couldn't see because he was lying in the pine needles. "When did it last rain—last week sometime, wasn't it? Look at the ashes. They haven't been disturbed."

Ulysses rolled to his hands and knees and steadied himself for a moment before getting to his feet. A muscle in his neck had seized up, and the pain was slowly crawling up the back of his skull.

Eli was right, of course. The ashes pretty clearly hadn't been rained on. He tried to remember the exact day—Wednesday? Friday? When had he and Sam seen the ghosts? Tentatively, he settled on Saturday for both, but the rain had preceded their outing by a few hours. Interesting. Had the church groundskeepers seen the burned spots? What did they make of them?

He fished his sunglasses out of his pocket and slid them on. When he opened his eyes again, Eli was frowning at him, so he said, "Good find," and started to turn away.

"Another headache?" Eli asked quietly.

"Something about this place." Ulysses shook his head. The last time he'd tried to touch the nexus, he'd had a migraine for two days. Hopefully that wasn't going to be the norm.

"Shall we take you home? Is Sam there?"

"I—no, he's out." Ulysses shifted uncomfortably from foot to foot, trying to keep everything he was feeling off his face. "I think I've seen enough." He swung toward Laz and Peregrine. "Hey, guys, are you—"

Eli cleared his throat meaningfully. Ulysses looked his way and froze. Julie Stricker was standing about ten or fifteen feet up the hill from them. She was alone, but Ulysses still moved fast to put himself between her and Eli, as though that might somehow make a difference in whatever happened next. Laz was next to him a moment later, shoulder to shoulder.

Stricker gazed dispassionately at the two of them, which was almost worse than anything else she could have done. If she'd smirked, he could have told himself she was pretending she knew something he didn't; if she'd looked angry or frustrated or menacing, those he could have dealt with. But she just stared at them.

She looked exactly the same as she had the last time he'd seen her: mid-fifties, blond bob, dark clothing. Her hair was even still permed, which was galling—how could someone who was supposed to be living undercover, on the lam from the police, just walk into a hair salon? She didn't look especially stressed or sleepless, which given how raw Ulysses was feeling seemed impossible.

"Ulysses Lenkov," she said after a silence whose duration seemed equivalent to his entire lifespan to date. "How is your granny doing? I understand she's sturdier than I gave her credit for."

That caused a new trickle of anxiety. "What did you do?"

She shrugged. "Nothing more than what she deserved."

Laz would have lunged forward at that, except that Ulysses had the presence of mind to put a hand on his arm. He wished he hadn't. "What do you want?" he asked.

"You have something I need."

"What would that be?" he asked, even though he was pretty sure he knew.

She looked appraisingly at him. She was going to ask for Sam. That was what she wanted—Sam's link to the Sterling bloodline, his inchoate godhood. But what she said was, "Your magic." She smiled. It was a cold expression on her face.

"I'm not going to *help* you," he said, shocked, and she laughed.

"I wouldn't ask you to. I just want your power." Her face turned hard. "It's an accident anyway. Nothing that was yours by right."

Laz muttered, "What is she talking about?"

Ulysses shook his head. "Nothing. She's bluffing."

"Ask your granny," Stricker advised.

That gave him pause. She was clearly trying to wind him up, but it was also such an odd thing to say. "What do you need it for?" he asked, shoving the thought down.

"A little project I'm working on." She shrugged. "I'll make you a deal. You come help me, I'll leave Dionysus Samuel Sterling-Lenkov alone."

Laz made a noise, but Ulysses couldn't figure out what it meant over his inner sense that he was falling, the anxiety widening into a vast river that was going to sweep through him and carry him away. "Why would I trust you?"

Stricker cocked her head to one side. "I think I've proven what I'm capable of. You know what will happen if you don't comply. You'll just have to take your chances on the rest."

Ulysses flexed his hands, cracked a couple of knuckles. There was a balloon inflating inside his skull, and he had neither time nor patience for this. "You'll have to forgive me if I don't find that convincing."

"I don't care how you find it." She studied her fingernails. "I have the book. I have the box. And I will get the power I need one way or another."

The box. The box they'd pulled out of the library? The one he'd very carefully installed in the specially protected cabinet beneath their sink? "How did you—" He broke off, unsure if he wanted to ask how she'd even known where it was or how she'd been able to recover it.

"I have people who do these things," she said, effectively answering both questions and neither.

Ulysses squeezed his eyes shut as his anxiety blossomed into full-blown panic. Where was Sam? What was happening at home? He reached for the bond—it was still there, which was reassuring. He was too far away to feel any emotions that way, but he'd know if Sam was in real trouble. Probably.

Shakily he asked, "Why are you doing this?"

"It's not a secret. I told you before, I want to live forever. Ask your soldier-brother or his pet doctor there; death is for chumps." Stricker's gaze flickered away, taking in the spot where Ulysses had been sitting, Eli and Laz, and then Peregrine, about whom he'd forgotten, oh *shit*, and then back to Ulysses's face. There was something deeply unsettling about her expression. "Think it over. But don't take too long. You have until July seventh."

They drove back in uncomfortable silence, Laz's lead foot keeping the car moving through the late afternoon traffic at a speed that was still slower than Ulysses's panic demanded. Eli radiated professional concern. Peregrine, never talkative, was wary, hunched over their equipment, barely responding to Laz. Ulysses thought he ought to say something reassuring, or even explanatory, but he didn't have any words. He didn't like that Peregrine had been involved in this in any respect. He tried to warn them as he got out of the car in front of the Baskerville—be careful of strangers, make sure your room is warded. Then he turned and ran up three flights of stairs.

Ulysses's headache had gone from pressure in his skull to a low-grade throb, a kick drum in the background of his thoughts, but at least the apartment was pleasantly cool. The windows were open, and a soft breeze off the lake moved through the living room. There was an odd scent of pine forests and decay; it took Ulysses a moment to place that as old magic hanging around. The vacuum had been left in the corner of the room.

Sam was sitting on one end of the sofa in a puddle of light from the floor lamp, reading, his long legs stretched out along the seat. He raised his eyes when Ulysses came in.

"They broke in and took the box."

Ulysses took a step toward him. "Are you all right?"

"They didn't touch me." Sam was tense, guilt and shame radiating off him. "I couldn't stop them. Hugh helped clean out the—whatever it was they did to overcome the wards. So everything's fine."

Fine. What a brittle word. Ulysses grappled through several possible responses and landed on, "*Hugh?*"

"He's in town for a few days. We got a beer." Sam's tone suggested everything was definitely not fine.

The break-in appeared to have been a neat enough job. Either Sam had already finished cleaning or they had barely put anything out of place. Ulysses wondered how they'd gotten past the wards in the first place. He would have to ask Celeste and Obe sometime.

"I should have been here," he said quietly. Not all of the guilt he could feel was Sam's.

"What would you have done? There were five of them." Sam rubbed his forehead and then met Ulysses's gaze, his eyes wild and desperate. "Even with Hugh here, our odds would have been unpromising."

"You might be right." Ulysses hoped he sounded serious and not placating. His headache was getting worse.

"How was your excursion?" Sam asked, and Ulysses realized he'd been silent for too long.

"Bad. Give me a sec." He kicked off his boots, went into the hall bathroom to wash his hands and splash cold water on his face. It didn't help.

When he got back, Sam was sitting up, book closed. Ulysses sat down next to him with a groan, closing his eyes against a world that was starting to go blurry around the edges. "I'm sure Stricker has worked out how to use the nexus directly as a power source, although damned if I know how. But it's a mess down there."

"Headache?" Sam asked quietly.

Ulysses slumped sideways until his head was resting in Sam's lap. "Eli gave me something for it."

There was a pause. "Did you take it?"

"Not yet. I wanted to . . . I don't remember. Say hello, maybe. Apologize." He made another involuntary noise as Sam shifted him back to a sitting position.

"Wait." Sam went into the kitchen and came back with a glass of water and a damp rag. "Drink." He thrust the glass at Ulysses and watched him obediently swallow the two small tablets from Eli.

When he'd finished the water, Sam took it, set it on the coffee table, and resumed his seat, tugging on Ulysses's shoulder until he lay down again. He didn't need much persuading. Sam carefully draped the rag across his forehead. Ulysses shut his eyes so he didn't have to stare at the blurry ceiling.

"Thanks." He cleared his throat, and the sound was grating in his ears. He let go of his grip on the bond, just a little, and felt a wave of confused emotions: Sam's irritation that Ulysses insisted on going to the graveyard without him, his concern for Ulysses, old fear, new anxiety. "I'm not really good at being taken care of."

"Could have fooled me," Sam said wryly. After a moment, he added, "I don't know if anyone is, once we're out of childhood."

Ulysses thought about his youth, and then shook his head. The motion sent a fresh frisson of pain up his neck. "Even then . . ."

"Me too." Sam laughed quietly, more air than sound. "What a pair we are."

"I didn't marry you to force you to take care of me," Ulysses told him. He couldn't feel his fingers anymore, he realized. Or his toes. Eli's drugs were quick. It was like being hit by a truck full of feathers.

"Nevertheless, that is what you get." Sam was quiet a long time, and Ulysses wondered if one of them had somehow fallen asleep without noticing. Sam had one hand on Ulysses's chest, heavy and warm. Ulysses could barely tell it was there. Finally, Sam said, "Isn't that the point of marriage?"

Ulysses didn't know, but the thought followed him down into the darkness.

Ulysses woke up the next morning in bed with no recollection of how he'd gotten there. He'd been stripped as far as his underwear and T-shirt. The light streaming through the windows was too fucking bright, but at least the headache was gone. He shut his eyes again.

He was going to have a talk with Eli the next time he offered him drugs.

Sam stepped out of the bathroom, a towel around his waist, and Ulysses tried to say good morning.

He managed part of "Good," maybe, and the corner of Sam's mouth twitched up.

"Still stoned, huh."

Ulysses took more time forming his next words. "I guess so." He rubbed his face with both hands. "What the hell did Eli give me?"

"Phenobarbital." Sam sat down on the edge of the bed, either because he was feeling chatty or because he didn't want Ulysses to attempt something too strenuous, such as standing up. "I called him after you passed out."

Ulysses searched his memory and came up blank. "When was that?"

Sam glanced at the alarm clock. "About twelve hours ago."

"I slept for *twelve hours?*"

"Close to." Sam didn't even bother to pretend he was surprised or concerned. "Eli said he told you to take *one* of the tablets, not both."

Ulysses didn't remember that either. "How did I get in here?" He sat up slowly, gripping one of Sam's hands.

"You weren't totally insensate. I levered you up and we staggered in so you could collapse on the bed." He shrugged. "It's not like I haven't had enough practice taking your pants off at this point. You're just usually more awake for it."

Ulysses laughed. Laughed until his sides ached, until he was clutching at Sam's hand and arm for support. Sam grinned, his eyes dancing. Ulysses leaned forward. He wanted to kiss Sam, but something in his brain was still off and he toppled forward, forehead diving into Sam's shoulder. When he righted himself, he found Sam watching.

"Eli warned me you might be dizzy," he said.

Ulysses wasn't a total stranger to the charms offered by recreational substances, but he generally avoided such things. Why invite hallucinations when he already saw ghosts? A glass of wine or vodka was fine when he wanted his mood altered by a drug. This was different, of course, but he didn't like it any better.

He hadn't realized he'd spoken any of that aloud until Sam said, "It'll be out of your system in a while."

"I'll just stay here until then," he murmured, and kissed the corner of Sam's jaw. "Thank you." Sam hummed in response, moving his head to grant better access. Sam's skin was smooth, still slightly damp, prickling in the cool air, smelling of soap and fresh water.

"I was debating taking the morning off," Sam said, running a gentle hand up his side. "But I think at some point I'm going to have to get up and eat something."

"I forbid it." He could keep track of himself in space if he moved slowly, so he did, shifting to his knees, kissing Sam's neck, his ear, the corner of his mouth. "You're taking a day off to keep an eye on me?"

"Someone has to." Sam cupped his shoulder, fingers pressing harder when Ulysses brushed something sensitive. "What happened on your outing last night?"

He sat back slowly, not wanting to stop touching Sam, not wanting to fall over. "I tried to commune with the nexus."

"And that's where the headache came from?" Sam took his hand, ran his thumb over Ulysses's knuckles.

"It doesn't want to be communed with." He shifted uncomfortably.

Sam looked down at their joined hands for a moment. "Is that everything?"

For a moment, Ulysses thought about not telling him, solely because it felt like the bad kind of burden-sharing, the kind that oppressed everyone and helped no one. But he couldn't really lie to Sam, not like this. Even before the bond, he wouldn't have been able to. "Julie Stricker showed up."

Sam's face faltered. "What did she want?"

"Me. My—she wants a battery. Scoop out all my magic." He took a deep breath, not entirely sure he was making sense. "I have a week or so to decide."

"You didn't say no on the spot?"

"If I do, she'll go after you. Or Peregrine. Or—I don't know. Someone else." The confession slipped out before he could stop it. The drugs again, probably. "If I thought it was only her living forever versus your safety, I'd say to hell with it."

"But it isn't."

"There's a lot more going on than I knew about." Ulysses bit his lip. "From ancient grudge break to new mutiny . . ."

Sam blinked, but finished the quotation: "Where civil blood makes civil hands unclean?"

"I need to talk to Babushka about this. I think she knows—well, she always knows more than she's willing to say. But I think she knows something important."

Sam regarded him for a long moment, clearly gauging Ulysses's ability to make it as far as Gooseberry House without falling over. "All right," he said. "Get dressed. I'll make coffee."

Chapter 20

ALTHOUGH ELI HAD BEEN reassuring, Sam still found Ulysses's inability to walk down the hallway from the bedroom to the kitchen in a straight line concerning. Ataxia, Eli had called it, and said it was to be expected. Sam hoped Eli was right.

Coffee seemed to help, but Sam still kept a watchful eye on Ulysses. When he bent to pull on his boots, frowning as if the laces were some sort of puzzle, Sam decided he would drive. To his surprise, Ulysses offered no resistance. It was probably for the best, actually; focusing on keeping the Triumph upright with both of them on it, shifting gears, the wind on his face, Ulysses's warmth pressed against his back, it all conspired to keep Sam focused on what he was actually doing rather than spiraling out into darkness.

There had been a moment, as they were opening the wall in the library, when Sam recalled his visions and found himself wondering why Memorial had selected that particular sequence of images for him. A forest, a bridge, a running stream: It had seemed tailor-made to catch his interest and lead him to the box. But what if they'd misinterpreted something? He'd assumed the library had wanted to be rid of the box. He'd certainly made some assumptions about the source of the vision.

He pushed his thoughts away.

Downtown traffic was light mid-morning, and the students had completed their yearly out migration, so there was plenty of parking along Pinkney Street. Sam slowed the bike as they cruised past Laz's GTO in the driveway, Aunt Cass's elderly brown Volkswagen parked on the curb, and a heavy black sedan. Sam pulled into a space behind it and held the bike steady while Ulysses slid off.

He looked better. Less pale, more engaged with his surroundings. Maybe the ride had been good for him. Sam pocketed the motorcycle's key and pulled off his helmet. "Are you ready for this?"

"No." Ulysses smiled tightly. "Talking to her never seems to yield the kind of conclusive answers that one desires."

"But it does produce something." Sam hung his helmet and Ulysses's from the handlebars and joined him on the sidewalk. "Hopefully, in this case we'll get a clue as to why those guys were so desperate to get their hands on the box."

Ulysses took a step, wobbled, and took Sam's arm. "I'm sure she won't tell us."

"Because she doesn't know?"

He made a sweeping gesture with his free arm. "If she knows and doesn't want to say, it'll be the same as if she doesn't know."

Ulysses sounded so miserable, Sam felt like he had to offer some response. "She's not doing it out of animus, at least."

Ulysses considered this for longer than Sam expected. "How much of a difference does that make?"

They came to a stop in front of the house, where Sam found himself distracted by Laz's updates. From the forest of stakes they'd seen him putting up a few days ago had grown a sturdy wooden ramp that ran all the way to the sidewalk. It was a startling addition to the house's otherwise symmetrical façade, but it was clearly well-made.

Sam put a hand on one stout wooden post. "Laz does good work."

"No wonder he looked so tired," Ulysses said. "He's going to paint it when he gets a good stretch with no rain."

"What does the house think?" Sam asked, and Ulysses raised an eyebrow. "I mean . . . does it have feelings about being added onto?"

Ulysses put a hand on the post next to Sam's, tilting his head. "It's happy to have Babushka back, I think. That's all."

Sam looked up at the house's face, the beautiful arched windows like questioning eyebrows. "Do houses know how they look?"

"Does anyone?" Ulysses shot back, leaning closer to him. "Do you?"

"I have a mirror," Sam said. Ulysses snorted, and in a rush of honesty, Sam added, "What I don't always understand is the effect I have on people."

Ulysses opened his mouth to reply. Then the door to the house closed, four steps above them. It wasn't a loud noise, but Sam jumped and looked up. Ulysses drew in a sharp breath, but for a long moment, Sam didn't quite understand who he was looking at—it was just a man in a suit. Graying, swept back hair, a well-tailored suit. Silver and green cufflinks that Sam had seen before. Why was Ulysses—

The man jogged quickly down the steps and nodded to them. "Good morning Samuel, Ulysses," Howard said, and got into the black sedan parked at the curb.

⟫⟫⟩ ⟨⟨⟨

WHEN ULYSSES LOOKED BACK, Sam seemed a bit shaken. But he wasn't clinging to the porch railing for dear life. As far as Ulysses could feel, reaching gingerly into the bond, he wasn't spiraling into panic.

"He was curious," Sam said. "When he heard she was hospitalized. He asked how she was doing. He said it was because she's my relative, but—" He shook his head. "Why does he even know who she is? It's not like they met at our wedding and hit it off."

Ulysses bit his lip. "Everyone knows Babushka." But the words felt hollow, and Sam gave him a look.

"All the magic people, maybe." He stared in the direction Howard had gone. "Howard hates magic people."

Ulysses wondered if that was true. Howard had married at least one member of the magic community, even if they'd kept her abilities hidden.

Their abilities, surely. Howard was the son of Julius Sterling, perhaps the greatest non-bloodline magician of his era. Had he really grown up knowing *nothing* about magic? "We should go inside," he said. Sam looked bleak. "Unless you want to go after Howard."

Sam was quiet for a long moment. "I think . . . we're here already. Let's talk to Babushka."

They went up the four steps to the door. Ulysses hesitated, placing one hand flat against the doorframe. But if the house still held a grudge against him, he couldn't feel it any longer.

Inside was quiet. The foyer was a small room with a coat closet, a door to a small powder room, a flight of dark wooden stairs running up to the second floor, and a doorway that led to the rest of the house. Generally, if there was anyone in the living room or kitchen, he could hear them from where he was standing. Today, there was nothing.

Ulysses wasn't in the habit of feeling trepidation upon entering the house in which he'd spent most of his life, but for a moment he wondered—

Surely there was someone with Babushka, keeping an eye on her. Howard hadn't been alone with her—she wasn't—

For just an instant, he felt like he was standing at the edge of a grave, gazing down. He didn't know where he was, only that there was level green grass spreading out around him and a coffin at the bottom of a pit, a long way beneath him.

Sam, a pace behind him, reached out and wordlessly took his elbow, steadying him. Ulysses tightened his mental shields. "I have an ill-divining soul," he muttered by way of explanation.

"Thou look'st pale," Sam murmured.

What had he even seen? No wonder Laz was always so reluctant to discuss his visions, if that was what they were like.

Ulysses fumbled his boots off and took a few quick sock-footed steps into the living room. Babushka was sitting calmly on the sofa, legs propped on an ottoman in front of her, a large silver teapot on the end table to her right along with three extra glasses in their little metal holders. Two armchairs had been drawn close. In one sat Dr. Edith Pearlman, delicately holding a tea glass; from the other, Dr. Nadiya Lesko looked back at him.

No one seemed surprised to see him, or Sam at his heels.

Ulysses drew a breath and tried not to blurt out the first thing that came into his head. But as the house's silence drew in around them, oppressive and thick, he couldn't shift his focus to anything else. He cleared his throat. "Why was Howard Sterling here?"

Dr. Pearlman glanced at Dr. Lesko. But it was Babushka who spoke: "He had concerns he wanted to lay before us."

"And what do you think of his concerns?" Ulysses looked from face to face. "Do you agree?"

Babushka gestured at the end of the sofa. "Sit down, child."

Ulysses glanced back at Sam, who lifted one shoulder slightly. He was paler than usual, but his lips were set in a thin, resolute line.

Sitting did not alleviate the tension. Nor did any of the women seem interested in breaking the silence. Ulysses let it build around them. He and Sam were crammed onto the far end of the couch, shoulders brushing, and he could feel the tension within his husband. But Sam was good at this game. Better than Ulysses.

He had a sudden memory of a time when he was about twelve or thirteen. He'd still been smarting from Mariah's departure for France. He'd spent most of the summer outside, away from the house with its oppressive chill and books and people who didn't understand why he was upset that his mother had moved to Paris. He and Celeste and Laz had pooled their money and bought a rowboat off old Mr. Mackenzie at the end of the block, and he'd spent hours trying to row to Governor's Island on the opposite shore of Lake Mendota, coming home exhausted and sunburned.

He had been a skinny kid, and the exercise and impending puberty was starting to put muscle on him. When he noticed, it was the first time he'd ever felt like he was in control of something.

And then there had been an afternoon when he'd dragged in and decided to stop in the kitchen for a snack before he went up to his room. On his way, he'd found these women in this configuration, a suspicious silence in the air, as if he'd interrupted something. There had been a samovar on the coffee table then, and a few glasses and other items he hadn't paid much attention to. Had there been a wooden box among them? Was his memory playing tricks on him?

They'd been younger then. Dr. Lesko must have just finished her PhD, and Dr. Pearlman was probably only a few years older than Ulysses was now. They'd both seemed old to him at the time, and Babushka in her fifties was ancient. Strange how things changed.

He had hesitated in the doorway, unsure if he should rush through, or go back outside and run around to the back door. And in that moment of indecision, Babushka had said, "Come here, Lyosha."

"*Ulysses*," he grumbled, but stepped fully into the room, aware of their eyes on them, aware that he was sweaty and smelled like lake water. They asked him a few questions—the perfunctory kind people ask children. What grade are you going into, how do you like your school, how is your magic these days? He stared at the toes of his sneakers and mumbled his way through the conversation. And then one of them looked at Babushka. He looked at her too. She nodded.

"He is strong," she said. He felt himself swell with pride and tried to hide it. But when he looked back at the others, they were slowly nodding as well.

He blinked the memory away. Babushka was watching him, mouth hidden behind her teacup. And before he could think better of it, he said, "What happened in 1954?"

"Howard Sterling came to us," Dr. Pearlman said. "He was concerned about his father."

Sam made a noise of dismay, and Dr. Lesko nodded. "I'm sure he'd been thinking about the situation for years. He didn't tell us everything—far from it. But he did say he feared Julius Sterling was doing something that would be actively harmful to his son Dio—to Samuel, rather than just . . . passively menacing him." She smiled genially at Sam, but Ulysses thought there was something odd and flat about the action. Dr. Lesko's eyes remained serious. "Howard had been keeping the boy protected as best he could. But Julius had intimated that wouldn't be enough."

"The magic community has long survived through self-policing," Dr. Pearlman put in.

Dr. Lesko continued, "We went with Howard to confront Julius Sterling. His old partner, Dr. Barth, was already there, and . . . things got out of hand."

Ekaterina poured a cup of tea and pushed it into Ulysses's numb hands. He handed it to Sam, then turned back in time to receive another. "Sympathetic power transfer," she said after a moment. "He'd built up a sizeable lake for himself. Without him, it was extremely unstable, and we had to do something with the power. And that was where Ulysses came in."

Sam looked confused. "Sorry, what's that mean?"

Ulysses said, "The easiest way to understand is that Julius made himself the object of a spell." He frowned to himself. "But what do you mean, the power? Where did it come from?"

To Sam, Dr. Pearlman said, "You're aware of Ulysses's innate magic, I'm sure."

"Of course." Sam looked nervously between them. "I can access his power because of the bond."

"You can access his power because Julius Sterling was already drawing power from you somehow," Dr. Lesko said. She sounded satisfied, like she'd solved a puzzle. "And Ulysses was the recipient of Sterling's power."

Ulysses opened his mouth and shut it again. He took a deep breath and wrapped his hands around his teacup to hide their shaking. "What—"

"The library talked to me before the bond started," Sam said.

Ulysses cleared his throat. That part, at least, he understood. "You were always already Dionysus."

"A fact Howard Sterling neglected to mention," Dr. Lesko muttered.

"What you're saying," Ulysses said slowly, "is that the bond was always going to happen. Or it was there to be uncovered from the beginning."

Distantly, it occurred to him that he should be angry. Instead, he just felt numb. Their entire relationship—certainly, especially, their marriage—had been shaped by these choices Babushka had made, and she'd never once mentioned . . .

"You boys certainly found some interesting ways to work around your problems," Dr. Lesko said.

He looked at Sam, unwilling to reach out through the bond to see what he was feeling about this development. But Sam's mind was clearly elsewhere. "When all this happened, I was . . . eight? Nine?" Sam said.

Dr. Pearlman nodded. "Howard believed that the ritual would have happened around your tenth birthday, although obviously he couldn't be certain. Even if it hadn't, he was right to be concerned about how hard being Julius Sterling's battery was on you."

"I *was* sick a lot," Sam murmured. Ulysses stared at his profile, the high forehead and strong nose, and tried to imagine him as a child, gradually having his magic siphoned off. Horror prickled over his skin, and he had to remind himself that Sam was fine now.

"There are some times in our lives when we are more sensitive than others," Dr. Pearlman put in. "Children from around that age to about fifteen happen to be very vulnerable."

Ulysses said, very slowly, "I was—thirteen?"

"You were."

What a time. He looked down at the knees of his jeans. They were getting frayed along the inseam. He could see three spots where the denim was starting to come apart into tiny puffs of white cotton thread, and another at the knee where the hole was wider. Soon he'd need to buy another pair.

Everyone was watching him. He could feel their eyes on his skin. He also felt understanding prickling down his spine, all the things they weren't saying. All the things they hadn't said all these years.

Sam reached out and put a hand on his arm. Ulysses swallowed and closed his eyes, trying to still the pounding of his heart, the whirling of his thoughts. When he thought he could hold it together, he opened his eyes and looked at his grandmother. "Why did you do this?"

This silence had a different quality. Or was he imagining that? The medication was still in his system. He took a sip of the tea, tasted smoke and citrus. He forced himself to breathe.

Babushka said, "We could not release his power into the nexus. With Barth still alive, it was too risky."

"But you could have given it back to Sam."

She shook her head minutely. "Howard Sterling would not permit this. It made Samuel too tempting a target."

Ulysses found he was gripping the teacup too tightly and tried to relax his fingers. "So you attached it to me." He'd jumped from a balcony once at the Roundhouse, a ten-foot drop to the ground below. Just long enough to wonder if he'd made a mistake before he landed. This was a similar sensation. Ulysses put his elbows on his knees and stared into the red-brown tea. She hadn't given him any leaves. Around him, the women carried on drinking from their glasses, a strange network of meaningful looks and conspiracy binding them together. He had so many questions about the particulars of what they'd done, how they had managed it. "Why me?" he asked instead.

"You were the right age. You already had some talents, some magic of your own. And I could protect you," she said simply.

Sam's hand pressed against his back, between his shoulder blades. He couldn't get any thoughts to cohere. Was he panicking? His hands were shaking, but he hadn't exactly been steady on his feet when he'd walked in.

What he was remembering, absurdly, was all the times he'd almost left Madison. He'd applied to a couple of other schools for undergrad, and she hadn't said anything about his choice either way. He'd considered living in the dorms before deciding the attic would be more comfortable and private. He'd almost left in that year after finishing his BA, but had held off until he figured out what he wanted.

She'd never said anything about his choices.

"What would you have done," he asked quietly, "if I'd decided to move somewhere else?"

Babushka shrugged. "It did not happen."

"But if it had," he pressed. It suddenly felt very important to know. Would she have changed his mind somehow? He couldn't imagine her trying a geas on him, but there were many types of persuasion.

"My goal was always to make you strong enough that if I was not there, you would be able to survive," his grandmother said, and sipped her tea.

Chapter 21

S AM STEPPED OUT AND leaned against the back door after it closed behind him. He'd seen Ulysses do this, seemingly drawing strength from the house itself. But while it did hold Sam up, he felt nothing unusual beyond the rough, cracked paint and the warmth of the sun. Apparently, his ability to commune with places unassisted began and ended with the library.

That was a relief, actually. Imagine feeling that kind of connection to every place you went into.

It was difficult to imagine having magic the way Ulysses did. Sam only stood on the banks of the river Ulysses swam in, and that was enough. Whatever he could have had, it was better this way. Probably.

He felt like something was choking him and loosened his tie. It was barely nine in the morning and humid. Madison was always humid; the isthmus had once been a swamp situated between two large lakes. But it was especially humid, and already quite warm, with a promise that it would be hot later on. It was almost July and the weather was shifting.

The greenhouse was at least *cool* and humid. At this time of year, it was filled with rows and rows of green, bushy plants. There were geraniums, orchids, and a handful of little cacti, along with many others he didn't recognize—tall plants with wide, ribbed leaves; smaller plants with black-purple leaves that looked like hands; tiny little plants that shivered as he passed. Things that were presumably too delicate to put out in the yard.

Cass was at the bench at the rear of the greenhouse, peering through a microscope at something. She beckoned to him as he approached. "Samuel, my dearest. You have strong, young eyes, don't you?"

"I—" Sam had to restrain himself from putting a hand to his temple. "I guess so."

"Come here and tell me what you see." She stepped back, making a space for him.

He had to hunch absurdly over the bench, but after adjusting the knobs on the side of the microscope, a slide came into focus. It was . . . maybe a cross-section of a plant? It had been dyed blue, and he could see all sorts of little structures, round and plump and lined up like a diagram of theater-goers around a stage. "It's—yeah." He raised his head, blinking. "What am I looking for?"

"A star pattern. It will be in the center. Some areas will be bluer than others, because of how they absorb the stain." He heard a pen moving over a piece of paper and looked up to see she'd sketched a rough diagram on the corner of her legal pad. "Something like this."

He fiddled with the knobs a bit more, squinting. Even knowing what he was looking for, it took an embarrassingly long time before he saw it. He felt himself growing tense and slightly anxious, sliding his eye across the little circles until suddenly they resolved into a coherent pattern. "Oh! I see it."

She made him draw it like he was a high school junior stuck in his first biology class, outlining all the little circles with different blue pencils. Then she switched the slide and said, "Does this one look different?"

It did. The star pattern was different, the stain having revealed something much more intricate. He struggled to draw it, feeling like a rube with Cass looking over his shoulder. "I'm a librarian," he groused at last, setting down the colored pencils.

"You did very well." She picked up the sheet of paper with the drawings on it and frowned at them. "Thank you."

"What are you looking for?" He yielded the stool and circled back to the other side of the bench.

"This is the cross-section of a ginseng root that was planted during the new moon and harvested during a subsequent new moon, and this is from one that was planted and harvested during a full moon." She bent forward and made notes on the paper, then peered through the microscope again, hand going to the focus knob. "I have to admit, I'd never really thought about it, but Eli suggested . . ." She trailed off and pulled back, making another note on Sam's diagram.

"Suggested?" he asked after a long silence.

"Hm? Oh." She looked up at him, distracted. "The full moon planting is traditional. He suggested I look into what's different, if anything. Because it's a lot of trouble to go to, so why . . ."

Sam nodded. "There's a lot of things like that," he said vaguely.

Cass seemed to notice for the first time that he was alone. "Where's your other half?"

The term made Sam grimace suddenly. "Talking to Babushka and her . . ." He hesitated. Coven? Former coven? His boss? "Her friends," he finished awkwardly.

"Ah." She studied him. "And they asked you to step away?"

Sam shrugged. "I could have stayed. Ulysses didn't mind. I just . . . my immediate emotional reaction wasn't . . ."

"What happened?"

He swallowed. "It's complicated, but it seems as though Ulysses wound up with some of my grandfather's magic. And that may have influenced our relationship, because it was originally my magic." He paused, watching her face for a reaction. "Is that weird?"

"Everything is weird," she said slowly, "especially you two." She put down her pencil and leaned against the workbench. "Who was Julius Sterling?" Sam opened his mouth, but she waved a hand before he could begin. "I mean, was he a bloodline magician?"

"No." Sam looked down at his hands, which were tan and powerless, unscarred and soft. "He was just—he was a magician. I think he called himself an amateur. From the Latin, amator, meaning 'lover.' "

Cass snorted. "Of course he did." She set her pen down, but for a long moment she didn't say anything. "You know, he came here once or twice."

"Did he?" Sam felt something brush against his ankle and looked down to see Tim, Cass's black cat, staring up at him with wide yellow eyes. Impulsively he reached down and lifted the creature. He was soft, and lighter than he looked. "What was he like?"

"Charismatic." His surprise must have shown, because she nodded ruefully. "He was incredibly charming when he wanted something. And if he thought you didn't have it, or you weren't going to help him, he didn't have anything to say to you. Just—" She waved a hand in front of her face. "Blank."

Tim was purring. Sam scratched him under the chin and he went pleasantly limp. "Why was he here?"

"He thought he could beguile Babushka." She laughed. "Can you imagine?"

Sam smiled uncomfortably. "And she didn't know—that is, she said she suspected, but . . . ?"

"Do you think she'd have let him leave here in one piece if she'd had proof? She did her best." Cass sighed and shook her head. "I'm sorry that this has hurt you."

"I just—I don't like the idea that we only—because Julius—ow!" Tim, not sorry at all, bit Sam's hand with his needle-like little teeth, and then ran up his arm to perch on his shoulder.

"I think that whatever brought you two together, it was more than just your power being dumped in Ulysses's body." Cass tapped her papers into a neat stack. "Power isn't quite like that, and the amount Julius Sterling would have needed—"

"Is this a private lecture?" Ulysses called from behind them. Sam whirled, feeling guilty without quite knowing why, and then winced as Tim leapt off him, landing on the table. "If you're explaining my inherent magic, I want to know."

Ulysses looked awful. Sleeping for twelve hours had done nothing for the dark rings under his eyes or the exhaustion that hung around him like a shroud. His skin was pale and clammy. But there was a brightness to his gaze, too, and a magnetism.

"How was the talk?" Sam asked. He kept his hands in his pockets, feeling like if he reached out, he wouldn't be able to stop the gabble of his emotions flooding across the bond. Ulysses did not look prepared for that.

"It was fine." Ulysses shifted his weight from foot to foot and looked at Cass. "I guess Sam told you."

"A bit," she said. Sam got the feeling she was trying to take Ulysses's measure, figure out how much he could take. "How angry are you with her?"

To Sam's surprise, Ulysses shrugged. "I think I'm relieved more than anything to finally have it in the open."

Sam snorted. "Should I ask you again on a day when you're not drugged to the gills?"

"Perhaps." Ulysses took a step closer. He was walking more steadily now, and when he reached out and put a hand on Sam's forearm, he felt calm. "I guess I reserve the right to revisit this later."

"Noted." Sam tried to fumble the radio to zero volume. The knob wobbled; his fingers couldn't grasp it. He bit the inside of his cheek.

Ulysses slid his hand down Sam's arm until their fingers tangled together. Ulysses's skin was cool to the touch. Sam must have been doing a worse job of shielding himself than he'd thought, because Ulysses's eyebrows went up. "Really?"

Sam looked down at the toes of his wingtips. "I'm angry on your behalf," he said quietly. "Who wouldn't be?"

"That *is* a bit creepy," Cass said, making Sam jump and blush. "Laz was complaining about you two, and I told him to get over it." She shook her head. "Guess I owe him an apology."

Ulysses rolled his eyes. "Or you could tell him where he can—"

"Ulysses!" Cass looked mildly shocked, although she was smiling.

"Sorry." He squeezed Sam's fingers. "I'll tell him myself sometime."

Even though he'd already called in, Sam went to work and tried to pretend everything was normal.

Everything *was* normal. No one was dead. Ekaterina's hip was healing. She and Ulysses were working out their shit. Sure, Howard was acting oddly cagey. And the revelations about Ulysses hadn't left a good taste in his mouth, but even there—wasn't it nice to have an explanation?

Really, everything was fine. The thought echoed through Sam as he walked into the library, as he greeted Buttercup and gave her a project for the day, as he sat in on a reference group meeting. Everything was fine. Some things could be better, but overall it was fine. He started many days by taking his drugged husband to visit his parental figure and her former (?) coven. By hearing it explained that the reason they'd gotten together was (maybe) his evil grandfather.

If Buttercup sensed anything was off, she had the mercy not to ask. Instead, as she was helping him choose books for an exhibit on the evolution of the title page, she said, "Galadriel called last night."

"Did she?" He looked up from the book he was examining, *An Essay on the Art of Ingeniously Tormenting*, which had been printed in 1753 and had an ornate title page and a bracingly lengthy title.

"She's coming back."

For the life of him, Sam couldn't tell if she was pleased by this or not. "What do you think about that?" seemed safe.

Buttercup bit her lower lip. "I miss her," she said quietly. "But I don't know if it's for the best."

Sam nodded. "You're worried about her."

"It was scary before we left. I want her to be okay, you know?" She exhaled. "I can't keep her safe."

"Probably not." He looked back at the book. "But that's always true, isn't it?"

"Maybe, yeah." Buttercup managed a wan smile. "I mean, our life is here. I'm sure she doesn't want to miss out."

"That's also a reasonable impulse." He shut the book and put it in the keep pile. "I suppose I'd rather be in danger than spend significant time away from Ulysses."

Behind them, someone snorted. "Where Ulysses goes, danger follows." Sam turned to see Ellen leaning against a display case.

"That's not true." Sam paused, then amended: "Well, not always true."

"My dataset—"

"Is limited," Sam said firmly. "Ellen, what are you doing here?"

"I just came to remind you that we have rehearsal tonight." She eyed him and added, "And to claim you for lunch, unless you're expecting the redoubtable Dr. Lenkov-Sterling."

Sam winced a little at the joke. "What time is it?" He pressed a hand to his stomach. He hadn't eaten anything since his run and suddenly felt queasy, vaguely lightheaded.

"It's almost noon," Buttercup said, looking at a little silver wristwatch. "I should be going."

Sam nodded. "Would you reshelve the rejects before you go? I'll take care of everything else this afternoon." Ellen was looking at him with a raised eyebrow, so he added, "Ellen, this is my assistant, Buttercup Diaz. She's a grad student. Buttercup, this is my good friend Ellen Balfrey."

"Grad student? Not one of Ulysses's?" Ellen asked.

Buttercup smiled, gathering up the books. "Kind of. He's on my committee. I'm in comp lit, officially."

"And unofficially?"

"I'm halfway between magic and history."

Ellen's eyes lit up. "Who are you working with in history? My husband just graduated from there."

"O'Brien."

Sam left them discussing hot department gossip to fetch his suit coat. He found Edith stepping out of his office as he headed in.

"I left you the agenda for the acquisitions committee meeting," she said cheerfully, gesturing at his desk. "Should be a fun one."

Sam tried not to let his feelings about that show on his face. It would only encourage her. "I'm off for lunch," he said, stepping aside to let her pass. "By the way, what was Howard doing at Gooseberry House this morning?"

Edith pressed her lips together for a moment. "He came by to wish Ekaterina well," she said finally.

"And?" When she didn't respond, he felt a touch of irritation creeping into his tone. "If Howard only wanted to wish her a speedy recovery, he would have had someone deliver flowers. Why did he decide to go in person?"

Edith looked up at the ceiling for a moment, as though searching for strength. "You should ask Howard Sterling directly about his reasons," she said finally. "I think you should hear it from him."

Sam narrowed his eyes, trying to find a way to say—he wasn't sure. He wanted to growl, to shout that she knew what was going on. Why wouldn't she tell him?

But she was still his boss. Beneath the informality they shared, and the family ties, there was a point past which he could not press. So he swallowed the feeling and tried to smile in acknowledgment. "I'll do that."

When Sam got back from lunch with Ellen, the department was quiet. Buttercup had departed. Edith was at a meeting, or—he didn't care that much, actually. There weren't any students around. He slunk back to his office.

On his desk, someone had left a sheaf of handwritten papers. On top was a note: *Buttercup found this under the card catalog. Thought you might find it interesting.—EP*

Sam sat down and studied the pages. Most lines contained at least two scripts—a tight, impatient hand that noted book titles, and a library hand that described the contents more thoroughly.

It was a collection inventory, a fairly detailed one. Leafing through, he spotted a title he recognized, written in a spiky, non-Roman script, followed by the notation *De Naturis Beluarum.* Of the nature of monsters.

The department was empty. But his voice still came out soft and strangled when he said, "Shit."

Chapter 22

U LYSSES STARED MUZZILY AT the ceiling of their bedroom, studying the pattern of shadows and light created by the half-open curtains. The revelations of the morning felt distant and muted. As though he'd been told something he'd known for a long time.

Perhaps he had.

It wasn't helping him get back to sleep, though.

Sam was upset. He hardly needed the bond to tell him that. Of course Sam was upset. This was his history too, this strange moment when their lives had brushed past each other. But it wasn't only that—if Babushka had announced she'd stabbed Julius Sterling in the chest, Sam would probably have hugged her.

Was Sam upset because of what Julius had done? Because Ulysses had something that was rightfully his? Did he regret the bond that had grown from this? Did he regret *meeting* Ulysses?

After about twenty minutes chasing his thoughts in circles, he figured he wasn't going to feel better unless he got up and forced himself to move. Washing his face helped, and getting dressed. There was food in the kitchen, most of which seemed ungodly complicated and unappetizing, but he found a banana and ate it on the stairs down to the street.

The gym was a place he specifically went so he didn't have to think. It was easy enough—put the plates on the bar, move the bar until he couldn't anymore, take the plates off. His muscles felt weak, but it was just a feeling.

Some of Sam's unhappiness was on Ulysses's behalf. Probably neither of them had been treated especially well in all of this. And the basis for their marriage was the bond, which no one had ever suggested—

Ulysses put forty-five more pounds on either end of the bar and did another set of deadlifts.

It was humid in the weight room, and he was sweating by the time he was halfway through his normal routine; his muscles were shaking by the time he'd finished.

Good. Job well done.

Not long after, he found himself pulling up in front of the magic building. There were a couple of bikes in the bike rack, but one of them had been abandoned there since early May. Mostly the place had the deserted feeling the campus sometimes got in the summer. He imagined that this was what it felt like to walk through the corridors of an abandoned temple from some ancient civilization.

The twelfth floor was quiet. The department did offer some summer classes, but no one seemed to be around. Perhaps they'd all gone home already. He wondered if Dr.

Lesko had come in after their unexpected meeting that morning.

He wondered if he had the guts to check.

The mail had come. He flipped through and discarded a few pieces of junk, glanced over a note from *Ritual* about revisions to a paper he'd submitted, and paused on a thick envelope with a flyer for a conference on ghosts and geography being held at a college in Santa Fe, New Mexico, along with a letter asking if he'd like to sit on a panel. It was the weekend before Sam's birthday—maybe he'd like to come along. Santa Fe was up in the mountains, wasn't it? Might be a nice place to visit.

If he made it that far. Laz's vision hung in the back of his head, and what was Sam going to say when he really understood everything Babushka had done? It was—

He folded everything back into the envelope and stuck it into the top drawer of his desk.

The remainder was a letter from Titania Usignole, written in a very small, cramped hand. He glanced over it—it held a few bits of gossip, nothing disastrous—and set it aside to take home for Sam.

There was a loud thud from somewhere outside his office. He sat, frozen, waiting, until it happened again, along with muffled cursing, and he got to his feet.

He followed the noises to the lab, where he found Peregrine sitting on one of the workbenches. They were barefoot in denim overalls, their hair pulled up on top of their head, looking at the ground where a collection of screwdrivers had fetched up. On the bench were the guts of a machine, wires and sensors and gears and springs and receivers.

"What are you working on?" Ulysses asked, bending over to retrieve the tools. "Is that the zaubergraph?"

"I was talking to Laz about the design," Peregrine said, selecting a small blue screwdriver, "and he gave me some parts to play around with. And a few ideas." They trailed off, focused on trapping a thin wire under the head of a screw as they tightened it. "This is going to revolutionize our ability to study how people use magic."

Ulysses looked at the jumble of parts on the bench. "Is it?"

"You have no idea." They pressed the lid onto the box and hopped off the bench. "Here, I'll show you. Sit down." They cast about the lab, but there weren't any chairs. Ulysses, obligingly, hoisted himself up to sit in the spot Peregrine had abandoned. "All right. So just let me—" There was a protracted period of muttering, and eventually a loud click as they found a switch somewhere on the large box. The machine began to hum and emit a faint smell of hot oil. "All right. Let's get a baseline . . ."

After a few moments, a strip of paper began to emerge from the back of the machine. It was similar to the previous zaubergraph output, except it had four wiggly lines instead of three. "What's the fourth line?"

"Watch." Peregrine handed Ulysses an electrode. It looked like the ones Eli had glued to Laz's scalp one afternoon last November when they'd tried the EEG. Peregrine said, "Just press it to your temple for now."

"All right . . ." Ulysses half expected to feel a tingle of current when he did, but there was nothing. The top pen, hitherto a straight line on the paper, gave a little wiggle.

Peregrine looked up from examining the output. "Do some magic."

"What?" Ulysses thought absurdly of Laz's coin trick. "I don't have a sacrifice with me."

"Don't you have some talent?" Peregrine picked up a long pointy tool and poked something in the box with it.

"I see ghosts. That's hard to do at the drop of a hat."

Peregrine actually glanced around. "No ghosts here?"

"Not right now."

"Hmm." They looked torn between picking up a pen to scribble that down and continuing to poke the long pointy thing into the box. "Do something else."

Ulysses snorted at the imperious tone, but settled back and closed his eyes. Gingerly, he reached out and felt around for Sam. Where was he? Somewhere east of them . . . maybe still at the library, but the feeling was slightly fainter than that. Maybe somewhere farther away. Ulysses felt the tug of it beneath his breastbone, sharp and not quite painful.

He opened his eyes when Peregrine made a pleased sound. All four pens were dancing merrily. "What's that mean?"

"It's capturing your innate magic and subtracting that signal from the rest. And the rest is better differentiated too." They jabbed a finger at the strip of paper and then started to hunt around. "Wait, I have a sample from before—"

They came back and presented him with another paper. He recognized his own pencil scrawl in the margins, noting the moment he and Sam had walked into the lab. It was difficult to know how to compare the data points, but the peak amplitude certainly seemed to be distributed differently in the new model.

"Here," Ulysses said impulsively, and handed the electrode to Peregrine. The top line quieted as soon as it left his hand. "You try."

"Me?" Peregrine took it, looking doubtful. "But I'm—I mean, I'm not—"

"Try anyway."

Peregrine looked nonplussed but pressed the electrode to their temple. The top pen jumped immediately, much more dramatically than it had for Ulysses, while the second one slowed as the machine subtracted Peregrine from the room's ambient magic.

"Is that—" Peregrine was wide-eyed, their almost frenzied energy arrested. "That's me?"

Ulysses looked at the output and found himself wishing Sam was there so hard he had the bond halfway open before he realized what he was doing. The second pen skittered and then subsided as he let go. "Yeah," he said. "That's you."

Peregrine stared at the output. Experimentally, they pulled the electrode away from their head and watched the styluses change speed, then put it back. "How is that right? That would mean that I . . . But you . . ."

Ulysses opened his mouth, shut it, tried again. "Yeah." He rubbed his face with both hands, fingertips rasping over the stubble on his jaw. "You deserve an explanation."

SAM STEPPED OUT OF Harry and Ellen's house after rehearsal to find Ulysses waiting with the motorcycle under a streetlight. He was sitting backward on the seat, reclining against the gas tank, ankles crossed, his attention on an old, tatty paperback. The sight triggered some old memory of a black and white movie, Marlon Brando or James Dean, back when everyone had wanted to look like they were part of a motorcycle gang.

Sam waved farewell to the last of the departing actors and made his way over. "You look like a dream I once had."

Ulysses looked at him and shut the book. "Hello to you too." He got up, stowing the book in an inner pocket. Sam caught the word *Ivan* in Russian on the cover, and *Tolst* before it vanished. Ulysses said, "You look nice."

"I feel like I ought to be wearing bobby socks or something." Sam smoothed a hand over the front of his slacks. "A pink poodle skirt, maybe."

Ulysses's eyes flickered over him as though he was imagining Sam dressed like a teenybopper. "Not your color," he said eventually. "But if you need a date to the sock hop, I'm your man."

He offered his hand, and Sam took it and let Ulysses spin him around. "I notice you don't object to the image of yourself as a greaser."

There was a party somewhere. Sam couldn't name the old blues tune that came drifting down the street to them, but he could hear drums and bass notes, a few bright guitar riffs floating over the top. He set a hand on Ulysses's shoulder and followed the sway of his body, let Ulysses spin him around. He could smell the leather of Ulysses's jacket, the low scent of sweat that might mean Ulysses had made it to the gym.

"Nothing makes one so vain as being told one is a sinner." Ulysses grinned rakishly, then sobered. "Although I wasn't a very good rebel."

"No?" Sam dipped him to muted saxophone wails.

When Sam went to straighten up, Ulysses put a hand on his cheek, stilling him. "I was always pretty convinced that the things Babushka was doing were right. Hard to rebel against that."

"I suppose you've led me to ruin with your radical ways anyway," Sam said lightly.

"I led you to something."

He sounded serious all of a sudden, like he was apologizing. The idea was suffocating. Sam pulled them both back to their feet, keeping his hands on Ulysses's waist, his lower back. Sam leaned close. "To be fair, I was pretty interested in going where you were headed."

Ulysses held his gaze when he let go, eyes pale in the streetlight. He wasn't quite smiling, but he seemed more at ease, like Sam had managed to say something that brought him some small relief. Sam watched him straighten his jacket and swing a leg over the bike. "You eat yet?"

They fetched up at the diner. Sam spotted the GTO in the parking lot, and inside Eli and Laz were sitting in a corner, hunched over a notebook in the middle of the table. As they approached, Sam caught a few words of the conversation, enough to understand they were discussing math. Ulysses slid into the booth next to Laz, so Sam sat opposite him.

Laz didn't look at his brother, just turned to an earlier page and slid the notebook in front of him without a word. It was some kind of schematic; Sam couldn't read the notations, but then he wasn't sure he would have been able to read them right side up either.

Eli said, "You look better than yesterday."

Ulysses frowned at the page before him. "No thanks to you."

"I told you what those pills do," Eli said mildly.

"I only remember you saying they'd help my headache, not that they'd knock me out." Ulysses picked up Laz's pencil and made a mark on the diagram.

Eli glanced over at Sam, a wry smile playing around the corners of his mouth. Sam laughed.

Eli still had his bow tie on, suggesting he'd just come from work. He looked tired, and he had one hand curled around a steaming mug of coffee. Laz looked like Laz, which was to say hassled, hairy, and one step from exhaustion. They both showed signs of being as scraped raw by Babushka's injury as Ulysses had been, continued to be. Sam was definitely not going to bring that up.

The waitress arrived and deposited omelets in front of both Laz and Eli, then with a certain restrained surliness fished out her order pad and took Sam and Ulysses's orders as well.

"This is your design?" Ulysses asked when she'd gone, gesturing at the notebook.

Laz was spreading jam on a slice of toast with an expression of fierce concentration. "Yeah."

"It's clever."

Laz looked pleased. Laz had to be used to being one of the smartest people in any given room, so it was a little funny to see how Ulysses's praise made him swell up. Sam tried to imagine getting praised for something by one of his siblings and couldn't.

Ulysses scribbled another note in the margin, then set the pencil down. "Are you going to talk to Peregrine about this?"

"Maybe." Laz paused to take a bite of his toast. "I'll have to systematize it if I'm ever going to be able to increase production beyond what I can accomplish on my own. Might as well think about that now, while I'm still getting all the components sorted out."

"Celeste might have ideas too," Ulysses said. Sam pulled the notebook around so he could look at it properly. The schematic was possibly some kind of battery. He vaguely remembered Laz having something to say about batteries and magic-powered prosthetics during a long, dreary drive back from Minnesota last November. Ulysses and Laz had covered the page with equations and a spellcraft notation that Sam had seen in some of the magic textbooks but couldn't read.

"Is this why the classes?" Sam asked, sliding the notebook back.

"I—sort of." Laz shut it, drumming his fingers on the cover. "I'd really like to make prosthetic limbs. For guys who got—who were injured in combat. But I have to figure out a power source that's reliable and lightweight first."

Eli said, "Well," with the air of someone wading back into a conversation they'd had before, and Laz rolled his eyes.

"Maybe I *will* take it up with Peregrine," he said. "I've never met a magician as interested in the intersection of magic and engineering as they are."

Ulysses nodded. He was still looking at the table, but Sam got the distinct sense he was no longer seeing it. "I went to see them," Ulysses said abruptly. "This afternoon."

Laz had opened the notebook again. "Oh?"

"They're working on updates to the zaubergraph. Improving the way it filters."

Laz nodded absently, eyebrows furrowed.

Sam took a deep breath. "Did you talk to them?"

"We spoke at some length." Ulysses snagged Laz's water glass and took a long swallow. "I asked them about their past. Their parents, magic, that kind of thing." Laz and Eli continued eating, seemingly unconcerned.

"And about the god thing?"

Out of the corner of his eye, Sam saw Laz's head turn toward them, heard Eli fumble his fork.

"I mentioned it." Ulysses sat back and started to crack his knuckles. Sam waited. Ulysses finally sighed. "It went very badly. I'd never seen them angry like that before. They shouted at me, said I had to be mistaken. I left the lab before they could start throwing things."

"All right," Sam said finally. "That sounds like a reasonable response, if I'm being honest."

"You aren't wrong." The waitress finally came back with coffee. Sam wrapped his hands loosely around his mug and watched Ulysses fuss with sugar packets. It felt like something was bunched up under Sam's skin, so he tried to soothe it down, knocking his wedding ring gently against the cup to distract himself. Ulysses glanced up at the sound, one eyebrow raised.

Sam shrugged. "Did you tell them about the party at Harry and Ellen's? I could talk to them."

"I invited them." Ulysses stirred his coffee. "Who knows if they'll come."

Sam looked down at his knuckles where they curled around the cup. "I received something interesting today."

He fished the list out of his pocket and slid it across the table.

Understanding broke across Ulysses's face with gratifying swiftness. "This is the inventory of all of Sterling's books. Where—"

"It was on my desk. I don't know if Buttercup actually found it, like the note claimed, or if Edith wanted to leave me some kind of peace offering and that was just a convenient excuse." He took a long drink of his coffee, watching Ulysses skim the document. "Not *very* useful, is it."

Laz cleared his throat. "Care to explain for those of us who didn't do the reading?"

Ulysses didn't look up. "The book Stricker's goons took from the library when they kidnapped Sam was handwritten and encoded. So presumably some kind of journal, maybe even a personal grimoire. We didn't have a list of all his books until now, so we couldn't work out what it was."

Laz made a face. "Not promising. If there are instructions on how to do any of this bullshit, that's where they'd be."

Eli set his fork on the edge of his plate. "What I'm stuck on is, why would she want to bring Sterling back?" Sam glanced at him in surprise, and he shrugged. "No offense. Your grandfather just doesn't seem like a very pleasant person."

"She wants exactly what Julius Sterling wanted: to live forever," Ulysses said. He sat back on his side of the booth, like a puppet with cut strings. "But spirits can't do magic. If she tried to do it alone, she'd leave her body and get stuck. Ergo, you need help."

Laz nodded slowly. "There are probably very few people who can do the spell. Babushka could—"

"But like hell is she helping," Ulysses put in. "And I could."

"Same problem," Laz said. "Maybe Sterling is a good bet, because she could turn around and do it for him afterward."

"A quid pro quo sort of thing." Eli took a bite of his toast. "Seems risky unless both parties really trust each other."

Sam turned that over in his mind for a moment. "Julius Sterling doesn't strike me as the trustworthy sort."

Ulysses glanced sidelong at him and nodded. "Stricker is no better."

"Canny, though. She probably has a plan."

They sat in silence for a long moment. Sam found himself staring at the tabletop, the little scratches and marks that had become part of the surface of the Formica.

Laz said, out of nowhere, "There's a full moon on the eighth."

It was hard not to shiver at the reminder of Laz's visions. And Peregrine's birthday was sometime in July, wasn't it? Sam took a deep breath. "I hate the waiting," he said suddenly. "Knowing something is going to happen . . ." He shook his head.

"Vietnam was like that, sometimes," Laz said. He was carefully cutting up his omelet into small pieces with his fork, not looking at anyone. "When I was flying the evac chopper, before they sent me to Thailand. Didn't ever know when I'd be called out."

That was practically the most Laz had said about the war in the ten months since he'd been home. Ulysses was staring at him. Eli sipped his coffee.

"What did you do to pass the time?" Sam heard himself ask.

"I learned the language. Developed a taste for the coffee. Worked on engines. Drank heavily. Slept around. You know." He lifted his eyes and grinned at Sam. "That kind of thing."

Sam nodded slowly. "Distractions."

"Exactly."

They stared at each other. "What are you doing for the Fourth?"

Laz licked his lower lip. "Getting very drunk, hopefully in a basement somewhere." Eli cleared his throat, and there was a moment of eye contact between them. Laz added, as though as an afterthought, "Eli wants to take me camping up north for the weekend."

Ulysses nodded jerkily. "Sounds like fun."

Chapter 23

S AM STOOD IN THE shower after his run the next morning for a long time, thinking about nothing in particular. The hot water beat a staccato rhythm against his back, steam curling around his body. He traced the lines of grout between the turquoise tiles and watched the last of the soap suds disappear down the drain. He thought about an amusing story Vikram had told during their run, something about a student he was doing an independent study with—the kid had been looking for a pipette, and—

It was gone. His mind was distressingly empty.

He turned off the water and opened the shower curtain.

Ulysses was standing in front of the sink screwing a new blade into his razor. He was wearing a pair of jeans and nothing else. Sam let his gaze travel from Ulysses's hands to the muscles of his arms and shoulders, lingering on the back of his neck, then his hair, which needed a trim.

"I didn't realize you were awake," Sam said finally, reaching for his towel.

Ulysses glanced at him in the little bit of mirror he'd wiped clear, a wry expression on his face. "I decided to shave before we went over there. After all, it's—" He hesitated. "It's Howard." When Sam didn't respond, Ulysses turned all the way to look at him. He was wearing a necklace Sam hadn't seen before, some sort of silver charm that brushed the top of his sternum. "We don't have to go today if you'd rather not."

"We should. It'll be easier to get his attention at home. It's just—" Sam broke off as he dried his hair, and then forced himself to say, "I had strange dreams last night."

"Nightmares?" Ulysses's voice was casual, but there was an undercurrent of concern that Sam found suddenly constricting.

"I dreamed I was driving across Lake Superior in Howard's car." He wrapped the towel around his waist and stepped out of the bathtub.

"A memory?" Ulysses turned back to the mirror, wiping more condensation away with his hand.

"I guess. I know I made that drive, it's just not . . ." Sam shrugged helplessly. "In the dream, Howard wasn't there. I was driving his car." He looked to his right, remembering. "Dionysus was in the passenger seat."

Ulysses opened the medicine cabinet and took out the shaving mug with the soap in it. "You were pretty out of it when Howard drove you to Madeline Island, right?"

Sam nodded.

"Is it possible that your body remembers somehow, and this is how it interprets that?" Ulysses fished the shaving brush out of the sink and started whisking the soap.

Sam watched him idly, leaning against the wall. "There's a lot missing from that night." He remembered how blue the ice was, spreading out around the car in all directions. It wasn't that far a drive, three or four miles at most from Howard's cabin to the graveyard on Madeline Island—he should have been able to see the island on the horizon. But in the dream, there was nothing but the strange twilight sky they were driving toward, and the ice. "It was . . ."

Ulysses suggested, "Unsettling?" into the silence.

"I was unsettled by it." Sam adjusted the chain on the nazar, which had gotten twisted while he was showering. It was the same temperature as his body, no warmer. "It was just a dream."

He felt steadier when he was dressed and leaning against the sink in the kitchen with a lukewarm cup of coffee in his hand. Ulysses joined him a few moments later, now in a black Stumbling Blindly T-shirt, smelling of clean water and soap and aftershave. He eyed Sam, but didn't say anything except, "Ready to go?"

Sitting pillion on the Triumph, Sam remembered the first time they'd come out to the family home this way. He'd had been new at riding on the motorcycle, feeling a combination of frightened and thrilled to be going so fast, plus the rush of being able to cling to Ulysses's hard body in public. It had been a good distraction from his troubles. It still was; his troubles were just harder to be distracted from.

They turned down Sherman Avenue and raced past all the fancy old houses and then Tenney Park, eventually taking a left into Maple Bluff. He wondered if Ulysses could feel Sam's rib cage expanding against his back, or tell that he was taking deep breaths to steady himself.

Maple Bluff. It was an upper class neighborhood full of wide green lawns, big ivy-covered houses, and people who were set to disapprove of one. Sam had grown up under a geas, but also under an almost equally strict commandment not to embarrass the family. Whatever that meant. Sam had always worked hard and kept to himself; probably he'd embarrassed the family anyway. It had been almost two years since he'd come to dinner in Maple Bluff, longer since he'd been to any of the little cocktail parties the neighbors were wont to throw, which one had to attend to hear one's sins picked apart.

Sam thought about Oscar Wilde's line, "The only thing worse than being talked about is not being talked about," and sighed. His life had changed so dramatically in the past two years. There was something distressing about the idea that perhaps his father had told no one. Not that he'd ever been the bragged-about child anyway, but he couldn't picture Howard lighting the cigarette of the head of the women's auxiliary down at the country club and saying, "Oh, Samuel? He's in rare and magical books. Married a magician. A professor, actually. Done rather well for himself, I suppose. Yes, we're all very proud of him."

Ulysses glanced over his shoulder and said, "Hey," in a low voice that reverberated through Sam.

"Sorry." Sam loosened his grip on Ulysses's waist, then realized what he meant. "Was I thinking too hard?"

"I can tell you're arguing with Howard in your head." Ulysses slowed as they turned a corner. "If you want to get drunk, or go for a hike, that's your choice. But we need to get through this interview first."

Without screaming, Sam surmised. "Sure." Ulysses brought the motorcycle to a gentle halt at the end of the Sterlings' driveway. Sam sat still and listened as the echoes died away. The Triumph wasn't a loud bike, as these things went, but there was still something pleasant about disturbing the neighborhood with it. It was barely eight thirty in the morning. Everyone was still eating breakfast, sleepy children under the aegis of stony-faced housekeepers, grim mothers in pearls missing the days when Mamie Eisenhower was in style, fathers ready to escape to the office.

Ulysses pulled off his helmet. He still looked tired, but the intensity was back in his eyes. "Come on," he told Sam, taking his hand. "This will be easy."

"Will it?"

"No." Ulysses gave him a wry little half smile. "But we can pretend."

Howard's house had been designed by a student of Frank Lloyd Wright. A long time ago, Sam had liked it—all those glowing windows when he came home nights, the long graceful lines, the way it mushroomed out of the landscape and hunched over the bluff, looking down at the lake. Now he wasn't sure. It was still a beautiful place, objectively speaking. But he was old enough that he knew the glowing windows weren't the same as actually being welcomed.

Sam rang the bell because he didn't live there anymore, and they stood on the low stoop for what felt like an eternity, waiting for some sign of movement within. Sam caught a sidelong glance from Ulysses. A car drove by, tires crunching on the street. Sam reached out and took Ulysses's hand.

It wasn't the housekeeper who opened the door, in the end. It was Howard himself, wearing a charcoal suit, as if he'd been preparing to walk out to his car. He stared at Sam for a long moment. Sam stared back.

This was, possibly, the first time he had been to the house since the night Howard had stabbed him. Sam still didn't exactly know what had happened, if it had been fate or some misguided plan of Howard's. He hadn't been able to look at the man since without recalling the mix of apology and awe on his face that night. In his nightmares, he remembered the moment of the knife reaching its apogee.

This morning, Howard just looked weary, a little gray around the edges. Sam didn't know why and didn't especially care, but he did feel—something. Sympathy, maybe. It must have been odd for Howard as well, even if Sam was the least favored of his children.

Well.

Sam offered him a weak smile. "Morning." He didn't let go of Ulysses's hand. He wasn't sure if he was holding Ulysses up or vice versa, but it seemed best not to risk it.

"Come in," Howard said at last, and led them through to the dining room, where Francie was eating toast points.

She looked better than the last time he'd seen her. It had been almost two years, he reminded himself. The gray cast was gone from her face, and instead of a quilted robe, she was wearing a rather pretty long-sleeved blue dress, cinched at the waist, with a matching handbag sitting on the table next to her plate.

He and Ulysses sat down across from Howard and Francie. There was a silver coffee pot in the middle of the table, gleaming in the cold light, surrounded by all its accoutrements. After an excruciating moment during which no one moved, Howard seized two glasses at random from the sideboard; Sam poured coffee for himself and Ulysses into one rocks glass and one brandy snifter. Francie didn't sneer, but she didn't look at them, either.

Sam exhaled. Where to start, that was the question. For whether 'twas nobler in the mind—

No.

He realized he was waiting for Ulysses to break the silence, to rescue him and Howard so they didn't have to—whatever it was they'd been avoiding. But Ulysses was stirring sugar and cream into his coffee, and anyway maybe it was time for Sam to face this.

"The night Julius died," he began. Across from him, Howard was also busy adding a sugar cube to his coffee, his face betraying nothing. There was a newspaper folded on the table in front of Francie, and she was studying the article revealed with a certain ferocity. The headline, upside down, trumpeted a Russian satellite launch. "What happened?" Sam asked simply.

"I was called down to the lab by Dr. Barth, because Julius had suffered a heart attack and collapsed," Howard said promptly. "He was dead when I arrived."

The answer felt rehearsed. It probably had been; presumably Howard had needed something to tell the police, perhaps the medical examiner or even a grand jury. "Was there much investigation?"

"It was so long ago." Howard set his spoon on the saucer. "I believe there were some questions asked, but not many. The assumption was that he'd been at the lab alone most of the evening and died of a heart attack, and there was no evidence to suggest otherwise."

"And you didn't have any reason to dissuade them."

Sam counted the individual beats of his heart as Howard eyed him. "What good would that have done?"

Sam decided not to press the point. "And after?"

The silence was cold, but when Howard spoke, his voice was mild. "You remember the funeral, don't you? You were old enough."

"I . . . a bit." He remembered his older brother Max tying a tie around his own neck, then slipping it off and putting it on Sam. He remembered the choir singing a kyrie, the light streaming through the huge windows behind the altar of the Unitarian meeting house. It had been July, and too warm, sweat prickling on his neck beneath the collar of his shirt. He remembered the cemetery. "And after the burial, Barth helped you dismantle the lab?"

"Of course he didn't," Francie said, startling him. "Dr. Barth hated Julius by then. He would have broken up everything and sold it for scrap to the highest bidder. *I* helped get rid of all that."

Sam felt Ulysses's attention shift, sharpen. He looked at Francie, too. It was impossible to see her for the first time again, to divorce twenty-two years of mutual distaste from the human being sitting in front of him. But he could see the sharp glitter in her eyes. He'd known she was shrewd, but this was something else. He didn't know what to say to this person.

"Do you know why they had a falling out?" Sam asked her. "Was it—no, don't tell me. Julius slept with Barth's wife, didn't he? And that's where Barth's daughter came from?"

For possibly the only time in their acquaintance, Francie gave him an approbatory nod. "Well done."

He felt anger and satisfaction in equal measure. "That's awful."

"Your grandfather could barely acknowledge that other people were real." Francie turned the toast point she'd been holding, finally set it back on the plate. She didn't look at Sam. "Apart from your grandmother, perhaps."

Ulysses, unperturbed by this deluge of family history, pressed ahead. "What did you find when you cleared out the lab?"

Howard glanced sidelong at her, but Francie looked unconcerned at the scrutiny. "All the records of his sordid experiments. Everything that went to the Historical Society. His books." She picked up a toast point, her other hand demurely in her lap. "Disgusting things you could not believe."

"I probably *would* believe them," Ulysses muttered. Louder, he said, "And you destroyed nearly everything."

"Everything we could." Howard's deep voice had a certain final quality when he rumbled, "We did what we had to."

"You just said there was no real investigation." Sam swirled the coffee in his glass. "What does that mean, you had to?"

Howard shook his head. "I had to protect the family."

They stared at each other. Sam wasn't sure how to understand that, for a moment. He was part of the family, but Howard didn't mean—that is, this wasn't—

Ulysses pressed his knee against Sam's under the table. Sam glanced at him and then away, forcing himself to take a sip of his coffee. He said, "Among the possessions, did you find a wooden box?"

"There were a lot of boxes. You'll have to be more specific." Howard folded his hands in front of him on the table, like he was being deposed.

Sam's coffee had an off, slightly burned flavor. "We found a box." He set the cup down.

"Did you."

"Wooden, covered with inlay flowers. In the library." Speaking of it aloud felt like a transgression. "We have reason to believe it was associated with Julius."

Howard took a sip from his own cup and set it neatly back on the saucer in front of him. "What makes you say that?"

Ulysses said, "Because I saw it on a table in Gooseberry House in 1954." His voice was soft, but firm.

"And the library told me about it. Or at least, I thought it was the library." Howard was silent, and abruptly—finally—Sam ran out of patience. "If you won't talk, we'll go." He pushed back his chair. Beside him, Ulysses was also getting to his feet, watching Sam cautiously like he was about to explode.

"Wait." Howard rubbed his forehead. "Sit. All right. I suppose you have a right to know. We found that box in your grandfather's lab. It's a reliquary of some sort."

"A reliquary," Sam said flatly. "What's the relic?"

To his shock, it was Francie who broke the subsequent silence. "In the early modern period, there was a hypothesis among some magicians and alchemists that the soul could be housed in a reliquary for at least some years after death."

Howard said, "We believed that the soul would be impossible to destroy, but potentially disastrous if it were to be released. Ekaterina Lenkov indicated that somehow, Julius's powers were still attached to his soul, and indicated that she would do what she could. I understood that it had been taken care of, and it was better if I remained unaware of the details."

Sam must have moved his hand, because his coffee was suddenly spreading across the table cloth. He watched the puddle, mind spinning. "What does it mean if Julius's soul is still there?"

Ulysses made a skeptical noise. "Plenty of these have been found, but none have ever been proven to contain anyone's soul."

Francie cocked her head to one side. "Then maybe you've got nothing to worry about."

From the apartment, Ulysses walked Sam all the way to Memorial. Sam was upset, his face drawn, and he said little; Ulysses would have suggested he call in except that he'd probably find being at the library soothing.

"What does it mean," Sam asked finally, "if Julie Stricker has Julius's soul?"

"We don't know—"

"Of course we do. That's how they found it." Sam's voice was practically sepulchral. "They have the body, and they used that to call the soul. The principle of similar things wanting to be together. I *just* read about it in your textbook."

"The principle of collocation?" Ulysses saw Sam's shoulders tense further as he opened his mouth to particularize the concept, and decided to skip it. "All right. Assuming Stricker has the soul, she still needs a lot of power to bring Julius back. There are various ways to get this, including blood sacrifice. She's asked if I would be willing to provide my power, presumably to this end, so she's unlikely to go to the trouble of kidnapping someone unrelated to all this until I tell her yes or no."

Sam nodded. They crossed Lake Street and started down the last stretch of State Street toward Library Mall. It wasn't until they'd turned the last corner to approach the front of Memorial that Sam finally spoke. "What are you going to tell her?"

"I don't know yet."

They were practically in front of the doors to the library now. Sam bit his lip and looked at the sky, the fountain, the grass at their feet. "I'm worried this wouldn't be a benign procedure for you. Actually, I'm worried she'd kill you, whether or not that was part of the deal."

"I know." Ulysses reached out and tilted his head up until they could look at each other. "She can try." He smiled. It was a bluff, and Sam probably knew it, but he smiled back anyway.

Ulysses stopped on the way back up State Street at the Coffee Co-op for a paper cup of coffee, which he regretted somewhat when he emerged. The sun was getting higher and hotter as he walked toward the Square. He'd left his jacket back at the apartment, but even in just a T-shirt with his jeans, it was going to be too warm soon.

There was another anti-war protest at the Capitol, just breaking up as he approached. The signs were brightly colored and varied—STOP THE WAR, FREE THE HARRISBURG 7, NIXON spelled with a swastika instead of an O, JAIL TO THE CHIEF. Ulysses stood for a moment, watching the protesters disperse. Somewhere, a woman with a guitar was plucking out a plaintive version of "Blowing in the Wind." Then he spotted Eli coming back up State Street, past the sketchy bookstore and record shop and head shop. He was wearing a short-sleeve button-down and a bow tie, no jacket. He walked with his hands in his pants pockets and his gaze fixed on something up above the street, so intent that he nearly walked into Ulysses.

"Whoa there," Ulysses said, grabbing the back of Eli's shirt before he could topple off the curb into traffic. "What's so interesting?"

Eli glanced at Ulysses, lingering just long enough he saw himself recognized. "Look there!"

Ulysses turned to see a startlingly large bird swoop down. For a moment, it sat there on the lawn of the capitol, looking around. Then it took off again, a hapless chipmunk or something in its claws. "What on earth?" Ulysses muttered.

"It's a red-tailed hawk."

Ulysses shook his head. "I've never seen anything like that before."

"There's been a significant drop in the populations of raptors in the US. There's compelling evidence it's related to the use of insecticides like DDT. I don't know if you read the book *Silent Spring*?" Eli paused, looking at him. "What?"

Ulysses shook his head. "I must have missed it. Sorry."

"It's rather convincing." Eli looked both ways before stepping off the curb, and for some reason Ulysses followed him.

"Were you walking Laz to the gallery?"

Eli shook his head. "Or, well, not exactly. I've been thinking of moving my practice and opening a clinic, so I was looking at a space farther down State."

"How was it?"

Eli pulled open the door to his office building and motioned Ulysses through in front of him. "It wasn't the best place I've seen, and it needed more than a little work. Still, the price wasn't terrible." He sighed, pushing the button on the elevator. "Laz gets very impassioned about all the repairs and starts drawing up lists of materials and tradespeople and making schedules . . ."

"A bit too quick to jump?"

"In a manner of speaking. He'd get started tomorrow if I said the word. But I'd just as soon not rush into anything." They stood in silence for a long moment in front of the elevator. It was from the era when everyday objects were still permitted to be beautiful, and its doors had graceful art deco ginkgo leaves done in different colors of metal.

When the doors slid open, Ulysses followed Eli in and leaned against the railing that ran around the interior. He could see both himself and Eli reflected in the plainer inside, hazy in the old, tarnished metal. "When you say a clinic . . ."

"Magicians are a community with particular medical needs that few people are studying in depth." Eli raised a hand as though to indicate Ulysses, then seemed to change his mind. "Most of my patients these days are bloodline magic users. I thought I could find a few other doctors who might be interested in helping that population."

Ulysses thought about it. Opened his mouth, shut it again, thinking about Laz and the state of the research. "Huh." He sipped his forgotten coffee. "You saw my grandmother last fall, didn't you?"

Eli gave him a level look. "I did."

The doors of the elevator slid open and Eli stepped out. Ulysses followed, a step behind as they walked along a quiet linoleum-floored hallway, past a gray desk in a gray-carpeted waiting room. Eli nodded distractedly to the receptionist. His office was at the end of the hall, a small but cozy space. Ulysses lingered in the doorway for a moment, then committed to stepping inside when Eli had to retrieve his white coat from behind the door.

"Don't take this the wrong way," Eli said, shrugging into the coat. "It's not that I don't enjoy seeing you. But was there something you wanted?"

Ulysses started to demur, saw the skeptical expression on Eli's face, and laughed. "All right, Doc. You know about ethics, right?"

Eli opened his mouth. Closed it again. Finally said, "I know a bit," in a guarded tone. "Why?"

Ulysses took a sip of his coffee. "The way I was brought up," he said, "it was with the knowledge that I was someone who had to look out for others. Laz and Celeste, obviously, but also other people in the community. I had better control over magic, or"—he had to force out the next phrase—"a larger innate pool of magic to draw on, and that meant that I needed to help."

"From each according to his abilities," Eli said, waving a hand.

Ulysses nodded. He fell silent for a moment, focusing on cracking the knuckles of his free hand. "You met Julie Stricker the other day. She's been sniffing around, threatening Sam. I'm sure she's the one who put Babushka in the hospital, and . . . let's say I have very good reason to believe she's dangerous and might hurt a number of people to get what she's after. So at first I thought, what if I just capitulate? Give her what she's asking for? But I don't trust her to keep her word and leave everyone else alone."

"And if she brought Sterling back, as you intimated . . ." Eli said, and then shook his head.

"Exactly."

There was a long silence, and Eli said, "So what was your question?"

"I was thinking . . . I mean, I can't just . . ." Ulysses's throat felt dry.

Eli gave him a long look. "Have you heard of the doctrine of double effect?"

"Vaguely."

"Ah, well." Eli rubbed his hands together. "A woman wrote a paper about it a few years ago. Foot was her name, I believe. Essentially she said that sometimes you do something good but it has an unwanted side effect. Her example was a trolley that will hit five people tied to the track, but you can throw a switch and hit one person instead. Many people would agree that's morally permissible, and even that not doing that would be bad. If you're there and able to throw the switch, you're morally responsible for doing it in some way."

Ulysses nodded. "Ask not what your community can do for you . . ."

"I suppose so." Eli stuck his hands into the pockets of his coat. He looked more remote and professional with it on, as though he'd just donned a suit of armor. "But you are still killing one person, in that scenario. And I don't need to remind you what that can do to a person."

He waited a moment, and then to make sure Ulysses had understood, "That is, the consequences of giving her the power may be worse than the consequences of withholding it, but—"

"Yeah." Ulysses thought about Julie Stricker again, a sinking sensation settling in his chest. "Thanks." He turned away, opening the door to leave.

"Ulysses?" When he looked back, Eli said, carefully, "It's pull the lever, not throw yourself in front of the trolley to save everyone."

Ulysses exhaled. "It's a thought experiment, Doc," he said, and let the door swing shut behind him.

Chapter 24

THE PROBLEM WAS, ULYSSES didn't know what to do with any of that. Or perhaps he did, and that was as big a problem. He paced around the apartment and did laundry. He met Sam at the library after work and took him out for dinner, smiling distractedly through the conversation. He bought groceries and went to the gym. The rest of June passed in a blur.

He was quiet at the Fourth of July party, up on the roof with Vikram and Sita and Ellen and Harry and a handful of the building's other residents. Sam eventually caught him staring out at the dark lake, Monona's municipal fireworks in the distance.

"Are you all right?" he asked for the tenth time, leaning into Ulysses's shoulder.

"Just thinking." He smiled wanly at Sam, then turned back to the lake. "The fireworks are nice."

Sam nodded. "Too bad Laz couldn't come."

"I think he knows what he's missing." Ulysses sipped the wine he'd poured into a coffee cup. It was something

Harry had brought—a light, sweet wine that tasted of honeysuckle. "Sam, after all this is over . . . if I die—"

"Don't."

"—Laz will keep an eye on you. Protect you, I mean. You can—" He kept his gaze on the distant fireworks, his hands on the railing that ran around the edge of the roof. It was hard to think about that future. Would Sam find someone else? It was hard to imagine him staying single for the next fifty or sixty years. Ulysses didn't like to think of him lonely; he just also didn't like— His throat went tight, and he sipped the wine again to try and combat it.

After a moment, Sam rested a hand on Ulysses's back, between his shoulder blades. Ulysses could feel the heat of the hand bleeding through the thin cotton of his T-shirt. Sam leaned closer and murmured, "I'm not going to let you die."

"Mmm." Down on the lake, a large flower burst open, blue and shimmering. "I don't know if you get a choice."

AT WORK ON TUESDAY, closed in his office, Sam closed his eyes and leaned back in his chair, thinking about the mental radio he had so painstakingly constructed a few weeks before. There was magic there, he could feel it. And although Ulysses had a plan and swore it was going to work, Sam thought they could both use some extra power, just in case.

There was something appropriate about trying this on a day like any other, when the sun was bright and the sky was clear. Outside, tired students wandered along the mall, squinting at the glare. A man with a guitar was busking on the steps of the church not quite opposite the library. Inside, Sam let himself sink down. He could visualize the radio easily now, the knobs that were waiting for him. He reached out.

The dial wouldn't turn. Sam pushed harder, but it was pointing at WULY and it wasn't going to move.

Anticlimactic.

He opened his eyes and stared at the paper-strewn surface of his desk. There was some set of conditions he wasn't meeting. That was the sense he was left with; not that it was impossible, not that the WDIO station shouldn't exist, but just—not now.

When he got home, Ulysses was lying on the chaise in his office listening to *Giant Steps*. He'd spent the day reading, if the books that had accumulated in stacks on the carpet within an arm's reach of him were any indication. Sam thought he recognized a few of the titles from back in the Dionysus days. Others were new: *Keine Hora: Counterspells and Remedies* and *The Great Knot of the World* had library bindings. *A Pocket Full of Tunes: Music and Spellcraft Examined* looked new.

Sam left him to it and went to figure out something for dinner.

After a while, the album changed to one Sam couldn't identify, but which sounded like Django Reinhart. Two or three tracks later, the stereo went off and Ulysses stepped into the kitchen. The lentil stew was bubbling away on the stove, and Sam was cleaning up.

"Any thoughts you care to share with the class?" Sam asked him.

"We should get a dishwasher." Sam raised an eyebrow, and Ulysses added, "Improvisation exists within a framework."

"It's called a key. You listen to more music than anyone I know. I'm surprised you're just realizing that." Sam turned off the faucet, set down the bowl in the dish drainer, and turned around. Ulysses was leaning against the kitchen doorjamb, arms crossed in a way that showed off his biceps. Sam licked his lower lip.

Ulysses snorted. "I suppose I was hoping there was some other, different definition of improvisation that I hadn't considered."

"Did something happen?"

Ulysses opened the refrigerator, took out a beer, then sighed and put it back. "I went to see Babushka. She didn't have any advice, just said I improvise well and she is not worried."

Sam nodded slowly. "She means she trusts your instincts."

"She shouldn't!" Ulysses flushed and looked away when Sam smiled at him.

"She's taking you seriously." Sam picked up the wooden spoon and gave the lentils a stir so they wouldn't stick and burn. It seemed like they needed more water.

When he turned back, Ulysses was still standing by the fridge, looking mildly gutted. "She doesn't know that I only made it through those other things by sheer luck."

"I don't believe that either, but . . ." Sam shrugged. "Any reason to think your luck has run out now?"

Ulysses didn't answer.

On Wednesday afternoon, Sam came out of the library as usual and found Ulysses sitting on one of the lower steps, waiting for him. He was wearing the old Bookends T-shirt that he for some reason regarded as one of his more formal ones.

It was heartening to see him out and about. He had barely, as far as Sam was aware, left the Baskerville for the past two weeks, except to run errands and take long, meandering walks. But now he looked . . . better would be overstating the case, but he looked all right. Except something about him reminded Sam of December 1969. Sam had been resigned to his impending death at the hands of Dionysus, trying to make the best of it. Ulysses had been frantic to find a solution. Neither of them had said it yet, but Sam had figured that if what they had wasn't love, it was close enough that he wanted to spend the time he had left enjoying it, rather than haring off after answers that were only going to evaporate into more questions when pressed. Insofar as he'd been aware of anything at the time, he'd known this approach drove Ulysses a little bit nuts. He'd felt Sam was capitulating, instead of being practical.

Sam understood now. Seeing Ulysses fold miserably in on himself was alarming, and watching him cycle through a hundred dangerous plans was equally difficult.

He raised a hand in greeting when he saw Sam coming. His face wasn't sad, but it wasn't anything else, either, except possibly tired. Resigned.

"Ah," Sam found himself saying. "That kind of day."

Ulysses did smile at that. "I *am* happy to see you. It's been a long day."

"Were you at the gym?" Sam watched Ulysses nod. For a very brief moment he looked almost heartbroken, and then a mask of relaxed coolness settled over his features. "Want to grab an early dinner somewhere?"

"Actually, I cooked."

Sam blinked. "You cooked?"

"I made borscht."

He opened his mouth and shut it again. "Sounds great."

They started around the building, toward State Street. As they turned the corner, a voice called out to them: "Hey, Lenkov! Sterling!"

Sam's pulse kicked up before he even consciously recognized the voice. Beside him, Ulysses stiffened. They turned to see Julie Stricker, sitting on the top step of the church across the street, legs crossed at the knee.

"Today is the day. Have you given my proposal any thought?" Her voice was conversational: no underlying threat of violence, no commanding presence. Sam was surprised.

Ulysses was equally calm. "If you're as smart as you seem to think you are, you'll stop this now. There's still time to walk away."

The man with the guitar was watching them curiously, and Sam felt a wave of paranoia. Who was he, and why was he so interested?

Stricker smiled coldly at Ulysses. "Is that a no?"

"It's—" Ulysses hesitated, and Sam put a hand on his shoulder. Whether he meant it as encouragement or as one last 'you don't have to do this' even he didn't know. Ulysses drew in a breath. "It's not a no."

Did she look surprised? The expression passed too fast for Sam to decide. "Very well." She got to her feet. "You will be summoned tomorrow evening."

"When?" Sam demanded, taking a step toward her. "To where?" The guitarist was trying to scoot away from them along the step as unobtrusively as possible.

"All will become clear," Stricker said. A moment later, she was gone, without ever having turned and walked away. Sam blinked.

"I didn't know people could do that." He remembered Laz vanishing the coin through sleight of hand. It hadn't occurred to him to ask why no one vanished things by magic until now. He glanced over at Ulysses, who looked nonplussed, like he wasn't sure how she'd managed it either.

"She shouldn't be able to." Ulysses frowned. "I know she's deeply into some pretty esoteric stuff, but that's very. . . . It's flashy."

Sam thought about that. "Cheap tricks?" he suggested.

Ulysses threw back his head and laughed.

Thursday was quiet. Sam had wanted to stay home and help Ulysses prepare. But there wasn't anything in particular to be done—Ulysses knew what he was going to do when he was summoned. He had his sigils and spellcraft ready, his sacrifices picked out. So Sam went to the library and did a credible impression of someone who was having a normal day at the office: He went to meetings. He cataloged a few books. He talked to a couple of researchers who stopped by with questions. He showed Buttercup the stacks and discussed a few ideas for reorganizing them. He definitely did not sit in his office at lunchtime and contemplate calling Ulysses just to say hello.

He *missed* Ulysses.

Since Ekaterina's revelations about the history of Ulysses's power—*some* of Ulysses's power—and the connection between him and Sam and Julius Sterling, Ulysses had barely touched him. Of course he still hugged Sam and murmured the usual assurances, but something was different. Guilt had wedged itself between them.

At the end of the day, Sam walked home through the warm streets to a quiet apartment, his tie pulled loose, coat draped over one arm. On the fourth floor, even with the blinds closed, it was stifling. He pulled his tie all the way off, padding down the hall to the bedroom, where the door was shut. Something was whirring on the other side of it.

Sam hesitated a moment without quite knowing why, then quietly pushed the door open. Stepping into the bedroom was like falling suddenly into cold water; a window AC unit Sam hadn't known they owned was chugging away. Possibly they hadn't owned it before.

Ulysses was asleep on the bed in a white undershirt and his boxer shorts. On top of the covers, even, lying on one side, knees bent, very still. Sam watched him, feeling like he was on the verge of a revelation. It was right there, like a word on the tip of his tongue.

But nothing came, so he stripped off the rest of his suit, vest and shirt and trousers, hanging them carefully in the closet, and curled up behind Ulysses, chest not quite against his back. Sam didn't want to disturb him, but after a moment he settled one hand on Ulysses's hip and pressed his face into the back of Ulysses's neck, letting the short hairs there tickle his forehead.

For a while, Sam shut his eyes and let himself drift. He wasn't quite asleep, but he wasn't all the way awake, either. It was nice.

Eventually, Ulysses woke up. It wasn't a big change, just a momentary pause in his breathing, and then—"Sam? What time is it?" in a sandpapered voice.

"Five thirty," Sam said. "Give or take."

For a moment, it seemed as though Ulysses was going to pull away. Sam tightened his grip on Ulysses's hip and tugged gently, hoping his fingers could convey the things he wanted to say but couldn't find a way to: 'Please don't leave me. Please, just give me a few moments now.'

With a drowsy sigh, Ulysses shifted, closing the bare inch Sam had left between them until they were pressed together chest to back, thigh to thigh. "When do we have to leave for the party?"

"Six fifteen or so." Sam wrapped his hand around Ulysses's waist, splaying his fingers across Ulysses's stomach. "Are we still going to Ellen and Harry's party?"

Ulysses made a dismissive noise. "Might as well. I'd like you and Sita to talk to Peregrine. Nothing's going to happen until after moonrise."

Magic being stronger, somehow, under a full moon. Sam didn't really understand it; the moon was full all the time, because it was an orbiting chunk of rock rather than a picture that changed very slowly. But that seemed to be the rule, or at least the belief, among magicians. "Harry and Ellen will be happy about that." Sam was ambivalent. Going to the party felt slightly frivolous. However, contemplating skipping it—and the performance—felt like a betrayal. Not that the reading really needed a stage manager. He'd already left the props there, ready to go. "Where did the air conditioner come from?"

"I made Laz drive me to Sears," Ulysses said. "What do you think?"

"It's nice." Actually, it was chilly, and Sam moved closer to Ulysses, not that there was far to go. Ulysses in turn made a pleased noise and rolled over, draping a leg over Sam's hips. "It's going to—" But Ulysses kissed him, and he lost track of where the complaint was going.

It was a strange feeling, to have all the edginess and tension of the last ten days coalesce into wanting, like a picture coming into focus. Sam hadn't expected it; it reminded him of the first time he'd really kissed Ulysses, in the smoking wreckage of a demon, the way the adrenaline, not yet faded, had transmuted into something entirely different.

Ulysses was muttering something about having almost forty-five minutes to kill, his words a delicious buzz against the hollow of Sam's jaw. Sam cupped his face and kissed him, a gentle hello that grew hotter, sharper, filthier, less controlled. Ulysses pressed him back into the bed and pinned his arms above his head one-handed, using the other to hike up Sam's undershirt. After a moment, Sam got the idea and relaxed, tucking his hands behind his head to prevent the temptation to move. Ulysses bent so he could tongue one of Sam's nipples and make him squirm, then moved across to the other, and kissed the hollow between his collarbones, beneath his sternum, his stomach, the spot just below his navel.

Sam watched, fingers twitching, Ulysses's brown hair, wide shoulders, the way his muscles flexed as he leaned forward, running a palm over Sam's hardening cock, replacing the hand with his mouth. All of it seemed premeditated to catch at Sam, draw tight the strands of desire that wound through him, between them. For days, Sam had been asking himself if there was something he should have done differently, back at their first meeting, or if the bond had been a foregone conclusion. But he couldn't see a world where he had met Ulysses but not wanted him, where in seeking comfort he had somehow been able to do without Ulysses's hands on him, where that wasn't everything he'd wanted since practically the moment they'd crashed into each other.

He pushed himself up to his elbows, clumsily reaching out to draw Ulysses toward him, to touch him, to find something warm and true in this cool, strange room.

He wanted desperately to know what Ulysses was thinking as their mouths met again. Even if Sam opened the bond wide, that wouldn't really tell him. And it was the full moon again, and with Laz's prophecy hanging above them—

They were on top of a precipice, holding their breath. Sam pulled back, hands on the hem of Ulysses's undershirt. "I want you to fuck me," he said.

Ulysses's pupils were wide, his breath light and fast. "Yes," he murmured, and let Sam strip his shirt off. Ulysses had to shift backward to get his shorts off; Sam pulled his own shirt off impatiently, anxious to be touching Ulysses again, to bury his fears somewhere deep. And then Ulysses was back, kneeling between Sam's thighs, and they were falling or flying down the other side of the precipice, stripping off the last of their clothing. Sam felt just shy of frantic as he twisted to grab the lube out of a drawer, saw that Ulysses's hands were unsteady as he slicked himself, and folded that away inside himself somewhere.

Ulysses shouldered one of Sam's legs and leaned into him, moving slowly, holding himself back. Sam caught his breath, watching the afternoon light that snuck past the curtains play on his face, lingering on the little silver charm around his neck, his chest, the way his flat stomach tapered down to lean hips. Sam abruptly spun the knob on the bond—not all the way, but enough to feel what Ulysses was feeling, lust and excitement and love.

Sam was loved, and it was both the greatest thing and the most tragic, because someday one of them would be alone. Whether it was in another fifty years or tonight, nothing lasted forever.

Sam was aware Dionysus might have some opinions on that, but they, perforce, couldn't be his, so he pushed it all away. Instead, he pulled Ulysses closer, as close as he could make them, and bit his shoulder when he came.

Chapter 25

ULYSSES PUSHED SAM'S DAMP hair off his forehead as they lay together, let his fingers trail down the back of Sam's neck to cup his shoulder. The bond was still too open, but it was for once a quiet, steady presence. Sam lay with his head on Ulysses's shoulder, their legs tangled together, idly toying with the silver chain of Ulysses's necklace.

"What does it mean?" he asked after a while.

"Radio," Ulysses said.

Sam raised his head to frown at the charm. "Why radio?"

Shrugging was an effort. "Celeste didn't want it." They needed to get up and shower, throw in a load of laundry with the wreckage of the bed, and leave for the party. He didn't move. "Laz was the one who translated it; I'm unclear on how much Chinese he knows."

Sam made an amused noise. "It's funny how we're both just willing to accept that he must have picked up some."

Ulysses shrugged. "It's probably all classified, the way he talks."

"The way he avoids talking," Sam said, largely into Ulysses's neck. "I wonder if we'll ever find out what all he got up to over there."

"Mm. We probably don't want to know." Ulysses turned his head and smelled Sam's hair, fresh sweat and sunshine. He wanted to say a lot of things—apologies, mostly, for things he couldn't change. He wanted to tell Sam how much he needed him, how his only regret in the wake of Babushka's revelations was that something had been taken from Sam that wasn't anyone's to take. But there wasn't time. "Sam, it's getting late . . ."

"Yeah, yeah." Sam grumbled and sighed and pushed himself up. "I guess I did swear to Ellen that we'd be there unless we were actively being attacked by demons."

Ulysses followed Sam into the bathroom. "That sounds like Ellen. A blood oath, but with a little carve out."

Sam laughed, bent over the sink already. "She knows better than most people."

"Of course she does. She's always wrapped up in it somehow." Ulysses sighed. "I'm gonna miss them."

Sam gave him a long, level look, and then nodded. "We can visit," he said carefully. "It's California, not—I don't know, Timbuktu."

Ulysses rubbed his chin. "They have good universities in Timbuktu?"

They parked the bike and walked around Harry and Ellen's little yellow house into the backyard.

Ulysses had always privately classed Harry and Ellen as *Sam's* friends. Sam shared them, because that was what he did, but they were Sam's. If Sam went out of town, Ulysses wouldn't get a dinner invite; if Sam divorced him, he'd never see them again. But walking into the party, Harry spotted them and came over with a couple of beers, slinging a friendly arm around Ulysses's shoulders. "Good to see you, man."

"Good to see you," Ulysses said.

Sam, on Harry's other side, was saying, "What are you—"

Harry said, "Smile," and someone clicked the shutter on a camera before Ulysses or Sam had a chance to react.

"That's going to be a good one," Sam said dryly. He examined the beer he'd been given. "What's this? I thought you were buying classier beer these days."

Harry hit him in the shoulder. "Taste it, you dolt."

"Oh, is this—?"

Ulysses looked between them with an eyebrow raised, his hand hesitating on the cap of his beer bottle. It was, he noticed, a different brand than Sam's, but the label was scuffed and partially peeling. "What?"

"Harry's been learning to brew his own beer," Sam said, and took a swig. Ulysses watched the long line of his neck, the way his hair curled against the back of his neck. "It's not bad; what's in it?" Sam ran his tongue over his lower lip.

Ulysses remembered he was holding a bottle too and took a drink. "Honey?" he suggested.

Harry looked extremely pleased. "Yes! Honey. Also wheat berries, barley, and malt." He grinned at Ulysses. "What do you think?"

Ulysses tasted it again. It was slightly sweet, with more spices than he expected in beer and none of the bitterness of hops. "It's nice." He frowned at the bottle. "Unusual. Where did you get the recipe?"

"It's Sumerian." Harry turned and saw someone else coming in behind them. "Hey, I'll be right back."

When he was gone, Ulysses glanced at Sam. "Sumerian?"

"One of the ancient history guys found a beer recipe in a hymn or something. I believe there was a bet." He took another sip of the beer and nodded approvingly. "It's good."

"For a—how old is the recipe? Four thousand years?" Ulysses took another drink. Something was pinging in the back of his mind, but he couldn't pin it down. So instead, he asked, "When is the reading?"

Sam glanced at his watch, eyes going wide, and went to check on something.

Ulysses wound his way through the crowd until he found Ellen. She was standing with one foot on the back stoop, conferring with someone still inside the house. Her long hair was loose around her shoulders, and it gleamed in the sinking sun as she turned toward him. "Hello," she said, and hugged him.

Ulysses blinked. "Happy anniversary. And happy getting the hell out of Madison, finally."

"Thanks." She smiled, a little bittersweet. "Berkeley isn't going to be the same."

Ulysses nodded. "I'm sure if you look around you'll find some freaks who want to borrow your car for inexplicable, quasi-legal purposes."

"Yeah, but who will have so much panache?" She was holding a bottle of Harry's brew too, and held it up to clink with his.

"I hope you don't mind, I invited someone to join us."

Ellen raised an eyebrow. "Laz and Eli are already here. And Vikram is over—"

"No, someone else," Ulysses said. He tried to remember if she'd ever met Laz. Maybe Sam had introduced them. "A student who needed . . . I didn't think they should be alone."

Ellen's face flickered through a few emotions before settling on compassion. "Of course it's fine. I invited Sam's intern." She gestured over his shoulder and he turned and saw Buttercup, standing back approximately where Sam had once been attacked by demons, Galadriel laughing at her side.

"Oh," Ulysses said. "I'm on her committee."

"So I hear. I thought she might like to meet some of the other ancient history guys." Ellen looked at him critically. "You're not going to make a big deal about this, are you?"

"No, absolutely not." He shook his head for emphasis. "I was just remembering being dragged to a wedding when I was ten, and then fifteen years later one of the brides became my PhD advisor."

He sighed as Ellen giggled. "Academia is like that," she said when she'd recovered. Then someone from across the yard caught her attention. "I have to go help with this. Bring your friend by after the reading, though. I'd like to meet them."

She vanished, and Ulysses sat down on the stoop with his ancient beer and watched the partygoers come and go. They were a colorful bunch, Harry and Ellen's crowd. Mostly actors and their lovers, friends, and other companions. Many of them he'd met back at the cast party for *My Kingdom for a Horse*, an ambitiously Frankensteined Shakespearian history they'd been working on back when he and Sam had first met. At the time, Sam had introduced him as a friend from out of town. No one had questioned it, just as they didn't seem to notice or care that the friend was still hanging around. Ulysses wondered what Sam had told the acting company about their changing relationship, or if he'd mentioned it at all.

He wondered, suddenly, what Sam was going to do for a theater troupe with Harry and Ellen gone. Or what the apartment would look like if Sam didn't have anything to fill his leisure time. Maybe Ulysses could convince him to adopt a cat or something. Or he could get a Ph.D. That would keep him occupied for a while.

He spotted Vikram over by the beer table and waved, feeling vaguely surprised when the other professor made his way across the backyard and slapped his back in greeting.

"Having a good summer?" Vikram looked tan and cheerful, a bottle in one hand. "Haven't seen you around. How's your grandmother?"

"Much better, thank you." Ulysses glanced around. "Did Sita come?"

"She got called into the office earlier," Vikram said. "She's planning to come by when she's done. She didn't want to miss the performance."

Ulysses took a swallow of his beer. "I had someone I wanted to introduce her to. But they're not here yet either."

Time dragged on. Ulysses finished his beer and let Vikram grab him another. Peregrine didn't arrive, and continued not to arrive. Laz and Eli stopped to say hello, then wandered off again. It was a beautiful afternoon, hot and clear. Somewhere in the yard, someone lit up a joint, and the smoke wafted here and there. Peregrine wasn't coming.

That was the part of everything that Ulysses had been most concerned about. Peregrine hadn't reacted well to the idea that they might be something other than human. Probably Ulysses hadn't done a good job of broaching the subject. Likely there *wasn't* a great way to explain . . . but then again, Sam had apparently had a very straightforward discussion with Sita when he'd told her, and there had been no shouting or angry recriminations. But Sita was—well, she was a lot of things, but she was considered in how she used her anger. It was a knife. And if Peregrine was already more than half in the grips of the god they were becoming, like Sam had been, that close to his birthday, even with Ulysses to ground him . . .

Ulysses was still mulling things over when the show began.

It was technically a staged reading, with six ensemble members at music stands and the audience spread out on blankets and lawn chairs around them. But for all the minimalism, Ellen and Harry had done an excellent job. The cut-down version of *Hamlet* was extremely funny, the limited choreography they'd put together was well executed, and Sam accompanied Ophelia's song with a little tune of Ellen's composition played on the guitar, both clever and sweetly performed.

And then, after a final battle with water pistols, it was done. Ulysses found himself applauding hard, abruptly conscious of what they were losing.

Harry and Ellen pulled Sam up in front of everyone to take a bow with them, and then kept him there as the applause died in response to Harry's raised hand. An expectant silence settled over the group.

"Thank you all for coming," Harry began, and waited out another little round of applause. "This means a lot to us. This is our last show in Madison, because in two weeks we're leaving for California." A mix of whoops and boos. "I just wanted to thank everyone in the cast. Greg here has been in every show we've done since the very first, when we did *All's Well That Never Ends*. Sophia has been in everything except El's choral performance of *The Tempest* last winter. I wasn't even in *The Tempest*, so that's pretty good. And then I have to mention Sam."

Sam, realizing suddenly that something was up, had started trying to slink away. Ellen grabbed his arm and arrested his progress.

"We met Sam two years and one month ago. He came to our wedding after knowing us for thirty days, and then he agreed to stage manage every show from *My Kingdom* onward." Ellen added something Ulysses didn't catch and Harry nodded. "And he co-directed *The Tempest*. He has designed special effects, hung lights, helped arrange music, played guitar. At this point, I don't think there's anything he can't do." Everyone applauded for Sam, who smiled bashfully. "Sam," Harry continued, "got married almost a year ago, and—" Ulysses saw Sam mouthing the words 'it was the end of September!' and Harry laughed. "No, shut up, ten months is almost a year. At any rate, he didn't have a party, so I didn't get to make any kind of embarrassing speech, or tell him how much his presence has meant to both Ellen and me. And unfortunately, moments where I get to recognize him publicly are pretty thin on the ground. So . . ." Harry looked out over the audience and pointed abruptly at Ulysses. "Get up here."

Ulysses made eye contact with Sam and, when no escape route magically appeared, forced himself to cross the distance between them. Sam, as a rule, was uncomfortable with being the center of attention like this. Apparently, there had been a lot of fuss when he was a child about bringing shame on the family name, or who really knew what, but Sam had learned real damn quick that staying out of the spotlight was generally safest. But now he just shrugged, a rueful smile tugging at his lips. Ulysses was aware he looked more than a little disreputable, with the deep purple rings under his eyes and a few days of scruff. He was acutely conscious of the purpling bite mark on his trapezius, hopefully hidden by the collar of his T-shirt. But when he had picked his way through thirty-odd hippies and yippies, Sam grabbed his hand and tugged him closer, until Ulysses was pressed up against Sam's side.

Harry looked at them both, then at Ellen, who said under her breath, "Keep it together." He wondered who she was speaking to.

Ulysses looked out at the audience. From this angle, the world was different. It always was, up on stage. He spotted Laz at the back of the crowd, arms crossed in front of his chest, head inclined to hear whatever Eli was saying. Vikram was with them, grinning. Nearby, Buttercup and Galadriel were sitting on a blanket. The audience was looking at the two of them, and Sam was looking down at Ulysses a little intensely.

"Doing okay?" he asked in a low voice. He touched Sam's hand where it curled around his waist, letting their rings clink together.

Sam nodded wordlessly.

"I was going to roast you guys, but I can't," Harry said finally. "Ellen and I are just so happy that Sam found someone worthy of him." He raised his beer. "A toast!"

Everyone cheered and raised their drinks. Under the noise, Sam leaned closer and murmured, "Rule three."

Ulysses dredged his memory. "Rituals carry meaning for participants as well as onlookers?" he managed, and then kissed Sam. Just a little thing, a brush of their lips, enough to make Sam lean closer into him, and then—

Reality lurched and shivered, like gelatin. The magical seabed rang like a bell.

Ulysses felt it, deep in the pit of his stomach and the marrow of his bones, which meant it was much stronger than it had been before. Sam staggered against him and almost fell, and Ulysses scrabbled for purchase on Sam's coat. When he opened his eyes, the audience was in disarray. Many people had fallen, clutching their heads or stomachs. Galadriel was vomiting next to the fence. Even the non-magical looked shaken. How the fuck had Stricker managed it? They'd probably heard that in Milwaukee.

Sam lifted his head from Ulysses's shoulder. "What the hell was *that?*"

"The summons." Ulysses waited until Sam was standing on his own again to release him. "We better go."

To his surprise, when he turned away, it was to see Ellen staring at them, face deadly serious. "It's time?"

Sam said, "Yes."

She nodded curtly. "I'll get my sword."

Chapter 26

ULYSSES HADN'T EXPECTED ANY of the other partygoers to come along, but they did. It was bewildering. There wasn't even any real discussion. In pairs or small groups, they made their way to their cars, then followed his bike in a long procession.

He felt how he imagined Howard must have felt that strange day driving across the ice to Madeline Island as the sun faded, all the maenads somewhere behind. Something was happening that he was fated to have a part in, and there wasn't anything he could do now to turn it aside or get out of its way. He was going to have to go through and hope everything worked out.

They turned into the parking lot of the church next to the sanitarium and stopped there. Nothing had changed since his last visit. The older, smaller church sat behind it, its stolid bricks sleeping until doomsday, and then the little cemetery on the hill. The mossy, faded headstones seemed to huddle together in the twilight. The cleared space was ringed with trees that got closer and closer together, eventually blending into the same woods Ulysses had once been dragged through on the way to a half-toppled pig shed.

Sam slid off the bike a moment before Ulysses did and waited alongside it while Ulysses pulled off his helmet. "What are you humming?" Sam asked after a moment. Ulysses didn't know how he could hear it, what with the screech of Harry's Datsun's brakes as he pulled into the parking lot behind the church, the slam of a car door somewhere, a bark of dark laughter—that was Laz, he was sure of it.

"I have no idea," he said, when his brain refused to circle back to whatever tune had been lodged there. "Was it Ophelia's song?"

Sam's eyes widened in recognition. He opened his mouth like he wanted to complain about it—a last minute addition, guitar half a step flat, singer didn't like the tempo, some behind-the-scenes story—but he stopped. Instead, he said, "There's a lot of people here."

Ulysses took a deep breath. "Ellen is a good bet to get them out of here when the shit hits the fan. She'll keep them in line." He set the kickstand, but found himself unwilling to swing his leg over the bike and stand up. Instead, he looked at Sam. All the things he'd wanted to say earlier were still swimming in his chest, but—he couldn't, or it wasn't the right time, or. So instead, he tipped his head and said, "Sterling-Lenkov, huh."

Sam's gaze, which had wandered, jerked back to him. "I didn't mean—"

"No." Ulysses tried to soften his voice. "I mean, I'm sorry. I should have kept my big mouth shut about it. You're the—" He exhaled, trying to get hold of himself. "You're brave, and smart, and a good person, and . . . I should be the one calling myself a Sterling."

Sam's face did a lot of complicated things Ulysses didn't want to dwell on. "Ulysses," he said in a low voice.

Ulysses shrugged. "I just wanted to tell you. Whatever else happens, I'm not sorry I married you. I don't regret any of this."

There was a trailhead at the back of the graveyard. He couldn't see what was happening beyond the first bend—it was high summer, and the world was a riot of green in the undergrowth. The path appeared well-trodden, although it hadn't rained in several days and Ulysses couldn't make out any footprints. He reached back and took Sam's hand. "Moonrise isn't until 9 p.m."

"What does that mean?" Sam's eyes were big and pale, almost glowing in the twilight.

"I don't know." They started down the path.

The woods were quiet. Ulysses remembered that from his last visit, but what he hadn't realized was how noisy quiet could be. Every so often, he heard a crunch or a thump as an acorn dropped from a branch or a squirrel scurried up a tree. He jumped and then chastised himself.

When he caught a voice on the breeze, indistinct but with a familiar, clipped cadence, it was a relief. He saw light flickering through the trees somewhere ahead. "Carefully now," he whispered, and Sam squeezed his fingers. They stepped off the path and picked their way through toward the undergrowth. If he didn't get killed by the ghost of Julius Sterling, he was going to wind up with poison ivy on his ankles.

At the edge of the woods, they crouched behind a pair of oak trees, peering into a clearing with a bonfire in the middle. The smell of smoke and decay hung over everything.

He'd been arrogant or hopeful enough to think they'd gotten most of the cult cleaned up the previous September. But either there had been a lot of members not present when they burned down the Quonset hut, or Stricker's recruiting drive had been significantly more successful than anyone had known. He recognized some of the figures from their little incident at the library; Stricker herself; and, next to her, Peregrine.

They'd been bound to a tree, arms twisted painfully behind their back. Ulysses tried to meet their eye, get a sense of how compos mentis they were. Next to him, Sam made an angry, strangled noise, and Ulysses grabbed his arm to stop him from doing anything rash.

"This was not the deal," Sam hissed.

"Get Ellen!" Sam looked stricken at the idea, and Ulysses squeezed his arm. "Go."

That was when Stricker looked over at them. Someone needed to keep her attention, protect Sam. Ulysses straightened his T-shirt and stepped into the clearing, and he didn't look back.

Peregrine's head whipped around, and Ulysses's stomach dropped. The grad student was shivering despite the warmth of the evening, their gaze vacant and searching, eyes quicksilver with no pupils. Ulysses had been ready to see them afraid or angry, but this was far worse. Peregrine seemed trapped between who they had been and whatever deity they might become.

The smell of rot was stronger near the fire, and Ulysses finally spotted a decaying casket. It had been left on the grass like a piece of forgotten sports equipment. Ulysses totaled up the number of people and the amount of power required for what he thought Stricker was planning, and started to do a little math about sacrifices.

At a motion from Stricker, a large man came across the circle and grabbed Ulysses's arms, pinning them behind his back. Ulysses winced and let him. His shoulders weren't that flexible to begin with. The man wrenched him around so he was facing the center of the clearing. There was an instant when Ulysses thought he could go limp, throw the man off-balance enough to get free. But that wasn't part of the plan. He needed to be here, face to face with Stricker when she tried to resurrect Julius Sterling. So instead, he looked up, searching the sky above the clearing for stars, and forced himself to take a deep breath, to try to ground himself in the stones of the city and the nexus deep beneath them. Places that knew him. Places he'd loved. "You rang?" he said, in as casual a tone as he could manage, just because he hoped it would infuriate Stricker.

"How lovely to see you." She smiled and waved a hand toward Peregrine. "As you can see, I've picked up a little insurance since we last spoke."

She was standing between him and the fire, face shadowed. Her followers were watching him attentively, but none of them looked alarmed that he was there—perhaps they'd been briefed. Ulysses supposed he wasn't too threatening a figure, if it came down to it, heavy engineer boots or no. Especially when some goon was wrenching his shoulders apart.

Somewhere, out in the darkness behind him, Ellen had a sword, and Laz probably had his throwing ax . . . and then there were a bunch of actors and willowy hippies, no one at all physically imposing. And there was Sam. "Let Peregrine go and we'll talk."

Stricker seemed bored. "I don't think you're in much position to bargain." She glanced over at Peregrine. "Do you really think that if I let them go, they're going to leave? They're becoming a god. They want to be where the magic is happening."

Ulysses tried to jerk away from the guy holding him and nearly dislocated his shoulder. Stricker snorted and made a motion, and the man let go. Ulysses staggered, caught himself, and closed the distance between himself and Peregrine.

"Nevertheless, that is my requirement." Up close, they looked clammy and desperate. They'd been bound with silver wire, and Ulysses didn't like the way it bit into their wrists as they tugged against it. When he touched their forehead, their skin was feverishly warm.

Stricker pressed her lips together, searching the edges of the clearing. "What about Sterling?"

Ulysses followed her gaze and couldn't see anyone outside of the clearing. The undergrowth was too dense. He couldn't hear any movement either. "I came alone."

"I doubt that." Her tone was acerbic, but her expression didn't change. "That's all you want?" She tipped her head to one side. "Them, not either of the other two?"

"Either of the—"

"I have been able to expand my plans." She waved an arm at two figures on a bench he hadn't even noticed before. It was on the far side of the clearing, the fire between him and them.

It took him longer than he was proud of to recognize what was happening, who he was being directed to look at. Hugh and Sita, tied back to back. Neither was entirely conscious; Hugh's head lolled heavily on his chest, and Sita was leaning back against him, eyes closed like she'd fallen asleep on the sofa. "How," he said, and then whipped around, panicked, just to ensure that Sam was still free.

"I'll tell you what. You can pick one and I'll let them go." She smiled. "As a gesture of my goodwill."

"I can't . . ." Ulysses couldn't help but remember Eli's doctrine of double effect. It had seemed so straightforward when they'd discussed it, but now the choice felt muddled, and not just by panic. How was he supposed to weigh the three of them: a friend, his student, someone he'd once nearly given his own life to save? What kind of a choice was this?

If he lived, he was definitely going to bother Eli about it.

"Peregrine goes free," he said finally.

"Interesting choice." She tilted her head. "You're certain?"

It wasn't about Peregrine's worthiness. The problem was their power—power that would be left behind if someone else got shoved into their body. Power that could be used against a lot of other people. "Yeah," he said. "I guess that's the deal. Iphigenia's Rule—blood given willingly makes a stronger sacrifice."

She hesitated for a surprisingly long time, looking between the three of them. Perhaps she'd anticipated him making a different choice.

"You came to me, acting as though my power would be satisfactory for whatever you're planning," Ulysses said. "Have you changed your mind about the dubious pleasure of seeing your biological father again?" A pained look crossed her face, fast enough he thought he'd imagined it. "If you want my power, you will let Peregrine go."

She shrugged. "If that's really what you want. But do you think that's wise?"

"I have a duty." Ulysses forced himself to take a deep breath. He could hit her, but some of the bigger goons from her collection were wandering closer, and he was pretty sure they'd win in that sort of confrontation. His death at this point wasn't likely to slow them down, not when they could grab his magic, then put his corpse in Julius's old casket and shove him back in the Sterling mausoleum. Also, he wasn't eager to begin the night by dying. Sam would be very angry, for one thing.

Stricker rolled her eyes. "Fine. They stay until the ritual is done, and then I'll release them." She gestured, and the man who'd grabbed him earlier pulled his arms behind his back again. Stricker looked at her watch, scowling, and Ulysses compulsively looked up at the sky. What time had they left Harry and Ellen's? Where was the moon? "It's time," she declared, and the clearing swarmed into action.

She produced the reliquary, turning it in her hands like she was looking for a seam. Ulysses waited for her to twist it open, not that he was sure how. The counterspell he'd prepared was waiting at the front of his mind, itching on his tongue.

He heard a noise from somewhere in the woods, then a scream from farther out. After a moment, a voice on another side of the clearing began to sing quietly. He recognized the soft, strange melody of Ophelia's song, but not the singer. "At his head a green-grass turf. At his heels a stone."

Ulysses bit the inside of his lip. He'd brought a bunch of maenads to a cult fight. Now how the hell was he going to keep them safe?

Stricker stopped next to the casket and motioned to the man holding Ulysses, who trundled him over. The sigil—he remembered it well—was already drawn on the old, wretched wood, the blood she'd done it with dripping down and soaking into the ground. Whose blood?

He'd thought she was waiting for the box to construct the ritual, but a glance into the open half of the casket showed him Julius's body somehow made whole. The eyes were still closed. She was going to bring him back into—that—first, and then force him to transfer her to one of the gods before she put him into the other. She didn't trust him. Probably smart.

"You've been busy," he said.

"Not all of us take summers off." A cultist stepped forward and presented her with a long, highly polished silver athame. She held it up, and Ulysses admired the filigreed handle, the moonlight glancing off the design. Stricker stepped closer. He tried to flinch backward but found himself held fast. She reached out, almost like she was going to pat him on the shoulder, but at the last moment raked the tip across his neck. It was a glancing blow, not a killing one, but he could feel the blood trickling down his neck as the shock faded and the pain spread.

The plans he'd made had somewhat depended on having his hands free and, ideally, his blood inside his body. But maybe he could repurpose *her* sigil. It would take exquisite timing, but if he managed to trigger his spell an instant before she did hers, it could steal her sacrifice.

He prepared the words in his mind as she swiped a finger through his blood and dabbed it onto the lotuses. He drew in a breath as she raised the box, mouthing the first syllables, and—

She brought it down unceremoniously in the center of the sigil. He thought it hit hard, maybe even cracked the casket, but he didn't hear a sound, possibly because he was busy screaming, his body involuntarily curling forward with such force that the man holding him lost his grip. The noise seemed to come from deep inside him, where the pain was, but also from somewhere far away. The box fractured into long, thin pieces, like a handful of spaghetti.

The pain stopped. Ulysses tried to breathe again. He was on his hands and knees in the grass, no longer held but unable to effect any sort of protest or escape. He looked up to check the progress of the ritual. It was impossible to tell if what he was hearing was magic or his own pulse in his ears.

Stricker muttered one long, hissing word and made a shooing motion toward the body; it seemed like she barely had to do anything before the body inhaled.

Ulysses had not been in a great frame of mind when he'd brought Hugh back, but everything seemed to happen a lot slower than he expected this time. Thirty seconds ticked past. Blood trickled down his neck and pooled on his collarbones. Another minute, and then Julius Sterling opened his eyes and sat up.

Ulysses wished that Sam was there. It felt wrong, somehow, to be witnessing this alone, when this was *Sam's* grandfather. The man who had, in some sense, made him. At the same time, he was glad Sam was elsewhere. This was grotesque.

Julius Sterling said, "What year is it?"

He had a dry voice, higher than Ulysses would have thought, with a biting edge to it. Julie Stricker said, "It's 1971," and he nodded, evidently unfazed by the fact he'd been dead nearly twenty years. His body was wizened, skin sallow and bruised here and there in big, purple patches that stood out grotesquely. His eyes were deeply sunken, his irises cloudy. A scant cloud of gray hair clung to the dome of his head. Ulysses shuddered.

"You . . ." He looked at Stricker, and then at Ulysses over her shoulder. The moment reminded Ulysses of their meeting with Barth. And then Julius recognized him, or at least figured out something about who he was, who his family were. "Things have changed in my absence, I see. Fascinating."

"More than you could imagine," Ulysses muttered. There was a scream from somewhere out in the woods. Ulysses didn't recognize the voice, but it still made him twitch in that direction, heart racing. Gods appearing occasionally raised the level of magic so high that demons appeared. He hadn't warned them.

"Always trust a Lenkov to do the noble thing." Sterling looked down at his legs, bent them experimentally. He raised a sardonic eyebrow. "Are you here as the advocatus diaboli?"

"I'm here to stop you."

The dead man sniffed. "Good job you're doing so far."

When Ulysses didn't answer, Julius Sterling growled to himself and levered his body up and out of the casket. Ulysses could remember Sam's first few days in his new body after Dionysus, how coltish he'd been, forgetting how high door knobs were, walking into tree branches. It didn't seem entirely fair that Julius would just be able to pick up where he left off. But he looked steady enough. Stricker had left the athame on the foot of the casket and he picked it up now, turning it in his hand.

"What is your plan?" he asked, looking at Stricker. "I presume you've brought me here for a reason."

"It's time," Stricker said. "I've got the god children." Sterling followed her a few paces toward Hugh and Sita. They were looking more alert than they had been, although they probably weren't awake enough to be helpful to Ulysses yet.

"Well done," Julius Sterling said. There was a pause, and he added, in a distant tone, "No Dionysus?"

Stricker started to speak, but Ulysses got there first. "He's dead. I killed him."

"A pity." Ulysses didn't know why he'd expected some show of sadness, but it wasn't there. Dionysus, such as he was, didn't exist for Julius as his grandson, just something to be used. Ulysses shuddered.

Stricker, on the other hand, didn't seem to care. Perhaps she was grateful that he'd provided her with a cover story so she wouldn't have to explain their deal and Sam's absence. "Everything will be as you and my father planned it. You'll transfer me into Lakshmi, and then I will transfer you into Arawn."

Ulysses frowned. "How are you planning to manage that?"

"What do you mean?" Stricker turned dark, angry eyes on him.

"I'm counting the transfers," he said. "And I get three: Sterling into his former body, which is already complete; you into Sita; and then Sterling into Hugh. I assume I'm the sacrifice for one of them, but what about the other two? You couldn't have used Sterling's body as a sacrifice to bring him back, and Peregrine and I are both still alive." Ulysses set his teeth mulishly. "What did you do?" There was a long silence. Sterling was looking at Stricker too, now, with interest. Ulysses said, "You didn't . . . tie the sacrifice to this body, did you? So that if he doesn't do what you want . . . oh no."

Stricker raised an eyebrow. "It's just a little insurance policy. He needs me as much as I need him now."

Sterling appeared to come to a very quick decision. He muttered something, reached out and touched her arm, and she crumpled. Not even time for a gasp, not even for her eyes to go wide.

"Holy shit!" Ulysses could smell the magic in the air, feel it at the back of his throat. He knelt to take her pulse. "You killed her."

He felt numb at the idea. Of course Julius Sterling had always seen people as disposable. That shouldn't be surprising. And yet Ulysses found himself looking at the old man as though he might have some sort of explanation.

"I don't respond well to pressure" was all Sterling said. He tottered off toward the tree where Peregrine was still tied.

"What—" Ulysses spluttered. When the old man turned his pointed gaze back, he managed to be more coherent: "You can't do the spell on yourself. You're stuck in that for however long it lasts."

"Can't I?"

Ulysses glanced at Stricker's body. "She couldn't. And I'm sure as fuck not going to help you."

"Mmm. I'm not concerned about the approbation of a Lenkov." He was walking around Peregrine now, eyeing their small, shivering form with an unpleasantly covetous expression. "Nor do I want your assistance. Who was that horrible old bat to you? Your mother?"

"Grandmother."

Julius Sterling spared him a glance. "Clearly the bloodline has not improved." He looked back at Peregrine, who was practically hissing at him. "Which one were you, eh?"

"What are you talking about?" Peregrine spat.

He grabbed their chin with a strength that belied how decrepit he looked. "What god am I speaking to? I command thee."

There was a long silence. "Mercury," Peregrine gritted out at last, and looked away.

Sterling nodded once, a proprietary gesture, and said, "You'll do."

"What?" Ulysses's mouth went dry. "You can't—Stricker promised—"

"On the contrary, Mr. Lenkov." His face twisted in an approximation of a smile. "You saw what happened to Julie. There's no one to gainsay me. No reason not to do what I've planned."

That was a problem. Ulysses had been counting on having Peregrine's extra power to work with when he took Sterling out.

"Please," Ulysses said. "Let Peregrine go. They're innocent."

Julius Sterling cocked his head at Ulysses. "Why do you care? Are you their boyfriend?"

"I'm their advisor. I have a duty to protect them." He thought, absurdly, of Dr. Lesko. "They don't deserve to be caught up in all this."

"Deserve," Julius hissed. "What deserve? Who deserves? Nobody, nothing. Use each man according to his deserts, boy—"

"And who shall 'scape whipping?" Ulysses put himself in between Julius and Peregrine, as though that was going to make some kind of difference. "I've heard that one before."

Julius's mouth turned up at one edge. "Good."

He took a deep breath. "But you're going to have to go through me if you want to sacrifice Peregrine." Somewhere out in the darkness, he could feel Sam running toward them. Or he hoped he could. "This is where it ends, Julius. Either you give up—go back to your grave—or I'll put you there. I am willing to die to do it, under the sight of all of these gods." That was a good declaration of intent. What were the other parts of an oath? He couldn't remember. He shoved his hand into his pocket, fingers closing around the little knife he always carried. He could feel the silver chain of the necklace holding the charm to his chest, hot against his skin, burning where his neck still bled.

The old man was scintillating with power. Ulysses didn't have to have any particular facility at sensing such things to know that. Whatever he'd done to Julie Stricker had given him a boost. But the magic was running through Julius like water, too, pouring out of him. He could have been dragging the entirety of the nexus behind him, and it still wouldn't have been enough to buy him more than a couple of hours. They locked eyes, Julius's dead ones gazing into Ulysses's.

"You're a lot of things, boy," Julius muttered, leaning too close for Ulysses's comfort, "but a god you're not, regardless of what you did to Dionysus. I admire the grit, but it's not going to come to anything. You'll have died in vain. Is that what you want?"

Ulysses pulled out the jack knife and sliced his palm. "Yes," he said simply, and reached up, wrapping his bloody hand around the sigil that wasn't a sigil. "Peace," he murmured, and grinned at Julius, knowing he must look half-feral and not caring. "The charm's wound up."

Julius sniffed. "Such devotion." Then he seized Ulysses by the lapels and, with a strength Ulysses hadn't expected, shoved the athame into him. He flinched at the pain in his ribs, stumbled backwards, and . . .

He fell.

He let himself fall?

He was never certain. He grabbed for a handhold that wasn't there. Shit. And then he was in motion.

He forgot the rest.

Chapter 27

SAM WAS AT THE edge of the clearing when Ulysses fell. Logically, he knew the moment didn't happen in slow motion, like something out of a film. The sound didn't really cut off around him when he saw Ulysses hit the ground. He—

Malfunctioning radio. He was a—

Eli—where the hell had he come from?—got to Ulysses first and started to assess him, fingers on his neck searching for a pulse. Sam couldn't think why this was a problem. Ulysses was going to get up in a second. He hadn't fallen far. Sam had seen him jump from ten feet and walk away with maybe a twisted ankle.

But Eli was dragging Ulysses's body into a better position, bending low over his face. Eli looked worried.

Sam skidded to a halt next to them. He dropped to his knees and grabbed Ulysses's hand. It was cold. Ulysses was breathing in uneven gasps, his eyes wide and panicky, lips tinged with blue. Eli murmured something apologetic as he picked up Ulysses's jack knife from the grass and used it to slice his T-shirt; Sam winced at the naked fear in Ulysses's face. The stab wound was bleeding a lot. Did it hurt? Sam was numb. Even with the bond open, it was all so distant and cold.

Laz arrived at a run a moment later, sliding into the spot next to Eli, bending to listen to his instructions. Sam's brain was buzzing. Nothing that was happening seemed quite real, and he still couldn't really hear. There was—there was actually a lot of blood. Ulysses tugged at his hand to get his attention.

Ulysses was fumbling with something at the neck of his shirt. "Rule," he managed, wrapping Sam's fingers around the little necklace. Eli pressed something against the wound. Ulysses took a sudden, convulsive breath and said, "Rule two."

Once you start a ritual, you have to finish it.

Sam's fingers came away bloody, but everything was kind of bloody now. "Rule two," he repeated softly, and nodded. Ulysses seemed to relax fractionally, so Sam leaned forward and kissed his forehead. "Give me a minute. I'll be right back."

He took the jack knife and got to his feet. Now would be a good time to tune in to WDIO, but the dial was still stuck.

What did gods want? Obe had told him once that gods desired offerings. Livia had said they demanded sacrifice. But their gods were not Sam's god.

What if Dionysus wanted something else?

All right, that made sense. But what?

He took a few absent, shuffling steps away from Ulysses, hoping to bring clarity to his thoughts through distance.

Magic was culturally embedded. What culture was *Sam* embedded in? He was not the child of a Russian defector. He was not a Haitian immigrant. He wasn't a Jewish Northumbrian physician. He was just some guy who lived in Wisconsin, in the weirder part of a city that was an aberration in a state that mostly cared about cheese, beer, and football. He was part Greek, but that was kind of an accident. Ulysses loved music, but Sam couldn't sing, not really. Sam . . . was into Shakespeare.

Dionysus liked theater. There were theaters built for him, structures that had survived thousands of years. And of course rituals were somewhat performative, weren't they?

Stricker was on the ground. No one was paying her any attention; Sam bent to check her pulse and discovered she didn't have one. Most of the cultists seemed to have fled in the wake of her death, apparently judging that their chances of immortality, or whatever she'd promised, had evaporated. Just as well. He turned back toward Ulysses and saw the clearing was filling up with their friends.

Ellen was standing a few steps away, huddled with Buttercup and Galadriel and Manaow and a few other women Sam recognized but couldn't put names to. Ellen's eyes were big and damp when he came over.

"Damn it, El. If you cry, I'm going to cry," he muttered, trying for dry humor and landing uncomfortably on the truth.

She scowled at him but said, "Harry's trying to get people to come this way, but there have been a few fights with the departing cultists."

He nodded. "What's the greatest Shakespearian soliloquy?"

Her expression was dumbfounded, but she recovered quickly. Her eyes darted to Ulysses before she said, "What a piece of work is a man."

Sam nodded. He took a few steps to one side and closed his eyes. It was the sort of thing he'd seen the actors do to center themselves, but he didn't find it especially helpful. When he opened them, he was surrounded by a half circle of women. Some of them were clutching weapons, actual or makeshift, or holding hands with their fellows. All of them were waiting for him to tell them what the plan was.

Sam looked at Ellen, who was still holding her sword, but lowered, watching him. He took a breath. "I have of late—but wherefore I know not—lost all my mirth, forgone all custom of exercises; and indeed it goes so heavily with my disposition that this goodly frame, the earth, seems to me a sterile promontory, this most excellent canopy, the air, look you, this brave o'erhanging firmament, this majestical roof fretted with golden fire, why, it appears no other thing to me than a foul and pestilent congregation of vapors." Was something happening? The women were listening, some confused, some enrapt. "What a piece of work is a man! how noble in reason! how infinite in faculty! in form and moving how express and admirable! in action how like an angel!" He paused, looked at Ellen again, and said, "In apprehension how like a god!"

The knob clicked over.

It wasn't like the first time he'd been Dionysus. There was no sense of being scraped and overwritten. And it wasn't like the previous summer when he'd been terribly high, swimming through a cloud of Ulysses's borrowed power. Dionysus was suddenly there, beside or within him. When Sam opened his eyes again, he looked at the group he'd gathered and Dionysus was looking along with him. They were maenads. He hadn't seen it before, but Dionysus understood the truth.

"You've been holding out on us," Ellen said, shakily, her eyebrows drawn together. "That was excellent."

Dionysus smiled. Sam smiled too.

When he turned to look at the scene behind him, it was with new eyes. Sam understood that there was magic going on, but Dionysus could smell the deep, salty tang of the magic underneath the spilled blood, see the lines of power that pooled around Ulysses and stretched out toward Peregrine. There were more lines, reaching out to Sam, reaching out to everyone, a whole interconnected network. And in the middle, shining like a lighthouse, was Julius Sterling.

Dionysus looked at Julius Sterling, and Sam felt his face settle into a scowl. Ulysses's life was running out of him like water, and Sterling was chalking runes on a large, flat stone near the fire.

"Go, find your friends," Sam heard himself say, looking at the women. Two had sticks, and Ellen had her sword. Weapons they hardly needed. Galadriel was holding the water pistol he'd modified for *Hamlet*. After a moment's hesitation, she pressed it into his hand, and then turned away, laughing. They dispersed into the woods, buoyed by a new energy. He heard one of them begin to sing a wild little tune and the others take it up.

The pistol was still full. He eyed it for a moment, wondering if he would have to explain the mechanism to Dionysus, and then stuck it into the waistband of his trousers. It pressed against his lower back, cold and rigid.

Dionysus turned and circled the clearing. Did Julius Sterling have any idea that there was something to be wary of? Sam remembered, suddenly, a wild bit of a Homeric hymn he'd read: Dionysus, as a young man, had been kidnapped by pirates who mistook him for a nobleman's son, someone who could be ransomed back to his father for a lot of money. Only the pilot of the boat suspected the captive was not who he seemed. When the time had come to reveal himself, Dionysus had turned into a lion and killed all the crew except the pilot.

Maybe it was a memory, rather than a myth. Sam could feel Dionysus's leonine grace as he crouched beside the bench Hugh and Sita were tied to. Sita whipped around to stare at him as he bent down, and he winked.

Sterling was muttering to himself, deeply engrossed in recreating a very large sigil in front of Peregrine. Sam recognized parts of it, but other parts were new, being copied out of a small book bound in ivory calfskin. Sam was annoyed to see the book that had been stolen, wondered also exactly how sigils were related to magic, what the rules were for how they combined. Dionysus observed the procedure with a measure of amusement and indulgence, like an adult watching children drawing with chalk on the sidewalk.

Hugh was rubbing his wrists, trying to get the circulation back. "What's the plan?"

Dionysus grinned. "We stop him."

"We were hoping for something a little more specific," Sita hissed, and Dionysus shrugged.

"Get Mercury free," he told them. "I'll distract him."

Julius looked up at his approach, irritable, as though Sam was an interrupting busybody. There was a long silence and then a tick in Julius's jaw as he realized who stood in front of him. "Not as dead as I was led to believe," the old man muttered, getting to his feet.

Dionysus shrugged. "He's protective," he said, voice warmly affectionate.

"So it would seem." He looked Dionysus over, frowning when he noticed the wedding ring on Sam's left hand. "You're taller than Howard, but not exactly what I expected."

Sam had a few rough things to say about what it had been like to add *five fucking inches* to his height years after he'd stopped growing, but Dionysus was running the show and he found the comment hilarious on a level Sam didn't really appreciate. "Thank you," he said softly. "I enjoy being unexpected."

Julius snorted. "I assume so." He frowned. "Don't know what I was thinking, trying to make a deal with Dionysus. Alexandria's influence, I'm sure. She was always such a devotee, but she never understood . . ." He kept muttering, but his monologue went inaudible.

Dionysus cocked his head to the side. Sam's head. Sam scowled, because while reminiscing about your dead wife was all very well and good, Sam's husband was currently bleeding to death, and no one except Eli and Laz seemed to have a sense of urgency about it. Dionysus might have once gone to the underworld to drag Ariadne's spirit out, but Sam didn't think that was within *his* remit. They needed to get rid of Julius, not stand around being nostalgic with him.

"Of course, you've no real power," Julius Sterling continued. "A failure. But why?" He leaned closer. "Did Lenkov steal it? Is that—"

"No," Sam said honestly. Dionysus's thoughts curled approvingly around his rib cage. Ulysses was welcome to whatever power Dionysus had; in a sense, he already had whatever there was to offer. It was weird to realize that Dionysus had chosen Ulysses for reasons that differed from Sam's, an idea that definitely merited exploration at another juncture. Preferably one with a lot of drugs. "Ulysses saved me."

Julius grunted. He was still eyeing Dionysus like he was a side of beef. Then he glanced at the empty bench and wheeled to look at where Hugh and Sita were, which was standing next to Peregrine.

Arawn, Lakshmi, and Mercury, Dionysus corrected him. Of course. He hadn't realized that there was a pathway for Sita to channel the goddess she'd once been promised to, but there she was, shining and beautiful.

"What do you intend to do to me?" Julius said, derisive as he'd ever been. "Even with Mercury at full strength, you don't have enough power. I have the land itself behind me."

Sam could smell the heavy, pungent magic Julie Stricker had pinned to Julius, cloying like roses. Dionysus associated it with the nexus. Beneath it was the crackling, ozone essence of Mercury, the earthy decaying scent of Arawn, the fragrant, clean aroma of Lakshmi. Dionysus's power smelled like green growing things. Or perhaps that was Ulysses's borrowed magic flowing through Sam. But all of it was overpowered by the presence of the nexus.

Almost before Sam had finished his thought, Arawn was nodding. "By blood and breath," he said, and raised an eyebrow.

Sam shivered, but Dionysus was digging the knife Ulysses had been stabbed with out of his pocket and tossing it to him. Arawn sliced his palm, letting the blood run down onto the ground. He handed the knife to Mercury, who said, "By fire and water," and repeated the gesture. Lakshmi added, "By fear and faith," and her own blood.

And then the knife returned to Dionysus. Sam looked down at it, seemingly from a long way away. "In fulfillment of oath." The blade bit into his palm, but he felt no pain.

It took only a few steps before the four of them were standing in a square around Julius. Julius wasn't near the sigil he'd been sketching out, but gods didn't need sigils to do magic. Mercury looked up suddenly, eyes focused on something beyond Dionysus's shoulder, and said, "They're here."

Maenads were filtering out of the woods, filling the clearing, drawn by the ritual. Many were dancing in the moonlight, their arms outstretched to one another. A few held trophies, the teeth or claws of demons, battered baseball caps. One had a tambourine.

Ghosts were appearing now too, Abbie in her long skirt, and others Sam had seen before, in their fine clothes. They were pale in the moonlight, but their faces were determined.

Dionysus smiled.

He tucked the knife into his coat pocket and took the water pistol from his waistband, training it on Julius Sterling as though it was a real gun. Sterling shook his head, frowning. He had a haughty air, as though he was entirely unconcerned by what was going on around them. The maenads were chanting more loudly now.

Julius Sterling met Dionysus's eyes and said, "Stop this. You cannot succeed."

It was something, to be willing to lock eyes with a god. Sam thought Dionysus was reluctantly impressed. It was also far too late.

"You stabbed Ulysses," Dionysus said. "Dance now."

"What?" The ghoul looked around, and for the first time he seemed to fear what was going on. "No. I—you can't do this. You don't have enough power. You're all a bunch of has-beens."

Dionysus said, "Doubt me not, mortal," and pulled the trigger. Julius Sterling flinched as the water hit him, and stumbled. Dionysus, recalling some other memory or story, said loudly so the assembled throng might hear him, "Come, look, my friends! We are in danger! A wild beast is attacking us!"

The maenads surged forward and seized Julius Sterling, and Sam did not see him alive again on the Earth.

When Sam opened his eyes, he was on his knees in the clearing. Alone, more or less, although the dance went on around him.

Dionysus was still with him. Julius Sterling was dead again, if the state he'd been a few minutes ago had actually been life. Sam thought he could feel Sterling's power pooling around their ankles as it drained back into ... whatever the nexus was. What that meant was a question for another time. There were more pressing issues to deal with.

Sam scrambled to his feet and closed the gap between himself and the spot where Ulysses had fallen in bounding steps. Eli was still kneeling over Ulysses, two fingers pressed to his unmoving throat. Laz was next to him, hands on Ulysses's rib cage like he was going to keep all the blood where it belonged by himself. Sam's heart lurched, and he knew for once Dionysus was entirely in accord with him.

Please, don't be dead yet.

Ulysses was pale and clammy, eyebrows drawn together as he gasped for breath, like he couldn't figure out why his lungs weren't working right. Even by the light of the moon and the dying fire, his lips were tinged with blue. When Sam looked up, the other gods were surrounding him. Arawn, Lakshmi, and Mercury. Friends. Siblings.

Lakshmi was watching the maenads with a wary expression. "Will they be okay?"

Arawn snorted. "They will."

"Others may not be," Mercury murmured, looking down at Ulysses.

Arawn and Lakshmi were fading now that the rite was over. Dionysus looked at Mercury, who was still shining with magic and glory. "May I beg a boon, my sibling?"

And Mercury, tiny beautiful thing that they were, said, "Do what you must. Repay the debt."

Dionysus reached out and very gently scooped out the extra power that had filled Mercury up. It was like picking up a small bird, like holding something alive that was only staying where it was because it was chose to. He bowed deeply to Mercury, noting as he straightened that the bright glow was fading from their eyes, and then returned to Ulysses.

Already as he leaned forward, the dance was starting to slow, the singing to wind down. Dionysus would be gone in a few moments too. Sam despaired, because things were moving so quickly, and there was so much yet to do.

Dionysus tipped his palm and poured the power into Ulysses. He reached out and pulled the makeshift bandage away, then smoothed his palm over the spot where the knife had gone in, watching as the skin knitted itself closed.

Silence. Stillness. Laz and Eli exchanged a look in his periphery.

He needed something else to finish it off, a sacrifice. What made a sacrifice worthy? It had to be personally meaningful. He had nothing. He had—

He looked down at his hands, which were empty except for the ring he wore.

Shakily, he removed the ring. It was heavy, warm from his body. The shiny silver surface was smeared with blood. It was a gift, a symbol, a promise. He weighed it a moment before closing his fingers around it. The edge bit into his palm. He took a deep breath.

"I give this to you that he might be healed." And then he tried to let the magic waft through him.

He felt the ring vanish, but heavy pang of knowing it was gone was immediately washed away when Ulysses took a shuddering breath and coughed weakly. His eyes opened. Dionysus grinned broadly, meeting Ulysses's bewildered gaze. "All right?"

Ulysses nodded and squeezed Sam's hand. "You?"

"Yeah," Sam managed. "I'm sorry about my ring." He might have been crying.

"I'll buy you another one." Ulysses coughed again. "Assuming you still want—"

"*Yes.*" Sam pulled Ulysses to a seated position so he could wrap his arms around him and bury his face in his shoulder. "You're never getting rid of me now."

"Good." Ulysses hugged him back.

And the radio clicked back to WULY.

Epilogue

IN THE END, THEY left everything there, Julie Stricker's body next to Julius Sterling's. Sam wasn't sure it was the right choice, but he also didn't want to explain anything to the police. What, after all, could he say? Madison's finest were free to figure it out without him. If he got a phone call from Howard in the morning, so be it.

Vikram had come tearing through the crowd to find Sita. Hugh had closed an arm around Peregrine's shoulders and taken them home. Someone had offered Ulysses a shirt. The maenads and magicians who had come for the spectacle fucked off again, to drink or sleep or tear down the government, Sam didn't know or care. And everyone else, which at that point was Ellen and Harry, Laz and Eli, and Sam and Ulysses, went back to Eli's place.

Eli had a small fire pit in his backyard, surrounded by rough log benches. Ulysses sat down heavily on one of them; Sam found a spot on the ground near Ulysses and lay back. He could smell the lake from where he was and hear the water lapping at the rocks that ran along the edge of Eli's property. Harry threw a ball for Oliver while Laz and Ellen built a little bonfire and Eli fussed around finding drinks for everyone. Then the world gave a sigh and everything settled down.

They'd been sitting for some time, and the fire was beginning to burn low. The air was warm and smelled like flowers and woodsmoke. The sky was clear. Sam watched the ripples on the lake, broken puddles of moonlight as the breeze shifted and died and picked up again.

No one had spoken for a while as the adrenaline of the battle ebbed, giving way to something quieter, stitched together from fatigue and introspection. Every so often, Sam caught Laz glancing at his brother, checking to make sure he was still there. Eli sat beside him, leaning against a log, bowtie askew, staring into the fire. Oliver was curled up against his other side, occasionally nosing Eli for ear scratches.

Ellen and Harry eventually got up, yawning, and made their excuses.

Sam walked them out to the street and lingered next to the Datsun. "I don't know what to say," he admitted.

"Sam," Ellen said, and hugged him wordlessly. When she let go, Harry hugged him too. Once they'd both released him, she looked sheepish. "I have to tell you something," she said. "I lied earlier."

"What about?"

She glanced at Harry, then looked down, smiling faintly. "My favorite soliloquy is actually 'Tomorrow and tomorrow and tomorrow.' But under the circumstances, it felt like bad luck."

"She should have died hereafter," Harry began, and made a face. "Yeah, I see what you mean."

Sam let out a bark of laughter. "El! That's—I mean, thank you."

Harry wrapped his arms around Ellen and kissed the side of her face. "I think you chose well," he said. He looked at Sam, eyes dancing. "Your recitation was great. I really felt it! If you want, we could work out some better blocking."

Ellen was laughing now too, leaning back against her husband. "So he can be ready for the next time he needs to summon a god," she choked out.

"Or if he decides to audition for something," Harry argued, grinning. "It's always good to have a monologue in your back pocket." Sam couldn't decide if he was serious or not.

Ellen pressed the heels of her palms against her eyes, and Sam offered her his handkerchief. "Lunch tomorrow?" he asked, because he wasn't ready to let them go.

Harry grinned. "Sure. Your treat."

Sam wanted to wrap them both in his arms and never let them go. He wanted to set them in the heavens where they'd always be safe. But instead, he said, "That seems fair," and told himself it was enough.

When he got back to the fire, no one had moved. He took up his spot again, supine on the grass, staring up at the moon.

Ulysses had been cradling a half-empty bottle of beer for a while, humming to himself as he stared out at the lake. Sam watched the shadows dancing on his face as thoughts flickered past like clouds. He'd been keeping the bond at a low ebb since Ulysses woke up, a reassuring quiet presence. He could feel emotions simmering in Ulysses that he couldn't put a name to, and he was waiting to see what would happen.

Finally, Ulysses shifted and set the bottle down next to his foot. "Eli, how deep is the water here?"

"Not deep," Eli said. Sam heard the doctor shift. He had looked almost asleep a moment ago. He'd been drinking something that smelled like hot whisky with lemon and honey in it, although he claimed it was tea. Mainly tea. And medicinal. "Decidedly not deep, so please don't go diving in. I don't relish having to backboard you, and I don't think Sam has enough"—he waved a hand—"*chutzpah* left to put you back together if you break your neck."

Laz, who had been leaning on Eli's shoulder, gently scratching the dog behind his ears, looked over at his brother, one eyebrow raised. "I think we've both had enough of your blood on our hands tonight."

Ulysses nodded and started to pull at his bootlaces.

"What are you doing?" Sam asked. He had a vague plan of just putting down roots and never moving again. Perhaps he could grow like a mushroom in Eli's backyard. But Ulysses taking off his clothes was always of interest.

"Going swimming." He stood up and pulled his borrowed T-shirt over his head in one fluid motion. "You coming?"

Sam propped himself up on an elbow and watched him skin off his pants and undershorts. "Am I . . ."

Ulysses hopped on one foot, then the other, removing his socks. "Swimming." He stuffed the socks into one boot and started for the edge of the water.

Sam watched him walk away, naked and unconcerned, then glanced back at Laz and Eli, who were talking in soft voices to each other. "I'll, uh. Keep an eye on him."

"No diving," Eli said again. After a moment he added, to no one in particular, "I could fetch some towels, I suppose."

"Sure." Sam stripped quickly. Ulysses was already in the lake by the time he reached its edge. Eli was right—it was barely hip deep. Ulysses was wading rather than swimming, the moonlight breaking across the flat muscled planes of his body. The water was cool but not cold, and Sam followed Ulysses through it, stones and algae slippery beneath his toes. Everything was quiet except for the sounds of their movements. Sam thought of Orpheus leading Eurydice up from hell. Or that strange night on Madeline Island when he'd fallen into Lake Superior and been reborn.

After they'd gone a hundred feet or so, out to where the bottom started to drop off, Ulysses turned back to glance at him. Their eyes met; for an instant, Sam had a hard time breathing. Ulysses was beautiful and whole, droplets of water rolling down his flank caught for a moment by the moonlight. Sam's heart fluttered, and he wanted to say—well, Ulysses already knew, and he had the rest of their lives to repeat it.

Sam tackled him around the waist and they both fell, laughing, into the water together.

Acknowledgments

If there is one thing I have learned at this point, it is that there is no one way to write a book. Each novel demands something different. Some are easy, or easy-ish. This one wasn't. I always owe gratitude to the usual crowd, but this time I feel I owe even more. Bryan, Rowan, and Blaine all read one or more drafts and gave excellent feedback and support. Eliot did an emergency developmental edit on this when I was panicking, and then eleven days later did a line/copy edit, which is pretty heroic. The Middle Lions (Justin, Monique, Wendy, and Alice) continue to be willing to read my stuff and offer encouragement and helpful advice. Patrick was my medical advisor again; there are a couple of, let's call them medical implausibilities in this book, but the hip fracture is explained correctly. Dr. Jesse corrected my Latin jokes and helped with the Greek. Remaining mistakes can be considered choices for dramatic effect and are my responsibility.

Although this is the last Sam/Ulysses solo outing, Wisconsin Gothic will ride again. Book 6, tentatively titled *The Whole Wide World*, will be out in late 2026 or early 2027. Check out my newsletter or follow me on social media to make sure you don't miss any updates. My website is at ehlupton.com; there, you can find links to my social media and newsletter registration as well as all the Wisconsin Gothic extras. I'm @pretense_soup on Instagram and @pretensesoup on Mastodon and Bluesky. If you enjoyed this book, I hope you'll tell a friend about it, leave a review, or at least tell me you had a good time.

About the Author

E. H. Lupton (she/they) lives in Madison, WI with her husband and children. Her debut novel, *Dionysus in Wisconsin*, was shortlisted for both the Lambda Literary Award and the Midwest Book Award. Her poems have been published in various journals, including *Asimov's Science Fiction*, *Utopia Science Fiction*, *Paranoid Tree*, and *House of Zolo's Journal of Speculative Literature*. She is one half of the duo behind the hit podcast *Ask a Medievalist*. In her free time, she enjoys running long distances and painting.

More From E. H. Lupton

The Joy of Fishes (Vagabondage Press, 2013)

Wisconsin Gothic series (Winnowing Fan Press):
Book 1: *Dionysus in Wisconsin* (2023)
Book 2: *Old Time Religion* (2024)
Book 3: *Troth* (2024)
Book 4: *Lazarus, Home from the War* (2025)
Book 4.5: *The Alignments* (2025)
Book 5: *Rénaissance* (2026)
Book 6: *The Whole Wide World* (TBD)

www.ingramcontent.com/pod-product-compliance
Lightning Source LLC
Chambersburg PA
CBHW031109160726
47991CB00004B/1292